A special thank you to Greg Collins for my
hysterical nickname and eventual title.

JEWBILLY

Rick Rosenberg

JEWBILLY

©2021 Rick Rosenberg

Print ISBN: 978-1-66780-680-8

eBook ISBN: 978-1-66780-681-5

CONTENTS

PROLOGUE

WE WERE WHISPER-ARGUING.

"Did not."

"Did too."

"Did not."

"Did too."

"Did not."

"Did too."

The argument continued, melodic, juvenile, and eventually without whispers, when for some self-incriminating reason, I raised my voice so everyone could hear me:

"I did not kill Jesus!"

The words echoed through the gym, traveling up through the bleachers and basketball nets, into every ear of every little, now giggling, hillbilly sitting on the floor. There were about twenty of them. Calvin Macafee was one - the main one - with the weird, squeaky laugh like Dick Dastardly's canine buddy, Muttley.

Calvin was two of me: a giant, freckled, redhead redneck of Scotch-Irish descent, an instigator and anarchist who would argue sunup to sundown that Lynyrd Skynyrd was better than Led Zeppelin. According to Calvin, simply because I was Jewish, I killed Jesus. Of course, that was impossible as it was 1973, I was a twelve-year-old Jewish kid from Brooklyn, and Jesus passed in, what, 32 AD or so?

Unfortunately, the gaggle of pre and current pubescents weren't the only ones who heard me. The gym teacher, Coach Lee, did as well. A young man made of muscle, with cinnamon hair, a matching mustache, and tight shorts, he had been pacing slowly in front of the class, pontificating on the necessity of wearing a jock in gym.

Coach stood with his hands on his hips, glaring at me and beckoning with an index finger. My heart went into overdrive and I might have crapped my pants had I not been constipated since our arrival. I had fucked up badly. The desire to fight or flee popped into my head, but left as quickly as it came in. I was a twiggish, muscle-free child with a squeaky Brooklyn accent and glasses too big for my black-haired head – there was no way I could win a battle, or get away.

"Me?" I mouthed. He nodded slightly, his lips pursed and ugly.

Trembling, I got up and navigated across the sea of cross-legged boys. Their laughing seemed to grow louder with every step I took.

I managed to arrive without making a further fool of myself and stood beside him.

"What's your name, son?" he asked with the messy, Southern drawl I was now surrounded by.

"Yosef Bamberger."

The class laughed loudly. Weirdo. Pariah. Jew.

"Joseph Bamberger," Coach repeated back, incorrectly. "You're new."

Everyone was new, I wanted to say, as this was 7th grade. The school was 7th through 9th, bonehead. Instead, I just nodded.

Coach looked out at the others. "Boys, I want y'all to meet Big Bertha."

I was confused. Did I just get a new nickname? How do you get Big Bertha from Yosef Bamberger? If it was, cool, although it seemed out of character and gender incorrect.

Coach kneeled down and reached into his long, black gym bag sitting beside him. He pulled something out and held it up for everyone to see.

A giant wooden paddle. With holes like swiss cheese.

If I was trembling before, now I'm a 10 on the Richter scale, capable of taking out long stretches of interstate.

I wondered why God would let this happen to me. I was a good Jew. Hell, I was a great Jew! Is this what he meant by the chosen people? Has he chosen me to make some kind of point for Coach Jethro here?!

"Hi, Big Bertha," the class yelled gleefully, with Calvin shouting the loudest which he followed with several 'give me skin' hand slaps with a slew of buddies.

Wobbly, I managed a few words. "I'm sorry, I'm really so—"

"Pull down your shorts," Coach said, interrupting me, smirking.

My body weakened like a wet, kugel noodle. Terrified and humiliated, I stared up at him with pleading eyes, shaking my head no. Have mercy on me, oh great sir.

"Pull. Down. Your. Shorts," he repeated, his face beginning to turn the color of his hair.

I waited another moment, just in case God had sent swarms of locusts to save me.

No?

Okay, how about boils?

Frogs?

Hail?

Pestilence?

Nothing. There was no way out.

So, slowly, I pulled my shorts down, revealing my tightie-whities.

The boys roared. You could see the missing-jock-strap look of disdain on the coach's face. Then, like the master of suspense he was, he paused as if he wasn't sure what he would say next, although he definitely knew.

"Underpants too. Then, bend over."

My eyelids fluttered shut, and for just a moment, I experienced an anger towards my mother so deep that it scared me almost as much as Big Bertha did. This was Mom's fault. She could've stopped it, but didn't.

The class waited, quiet now, mouths agape, but partially smiling, each grateful it wasn't him. I managed to muster a desperate headshake, a sad, lame attempt to stop the madness.

"Don't make me do it for ya," Coach said.

At least I had the wherewithal to know that was a bad idea, so, with one hand, I lowered my underwear, immediately covering myself with my free hand.

Tears flowed now as I bent over, panicked, nauseous, lost.

So … you're likely wondering - how exactly did a sweet and scrawny Jewish kid from Brooklyn get here?

It wasn't easy.

And this was just the beginning. The next year and a half would be nothing short of juvenile hysteria full of deer ticks, heartbreak, LSD, and a thorough mangling of Semitic expectation and tradition. Not the typical or expected trajectory for someone of my status.

I was a gefilte fish out of water. My name is Yosef Bamberger, and this is my crucible.

MISHPOCHEH - CAN YOU DIG IT?

TWO-POINT-FIVE INCHES?! I WANTED TO SCREAM. AGAIN. BUT I didn't. No kid wants seven, worried New York Jews rushing into his room, wondering what's wrong at 6:30 in the morning.

"Sharpies?! Where is he? I'll knock him out!"

"*Du Zol Nicht Vissen Frum Tsores!*"

"Another nightmare?"

"Fall out of bed again, Yo-yo?"

"He's having a stroke!"

"What eleven-year-old has a stroke?"

"Why would you argue with me while our only son could be dying?!"

It was my birthday, the sixth of May, and I was hoping my first gift would be one of extension. But it wasn't to be, even though I was twelve, and it was the beginning of the last year before I was to become a man.

Two Saturdays ago, the whole family went to Micah Greenberg's Bar Mitzvah. A fidgety, chubby Ashkenazi, Micah was one of the Three Meshuggeners; our group's name based shamelessly, and obviously, on *The Three Musketeers*. The other two meshuggeners were myself and Mitchell Sheiner, a brilliant math prodigy on the inside, Goofy the dog on the outside. Our band of brothers was based loosely on the Michael York movie which we all loved. Also, to some extent, the candy bar which we loved, except that Mitchell once had seven in a row and threw up, so he was more partial to the film.

The meshuggeners may not have been as famous as our inspirations, but as gallant? Yes. Brave? Indeed. Ridiculous? Naturally.

Of course, meshuggening was put on hold when it came to Bar Mitzvahs in 1970s Canarsie, Brooklyn. The Starship Enterprise of synagogues, our beloved Ahavath Achim Anshei was a towering, white-bricked temple that took up half a block. Inside, it was a vision of Jewish Orthodoxy with a smattering of '70s groovyness; soaring, stained-glass windows between wood-paneled walls; red carpeting and wooden pews separated by a gender partition - a sea of yarmulkes on one side, babushkas on the other. Our divider was shelving with some very nice ficus plants on top.

We were in the second row. I sat between my father and grandfather as Micah sang his off-key Hebrew chants to the congregation. Slowly, though, he began to fade away as I envisioned myself up there: Yosef Bamberger, proud, not making a single mistake, mesmerizing the crowd with what could only be described as deeply felt religious, musical, Jewish beauty. And on key, I might add. It was so meaningful and close to God. In fact, a few women were even weeping from happiness - my mother mostly.

Gramps poked me. "Shush," he said.

Apparently, I was chanting along with Micah, too loudly and drowning him out for the folks nearest me. Micah was one of my best friends. It was unintentional, but people were staring. I smiled, nodded with silent apologies. It was an intoxicating premonition, people. You will all see in a year or so.

That's right. My Bar Mitzvah would be more thrilling than Moses's. If he had one. I like to think he did, even though the first recorded Bar Mitzvah was in 13th century France when a French dad decided his thirteen-year-old son was no longer his responsibility. Deadbeat dad, much?

Regardless of its origins, my Bar Mitzvah would be in the top five ever. That, I was sure of.

Still under my bed covers, I reached out to my rickety, old bedside table and grabbed my even older copy of *Anne Frank: The Diary of a Young Girl*. Part two of my waking ritual. I read a passage from the revered text:

August 21ˢᵗ, 1942: "Now our Secret Annex has truly become secret. Because so many houses are being searched for hidden bicycles, Mr. Kugler thought it would be better to have a bookcase built in front of the entrance to our hiding place. It swings out on its hinges and opens like a door. Mr. Voskuijl did the carpentry work. (Mr. Voskuijl has been told that the seven of us are in hiding, and he's been more helpful.) Now whenever we want to go downstairs we have to duck and then jump. After the first three days we were all walking around with bumps on our foreheads from banging our heads against the low doorway. Then Peter cushioned it by nailing a towel stuffed with wood shavings to the doorframe. Let's see if it helps!"

It was one of her more playful passages and I read it often, but the gravity of her experience never escaped me.

My grandmother Gertrude would often tell the story of when her, Gramps, and my mother were swept off to Auschwitz. In emotional, part-English, part-Yiddish, part sighs, she would tell of being bitten by rats through the night, the horror of selection days when SS officers chose who was killed, and the hang-in-the-air stench of death that would permeate every inch of the camp. But then, she'd always end the conversation with gratitude. Grateful that Mom was too young to have any memory of it. Grateful Soviet forces eventually arrived and saved them from eventual death. In the end, she'd say, they were the lucky ones, indeed, the chosen ones.

My bedroom door swung open suddenly, interrupting me, as it did every weekday ... it's the pasty, overweight, might have a heart attack any moment thirty-nine-year-old Bamberger patriarch, my dad – the civil, mechanical, and eventual nuclear engineer – Murray. Yarmulke, polyester suit and tie clad, stressed and exhausted, even before the workday began.

"Time to get up, Zees." That's short for *zeeskeit*; it means sweetness or cherished one.

Always in a hurry in the morning, Dad never ate, but never skipped the kissing, never missed a crown or cheek.

I pulled my head out from under my faded blue, cotton blanket, and screamed at him, "Dad! I told you to knock from now on! I'm not a baby anymore."

"Okay, adult," he smiled. "Time to get up. And happy birthday." Milestones made dad emotional. If he spent too much time with these types of things, he would embarrass himself, and worse, be late, so he closed the door and headed down the hall to wake my sisters.

I laid Ms. Frank's diary back on the table and delighted in my room. It was tiny and cramped, as were most 1880s New York brownstones. But it was my tiny and cramped room, and I loved it. An ornate, antique desk sat just inches from my twin bed. The walls were filled with posters of the Brooklyn Bridge, Nikola Tesla, old Jerusalem, and a blacklight poster of a tiger my sister Susan got me. On my one shelf was a replica of the Talmud, three splintery wooden dreidels from the '30s, a Firebird Hot Wheels, and an Evel Knievel Stunt Cycle. Dusty relics of my childhood, I hadn't touched the toys in months, yet I wasn't ready to discard them either.

I bent down and slid my ruler and flashlight way, way underneath the bed – somebody finding them (Mom!) would be devastating. Didn't want to have to explain that. Yes, my penis was still only 2.5 inches, but I was in a grand mood regardless. My Herve Villachez of schlongs would not deter me from having a great day! I would check again tomorrow morning, as I did always, part one of my ritual. I knew I was moving up in line to receive that gift of growth, of manhood. It wouldn't be long now. And it would be glorious.

Finally, part three of the waking ritual was relishing in the sensory overload that was my awakening family. Every morning, a comforting symphony of chattering and singing, combined with the heavy, sublime smells of Gram's Yiddishe cooking.

I jumped out of bed, lanky and awkward in my red and white striped PJs, and went out to greet the day. A day that that would end up being my apocalyptic twelfth birthday.

Our apartment went up at the dawn of the 20th century. With the new subway system, New York was becoming more than Manhattan, and expanding into the other boroughs. Brooklyn was one such beneficiary, bursting from its embryonic ways, with unbounded industry, elaborate trolley lines, and Italian-inspired brownstones like ours.

Seventy years later, the place still stood, full of grace and vainglory. It had been home to the best and worst; moguls, hoteliers, mobsters. Irish, Russian, Chinese, Black. New York in all its flavors.

As I bounded toward the kitchen, the creaks in the floor surprised me with every step. They were never in the same place; impossible to memorize, as hard as I tried. Even old wood flooring had its secrets, I suppose. But, in the morning, it didn't matter.

When I entered, Mom (aka Sandy) was in the kitchen serenading the household - just like she did every morning. She wasn't singing Elvis, or Frank, or Harry Belafonte as you might expect from a woman in her late-ish thirties in 1973. No.

Today was ZZ Top. The day before that, Lou Reed. Uriah Heep, the day before. Growing up in the fifties, Mom felt she was one of the mothers of rock and roll, as if her and Wolfman Jack hooked up one night, and nine months later, gave birth to a whole genre of music. That ownership, coupled with her soaring contralto voice absent of any Brooklyn accent, was how she expressed her musical self. At the time, though, I assumed every kid's mom screamed *want a whole lotta love* as they served goat cheese breakfast bourekas.

The living and dining rooms weren't really rooms as much as they were areas, blending together due to a lack of square footage. It was crowded, but cozy.

We had mostly mid-century furniture at the time: a brown sofa, a faded, flowery lounge chair, and a long cabinet where our Sabbath candlesticks, Jewish texts, Jewish calendar, and menorah were situated.

Hanging on three of the walls were a collage of fading black and white family photos shoved between various paintings of ancient rabbis and destroyed European villages.

On the fourth wall, well, that was particularly special. Hanging all by itself, framed in glass, was an antique black and white poster of a short 1920s boxer with negative body fat. Jack Solomon, my grandfather. Topless with tight black shorts, long-laced shoes and showing off his leather, gold-plated championship belt, Gramps stands at the ready in his best *come at me* pose. A big, bold headline says *Behold the Battling Solomon!*

I sat down at our six-person, wooden, dining table. (There were seven of us).

Mom bolted in from the kitchen.

"Happy birthday, Yosef!" she shrieked, planting a giant kiss on my cheek, and a plate of strawberries and sour cream blintzes in front of me. "My baby is twelve-years-old! *Oy gevalt!*"

"That doesn't make sense, Mom," I cracked back. She laughed it off, smacking me gently on the back of the head. I dug in as she went back to the kitchen, continuing her song.

"Just let me know, if you want to go, to that home out on the range... "

Tall, with early osteoporosis creeping in, my sixty-four-year-old Gram came in from the kitchen. She put her blintzes down, grabbed my face with both hands, and kissed me on the lips. "Happy birthday, *Zeeskeit*," she said, her brown eyes widening, as they did when family was on her mind - which was always. She sat and dug in.

Gramps was next, emerging slowly from the hallway. His mangled nose three times broken, with Shar Pei wrinkles under a gray mop, he was eighty now, forty-seven years and twenty pounds away from being the 5-foot, 6-inch bantamweight boxing champ of the world.

Yet, he still had the belt. And he still wore it. Every day. Everywhere he went.

About a year ago, while he and Gram were out for a walk, he strolled up to a man and slugged him right in the jaw. Knocked him out. There were police. Charges were pressed. He explained that the man was actually an old opponent of his, Sonny Lipzano. Gramps had lost that match and thought he'd get in one last punch. Almost fifty years later. It took some doing with some family lawyers, but they convinced the judge that Gramps was just a senile old man. He eventually got out of it. Of course, that was a lie. He might have had some creeping dementia here and there, but senile he was not. A while back, I asked him why he did it.

His answer: *Better late than never.* Made sense to me.

"Morning, champ!" We recited in unison, as I stood and put up my dukes. Gramps fisted up and we commenced our regular five seconds of fake jabs and hooks. In those days, he was a just over a foot taller than me, so I could really get into it. Even better, it gave me lifetime bragging rights: *I fought the 1926 bantamweight boxing champ of the world!*

It was a draw.

As Gramps sat down to eat, Dad ran in, briefcase in hand. He rushed over and kissed me on top of my head. "Goodbye, Zees."

He kissed Gram. "Goodbye."

He disappeared into the kitchen, kissed mom. "Goodbye."

Her response: "Don't forget the paper plates."

He shot back out of the kitchen, kissed Gramps, "Goodbye," then pointed his head toward the back of the apartment. "Goodbye girls!"

One more kiss to go, he opened the front door, put a hand on our green, enamel Mezuzah, then kissed his hand and took off.

"Bye, Dad!" I mumbled with my mouth full as he disappeared out the door. I was usually the only one who said goodbye back. God forbid, if anything happened to him while on his way to work, or at work, at least I said goodbye.

More singing was coming from the kitchen: "They got a lot of nice girls-a."

"Mom! Where are my white boots?!" The voice came from the back. My sister, Lynn, the eldest child.

"How should I know?!" Mom yelled back.

"She's lucky she has shoes to wear every day," Gram said to me quietly.

I nodded, understanding she was referring to the concentration camps.

"Found 'em!" Lynn bellowed back. And there she was, strutting into the living room, pulling on her boots. Lynn Bamberger, seventeen, going on twenty-nine. She was brand new sexy. Lacy blouse, hot pants, straight, long brown hair, and a beautiful, but acned face. Lynn was only a partial buy-in of the "Me Generation." She could be generous and loving, but in the next moment, she'd make a fiercely selfish decision with no thought whatsoever. Also, don't ask her to be Jewish outside Shul; that was not going to happen.

As was the new ritual, Gram offered her disapproving hands to God.

"Such a *shanda*," she'd say, turning away from her granddaughter and shaking her head. *Shanda* is Yiddish for shame or scandal. I was torn, as I agreed with Gram, but Lynn was just following the fashion trends of the day.

Lynn went over to Gram, kissed her on the head. "Sorry, Gram. Susan!" She came over, smiled, and kissed me. "Happy birthday, Yos."

She smirked and winked like we were in on a secret together, and we were. We had a connection that went beyond sister and brother. She was like a second mom, and sometimes, arguably, a better one. I always knew I could count on her.

Some people believe we're all souls living many lives, and our closest connections reappear as different relations in different lives. Brothers become fathers. Mothers become best friends, etc. Well, if it is true, for me, Lynn is definitely one of those reoccurring souls.

My other sister, Susan, appeared from the hallway. Fifteen, pretty like her sister but a bit rounder, Susan was a malcontent and an anti-smiler; all she wanted was to get through it, whatever *it* was. No matter if it was Shul, dinner, or homework, it was always, *Are we done yet?* Everything and everyone were simply ridiculous. She needed to get back to snacking on sunflower seeds and reading teen mags, her new introvert obsession. A couple years ago, she snuck into a theatre to see *The Last Picture Show* starring Cybil Shepherd. Ever since then, she wanted to *be* Cybil Shepherd. Whenever possible, she'd recite her dialogue from the movie and emulate Cybil's fashion choices: White blouses with colorful patterns, neck scarves, and hair bands - all matching of course. Also, earth shoes. One day, I heard her complain to Lynn that *Seventeen* didn't have enough pictures of Cybil's footwear choice, so Susan had to guess. Incorrectly, I'm going to assume.

She and Lynn headed out together. "Bye," they said at the same time.

"Neither eating?" Mom asked, out from the kitchen now, holding two plates of blintzes. For the record, I have no memory of ever having breakfast with my sisters during this period. Nevertheless, Mom felt that Jewish impulse to bring it up and go so far as to prepare platefuls of food that she knew, under no circumstances other than the food being shoved down their throats, would be eaten.

"Don't forget your brother's birthday party tonight!" she yelled after them.

"We know," they shouted back as they slammed the door behind them.

Mom finally sat with her own plate of blintzes.

Gram shook her head and said, "*Di liebe is zees, nor zi iz gut mit broyt.*"

Love is good, but better with bread.

We all laughed.

"Such a *shanda*," Gram said again because, God forbid, we stayed in a joyous place for too long.

Mom replied in half Bob Dylan sing-song and half Brooklyn Jewish dialect, "The times they are a' changin, Mom."

Unsurprisingly, the artistic mecca that was and is Manhattan had no effect on your average 1970s Brooklyn Hebrew Day School suit. Yosef Bamberger, a sight in fashion apathy, dressed in a bleached white shirt tucked unevenly into chocolate polyester slacks, a frayed brown yarmulke, and unremarkable black shoes.

I bounced down the steps of our brownstone, not skipping a one. They were too grand, too important not to acknowledge. It was one of those impeccable spring mornings: cloudless, crisp, temperature in the mid-perfects. As I strode down the sidewalk, I breathed in that glorious hybrid scent of Callery Pear trees, car exhaust, and pee. Ah, my beloved New York.

The same New York that was suffering hundreds of thousands of disappearing manufacturing jobs, a million plus welfare homes, and tripling rates of rape, burglaries, car thefts, and felony assaults. But for me and my friends, it was all merrily, merrily, merrily, life is but a dream.

Four houses down the block, Micah joined me, bouncing down his own, very similar steps. And then three houses down from there, Mitchell joined us. The camaraderie we shared would change, and quite abruptly, but on this day, it could not have been more perfect. The meshuggeners wished me a happy birthday, and we commenced running the short distance to school, past the butcher, laundromat, and deli; past the trash, aggressive pigeons, and newspaper machines; all the while air-stabbing each other with fake swords and yammering on about endless amounts of meaningless shit.

"In 'Israel: The Ever-Dying People,' the author tells us that every stage of Jewish existence has believed it will be the last."

The short, sprite Mr. Stein looked up from his notes and peered out at us, waiting for a response, as he did with every vital message.

There were nods, headshakes, oy veys – he got them all.

I can't speak for the rest of the class, but my responses to Mr. Stein were always genuine. Torah studies was my favorite; the material was always fascinating and helpful, and I was flanked by Micah and Mitchell. What's not to love?

But this day was different. About mid class, lightning struck.

The hair on the back of my head and even the ones covered by my kippa stood straight up. It was an intense feeling, enough to actually take my mind off of Jewish history and philosophy - a difficult if not impossible task at the time.

Someone was looking at me and it wasn't one of the two other meshuggeners. Discombobulated, I turned my head slightly back and to the right to see who or what had sent this firebolt through me.

And there she was, my everything, my future wife, the mother of my three beautiful children Avi, Rebecca, and Shira, the eventual woman who would douse me with love and give me Judaic purpose.

Everything around her fell out of focus as her crooked smile, deep-set green eyes, and puss-filled pimples filled my vision. Apparently, Barbi Benton and Barbara Streisand had a love child, Rachel Lederman, the future Rachel Bamberger. She was looking right at me; I was sure of it. Smiling. At me. Awkward, inelegant, tiny-penised me. Thrilled and terrified, I turned back toward Mr. Stein as quickly as I had looked away.

Maybe it was my imagination.

❦

"Sit on it!" Micah screamed at me in his heavy Brooklyn brogue as the three meshuggeners bumped and pushed our way through the Semitic youth, trying to squeeze our way out of the school lobby.

School was over and the vital topic of debate was whether or not Rachel Lederman was actually smiling at me or someone directly behind me. That person would've been Dory Fine, and the girls were indeed friends. So, maybe. It was a mystery made for Columbo.

"I'm telling you, it was me," I answered assuredly, even though I doubted it probably more than my friends did. "And keep it down," I said looking around nervously, "she could be right behind us."

"Why would she be smiling at you?!" Mitchell asked loudly.

"Good question," Micah said.

It *was* a good question. I shook my head like a baseball bobblehead. "I don't know ... I felt it."

Wrong answer.

"Yeah, you're feeling it," Mitchell screamed, "every night with a box of Kleenex!"

They both blew up with laughter. Mitchell had an older brother who he'd caught masturbating in the bathroom once. One night over potato latkes at a slumber party, he had described it to us in great detail. I thought it was all very gross. Regardless, I decided to join in the laughter. Didn't want to be the victim.

We finally made it outside. The sun was still shining, and I remembered, it was my birthday!

Then came the tap. The sweetest, kindest, most loving shoulder tap I've ever experienced, even to this day.

I turned and there she was, closer now. Rachel Lederman sent from one of the seven heavens, a masterpiece in dark blue babushka, matching blouse, and knee-level skirt.

This tap, it was not meant for Dory Fine's shoulder. Or any of the other thousands of kid shoulders Rachel Lederman could have tapped. No, this was my shoulder, Yosef Bamberger's droopy, lily-white-shirted shoulder. Her smile filled my vision.

I was more than familiar with the magnificent power a Jewish female can possess. But this was something else. This was that power to the hundredth degree. It was confusing. I didn't understand it, but I knew I wanted it.

Melting, I tried to smile back. Instead, I spit a little. A bit of lunch landed on her shirt, cheesecake. (It's usually the last thing you ate). Thank God and Moses, she didn't notice.

"Shalom," she giggled. I looked to my sides for moral and verbal support from my friends. Micah was drooling. Mitchell's eyeballs had popped out of his head. I was on my own.

"Shalom," I managed. Breathe, Yosef, breathe.

"I'm Rachel."

I nodded, tried to think of a proper response. "I'm twelve. I mean, I just turned twelve. Today!"

"Oh, happy birthday!"

"You, too," I answered.

She laughed again. What an idiot.

"I mean, thanks. I'm Yosef."

"I know. We're in Torah class together."

God, could she be any more perfect?

"Okay, bye," I stammered, turning and grabbing my friends to go. We were silent for several yards, moving fast, a trio of boy-shrieks about to explode like so much prepubescent vomit.

"Yosef!" Rachel shouted, still standing in the same spot.

I stopped, frozen.

"Yosef!" she yelled again.

"Go!" Mitchell scolded.

I turned and ran back.

"Yeah?" I asked.

She looked at me a second, squinting, as if not sure she should ask.

"Do you, uh, want to have lunch, you know, in the cafeteria, tomorrow?"

An unfamiliar, tingling sensation shot through my body. I wanted to scream in joy, pump my fists, dance like Tevye!

"Far out," I said finally.

She looked confused. "Does that mean 'yes?" Rachel asked with all sincerity.

"Yeah, sorry. It means yes. My sisters say that sometimes."

"Oh, okay," she said, with that adorable giggle of hers.

"I got to go. Shalom!" I said, running off again.

"Shalom. See you tomorrow!"

I rejoined the two meshuggeners and we moved quickly down the sidewalk, me in the middle, each of us completely freaking out.

Now they wouldn't shut up:

"What did she want?!"

"Yeah, what was that all about?!"

"Come on, spill the beans, Potsie!"

"Lay it on us!"

I felt like a king. This twelve-years-old thing was working out quite well, so far.

"Calm down, weirdos," I joked. "She wanted to know if there was homework in Torah class. She couldn't remember."

"Yes, there's homework. Wasn't she there?" Mitchell said condescendingly.

"Maybe she had something else on her mind, someone else," I snarked back.

Micah chimed in, "That was it? Homework?"

"No," I answered, baiting, conjuring. "I asked her to have lunch with me."

"What?!"

"No way, Jose!"

"Stop it!"

"Yep," I answered.

Mitchell stopped us in the middle of the gum-spotted sidewalk, his next words coming slowly: "You asked a girl on a date?"

I nodded, almost as slowly.

"What did she say?" Micah asked.

"Yes."

And with that, a vernal, riotous celebration erupted. If you could imagine a combination of America's reaction to the first moon landing, and Alex in *A Clockwork Orange* chasing a woman with a giant penis, you'll pretty much get the gist.

So for a couple years now, the three Meshuggeners had a Linden Boulevard afternoon ritual. It was as follows:

First, we'd run into the laundromat wash-and-fold and see how fast we could check all the machines for lost quarters. Customers would stare, frown and curse the hooligans. Teddy, a stout old woman with a long, gray ponytail would come out from the back and scream at us. Then, when her customers would nod in appalled agreement, she would laugh, wave them off, and tell us to have fun.

"Thanks, Teddy! Bye, Teddy!"

Second was hit the arcade and play the outta sight Orbit pinball machine. Unless we didn't have any quarters, in which case, we'd stand there, cheer, and hit the flippers as if we were playing. Ten minutes max.

Third stop was good ol' Zucker's deli. Behind the counter was jolly Jerry Zucker himself, a gathering snowball of a man due to sixty years of chopped liver sandwiches and oversized matzo balls. Each day, he'd hand us treats, then spend the rest of the time obsessively pulling his two thin, black streaks of hair across his otherwise bald head.

Today played out a little differently.

"Hello, boys," Jerry sung out in his heavy Brooklyn brogue.

"Hi, Jerry!" we answered in unison as he handed us each a chocolate babka straw.

"Yosef's got a girlfriend!" Mitchell blurted out.

"And it's his birthday!" Micah added.

"Well, well, well!" Jerry shouted with glee.

"I do not have a girlfriend," I said. "I have a date."

"Either way, babkas on me today! Happy birthday and good luck with the girlfriend."

"Thanks, Jerry," I said.

"So what's her name?"

"Rachel Lederman," I said, my head cocked and nodding, thinking her name was impressive all by itself.

"Yosef's been puckering all day, getting ready for the big kiss!" Michell said.

I popped him on the shoulder. "Shut up!"

"You have a girlfriend, Mitchell?" Jerry asked.

Mitchell shrunk. "No."

"Well ... maybe when you're fifty-eight or so. Give or take," Jerry smacked back. We all lost it laughing.

Jerry winked at me. "All right, get out of here," he said, "I got customers."

He didn't.

"Thanks, Jerry! Bye, Jerry!" We said in concert as we ran out.

We continued down the street, jamming chocolate crunchiness in our face holes. Mitchell walked backward facing us, lurching his lips at me, moaning and making moist, smacky sounds.

Was that how you did it? (Turns out, no.)

That was when he tripped. Backwards. As he went flying, his remaining Babka bounced off the pavement and landed a foot away. Micah and I burst into hysterical laughter, the kind where you can't breathe, no matter how hard you try. Doesn't get any better than that.

"Such a spaz!" Micah screamed. As Mitchell started picking up the pieces of his broken treat, a pigeon dove down, grabbed it and flew off. I didn't think we could laugh harder. But we did.

Our fourth and final stop was the synagogue. Our home away from home where we'd help the rabbi with chores around the shul. In the autumn, we'd rake the few leaves that would make the trip from far away trees. In winter, we'd shovel snow and ice off the sidewalk.

The task today: clean the ladies' room. Gross. Armed with scrub brushes and pails of soapy water, I attacked the commode, while Micah and Mitchell scrubbed the sink and floor, respectively.

"So what do you think you guys'll talk about?" Micah asked me.

"Can we just drop it already? It's one date, one lunch." My baby self was getting nervous. Was I ready for this? He had a point: What *were* we going to talk about?

The Holocaust? Sure. Then what?

I could talk about the small part of the Boeing 747 that my dad helped design, and how I was so impressed when he brought it home that it's what made me want to be an engineer.

We could talk about Gramps and how he was such a great boxer. That tended to be a popular topic for people of all ages. No it's not, you spaz!

Regardless, no way did I have enough material to last a whole lunchtime.

"Drop what?" asked a deep voice coming from the doorway. It was, of course, our beloved Rabbi Berkwitz, my third father figure. Forties, hobbit-ish, wearing a black suit and tie, and black yarmulke over a balding crown. His bushy black beard surrounded a smile that could produce a Middle East peace plan all by itself – if only they knew him.

We all stopped and looked over.

"Oh, hi Rabbi," I said smiling. "Just kibitzing." We went back to work, our scrubbing sounds echoing off the high ceiling washroom.

The rabbi nodded, smiled. "She pretty?" he asked.

"Oh. Yes. Very," I said.

Micah and Mitchell nodded and smiled in agreement.

"Of course she is," the Rabbi said. "You, young man!"

"What?" I asked, knowing exactly what he was referring to.

"It's time to start getting serious about your Bar Mitzvah studies."

There it is! From the rabbi's mouth to my pre-Bar Mitzvah ears!

Naturally, I was already taking it very seriously and he knew that better than anyone. I might've even been able to nail my Haf Torah right there in the girl's bathroom, knew it better than I knew myself. But it would have to wait.

"Yes, Rabbi. So excited."

"Good! It's going to be grand."

With that, he broke into song: "*Happy birthday toooo yoooou* ... come on boys, join with me ..." Mitchell and Micah stopped scrubbing and joined in. "*Happy birthday to you!*"

They sounded like three yowling cats, enough to send most running, but to me, it was divine.

When they were done, they applauded. The Rabbi left without another word, and me and my brothers in arms went back to the business at hand.

The day could not have been more perfect. And I hadn't even celebrated with my family yet.

THROW SALT IN HIS EYES, PEPPER IN HIS NOSE

"WHY ARE YOU LYING TO ME?" MOM SAID, HER LIPS TIGHT and jittery.

Standing in the living room, with one hand on her hip and one on the phone, she was in full interrogation mode, something I'd seen before. Gram and Gramps were sitting on the sofa.

I was at the dining room table, trying to do my homework. The smell of Gram's simmering chicken was practically narcotic, and it was impossible not to listen to Mom's one-sided argument. Homework could wait.

"Why is it, that for weeks, every time I've called, he's been in a meeting? How is that possible?"

As she listened to the response, the sound of Gramps' breathing filled the silence. It was nice, calmed things down a little.

"Yes! I have brought it up with him. He says he has lots of meetings these days. That's a lot of dreck, Patricia!"

Breathing, breathing.

"Well, it's almost five o'clock, and it's his son's birthday! I'm simply calling to remind him to pick up the paper plates! I have his gift! Mom made the cake! All he has to do is pick up the Goddamn paper plates! Do you think he could do that, Mr. busy busy meeting man?!"

Breathing, breathing.

"Is he telling you to tell me this? Is he telling you to tell me this?! Sh-sh-shush! I'm asking you - is he telling you to tell me that?!"

Patricia was dad's secretary at the engineering firm. I only met her once over the years, and all I remember was her green eye shadow. Both eyes. She looked like an alien from *Lost in Space*. That said, just because she was from another planet, that didn't mean she should have to suffer the wrath of Sandy Bamberger. Part of me enjoyed watching the Sandy show in those early days. It was a true study in pissed off, Jewish New Yorker; brimming with righteousness, persistence, superiority, and volume.

Suddenly, Mom slammed the phone down, charging the air with that resonating ringtone rotary phones made when they hit the cradle. Gram and Gramps winced.

She took a deep breath in and out, smiled at her parents, and joined me at the table. Apparently, at least for now, she wanted to forget it. Maybe, because it was my birthday. Or maybe she sensed something else and just didn't want to talk about it with us.

Grabbing the latest Sears catalogue from the table, she flipped to the men's underwear section. The Three Musheggeners had had our boy giggles with that edition, as we did with every edition: boys, as well as grown men, showing off their tightie whities. It was hilarious. Although, we did also spend several minutes in the women's underwear section.

"Need underwear, sweetie?" Mom asked me, her previous frustration now completely gone.

"No," I answered. I probably did, but I was becoming more and more uncomfortable with Mom having anything to do with it. Micah had said there was actually another way to buy underwear. Say what?! Yes, according to rumor, you could actually go to a store and buy underwear.

"Go in your father's underpants drawer, the top one. Tell me his size."

"Gross. Why?"

"Because he needs underpants. Just because you don't, he doesn't?"

"You don't know his size?"

"I forgot," she shot back.

"Fi-i-i-i-i-ine."

Exasperated, I got up and headed down the hallway.

Mom and Dad's room was the darkest in the house. Jammed up against the neighbor's house on one end, it was the only window faced north, so there wasn't much sun. It was yet another room stuffed like a kasha knish. There was Mom's giant, antique armoire, Dad's chest of drawers, a secretariat, a double bed, several random chairs, and framed family photos on every inch of every wall. For me, the room was the womb: always comfortable, warm, safe, bursting with love.

I went to my dad's chest and as I was about to open the top drawer, I noticed the bottom drawer was open a bit, so I went to close it, but something inside caught my eye.

I knelt down and pulled the drawer all the way open. It looked like papers of some sort, creeping out from under one of Dad's polo shirts. I moved the shirt aside and saw it was a magazine. On the cover was a young woman smiling and posing, her breasts only half covered. In giant type, above her, the title read: JUGGS.

My breath caught.

I looked toward the hall to make sure no one was coming, then slowly picked it up. This was obviously an important book, sacramental, much like the Torah. It needed careful handling. My hands trembled as it opened naturally to the centerfold.

And there she was, jugs and more.

"*Oy gevalt.*"

As I kneeled there, drooling, a subscription card slipped out and fell to the floor. Knowing Mom was going to wonder what was taking so long, I hurriedly grabbed it to put it back, but then noticed - it wasn't a subscription card, it was some kind of ticket. It said:

DELTA Coach rear cabin 34A JFK-TYS

"Yosef!"

I jumped, dropped everything. Mom was screaming from the dining room.

25

"Shouldn't be that hard!"

"Coming!" I screamed back.

I picked everything up, shoved the ticket thing back into the mag, slid it back under the clothes, slammed the drawer shut and ran out.

"What's wrong?" Mom asked as I approached, seeing something was off from the weird mix of excitement and confusion on my face.

"Nothing." I sat down, tried to breathe naturally and focus on my homework. She continued to stare at me.

"So?"

"So what?"

"His underwear size?"

"Oh!" I nodded, remembering. "Forty-six."

Mom nodded slightly, her eyes slivery, skeptical. She knew I was lying. I didn't lie much in those days, so I don't know how she got so good at it, so quickly. I focused back on my schoolwork, and after another moment, she was back to buying underpants.

At the time, I had never flown on a plane and had no idea what a boarding pass looked like. Because of where I found it, I figured it was some kind of ticket to boobs. But whose? The model's? Someone else's? Were Mom's not good enough for some reason? This was obviously a secret, or Dad wouldn't have hidden the magazine in the first place. It was bothering me so much I couldn't focus on my studies.

Finally, I decided I would keep a close eye on him and report back to Mom if I noticed any further unfavorable behavior.

⁂

Like mornings, we also had an evening routine. Gram and Mom would be in the kitchen. The girls would be in their rooms studying. Dad would be on his way home. Gramps would be in his and Gram's room, shining his championship belt. And I'd be going from room to room, being a general noodge.

Of course, since it was my birthday, this night was different. Gram and Mom were putting together a special, more intricate dinner. My sisters hadn't kicked me out of their rooms quite as quickly as they usually did. Dad was late because he was buying paper plates. (At least, that's what we thought.) Gramps was doing what he always did. And I was hopping around the house, like some kind of deranged birthday kangaroo, the suspense of it all too heady for stillness.

"Hi, Gramps," I said, bouncing into his room.

"*Zeeskeit!*" he said, rubbing his belt in circles with a small cloth. "Ready for the big celebration?"

"Can't wait!"

"You don't have a choice," he said, smiling. "Sit."

I plotzed onto the bed and watched him, mesmerized by the zen-like polishing. It calmed me, which I think, was his intent.

It also got me thinking.

"What you thinking about? Girls?" he asked, not looking up.

I laughed. "No," I answered, although the two subjects would become intricately connected. "Gramps?"

"Yes?"

"Were you, uh … were you, you know … little when you were my age?"

"Short then, shorter now."

I could tell he thought I was talking about height. "That's not exactly what I mean," I said, hoping he'd figure it out.

It took him a couple seconds, then, "Oh! You mean my penis!"

"Shhhhh!" I laughed, putting a shaky finger to my lips, and nodding.

"Oh, sure, schmekel for years, until, let's see … got to jar the memory, here. I guess my penis grew when I was … hmm … thirteen, fourteen? Yeah. Somewhere in there."

"Oh. Okay." It wasn't the answer I'd hoped for.

I was about to get up, but then stopped with another question. "Well, before it grew, did you, you know, do anything to *make* it grow?"

"Do anything?"

"Forget it. It's okay," I said, getting up this time.

"No, no, no. Sit down," he said, putting his belt on the bed now.

I sat.

"Listen, don't judge your penis based on me. I'll tell you why. I don't know if you knew this ... but your Gramps is always late, have been my whole life." He counted on his fingers. "I was late to puberty, also boxing, marriage, having a child. Sometimes, I'm even late to conversations."

I laughed.

"That's just me," he said, "not you. For you, it could be any second now."

"That'd be cool," I said, hopeful.

"You know," Gramps said, puffing out his chest. "Eventually, I grew to be the size of the frickin' Empire State Building."

"Gramps!" I shouted, laughing.

"It's true. Jewish men tend to be sizeable in that department. So ... it's worth the wait. Of course, today, it's back to nothing. *Meshuggeneh velt.*"

He joined me in the laughter now. It's cyclical. Who knew?

In time, we calmed and caught our breath. I hugged him and left him to his nightly task.

It was almost time for the party.

❧❦❧

The Jewish people have always been very good at tension. With the slavery in Egypt, Torquemada's pet project expelling Jews from Spain and, of course, the devastating Holocaust, there's been ample opportunity to perfect it.

Naturally, we were experts.

That evening, me, Mom, Gram, Gramps, Susan, Lynn, and her boyfriend, Jacob Feldman, all sat, silent at the dining room table. A gorgeous, Gram-prepared, kosher meal was laid out before us: perfectly-browned chicken, steamed carrots (yuck – then and now), and bread from Zabars. The only thing missing? Dad - the current reason for the inquisition-level tension.

The quiet was killing me.

"Smells really good, Gram," I said.

"I hope that it also tastes good," she said.

Someone's stomach growled.

"How long are we gonna wait?" Susan asked, looking at Mom.

"He had to get paper plates for cake," Mom shot back.

"He's over an hour late," Susan responded.

"Do you really think he'd miss his own son's birthday dinner?!" Mom screamed.

"Not on purpose," Susan answered, kicking the elephant in the room.

"Maybe we should pray," said Jacob suddenly. I caught an eye roll from Susan. I scowled at her; something I did often.

Jacob was a dark-skinned beauty, a short, twenty, Sephardic Jew, with a paisley yarmulke and eyebrows that doubled as caterpillars. He had an unusual accent - a French infused Moroccan dialect. Before I met him, I'd never heard anything like it. Everyone liked Jacob, even if he wasn't an Ashkenazi, European Jew like us and most of the people we knew. That year, he got me a book for my birthday: *The Apollo Space Program.* I loved it. Still have it.

Lynn gazed lovingly at Jacob, as the idea of praying sat with the group. I was against it as it meant there was an actual reason to be praying. Praying for what exactly?

"I think we should," Gramps said, finally. Until that moment, Mom hadn't become visibly worried. Now, I noticed a periodic shake, as if a Nor'easter was blasting her in the face every few seconds.

"Which prayer, Jacob?" Gram asked.

"Oh, well, I suppose Tefilat HaDerech, the traveler's prayer. He's traveling from Manhattan, yes?"

Nods all around.

"So, in English, let's see..." Jacob began as we all stood.

"May it be Your will, Lord, our God and God of our ancestors…" he paused as we all repeated his words, everyone but Lynn and Susan swaying as they prayed.

"May it be Your will, Lord, our God and God of our ancestors…"

Jacob continued: "…that You lead us toward peace, guide our footsteps toward peace…" "… that You lead us toward peace, guide our footsteps toward peace…"

"… and make us reach our desired destination for life, gladness and peace."

"… and make us reach our desired destination for life, gladness and peace."

Everyone sat down. Unfortunately, the prayer made me feel worse. A burgeoning fear was now, slowly digging its claws into me. What could've happened?

Were the paper plates too expensive at the first store he tried, and he had to go to another place?

Was he mugged and killed?

Had he fallen into the East River and sunk to the nasty, muddy bottom? Maybe, at least, remembering my birthday, his desperate, bubbly, last words were *Happy birthday, Zees.*

If he was dead, I knew one thing: we would not have my birthday dinner without him. That would be disrespectful. No, we'd wait until we, also, passed into eternal rest. I could see us all sitting there, disintegrating, gray brittlely bones hunched over the rotted brisket, cobwebs the only thing now connecting us, sans Dad, of course.

"Maybe he's still at work!" I blurted out. "Let's call him!"

"It's seven," answered Lynn.

"The office is closed. I called before we sat down," Mom said.

Gram muttered painfully, "*Du Zol Nicht Vissen Frum Tsores.*"

Suddenly, Mom grabbed the serving fork and knife and started cutting the chicken.

She served the birthday boy first. Then everyone else.

And we ate, in excruciating, heartburn-inducing, terror-filled silence.

It takes a lot to keep Jews from eating.

At the end of the meal - as was tradition when we had chicken - Susan and I each held a side of the wishbone and made our silent wishes. Mine was a combo about Rachel and Dad still being alive. I expected Susan wished she could stop doing our stupid little custom. It didn't exactly jibe with her being a cranky, I-hate-my-little-brother teenager. But she took a hold of the bone without pause.

"Ready? Go," I said. We tore it apart, the bone snapping loudly. She got the bigger side.

Mom had disappeared into the kitchen and was now walking out, carrying a giant chocolate cake with twelve lit candles.

And then, even with all this *tsures*, in that amazing voice, she sang: "*Happy birthday to you...*"

Everyone joined in: "*Happy birthday to you, happy birthday Dear Yosef, happy birthday to you.*"

I smiled weakly, then blew out the candles. No wish this time.

We ate cake.

On our regular plates.

That Mom would have to wash.

There wasn't much conversation. At this point, we were all just trying to get through the evening before the police would come to the door with news of Dad's demise.

A couple bites in, Mom handed me my gift. A gold, round box about the size of a grown turtle.

"What is it?" I asked.

"Open it," she answered. I ripped it open and pulled out a brand new, sky blue yarmulke. I held back tears as I gazed at its beauty, its significance. "Thanks, Mom."

"You got to have a new kippah for your Bar Mitzvah," she said, nodding, smiling sadly.

Everyone was smiling actually, even Susan, a little. They all knew what it meant to me.

I took off my old one, and just as I put the new one on … the front door swung wildly open, banging the opposite wall causing everyone to jump and scream out.

"Dad!" Me, Lynn and Susan shouted. I shot out of my chair and ran over to him, hugging him tighter than I ever had.

"Where the hell have you been?!" Mom fumed.

"*Du Zol Nicht Vissen Frum Tsores!*" Gram said louder than normal.

Jacob and Gramps were the only quiet ones. Jacob barely knew Dad, but happy Lynn was happy. Gramps sat back down, nodding and sighing a loud relief.

Out of breath, Dad closed the door behind him as the various pleadings and insults continued. He was surprisingly not wet or muddy, with no visible concrete from a mob encounter. Instead, he was sweaty, stinky, and chock full of *shpilkes* (anxiety).

And sans paper plates.

Dad raised his hands, trying to calm everyone. "I'm okay! I'm okay. Everybody, sit, sit."

He took a few steps further in, like a man might enter a housefire to save a beloved cat, tentative with no choice. He managed to avoid eye contact with Mom as we all stood, defiant, demanding answers.

"Well?!" Mom asked.

He caught his breath, swallowed. "I had to catch a later flight, didn't have time to call."

"Flight?" Mom, Lynn, and Susan all said at once.

Dad looked down at me, "Happy birthday, Zees. Really sorry I'm late. Your new kippah looks fabulous on you."

"Thanks." I wanted to know what flight too.

Mom again, "Flight from where?!"

He paused yet again, then spit it out, "Oak Ridge, Tennessee."

The room filled with blank, unaware of anything south of Philly, New Yorker stares.

"For work?" I asked.

"Yes," Dad answered. "Oak Ridge is a town in East Tennessee, very famous town, actually. During World War II, they enriched the uranium for the Atomic Bomb. Kept the whole town, the whole town!... under wraps to make sure the Germans couldn't find it."

"*Du Zol Nicht Vissen Frum Tsores!*" Gram interrupted, her hand up to God.

Dad nodded sadly to her, then continued, "They called it the secret city. Fascinating, right?"

I see now he was trying to get us excited about this odd little place. For me, it worked, at least for the moment. I was always fascinated by history, and of course, engineering. I wanted to know more, but soon enough, the gist of the conversation shifted.

"And you were there on some kind of project?" Mom asked, suspiciously.

Dad went quiet as he seemed to develop a *tell*, an invisible string pulling at his right cheek. Even I realized he was delaying. Then I remembered ... *Delta coach rear cabin 34A.*

"Murray! What?!" Mom yelled.

"I got a job," Dad spewed quickly, stepping back.

Instead, it was dead air. Catatonic stares. Confusion.

Dad walked to the dining table and leaned against his chair at the head, as if to remind us who the patriarch was.

"I was laid off from my job, here, months ago. I was ashamed ... so I pretended to go to work every day. I'd go to the park. Coffee shop. The movies."

He looked up, gauging our faces. I felt bad for him. He had been lying to us, but was unhappy and obviously hurting.

"I looked everywhere in New York," he said. "There's nothing."

Mom glared at him with narrowed eyes, slivers of rage, her mouth slightly open like a deadly snake about to strike across the table.

Dad went on. Verbal vomit, it had to come out. "Finally, a recruitment company called me about the Oak Ridge job. So, um … we're moving."

Wait. What?

Moving?

Moving?

Moving?!

As it sunk in, an avalanche of emotions started to bury me alive. Confusion. Terror. Anger. Sadness. Shock. Contempt. Extra terror. A lot more anger. Too bad about that East River drowning that never happened!

Tears followed, monsoon levels. This couldn't be happening.

"What the hell are you talking about, moving?" Mom managed.

"I accepted the new position so we … we are moving to Tennessee." There were equal parts fear and defiance in his voice. "I start at the K-25 engineering plant in a few weeks."

Mom dropped her face into her hands. It was so loud it made a slapping sound. She was crying and shaking her head, back and forth.

"Don't hillbillies live there?" Susan asked.

"You mean like the *Beverly Hillbillies*?" I asked her.

"No," she said, "I think it's more like *Green Acres.*"

"Stop, you two!" Dad snapped. "It's a mix of people!"

"I have a life here. I have a boyfriend," Lynn said, looking at Dad only a moment before locking eyes with the equally freaked out Jacob.

Gram was squeezing her husband's hand. "Do they have gefilte fish there? Spinach log? Tongue?" she asked.

"All of it!" Dad assured her.

"This is ridiculous, ridiculous, this is ridiculous," Mom muttered over and over, her face still buried.

My crying had become gaspy. I was feeling nauseous, and I could hear my heart beating. This had to be a nightmare. It had to be. This couldn't be happening. We were too New York. Too Brooklyn. Too sewn into the Jewish culture quilt. It was everything. We knew not a soul in this place, this Tennessee place. I couldn't fathom how I'd survive there.

I was trying to find the strength to form words. It took some doing, finally managing to squeak out, "What about my Bar Mitzvah?"

Mom looked up at me, her face a wet, furious mess. Everyone stared at Dad, waiting for an answer.

"We'll come back for it," Mom said.

Oh, good. Thank God.

"That won't work," Dad answered, gutting me again. "You can't plan for a Bar Mitzvah a thousand miles away. It would be too expensive. I haven't worked for months. But there's good news! The company's paying for our move! How great is that?!"

No one thought it was great. Lynn joined the crying team now, then shot up out of her chair and ran into her room. Jacob followed. The half-father, half-gargoyle watched them, trying to think of something to say. Nothing came.

He looked back at me. "Zees, they have a synagogue."

"So! It's not our synagogue!"

"It's nice. I've seen it. Maybe a little smaller. It's cute, you know."

I was staring at him in disbelief. Cute?! Who describes a synagogue as cute? Puppies, baby subway rats, they're cute. Synagogues, no. Tell me, how does a Brooklyn boy become a Brooklyn man in a synagogue that's cute?! How exactly would the three meshuggeners have a grand celebration in a synagogue that's cute?! And if, by cute, you really mean dilapidated shack like Oliver and Lisa Douglas might live in, then no thank you! Next thing you're going to tell me Sam Drucker is the cantor, and Mr. Haney's the rabbi.

I ripped the new yarmulke from my head and stood up screaming, "This isn't fair! This isn't fair!" Not sure how many times I said it. More than two, less than sixty-seven.

I ran into my room and slammed the door behind me as hard as I could – as if *that* would convince Dad to reconsider destroying our lives.

"Ahhhhhhhhhhhhhhhhhhhh!!!!!!!"

I erupted into full tilt Godzilla. Guttural from the soul screaming, grabbing every chachki and toy from my chest of drawers and shelves and throwing them across the room like tiny, crashing airplanes. I tore the posters from my walls, crumpled them into giant balls of paper, stomped on them. I even flung my Anne Frank book across the room.

"Ahhhhhhhhhhhhhhhhhhhh!!!!!!!"

Exhausted, I fell onto my bed and continued screaming, now unintelligibly into my pillow.

It wasn't long before I heard the yelling coming from Mom and Dad's room. I shot up and plastered my ear to the wall that separated our rooms. Mom would take of this. She would scream some sense into him.

I listened with hope.

"You lied to me!" she shouted. "I knew it!"

"I'm sorry," Dad said, "I wasn't ready—"

"You weren't ready! You weren't ready! You lose your job, you tell your wife, Goddamit! Goddamn you! Maybe we could've figured something out together?! Ever think about that?! I know why you didn't tell me."

"Oh?"

"Because if you did," she snarked, "I would've stopped you before you could accept the job. I'm right!"

Dad didn't answer. This was something he'd figured out long ago. Just do it. Better to ask forgiveness than permission.

"Murray, this is insane. We don't know anyone there! No one!"

"You don't think I'm nervous? I've never lived anywhere else either. This was not an easy decision."

"Jews do not live in Oak Range, Tennessee!" Mom screamed.

"Oak *Ridge*. And yes, there are Jewish people there."

"Oh? How many?"

"I don't know exactly," Dad answered. Turns out, he did ask his boss, who answered with one word: *Plenty*. Hmm. Pretty subjective. He could've meant plenty as in there are too many for his taste. Or he could've meant

36

there were thousands and he often joined them for Friday night services at the cute synagogue.

"You know the Cohens," Dad asked, "from the Bronx?"

"Of course I know the Cohens from the Bronx. What am I, suddenly senile?"

"When their ancestors came over from Russia, they settled in Gastonia, North Carolina."

"Right! *North* Carolina!" she screamed. "Murray Bamberger, you have lost your mind!"

There was a long pause. I thought it might be over, but then Dad spoke again, quietly, trying to calm her.

"Sandy, darling, I know this is hard. But it's not going to be as bad as you think."

"It's going to be very bad! Very, very bad! How can you do this to your family?!" She was crying again.

"I'm doing it *for* my family. We are running out of money staying here. Would you rather be a bum on the street, or move where I have a good job with a good salary?"

"What about our friends?! We have friends here! If money is that low, someone will take us in until you found something."

"I've been looking for months. There's nothing, I'm telling you. Sandy, it's a nice place, you'll see. There are birds and squirrels and ...all kinds of nice things."

"We have birds and squirrels and nice things!"

"Not like there. And the neighborhoods, much safer."

"Shut up, shut up, shut up!" she screamed, so loud this time, I pulled my ear from the wall. But just for a moment.

I listened closely again, barely hearing her last words that night.

"Just leave me alone," she whimpered. "Leave me alone." She had finally ran out of anger.

As Dad walked out, closing the bedroom door behind him, a shiver went through me, head to toe. I had never heard her so defeated. Mom and I were still so very connected, joined by a kind of spiritual umbilical cord, and this yielding made me feel even more weak, vulnerable, and threatened than I already was. Ironically, this would be the beginning of our separation.

But then, laying back down on my bed, I had a different thought. This was my mother. The strong, Jewish matriarch, get-out-of-my-fucking-way Sandy Solomon Bamberger. She had more fight in her. She would devise a plan to stop this madness. That was Mom, there was always a plan.

And, maybe, just maybe, if we both had plans to thwart the evil father, it would have twice the effect, and therefore be more likely to succeed.

BOONE LEARNS

BOONE MACAFEE'S FATHER WAS KILLED ON MAY 1ST, 1945, ONE day after Hitler committed suicide. Unaware their führer was gone, the Germans had continued to fight and Callum Macafee's throat got in the way of one of the last bullets fired. It wouldn't be till May 8th when the Germans would finally stand down. Boone was barely a sprout at the time, under four feet, scrawny, dirty, with shaved head above silver-blue eyes and unbrushed teeth. He was only seven, but he remembered it well since he lost his mother that same week.

An hour after she received the news of her husband's passing, the twenty-five-year-old Isla filled an old sack with a few dresses and told Boone to go stay with his uncle.

"Muir's a good Southern Baptist, everything he does is for Jesus. He'll take fine care of you, just fine," she said. Then she kissed his head, smiled because she was supposed to, and disappeared out the rickety shack door. He would never see her again.

Back then, Oliver Springs was a coal mining town. Muir worked in the mine and lived in a slightly nicer shanty than Boone had lived in with his folks. The insulation was better, so Boone didn't mind being there in wintertime. It was just the two of them as Muir had never married and never cared to. He was a quiet loner, wasn't much for children, but having just lost his only brother, he felt compelled to take the boy in. It's what Jesus would do. But it didn't take him long to see that having Boone in his life was also an opportunity.

"Son, if there's one thing you ever learn," Muir said one night at supper, "it's that niggers and jews...they's soulless creatures, cursed by God, not even human. They might appear to be, but that's what the devil does, you see. This war, the war we're in right here, right now, is us - the children of light - against them, the children of darkness. Purification is a necessity. You understand me?" Muir was pop-eyed, his face taut with animus as he waited for a response.

Boone nodded passionately, feeling and connecting with the resentment against the enemy, and just as much wanting to please the man he considered his new father.

Muir had gone on to explain that the Klan had actually been fading in the past few years because fewer men were joining the rallies, likely due to so many going off to fight in the world war. But the few that were still in Tennessee, they would soldier on. He said their war was actually more important than the bigger one because the enemy was here, on American soil. You couldn't say that about the Germans or the Japs. This wasn't exactly true, but even if Muir had known of the Duquesne Spy Ring or the bombing of Ellwood Oil Field, his goal was one of recruitment, not facts.

A few hours after supper, Muir grabbed a sack he had by the front door. Then, the two of them jumped into his crumbling, old Ford truck and headed out into the dark night. Earlier, when Boone asked Muir why he was allowed to stay up so late, he wouldn't tell him. He also wouldn't tell him where they were going, just that it would be part of his schoolin'. Boone was practically trembling with anticipation. He couldn't imagine anything having to do with school being this exciting.

Soon, Muir pulled over to the side of the road and parked between a slew of other automobiles, some old, some new. There was even a motorcycle. Boone had never seen one of those before.

Muir led Boone into an open, pitch-black field and started walking. Boone couldn't see a thing, his uncle included, but he could hear him, so he kept close using his ears. He might've been a little scared, but he wasn't about to tell his uncle that.

Finally, after what felt like an hour, right when he thought he might drop from exhaustion, Boone smelled the thick smoke and saw the red glow up ahead. A rally was underway.

As they joined the outskirts of the fifty-plus crowd, Muir knelt and pulled their very own sheets and hats out of the sack. He put on Boone's outfit, then his own.

This was like dressing up for Halloween, Boone thought. He had never celebrated Halloween before because there was a sugar shortage during the war. No sugar, no candy. No candy, no Halloween. But now, since the war had ended, Boone figured they'd have plenty of sugar for candy again, and the holiday would come back into fashion come October. He had heard some older kids talking about it. Apparently, the way it worked was you dress up as a ghost or a monster or an old dog or something, and you go from house to house where they give you the candy. For free!

Near the fire, in the middle of the crowd, one of the men was screaming atop a crate of some sort. Boone watched as the fire threw its jumpy orange flares across the long grass and bleached linen. It was all so intoxicating. The late hour, midnight, when he'd normally be in bed. The thundering crickets and frogs. The sea of white men with a purpose, a common enemy. He felt connected immediately.

He remembered that Uncle Muir had told him not to say anything - just watch, listen, and learn. So he decided to listen. There could be a quiz later, or worse, a test.

The man was describing the latest *Black horror* as he put it. Someone saw a nigger boy, not much older than Boone, gawk at a white girl as she entered the Piggly Wiggly grocery store. This would not do. One minute, a look. The next, a rape. The next, mixed race babies roaming the great Southern United States. No, this would not do. The plan was to capture the boy and lynch him. It would be done this coming Saturday.

Boone didn't know what the word lynch meant, but he saw that Uncle Muir did, and it thrilled him. Boone figured he should act excited as well, so he screamed and jumped up and down.

The angry man on the crate went on shouting, and soon, Boone began to have trouble concentrating. He couldn't see very well out of the eye holes in his hood, so he adjusted it, hoping that would help. It did a little, but he was getting tired again and wanted nothing but to lay down and sleep. Maybe they wouldn't notice.

His eyes began to flutter closed. This went on for a while. He'd pull them open with a head shake, then they'd slowly close again. He realized if his uncle caught him, he'd be in big ol' trouble. Finally, he smacked himself hard in the face. It stung terribly, but it worked. A man standing a few feet away saw him do it, but Boone thought he saw the man chuckle under his hood. *Thank you, Jesus*, he thought. *Thank you, Jesus.*

❧❧❧

White men with black faces and vacant stares dragged themselves from the mine, every one of them exhausted and happy to be heading home. Boone broke from the group and trudged across the rocky parking lot toward his car, a beat-up old Chevy.

It was 1960, and Boone was twenty-two, a strong, broad, young man with an overcast demeanor, unkempt teeth, and those knifelike blue eyes. He'd been walking out of that damn mine since he was thirteen-years-old, Uncle Muir, by his side, every day.

That is, up until about three months ago. Muir had suddenly retired, and Boone only found out when his uncle stopped showing up for work. He had to go see him to get the full story, and even then all Muir said was *I ain't breathin' right.* In those days, black lung disease wasn't understood much, nor was it your typical conversation over after work beers.

For the two men, family didn't exactly equate to fondness. Regardless, Boone was slow to become accustomed to Muir's absence. He had been the major influence in his life.

This evening, though, something else was different – there was a whiff of resolve around Boone. He'd made a decision, or was close to one at least.

When he reached his car, he fell in, making a grunting sound normally reserved for old men. He wiped his face with the back of his hand, then hacked up something nasty, and spit it out his window.

Before long, Boone was curving slowly down Highway 61, passing the oak and poplar trees, the sun dropping behind him. He liked to take it slow on the short ride home to Oak Ridge. It was the only time he could truly be alone. He could pick his nose if he wanted, pass gas, pray, whatever fancied him in the moment. Today, it was all mind chatter. Would he have the guts to quit? Would his boss try to talk him out of it? Would he be able to make enough in his new career to support he and his wife?

Genesis 2:24 came to mind, and he spoke it aloud as he gazed out at the asphalt before him. "Therefore a man shall leave his father and mother, and hold fast to his wife, and they shall become one flesh." Boone nodded slightly. He had dozens of biblical passages memorized, but this was one he had recited, not only at his wedding, but several times since. Unlike so many men at the mine, Boone took his marital commitment seriously. Jesus would have it no other way.

Two and half miles later, he pulled into a skinny driveway at 133 Michigan Avenue. The house was a modest, peach-colored single-family ranch style home. It was built during the war for workers who were helping to build the Atomic Bomb, although none of them knew it at the time. Boone had little knowledge or interest of Oak Ridge as the *Secret City*, as they called it. Only that it just happened to be where his wife worked and wanted to live.

But the house, now that was something he'd dreamed about. It was a far cry from the decrepit shacks he grew up in. Wood floors instead of dirt. Two bedrooms instead of one. Furnace heat instead of a wood-burning stove. A bathroom instead of an outhouse. There were even acres of woods behind the house for hunting. When they moved in, it was the first time in Boone's life he'd felt like he'd achieved something. All that time in the mine had actually paid off.

That feeling lasted about three weeks. Then darkness overtook him again.

Boone walked inside, headed straight for the small dining area and plopped into a chair.

A stunning, wide-eyed twenty-year-old girl-woman floated in with a can of Coca-Cola.

"Hey darlin'," she sang in her perfect, lilting Southern accent. She kissed Boone's filthy forehead and opened the soda for him.

Dorothy Ogle Macafee. Flour-covered apron over a petite, thin frame. Dirty blonde hair. Sublime smile. Her most noticeable attribute, a red sea of face freckles. Dorothy's parents moved to Oak Ridge from a small town in Virginia, just after the war when she was six. Her father worked in the same coal mine as Boone. That's how they met.

Dorothy sat down, wiggly and excited - the lively behavior unusual for her. Boone didn't notice.

"I have something to tell you," she teased.

Boone stared into his open Coke.

"What's wrong?" she asked.

"I can't do this no more," he said with his warbly, Southern drawl.

"Do what?" she said, suddenly shaken.

"Work in that damn mine," Boone said.

"Oh," she said, relieved. "Darlin', I understand. It's hard. Daddy used to tell me about it all the time."

Boone took a long swig as they sat in silence: the devoted wife anxious to tell of her news, and the miserable husband stuck in his muddy black, coal mine existence.

"Boone Macafee, you are a good man. You are a smart man. You are a man of Jesus. You can do anything you want because Jesus loves you. And he's not the only one."

This made him chuckle, buried though, down in his throat. He looked up at her.

"You think I could be a preacher?"

44

"What? Oh … well, sure!" Dorothy said loudly, smiling. "I think you'd be great. Do you got to study for that?"

"I don't know. I know the Bible inside and out," Boone said, proudly.

"Yes, you do."

Boone started to get excited, a rare thing. "I's thinkin' of lookin' into it."

Dorothy added, "You should. Meantime, you could maybe do custodial work at K-25 or X-10. I heard they's hiring." Dorothy took his hand, squeezing it. "You do not need to be going up into Oliver Springs every day for work when there's work in Oak Ridge. Especially in that dirty ol' mine."

Boone nodded as he took another hit of Coke. He looked up at her, his expression now, slowly turning lascivious.

Dorothy recognized that look. Alarmed, she stood up quickly. "Why'nt you go get cleaned up. Dinner be ready soon, okay? We'll talk more."

Before she could turn away, Boone grabbed her hand, put his soda on the table, and stood up. He started kissing her aggressively, all around her face.

She kissed him back, sweetly, but dismissively. "Go on now."

"Oh no you don't," Boone said playfully, now pushing her against the wall and removing her apron. "Let's have some fun. You like it when I'm dirty like this. You said so."

Dorothy tried to push him away - ever so slightly. She was pleading, "Darlin', I love you so much, I just … this is … not, not now."

Boone pinned her wrists above her head, began kissing around her breasts as he unbuttoned her blouse.

Sex with Boone was always the same: part lust, part violence. Dorothy would often be bruised afterward. She'd never understand how someone she loved so deeply could express himself that way.

But she dealt with it, that's just what a good Southern girl did if she found herself in that situation. She figured he loved her and that was all that mattered.

But now, she had something else to consider, *someone* else to consider.

"I'm pregnant!" she blurted out.

This stopped Boone.

"What?" he looked at her stunned.

"I'm pregnant, darlin'," she said, tears pooling.

It took a couple more seconds for it to sink in. "You serious?"

"I am serious!" she yelled, throwing her now loose arms around him. "I think it's a boy!"

They hugged for a long while. Dorothy continued to weep. Boone was in shock.

Suddenly, he pulled out of the embrace. "You need to get on the sofa! Get your feet up!"

"Oh, darlin'," Dorothy giggled, "there's no need for that now."

Boone ignored the comment and led her gingerly to the living room, then sat her down.

"What do you want? You want some water? I can go get some pickles and ice cream. You want some of that? You just tell me."

Dorothy laughed again. She wasn't hating the attention. "Some ice cream'd be nice."

"Be right back," Boone said as he took off toward the front door. "Wait," he said stopping and turning back. "What flavor?"

"I don't know. You decide."

"You like that, uh, Neo stuff, what is it?"

"Neapolitan," Dorothy answered, smiling.

"Right! Neapolitan! Comin' up!"

And with that, he was gone.

Judging by Boone's anxiety level, you'd think Dorothy's water just broke, but he did eventually calm down.

Boone knew he didn't know a lot. He sometimes got confused about things, but he did know things were about to change … big time. The baby only cemented his decision to find other, safer, cleaner work. Although he never considered himself the parental type, this made him happy. He had a fine girl, a house, and soon, a boy. And maybe he'd even become a successful preacher, spreading love through the word of Jesus. It was the most joy he'd ever felt.

THE BATTLE OF BROOKLYN

FOR THE FIRST FEW MOMENTS, I DIDN'T KNOW WHERE I WAS. Everything was blurry, jittery, like I was drunk, but that couldn't be, cause at the time, I didn't know what that felt like. Although, when I was eleven, I did have one sip of Mogen David wine at someone's wedding. Dad had snuck it to me when Mom wasn't looking.

A crowd was roaring, and I realized I was at Shea Stadium, where the New York Mets play. Everything was still fuzzy, but I could see that pitcher Tug McGraw was on the mound. He pulled back and threw a fast ball …

That's when I woke up, breathing hard, scared shitless. About what, I didn't know. Baseball's not typically terrifying.

I shot out of bed and went out into the hall.

In my white, blue-striped PJs, I tip-toed slowly toward Mom and Dad's room. It was 2am or so, the only noises being our creaky floor and a few sirens in the distance.

I opened their door slowly and peeked in. Only Mom was in bed, restless, but asleep. I figured Dad was on the sofa in the living room. Satisfied, I moved further down the hall. Creak, creak, you never knew where.

I peeked into Gram and Gramps's room. They were sleeping soundly.

Suddenly, right behind me, I heard a whisper. "Yos."

Unsurprised, I turned to see Lynn, standing in her full-length, yellow nightgown. My sister, the beautiful light-sleeper in lemon. She put her hand on my shoulder and walked me back to my room.

I slipped back into bed as she sat on the edge and looked at me smiling. "Same nightmare?" she asked, lovingly.

I nodded.

"I figured you'd have one tonight, of all nights."

My nightmares had become routine, a couple a week. After each one, I'd jump out of bed and make sure everyone was alive and present. Then Lynn would hear me in the hall, get up and get me back to bed.

She looked around my destroyed room. "Damn."

I shrugged, indignant, resentful.

"I get it. It's probably a good way to get out your anger. Better than punching someone." She was making an obvious reference to Gramps. Lynn was never a fan of his violent career.

My eyes must have told it, but I wasn't ready for her to leave. She sat there, looking perfectly maternal, waiting for me to talk.

"Are you nervous," I asked, "you know, about moving?"

Lynn nodded fiercely. "Definitely. It's so weird, isn't it? I can't even imagine not living here. Or living there."

"Me either," I said, desperately hoping she was going to suddenly have the perfect solution.

Instead, she sighed loudly, the type where one's voice mingles with the breath for emphasis.

"We'll figure it out," she said. "We don't have a choice."

With that, she bent down, her long hair tickling my face, and kissed my forehead. "Good night, John Boy."

"Good night, John Boy," I replied in kind.

Months ago, when the nightmares first occurred, we started making fun of *The Walton's* TV show. Lynn's idea – to make me feel better.

She left and closed the door behind her. I could hear the floor creak as she walked slowly back to her room. I closed my eyes, trying to keep calm, and let the ambulance and police sirens lull me back to sleep.

There's been an ongoing debate within Judaism for years of whether or not there's a Hell. Well, this I can tell you: there was that next morning in the Bamberger household.

⁂

So, my penis. You remember, the microscopic one? Not only had it not budged, but it decided to turtle all morning. Hello! Hello!

No answer.

Clearly, it was mimicking the way I was feeling, or mocking me, I'm not sure.

Regardless, I performed my morning rituals and got up to face the day. How else would I know if the whole thing wasn't some crazy nightmare, and we would remain safe and sound in our beloved Brooklyn?

I knew soon enough.

At breakfast, Gram was moving slowly around the kitchen as if she'd aged ten years overnight. Runny scrambled eggs in hand, Mom served, zombie-like, liquid fury dripping from every pore. Lynn left for school as she always did - starved, but fashionable. Susan was right behind her. They were moving faster than normal. Gramps and I had our morning boxing ritual, although it was short, silent and uninspired. Dad was nowhere to be found. He didn't start the new job for two weeks so I'm assuming he left to escape the sadness and hostility.

I couldn't eat. I just sat there looking to Mom, then Gramps, then Gram, hoping, again, for some remedy, a magic bullet that would come soaring into the room and take the life out of Dad's absurd need "to work".

Mostly, it was the silence that was killing me. No Mom singing. No Dad floating from cheek to cheek, kissing his goodbyes. No Lynn screaming from her bedroom. No Gram complaining in Yiddish.

The morning hullabaloo was one of the things that defined my family, it was love itself. And now, it was gone. For me, that translated to physical pain. Every quiet moment was another organ being ripped from my body - sans anesthesia.

I couldn't stand it anymore and left the table. No one tried to stop me.

⁂

The other two meshuggeners knew something was amiss. Probably because I was having trouble walking, breathing, forming syllables. Each, at separate times during the day, asked me if I was okay. I told them I wasn't feeling well, maybe coming down with something.

I couldn't tell them the truth, not yet, as I needed to first see if my sabotage would work. That, combined with whatever Mom was hopefully planning, would prove to be the unraveling of Dad's dastardly plan.

Oy gevalt!

Lunch with Rachel!

I had completely forgotten, until when walking out of history, I was greeted with her smile from across the hall. It was an *I'll see you soon* smile that filled my heart with love and passion. Unfortunately, devastatingly, romance would have to wait. The hillbilly clock was ticking, and I needed lunchtime to fully devise my plan. I approached her.

"Shalom, Yosef," she said, tilting her head to one side. Her *Gee, your hair smells terrific* hair floating past her perfect shoulder.

"Sh-shalom," I said weakly, lying to my love before even had our first kiss. "I'm not ... I'm not feeling good. Probably just a cold or something. I don't think we should have lunch today."

Her face wilted like a time-lapse rose. "Oh … really? Okay, I guess. Sorry you don't feel well."

"We'll do it in a couple days," I assured her.

I wanted so badly to tell her the truth. I would break down weeping and she would pull me into a gentle, nurturing embrace, and I would bury my face into the crook of her neck and breathe in her beauty. And then she would whisper, *Everything's going to be all right, Yosef. It's going to fine. Don't worry. You worry too much.*

"Okay, bye, shalom," I spewed the words out quickly and took off down the hall. I think I heard her vaguely say shalom back, but I'm not really sure.

Our mutual disappointment was hard to take.

My lunchtime masterminding was fruitful. As was my solo trip to the New York Public Library - phonebook section.

That evening, I took it one step further, sitting up in bed with pencil and paper, writing the letter.

It didn't take long. I knew what I needed to say.

Once completed, I signed my name, shot out of bed, and grabbed an envelope from one of my desk drawers.

Fold, insert, lick.

Now, a stamp. It was around 8pm and the house was morgue-like, so I didn't think it would be difficult to get one. Letter in hand, I left my room.

Hallway: Empty.

Living room: Empty.

Kitchen: Empty.

Plan so far: Flawless.

Entering the kitchen, I went to the junk drawer, opened it and started moving things around, looking for a roll of stamps. Mom always kept a couple rolls...

"What are you doing?"

Startled, I turned to see Susan behind me, grabbing a banana off the counter.

"Nothing," I responded quickly, closing the drawer.

"What?" she asked.

"What what?" I responded.

"You're being weird."

"No I'm not."

She pointed to the letter in my hand. "What's that?"

"A letter. What does it look like?"

"To?" she asked.

"To none of your business," I responded oh-so-cleverly. Luckily, I hadn't addressed it yet.

Susan's face tightened with suspicion. "You were obviously in there looking for a stamp. But you didn't get one, and you won't tell me who the letter's to. What's going on?"

I probably could've come clean with Susan. She might have even relished in my plan, but I couldn't take the chance. Like all of us, she was shocked at Dad's news. But now, she didn't seem very bothered. Susan wasn't fond of life in general, so I suppose it didn't matter where we lived. We could be moving to Quang Binh province, and chances are, it wouldn't matter to her.

I took my glasses off, started rubbing my eyes. "Just leave me alone."

Susan glared at me another few seconds, then said, "Whatever, Yo-yo."

And she was gone. The ol' *exhausted and stressed eye rubbing ploy* - works every time.

Yo-yo was the accidentally apropos nickname she gave me years ago. When we were younger, at night after Mom put away the Silly Putty and Slinky, I was the only toy available. Susan would drag me across the floor, splash me with dirty rainwater, poke me hard on my forehead - all for her endless joy - until I cried, and Mom or Dad, sometimes Lynn, would come to my rescue.

Everyone shows their love differently, I guess.

I opened the kitchen drawer again and finally found the stamps. I ripped one off the roll, licked it, and stuck it on the envelope.

Back in my room now, I dug into my pants pocket, pulled out the tiny piece of paper I wrote the address on, and copied it onto the envelope.

I took a deep breath and nodded to myself. This was the right thing to do.

The next morning, avoiding the meshuggeners once again, I went to a mailbox near school, and popped the letter in.

As I let go of the metal hatch, I felt a mix of relief and dread, the dread the weightier of the two.

What if it didn't work and we had to move anyway?

What if it did and Dad never forgave me?

What if it worked and we ended up going broke, then ended up as bums on the streets of New York, pleading for someone to buy us an H&H bagel?! Gram and Gramps couldn't survive in that type of environment.

I started panicking, wondering if I could get the letter back. I pulled the hatch open again and stuck my arm in as far as I could. Stretching … streeeeeetching… people stared, assuming incorrectly that I was trying to steal mail.

Naturally, I couldn't reach anything.

No, the letter would be mailed, and I would have to lay in the potentially dystopian bed I made. I decided to think positively.

⁂

It was a few days later, and things at the house were better. Not good, but not as terrible as they were. Most of us were still in denial, I suppose. At least there was some conversation. And even just a tiny bit of quiet Mom-singing *Ain't No Sunshine*. Make of that what you will.

I was sitting on the sofa in the living room, reading my new space book. Gramps was next to me reading the paper, and Mom and Gram were in the kitchen preparing dinner when the phone rang.

"I'll get it," Dad yelled as he left his bedroom and headed down the hall. Our only phone was in the living room. Lynn had pleaded for one in her room, but Dad said we couldn't afford it. Maybe if he didn't get himself fired!

Sorry … laid off.

Lynn and Susan followed him in, hoping the call might be for them.

Dad picked up the phone. "Hello?"

I watched him as he stood suddenly straighter, soldier-like. "Yes, Roger. Hello."

No idea who Roger was. Lynn and Susan disappeared back into their rooms as Mom walked in from the kitchen, curious.

Dad's face scrunched up with confusion as he listened. "Okay ... okay," he responded.

There was a long pause now as his gaze slowly turned to me, furious and growing steadily more so. "I see," he said.

Oh shit. *That's* who Roger is.

I averted Dad's gaze and focused on a picture of Apollo 13, an aborted mission.

Once again, he was silent, listening. It was excruciating, now that I knew what was happening.

Finally, he spoke again, jittery, but adamant. "No, no, everything's fine. See you in a couple weeks. I'll take care of this. Thank you, Roger. Goodbye."

He hung up calmly. That's how Dad got mad, calmly. The more upset he got, the more composed he became. It's like he knew that, if he didn't, he'd lose it and start bashing his subject in the head with a menorah until they bled to death. Of course, if it was one of the eight nights of Hanukkah, the person's head would probably catch fire first, and they'd die that way.

"That was Roger Carlsmith, my new boss," he said, his eyes super-glued to me. "He received a letter addressed to 'Man who's about to hire Murray Bamberger.'"

I could feel Mom and Gramps staring at me now, too. I couldn't look up. I knew Dad was waiting for me to say something.

I thought the letter spoke for itself.

Dad went on, "It said, 'I am writing you to beg you to please not hire him. I will lose my friends, my synagogue and my new girlfriend.'"

"Oh, Yosef," Mom said, displeased. That was a whole different knife in the gut - I thought she'd be proud.

I corrected Dad, "*Maybe* new girlfriend. Pretty sure I wrote maybe."

"Stop with the maybe. There's no maybe," Gramps said, winking at me.

"Anyway," Dad continued, "it ended with 'please change your mind, signed Yosef Bamberger.'"

He was shaking his head slowly, so disappointed in me. I wanted to bolt out of the house and even into another dimension. Instead, tears. I know, I know, lots of little Semitic boy tears. You might want to get used to it.

"What am I supposed to do, Dad?!" I screamed. "Nobody wants to go!" I looked at Mom, "You don't want to!"

Dad moved closer to me, blocking my view of her. "Okay," he said, "I will tell you what you're supposed to do. You're supposed to follow the rules and the rules are - Mom and Dad make the rules. And one of those rules is you don't write your dad's supervisor a letter asking him to not hire him. Period."

That used to drive me crazy – when he'd say *period*. As if I didn't know he was ending a sentence.

"What's going on?" It was Lynn. She and Susan had come out of their rooms, wondering what the commotion was about.

I stood up, facing Dad. "Nobody was doing anything! Somebody had to do something!"

"Well, you were almost successful," he said, still shaking his head.

"Successful at what? What's going on?" Susan asked.

Gramps filled them in. "Your brother wrote a letter to your father's new boss, trying to put the kibosh on the big move."

"You did what?" Susan asked me, disgusted.

Lynn didn't say anything, but I'm pretty sure she smiled, just a little.

Dad pointed a finger at me. "You're grounded."

I thought about that a moment, then said, "So I don't have to go."

The girls smirked.

"Enough from you, Mr. Smartypants," Dad said, done with the conversation.

I continued crying for sympathy, but it was to no avail. I sat back down. I was out of ideas. That was when Dad turned to Mom and said, "And I happen to know what you did, as well."

I knew it! I knew she tried something sneaky!

"What do you mean?" she asked, with a Goebbels-like guiltiness.

"Patricia was gracious enough to call me and tell me what you did."

"So what!" Mom shot back, crossing her arms in pissed-off defiance.

"You too?" Gramps asked.

"What did you do?" I asked, excited, hoping her labors would be more successful than mine.

Dad answered for her. "She went to my old job, a job I haven't had for months, and asked, no, begged, for them to give it back. A job that I was laid off from months ago."

He glared at her. No response. Just flames of fury shooting from her every pore.

Lynn and Susan were loving every second of it.

Dad continued, "She was dragged out of there, screaming."

I pictured Mom stomping across the tile floor, past the wood-paneled walls and plastic plants. Patricia, with her high heels and higher hair, chasing after her. Mom practically running to Dad's ex-boss's corner office, storming in, dropping to her knees and begging him to give Dad his job back. When that didn't work, she broke into Three Dog Night's *Joy to The World*, hoping her performance would be so breathtaking they would have to ask Murray back just so they could, at times, hear his wife sing. As they dragged her out, her sultry voice faded in the background as the balding boss sat back in his big chair, expensive paintings behind him, wondering what in the hell just happened.

"I wasn't screaming, I was singing!" Mom screamed at Dad. "I thought a nice song might convince them that we are a good and talented people, and we should be treated better!"

Did I know my mom, or what?

Gramps shrugged; he'd seen worse. Dad could only keep shaking his head. As far as I knew, he'd never run up against this kind of opposition before. Regardless, he knew not to push Mom too hard: Jewish matriarch, femme fatale, all that.

I had stopped crying, ecstatic the desperate times/desperate measures behavior wasn't all on me. Was Mom grounded too? Turns out, neither of us were. I think Dad realized we were reacting out of anxiety and despair and he should let it go – especially since neither act of sabotage was effective. But he did have some final words on the subject:

"Okay, okay, okay. Listen to me ... everybody." He had our attention.

"I am an engineer, and there are no engineer jobs here, in New York, for me. I need you all to understand this. You want I should do dishes at the Plaza? Maybe pick up the garbage? Guess what? They don't hire engineers. I got a good job in a nice town. We're a family and we are moving. It is Jewish law - Shalom Bayit. Period."

Shalom bavit is the concept of domestic harmony and good relations between husband, wife, and family. It was the first time he would bring that up, but not the last. He looked at Mom and repeated it slowly, directly to her, "Shalom Bayit."

Mom took a long, deep breath in, then out and ...

... reluctantly ...

... grudgingly ...

... hesitantly ...

... petulantly ... nodded in adverbial agreement.

We all saw it. It was hard for her.

My mother had a lot of discrepancies, but being Jewish, sticking with family through thick and thin, that was at the top of her everyday to-do list. It was nothing less than paramount. In fact, visiting Dad's old firm was proof of just that. Somehow, call it mother's intuition, she knew the move would tug at that thread and steadily pull our family apart. But, at this point, she saw there was no other choice. We would all have to walk into the fire and hope for the best.

"Ow!!!!" A short, loud scream came from the kitchen.

We all ran over to see Gram staggering toward us, holding her bleeding right hand in front of her.

"What the hell?!" Gramps yelled as he went to her.

"I ... I cut myself," Gram stuttered, her chest heaving with panic.

"*Oy gevalt!*" Mom cried, as her and Gramps led Gram to the dining table.

"What do we do?!" I asked, alarmed.

"Someone get a towel!" Mom shouted.

"*Du Zol Nicht Vissen Frum Tsores,*" Gram said, weakly.

"Towel!" Mom reminded ... anyone.

"I got it," Dad screamed, grabbing a dish towel and wrapping it around Gram's hand.

"Ow!"

"Sorry!"

"Let me see," Mom said, her voice cracking with worry.

"It's wrapped up, you can't see," Dad answered correctly, though you could see blood seeping through the towel.

"I can see that, Murray!" Mom thundered back.

Gram was staring at it and starting to tremble.

"What should we do?!" I cried.

"Put pressure on it!" Mom screamed.

Gramps put pressure on it.

"Stop!" Gram yelled again.

"I got to put pressure!"

"She needs an ambulance!" Susan said.

"I need an ambulance," Gram nodded, shaking.

Lynn chimed in, "No, we should take her. There's no time."

"No time? No time for what?" I asked.

"Lynn is right. Come on," Mom said, standing her up.

Her, Gram, and Gramps headed toward the front door.

Then ...

"Ahhhhhhhhhhhhh!" This time, it was me. I was standing at the kitchen opening.

All heads swung my way.

"What?!" Dad screamed.

I pointed a shaky index finger at the now crimson cutting board. "The tip! Her fingertip! It's right there!"

The girls made gross out noises as Dad came over. "I don't see it."

I pointed harder. "Right there! Next to the onion!"

"Wrap it in something and bring it," he said, leaving and joining the others.

I froze. Who am I, Marcus Welby, M.D.?

"Jesus, Yo-yo, just do it!" Susan yelled, as she headed to the front door.

I entered the kitchen slowly, as if moving faster might motivate the fingertip to come alive like in the movie *Alien,* jumping up with it's sharp, bloody teeth and then attacking me violently, poking me to death.

I couldn't see anything to wrap it in and everyone was already out the door. Panicking and fearing my delay would make things worse for Gram, I grabbed the only thing that was there - a nearby onion skin. I dropped it onto the flesh, picked it up, keeping it at arm's length, and ran out to join the family.

As we all left, Mom did her best to comfort Gram. "You survived Auschwitz, you can survive this."

⁂

Two separate cabs picked us up and rushed us to the hospital. I made a point of hiding the bloody digit from the cabbie. I was afraid he might kick me onto the street if he knew.

Ten minutes later we were at the E.R. and I handed the finger to a nurse. I was happy to get rid of it, but sad it was no longer attached to its owner.

Once Gram was taken back, it was maybe three seconds before Mom lit into Dad; it was all his fault, of course. The moving nonsense had caused so much stress Gram wasn't able to focus on preparing the chicken and, wouldn't you know it, chopped herself all up.

Dad was silent. I think he agreed with her.

I know I did.

Three hours later, we were all headed home again.

The surgeon was unable to reattach the fingertip.

❦

It was late as we walked in the house. Everyone was exhausted. Gram's hand was swollen with white bandages.

"We're glad you're okay, Gram," Lynn said, rubbing Gram's back.

"Let's get you to bed," Mom said.

"No, I want to sit on the sofa for a while," Gram said, uncomfortably, needing some normalcy.

Everyone settled in the living room.

But Lynn.

For some reason - we were about to find out - she stood by her lonesome, fidgety, next to the dining table.

Her body language was something I hadn't seen before: inflexible, defiant.

"I'm not going," Lynn mumbled.

"What? Speak up, Sweetie," Gramps said.

"I said I'm not going," Lynn said with more volume.

"What are you talking about?" asked Mom.

"I'm not moving to Tennessee," she said, tears flowing now, her words hanging in the air like stale cigar smoke.

"Is this some kind of sick joke? You know your grandmother just lost a body part!"

"I'm sorry!" Lynn screamed. "I can't hold it in anymore!"

Dad wasn't having it. "You're coming. Period."

"Of course you're coming," Mom agreed.

"You're coming," Gram added.

"I'm not coming! I'm almost eighteen. I have a boyfriend. School's almost over. I've been accepted to NYU - in case you forgot."

I wanted to say something, but I couldn't breathe.

"Who will cook for you?" Gram asked.

"Where will you live?! We're selling the house!" Mom screamed.

"Cousin Michael's. He has an extra room," Lynn answered.

"Michael's an idiot," Mom said, as if that, true as it was, had anything to do with Lynn living with him.

"What about expenses?" Dad asked.

"You were gonna support me in Tennessee. Support me here instead. What's the difference?"

"Who does this to their family?" Martyr Mom asked, not rhetorically.

"You're not exactly thrilled to go!" Lynn shrieked, throwing her arms in the air.

"You're making things worse!" Mom fired back. "You're coming and that's that!"

"If you force me to come," Lynn said directly to Mom, "the second I turn eighteen next month, I'm coming right back."

Their relationship had been compromised for years. When Lynn was twelve, she figured out that if she blew off her homework, but aced her tests, she would still get B's. And that was good enough for her since that meant she could spend more time with friends. Eventually, Mom found out and punished Lynn by keeping her from being in the school play. That was the end of the world for Lynn.

In revenge, Lynn started stealing from Mom's purse, a $20 bill here, $10 bill there. Just enough to cause confusion. *Sorry, Jerry, I thought I had a twenty.* When Mom figured it out, she confronted Lynn who gleefully confessed. Then Lynn was punished again. Then Lynn would rebel again. It was a vicious cycle for years.

"You have to come!" I screamed suddenly.

Lynn looked at me sadly, shaking her head no. It was a combination, a look that said I'm sorry/no, I don't have to come - you're wrong.

Sadness filled the room like water on the lowest level of the Titanic.

Mom buried her face in Dad's shoulder. Dad buried his head in his hands.

Gramps squeezed his championship belt for comfort.

Susan was speechless, glaring at her big sister with disdain.

I stared at the floor, trying not to vomit.

"Yet another *shanda*," Gram said weakly, then looked at Mom and added, "Good job."

"This isn't easy for me either!" Lynn screamed, then took off down the hall toward her room. The wood floor creaked in all its surprising places, punctuated by her bedroom door slamming shut.

First was the news that we were moving. Then it was the Great Onion Catastrophe of 1973. Now, a whole new kind of heartache.

They say bad things happen in threes. But you can only know that, for sure, after a fair amount of time has passed. Otherwise, there could be bad things happening in fours, fives, and sixes.

Du Zol Nicht Vissen Frum Tsores.

❦

"Where?!" Micah asked incredulously, his face bunched up like a wet *shmata*.

I had held off telling them as long as I could. I knew it was going to be heart-wrenching and I'd have to fight off questions and tears, but I couldn't just disappear. Not that I didn't think about it. That morning, deciding whether to get out of bed, I contemplated pulling an Amelia Earhart. I would be legendary, hailed a hero, instead of a shmuck that left New York to practice poor dental hygiene with the hill people. All I needed was an airplane.

"Tennessee," I said.

"I've heard of that. Where is it?" Mitchell chimed in, cluelessly.

"In the South," I said, fiddling with my new yarmulke as I held back the waterworks. There it was. The scene I was trying to avoid for days. Right there in the school hallway, the three meshuggenahs - on its way to two.

"But, why?" Mitchell said, his mouth staying open after he said it.

"I just told you – he lost his job here and he got a job there."

"Why can't he find another job here?" Micah asked.

"He tried, I guess. Look, it's not like we want to move."

"Well, can you drive there?" Mitchell asked.

"I think so," I said. "It's 728 miles. I looked on the map."

"That's far," Micah said.

"When are you going?" Mitchell asked, failing to hide his sadness.

"Soon," I said, my voice turning shaky, "Couple-few weeks, I guess."

Crying in front of a hundred Hebrew school Jewish kids was way, way down on my to-do list, but, oh well. Quickly, I wiped the tears away with my shirt sleeve. God forbid, Rachel saw me. In an attempt at regaining any semblance of cool, I leaned against the wall of lockers, but I was further away than I realized and tripped backwards, slamming hard against them.

Micah and Mitchell laughed, and I joined in, helping to diffuse the gripping sadness of it all.

Then Mitchell had to bring up the elephant in the hallway.

"What about your Bar Mitzvah? Will you come back to New York for it?"

Punch in the head. Faucets - full steam ahead. "I want to, but my dad says there's too much planning, and we can't afford to go back and forth. Besides, there's a synagogue there, I guess."

I looked up at both of them, so much sympathy in their eyes. "You guys can still come," I said. "The three meshugganahs got to stick together."

"Yeah," Micah screamed, "yeah!"

"Of course, Potsie breath!" Mitchell agreed.

We all laughed, smacking each other, and falling into a quick, hope-no-one-sees-us hug.

I think Micah was crying too, but he wouldn't cop to it. Not even today.

(Micah, if you're reading this, I think you can admit it now. No one will judge you.)

"Yosef," said a voice behind us, quick and stern and way too much like my mother. It was Rachel. I had blown off our lunch date a couple days ago. I figured it would be easiest if I acted as if she never asked me in the first place. Twelve-year-old cognition. Aka dumbass wishful thinking.

"Later," Micah and Mitchell said simultaneously, shooting down the hall.

"Shalom," I said to Rachel, smiling, acting as if nothing was wrong.

"We had a lunch date," she said, her eyes wide with accusation.

"We did, yeah," I said, bumbling. "When? Can't remember."

"Sit on it, Yosef! You know when it was."

Barbra Streisand and Medusa rolled into one. I looked down at my ugly black shoes. In that moment, everything was ugly. Mostly me. I couldn't face the fact that I had to reject the one and only girl who ever showed a smidgen of interest in me. On the other hand, if I had thought too much about it, I would've become furious, and in a sweaty, late-night frenzy, grabbed the kitchen knife that destroyed my grandmother's cooking career and stabbed my father to death, Manson style.

"My ... my family's moving," I told Rachel, stammering.

"Oh." She was shocked. "That's too bad."

God, there was so much in those three words: sympathy, compassion, the sexiest boy on Earth who managed to get away.

Tears! Stop! Do! Not! Come!

"Well, you could've just told me," she said.

"Sorry," I said with a lame whisper. Then, in behavior befitting a boy about to vomit on a gorgeous girl, I bolted.

Out of the cafeteria. Down the hall. And into the bathroom.

I leaned against the tiled wall, caught my breath and cried yet again. No vomit, unless you consider sobs of great sorrow - hurl. I couldn't stand her seeing me like that.

I never spoke to Rachel again. Or to be more specific, not to *that* Rachel. It was a very common Jewish name in the '70s. I heard she married

an anesthesiologist, had three kids, five grandchildren, and lives somewhere in Bergen County, New Jersey.

Apparently, she moved too. Sort of.

⁂

"Haggadol hazzeh! Mi haraq et-ha anasim ha elleeeeeeeeeeeeeeh!"

I held the last note as long as I could. It was unusual and, under
normal circumstances, unnecessary, but ending my impromptu Haftarah
audition with thespian embellishment was critical.

Don't get me wrong: I sounded horrible. Besides female anatomy,
singing was one of the few things I did not inherit from Mom, but the
climax worked; it was big and thrilling and the other two mesheggeners
applauded energetically.

But this was for an audience of one: Rabbi Berkwitz.

Me, Micah, and Mitchell had decided we'd go to the synagogue and
convince the Rabbi to have my Bar Mitzvah early.

Twelve, thirteen, does it really matter?

Except for the possible giveaway of my shrieky boyish voice, no one
would be the wiser. I'll show the Rabbi how much of the material I already
know (thank you, Hebrew school), and he'll certainly agree to it.

"Not a chance," the Rabbi said, smiling sadly from behind his wooden
office desk. "Not that that wasn't very nice. It was. It was very nice. You'll do
well - when it's time."

I implored him. "Rabbi, you have to let me! You have to!"

"Yeah, Rabbi! Please!" Micah screamed.

"It would be so far out," Mitchell said, rolling his eyes up in his head
for effect. (Such a weird kid.)

Rabbi Berkwitz stood up, walked around the desk to be closer, and
put his hands on my shoulders. "Yosef, of course I want you to have your
Bar Mitzvah here, but having it early is not the answer. You are not ready
- a man is not a man until he's thirteen. Besides, there's no time to plan

the other festivities that go along with it. Your parents are busy packing, *oy gevalt!*"

My head was pounding, aching. This was it, my last-ditch effort. If the three meshuggeners couldn't make it happen, it wasn't going to happen. I had to accept the move and somehow, some way, get used to it. I couldn't imagine what that looked like.

Maybe we could visit at times, but we were about to embark on a new life. A new way of living, and at twelve-years-old, it simply wasn't up for discussion.

I loved my friends and my life so much; it felt like I was being sent to bed without dinner – for every day of the rest of my life. A life that wouldn't be long since I would certainly starve to death of camaraderie, religious intimacy, and the ease and joy of familiarity.

❦

The big move was only days away now. Dozens of giant cardboard boxes filled the house, each plastered with the moving company name: United.

Irony, served up daily at the Bamberger home.

The place had become an obstacle course. If you had an appointment, say, in the living room, but you originated in Susan's room, you might consider going to the bathroom first, and leaving early.

To make matters worse - if that was possible - Gram's self-mutilation was having its effect. When it first happened, I was terrified, of course, but later became secretly happy about it. I thought it might convince Dad to stay. It didn't.

But it did cause Mom to begin doing the cooking, if you can call it that. My mother and kitchens never really had a chance to get to know each other. Mild acquaintances, if that. Gram taught her everything she knew, but Gram's constant presence in the kitchen kept Mom from ever putting what she knew into practice. An old woman suddenly loses a fingertip, and instead of actual food, overcooked beasts from the Netherworld end up on the good China.

Exacerbating the Bamberger milieu even more, Mom and Susan weren't talking to Lynn. Neither I, nor Gram were talking to Dad. And Mom and Dad had a freaky episode a few days ago. Lynn spied the whole thing and reported back. Apparently, he was showing Mom 8 X 10 glossies of possible houses to buy in Oak Ridge, and instead of paying attention, Mom tried to initiate lovemaking. Ick.

When Dad rejected her in order to focus on the real estate, she threw a water glass at him. It missed his head by an inch and shattered against the wall. It was a cheap tchotchke from a flea market, so not a big deal, but still.

Although I didn't realize it at the time, just like my and Mom's lame attempts at sabotage, Lynn's threat to stay and Gram's act of severance, were also acts of obstruction. Theirs were different, of course, enduring, but if Dad was someone else, I could see how they might've worked better than my ridiculous, little letter.

I had finished 7th grade without fanfare. Said goodbye to a few teachers I liked, also Teddy from the laundromat, and Jerry from the deli. That previous Saturday, we had all said goodbye to the Rabbi and our many friends at the synagogue. With so much sadness I couldn't help but wonder why we were doing this, but then I remembered: Dad working equals money. Money equals food and shelter. Food and shelter equal the continuation of life.

Finally, it was the night before we left, and I had to have another bizarro baseball nightmare. It was worse than the previous one, understandable considering the turmoil that my life was. There were quick, unsettling images of the stadium crowd this time, and players running bases. Why this was a nightmare and not a dream, I had no idea. But when I awoke, I was, as always, scared shitless.

I shot out of bed, did my regular family checkup. The creaking floor woke Lynn – as it did – and she tucked me back in. As she did.

This time, though, we didn't say a word. Not even our *Good night John Boys*.

Since she wasn't joining us in Tennessee, it would be the last time she would save me from my night terrors. Leaving my friends and losing any opportunity I might have had with Rachel were bad enough. I just couldn't handle the thought of losing my big sister, so I decided not to think about it. Simple. Buried. Done.

SANDY SINGS

IT WAS A SEEMINGLY ENDLESS LINE. THE TRAIN OF WANNABE girls snaked out of the building, around the corner and halfway down the block, finally stopping in front of a new public housing monstrosity.

Seventeen-year-old Sandy Solomon stood at the end, sweating in her striped cotton pullover, cotton pants, and saddle shoes. Not that it was hot or humid. It was the Julliard School of Music, and it was a very big deal for Sandy. She'd never auditioned for anything before, unless you call first dates and cooking the family brisket auditions.

Her dad had managed to save quite a bit of boxing money, and he was able to finance her dream. Secret dream, to be more precise; her mother, Gertrude, had no idea. Gertrude wished only for her daughter to marry a Jewish moneyed whatever who smiled every once in a while, and could extend the family line of curly, dark-haired *shayna punims*.

Sandy needed distraction, badly. The girl in front of her in line had a Lucille Ball Poodle Clip haircut, all rusty red and crazy curls, and that was a fine gaze for a bit, but it wouldn't keep her attention for long. Soon, she started counting taxis as they drove by. Then she'd count cigarette butts on the sidewalk. When that got old, she sang quietly to some of her favorite songs: first *Mona Lisa* by Nat King Cole, then *Sam's Song* by Bing Crosby, then *Cry* by Johnnie Ray. They were all great songs, but they too, didn't last. Eventually, Sandy would start thinking about her audition and become nervous again.

Almost two hours later, Sandy had finally made her way into the second-floor room.

The vocal teacher, Mrs. Sinclair, was talking with her two male colleagues who were sitting behind a long, wooden folding table. It was unfortunate they were in such a claustrophobic, brick-laden classroom, Sandy thought. An unimpressive room. The acoustics wouldn't be good. Regardless, she had waited a very long time for this.

"What will you be singing today?" Mrs. Sinclair asked, looking up now, grinning sweetly at Sandy.

Sandy smiled back, attempting to hide her anxiety with a friendly nod and slight move forward in body language.

Then in her heavy Brooklynese, she said, "*They Can't Take That Away from Me*, by Frank Sinatra? Actually, Ira and George Gershwin wrote it - I'm doing Mr. Sinatra's version."

"Whenever you're ready," the teacher said, picking up her blue mechanical pencil.

Sandy stood up straight, took a deep breath in, then out … and as the first lyric began to form, the door behind her suddenly swung open and a young man walked in.

"Hello! I'm—" he interrupted himself, embarrassed.

Sandy turned. The judges all looked up.

"Oh, my, I'm so sorry!" the man said, retreating and closing the door quietly.

Mrs. Sinclair rolled her eyes. "Everyone gets their turn. They just don't want to wait for it. Sorry, begin."

Sandy laughed lightly, tried to shake off the disruption. It didn't help, that's for sure.

She took another deep breath in and out, stood up straight, put her left hand in front of her and, like a human metronome, started snapping a slow beat.

Then, in a hypnotizing contralto, sans accent, she sang, "*The way you wear your hat ... the way you sip your tea ... the memory of all that ... no, they can't take that away from me ...*"

As she glided beautifully through the rest of the song, the judges watched and listened, taking notes. Each without expression, they purposely held in any reaction, pleased or otherwise. Sandy was unconcerned. She knew she sounded good. What's more, her singing always took her to other places - never the present.

She wasn't even there.

❧❧❧

Spring had sprung with deluges of every other day rain. It was a week later as Sandy bounded up the steps of her family's four-bedroom, forgettable Brooklyn box on east 91st St.

She had tried to forget about the audition and had been somewhat successful. Since she and her father were keeping it from her mother, it wasn't exactly a topic of conversation.

But that was about to change.

Her dad was sitting in the living room reading *The New York Times* when she entered. They got the newspaper for free as that was Jack's profession now, with his boxing career long over. Along with several other men, he helped run the printing presses at the Times. His bruised and bloodied boxing hands had now become black stained instead.

"Hi, Dad," Sandy said as she bent and kissed him on the cheek.

"*Zeeskeit,*" he answered air-kissing her, not because he wanted to, but because she was halfway into the kitchen before he could react.

"Hi, Mom," Sandy said as she entered the tiny kitchen. Gertrude was sweating over a raw chicken she was cutting up for dinner. Just in her mid-forties, Gert was already bent like an old woman. Sandy often wondered why. Good old-fashioned unhappiness? Guilt? The weight of countless persecuted Jews on her mother's back?

"*Ir zent shpet?*" Gert asked, stating a fact in the form of a question.

"Why do you speak Yiddish to me?" Sandy asked. "You know I don't know what that means." Sandy was spending her teenage years doing her best to modernize. She cherished her religion and culture, but she didn't want to be an outcast, a hold out from the old country. Those types never became famous singers.

Gertrude humphed. Her own daughter couldn't learn a little Yiddish?

"You're late," she translated.

"Ten minutes," Sandy answered. "The train was really late and crowded. I did meet Judith on the corner when we got off and we talked for a bit—"

"Fourteen," Gert interrupted, correcting her daughter on the exact extend of her lateness.

Sandy knew better than to push it. She had lost that battle too many times. It wasn't worth it.

"I went to Mansoura's today," Gertrude said as she separated the chicken's thigh bone from the body. "Got some *knafeh*."

"Did you?" Sandy said as she wrapped a clean apron around her body.

"I did."

"It's always very good," Sandy said with a big smile.

"Cut it," Gertrude said.

Sandy enjoyed her Arabic desserts, but for her mother, supporting Mansoura's was about supporting Jews, the Mansoura's having fled Egypt only a few years ago. *Jewish people had to escape Egypt more than once,* Gertrude would sometimes say when Mansoura's would come up. Of course, Sandy knew the family didn't *have* to leave Egypt, but from what she understood, animosity toward Egyptian Jews was growing again. This, not 15 years after the Holocaust. It was upsetting.

"The Mansoura's, they escaped Egypt, you know."

"Yes, Mom, I know," Sandy said, respectfully.

"*Du Zol Nicht Vissen Frum Tsores,*" Gertrude lamented.

Just then, Jack appeared in the kitchen, smiling, almost giddy.

The girls stopped, looked at him.

"Yeh?" Gert inquired.

Sandy's dad held up a letter, looked at Sandy. "It's for you."

Sandy's eyes brightened. She grabbed the letter from Jack and read the return address. She looked back at her mother who was curious now.

Sandy tore open the envelope, pulled the letter out, and started to read. As if she was in early menopause, her body flamed up with anxiety.

"Who's it from?" Gertrude asked, waiting, holding her chicken-greased hands in the air.

Sandy finished reading and pulled her father into a hug as she broke down crying. Jack couldn't tell if it was a yes or a no.

"*Vas iz geshen?!*" Gertrude was now concerned. Sandy let go of her dad, took a step toward her mother, and took her oily hands in hers. She swallowed once.

"Mom, I was accepted into the Julliard School of Music. The Singing Program."

"Oh! Mazel Tov!" screamed Jack, relieved and ecstatic.

Her mother's expression didn't change. "Vas iz Julie School of Music?"

"Julliard," Sandy corrected her, "it's the best music school in the country, maybe the world." She stopped, knowing a calm, measured presentation would be the most effective.

"I want to sing, Mom. This is it. This is my chance."

"You knew about this?" Gert looked at her husband.

Jack shrugged, noncommittal.

"And may I ask why I may not consulted?"

Sometimes, Gertrude's English could become compromised when she was upset.

"You would've said no?" Jack asked.

"We can't afford this," Gertrude said dismissively.

"We have some money," Jack said.

Gertrude looked at her daughter. Sandy knew what was coming.

"What about having a family?"

"I want a family, Mom, I do. This first, that's all. It's my dream. You know I can sing. You love my singing!"

There was a long pause while the three of them stood silent; Jack and Sandy staring at Gert, Gert now staring at her chicken.

"Jack, go back to your newspaper," she said.

Jack threw up his hands in silent surrender and left the kitchen.

Gertrude went to the sink, washed her hands, then dried them on her apron. She then walked back to Sandy.

"*Zitsn,*" she said.

Sandy sat at the small dining table. Gert sat across from her and took her hands in hers.

Gertrude spoke slowly, deliberately, working hard to remember her English. "This singing ... it will honor the Jewish people? Is this what millions of our people died for in the concentration camps, so you, Sandy Solomon, could spend money and time on songs?"

Sandy knew the question came from an authentic place. And she knew it shouldn't have surprised her because, whenever there was a special 'sitting down' with her mother, the Holocaust was always part of the conversation.

And that was okay with her.

Sandy gathered her thoughts and squeezed her mother's hands.

"God gave me a singing voice," she began. "And I know that if I make the most of it, I'm honoring Him, and by honoring God, I honor his chosen ones, those who died and also those who survived. So, yes, I think making the most of my gift ... honors the Jewish people."

Sandy didn't know whether she was going to need it, but she had actually worked on that speech. It was genuine, make no mistake. She believed it. It just wasn't the first thing she thought of when thinking of her singing career.

They looked into each other's eyes, connecting on that level only a parent and child can. Gertrude nodded slowly, an inkling of a smile creeping slowly onto her face.

"Okay," she said simply, then stood up and went back to the kitchen.

Sandy shot out of her seat, screaming with joy. She couldn't hold it in. She threw her arms around her mother in a one-person hug, as Gertrude was back to her chicken prep.

"Thanks, Mom! I love you! I love you! I love you!"

"There's a boy ... " Gertrude said.

Sandy pulled from the hug. "What?"

"Murray Bamberger," Gert said. "He goes to our shul. He's going to college to be an engineer. He wants to meet you."

Sandy froze, terrified she had dreamed the past thirty minutes. What did this mean? Then she realized - this was a quid pro quo: she could go to Julliard if she went on a date with Murray Bamberger.

"You'll meet this Murray fellow," Gert said loudly, making sure she was heard.

"I'd like that, Mom. No reason I can't do both. Right?" Sandy asked.

Gertrude answered in Yiddish: "*A yid hot akht un tsvantsik protsent pakhed, tsvey protsent tsuker, un zibetsik protsent khutspe.*"

"Translation? Please?"

Gert spoke slowly. She wasn't good with numbers in English. "A Jew is 28% fear, 2% sugar … but 70% chutzpah."

"Oh! Okay," Sandy said. "Well, for me, maybe 100% chutzpah."

Sandy broke into a big laugh. Gertrude managed a small chuckle.

Sandy was perfectly fine meeting a young man. At seventeen, she had obviously thought about boys - a lot - so a date would be nice. But those feelings were always second fiddle to her singing.

That night, she slept for no hours and no minutes, which is not to say she wasn't dreaming. She dreamt of Radio City, Carnegie Hall, and temporarily nameless Hollywood stages that she would become familiar soon enough. She would perform at all of them. Singing her heart out. This was her soul's destiny, and she knew this more than anything.

That musty smell would always remind her of him. Not every classroom had it, only his, as he liked to keep a window cracked for fresh air, and he never closed it, even in rain or snow.

Sandy sat in the front row, center seat, first because she found music theory fascinating: reading music, understanding chords, time signatures. All of it excited her so much. But within her first week, she also found something else quite fascinating, or someone else that is.

The professor, forty-seven-year-old Burt Zimmerman, was a tall, Jewish Englishman with an inky black pompadour, daily black suit, never a wrinkle, and dimples deep enough for bathwater. He was an accomplished pianist who'd come over from London to teach. Sandy had never met anyone like him. Or seen anyone like him. So much passion, adventure, elegance. She figured he must live in a plush Manhattan apartment with a gorgeous wife who wears only long, glittery gowns while they dine at their Henry VIII wooden table, a massive menorah squarely in the middle. The 8th day of Hanukkah must have been a sight to see.

She enjoyed watching and listening to him speak his dialect and began to wonder what it would be like to kiss him. While his teeth were as uneven as the New York skyline, his lips made up for it; plump and graceful. Her eyes would often find their way to his privates, curious what pleasures lay behind the fabric. These feelings took her by surprise, and she struggled to dampen them. Every day, her studies and Mr. Zimmerman battled for her attention. She had the allied forces on her side - her father, mother, her ambitions - but still, it seemed, he was winning.

Fortunately or unfortunately - depending on whom you asked - the feelings were mutual.

"Sandy?" He was looking down at her, smiling, waiting.

It took her a moment to return from Shangri-La. Apparently, this was at least the second, time he called on her.

"Yes?!" She looked up, embarrassed. The class chuckled.

"Can you describe arpeggio for me?" the professor asked patiently.

Sandy sat up straight, tossed her long black hair to the side, and said, with as little Brooklyn accent as she could muster, "Yes, sir. An arpeggio is a type of broken chord where the notes ... where the notes that compose the chord are sung in a rising or descending order."

"Or played," he said.

"Pardon me?"

"Sung or played. Arpeggio is also for instruments, not just voice."

"Oh, yes," Sandy agreed. "Sung or played. Of course."

Zimmerman gazed at her with a slow nod. "Excellent."

"Thank you," she said.

"I'm guessing you're a vocal student?" the professor asked as the class laughed.

"Yes, sir," Sandy replied.

"Quite right. Then why don't you sing us an arpeggio?"

Sandy shot out of her seat. "Which chord?"

Burt laughed this time. He was impressed with her comfort. Indeed, when Sandy was accepted into the school, any nervousness she had about singing disappeared. If Julliard says you can sing, you can sing.

The professor thought a moment, then said, "C major."

Sandy cleared her throat and hummed a couple notes until she found a "C." She repeated it once, then sang a perfect arpeggio - first rising ... then descending.

The class applauded. That was a surprise, but she acknowledged them, smiling, then sat down quickly.

Zimmerman didn't respond immediately. He was quite taken with this girl so many years his junior. The class waited. Sandy waited.

Finally, quietly, he said, "Flawless."

***

Sandy's time with him was always short, but sublime. Every Friday, she would tell her parents that she was staying with her friend Helen. Instead, she and Burt would meet at a synagogue in Queens where no one knew them, and they could worship. Afterwards, they'd go to a nearby Kosher Italian restaurant. Burt would drink wine, and they'd talk for hours about everything: music, of course, but also art, Eisenhower, the Rosenberg executions, Judaism in mid-century England, and a new crusade they were calling the civil rights movement.

Finally, they'd take the subway back to his place in Manhattan. Occasionally, Sandy saw how damn storybook it all was, so Romeo and Juliet, hopefully without the suicides. It couldn't last. But that thought was always fleeting, quickly dismissed by the overpowering romance, and the intoxicating immorality.

Her initial visit to his home was a bit of a shock, as there was definitely nothing plush about the place. Dusty, ancient books lined brick walls, and several faded, tattered rugs covered the cracked wood floors. There was no wife, thank God, but there were cockroaches, everywhere - scattering constantly, trying to avoid death by shoe squish. And then, of course, there were the windows, like in Burt's classroom, always cracked open to let in that exhilarating, industrial air. Sandy could've been in the squalor of a Dickensian orphanage, and she wouldn't have cared.

In the beginning, they would sit on his sofa, kiss for a long while, then fall asleep clothed. It was like this for several weeks. Then, something shifted.

Sandy wanted more. She could feel that the time was coming, and it would be on her terms. She had decided she'd be sexy and make all the first moves so she was clear on her intentions. But, as these things turn out, when the time did come, she froze like a butterfly in a sudden ice storm. As much as she wanted to be a mature and tough New Yorker, she was really no different than any other virgin.

Burt found her awkwardness amusing. He was more than happy to take the reins and, much to Sandy's gratitude, did so in that oh-so-British, courteous manner.

I'm going to put my hand here - would that be all right?

I fancy removing your brassiere. Comfortable with that?

I wonder if I might kiss you here.

Of course, yes, yes, yes was the answer to everything. Eventually, she told him to shut up and just get on with it. There's that New Yorker. They had a good laugh, and although it was a bit painful for Sandy - as first times tend to be - it wasn't sex, not at all. Not ever.

It was lovemaking. In her early teens, she had read about lovemaking during frequent clandestine episodes with girlfriends in the New York Public Library. They would sneak into the stacks and take turns reading Lady Chatterley's Lover, pointing and giggling. She had seen countless kissing scenes in the movies, even fantasized about kissing Humphrey Bogart, wishing he could teach her.

But she had no idea how blissful being in love would actually feel; how it would change every moment of her life; how a dreary day with sideways sleet felt like a warm embrace; how every nothing-comment someone made at school, or a moldy complaint from her Yiddishe mother, all would make her laugh, just because. Because she now knew what love was.

And it was all-consuming. Even while she was singing at school, Burt would be in the back of her mind, always there, always supportive, always protecting her. Always a dreamboat.

Now, months later, her feelings hadn't subsided one bit.

The hide-a-bed creaked as Sandy turned on her side to face Burt. He was still sleeping, a soft snore resonating from his nose. It made her smile and she raised a finger, poked his cheek gently. He stirred, grunting quietly. She moved closer to him, poked him again, this time on the other cheek. Finally, he slowly opened his eyes.

"Good morning," he said with a froggy morning throat.

"Morning," Sandy answered, petting his face now.

"What time is it?" Burt said as he looked up toward the shelves where a clock was. "Oh, eight. We should get up, I suppose. Get you home."

"No," Sandy said, wanting desperately to stay right there.

"Right," Burt said, turning on his back and closing his eyes. "Suppose we could get a little more sleep,"

"Well, that's not very interesting," Sandy said, snuggling into his hairy chest.

"Curious. I hear someone speaking, but I'm quite sure it's not Sandy. She's at Helen's."

Sandy laughed. "Depends on who you ask."

"Clever girl," Burt responded, opening his eyes now and brushing his fingers slowly through her hair. "You don't want to spend any more time than necessary laying around with a boring, old Englishman. Do you?"

Sandy humphed, slapped him gently, but firmly on the chest. "You are not old."

"So, I'm boring?"

"What? No. I didn't mean that," Sandy said.

"Good. But, unfortunately, we really do need to get moving, my dear. I have some grading to get done. Oh cheer."

Sandy nodded, sadly, sitting up.

"Sandy," Burt said, turning onto his side.

"Yeah?" Sandy said when he didn't continue.

"Are you, uh, uncomfortable with our age difference?"

"No!" she answered swiftly. "I mean, no, it's just, you know, the way it is."

Burt nodded, but his face betrayed an uneasiness.

Less ambiguous, Sandy's expression was full of fear. "Are you?" she asked.

Burt was quick to answer. "Absolutely not! But ..."

"But what?"

"I'm concerned about your mum and dad. When do we tell them? Do we tell them? It's been months. How long are we going to do this? Clandestine relationship, in the shadows," Burt said the last part dramatically, trying to keep things light, make Sandy laugh.

She didn't.

The truth was, that part of the relationship, she had pushed away. Complete denial. She was lost in love. But now, hearing Burt's concerns, she became concerned. Not about her parents, but that he might consider breaking it off.

"It's fine, sweetie," she said, laying back down with him. "We'll know when it's time to talk to them. Don't … just … try not to worry about it. Please?"

He nodded, but he didn't look convinced.

They laid there quietly a few moments as Sandy gathered her thoughts. She was starting to feel a loss of control. Summoning those New York cajones, she sat up again and looked down at him. "Do you love me?" she asked firmly, her eyebrows raised, waiting.

Burt smiled. "Very much."

"Say it," she demanded, "you've never said it, you know?"

"I haven't?" he said, surprised. "Are you sure? Positive? Maybe you were at Helen's when I said it."

"Stop using the same joke. Just say it."

"Sorry, I'm very old, I forgot - what is it you wanted me to say?"

Sandy couldn't help but laugh. She popped him playfully on the chest. "Say it! Say you love me!"

Burt sat up suddenly, grabbed Sandy, and threw her down on the bed.

Hovering over her now, he said emphatically, slowly, "I love you Sandy, my dear. More than you will ever know … more than even … lima beans."

"Eeeeooooh!" Sandy shrieked.

Burt bent and kissed her lovingly. As she always did, Sandy matched his passion, and they made love until they collapsed, falling asleep in each other's arms.

Hours later and hours late, Sandy would find herself rushing home, in a cab, on what had become Saturday night.

Her friend Helen was in on the whole charade. Sandy was smart enough to set that up months ago. Frantically, before she left Burt's that night, she called Helen and asked if Sandy's father had called. Indeed, he had. But luck was on Sandy's side. When he rang, Helen answered and told him that Sandy had left a while ago. Sandy thanked Helen several times, hung up, kissed Burt one last time, and shot out the door.

Now, halfway over the Brooklyn Bridge, she was devising a plan. She would tell them the reason she was so late was because the subway broke down, and there was no way to call. It was suffocating, and terrifying, and many strap-hangers thought they might not survive. But, finally, thank God, the train began moving again and everyone made it out safe. Sandy had heard this happened often. So often, it didn't always make the papers, so she thought it was as good a plan as any.

⁂

Sandy was performing well in her classes. Her singing voice was becoming more powerful, more professional. An important recital was coming up and Sandy was excited to show her parents how she'd progressed.

It was a warm Tuesday evening. Sandy had been at the library after classes and was on her way home for dinner, as she did most school nights. She walked with a bounce down the skinny sidewalk, passing all the other mostly Jewish homes. Her neighbors' lives flowed from the open windows, and she enjoyed listening. There were the out-of-context fragments of Jewish kvetching. The clanging of silverware on plates. The television snippets of *Gunsmoke* and *The Red Skelton Show*. Her family didn't have TV yet, so, every once in a while, she'd stop on the sidewalk and watch through an undraped window. It was like having the movies right in your own home, she thought.

When she walked in the house, she knew something was amiss. There was no smell of dinner. No sounds of her mother in the kitchen, shuffling and chopping and grumbling. As she put her books on the dining room table, she was startled by Jack sitting in the living room, staring at her.

"Dad, you frightened me," she said. "What's wrong?"

"Sit," he said, his voice dry and gravelly. He cleared his throat.

Sandy sat on the sofa across from him. "Where's Mom?" she insisted.

83

"Your mother ran into Helen's mother at the market today." He glared at her, waiting to see what her reaction would be. Jack knew his daughter. She had no poker face.

An odd-pitched noise came out of her mouth and nostrils as she shook her head, trying to dismiss the market run-in as nothing. "Yeah?"

"She said you were not at their house this past weekend."

Sandy looked down at a scratch in the wood floor. The photo covered walls. Anywhere but at her father who trusted her with going to Julliard, who paid for all of it with money that could've gone to other things.

"There was no subway break down, was there?" Jack asked, knowing the answer.

Sandy shook her head no. Jack crossed his arms, sighed, disappointed. "So, tell me the truth."

Sandy looked at him now. "I've been ... I was with ... a boy."

Jack nodded slightly, then closed his eyes. The disrespect was staggering. "All these Friday nights? With this boy?"

"I'm eighteen, Dad," Sandy reminded him.

"And unmarried!" he said, raising his voice and opening his eyes now. "What would the Rabbi say?!"

She didn't answer.

"Hmm?!"

"He wouldn't approve," Sandy said quietly.

"That's right!"

Boy, would he not approve, Sandy thought.

"We go to Shul," she said.

"What's his name?" Jack asked, doing his damndest to calm down.

"Charles," she said, "Charles Handelsman. He lives in Queens."

"So, what's wrong with going on a date?" Jack asked, wringing his ink-stained hands. "People still date, no? How come you can't just have a date?"

Sandy didn't know how to answer that one.

"You tell Mr. Handelsman he needs to come to this house, meet your parents, and if we approve, he can take you on a regular date. Go see a movie. Get a soda. Something normal. Home by 9pm. Understand me?"

Although he was trying to hide it, Sandy could see the disgust on her father's face, and it broke her heart. If only she could tell him the truth.

"I understand," she answered.

"Okay," Jack said, leaning back.

"Mom's real upset, I guess," Sandy said, worry creeping up in her voice.

"Very."

"Upset enough to ... make me quit Julliard?"

"She didn't say anything about that," Jack answered.

"Should I go in and talk to her?"

"No. Don't push it. Go to bed," Jack said. "She'll talk to you when she's ready."

Sandy nodded and stood up.

"Sorry, Dad," she said, "really."

Jack looked at her without expression. "G'night," he said quietly.

Sandy turned and headed out of the room.

Gertrude would never speak a word about it to her daughter. These weren't things Orthodox Jews talked about with their daughters. But, Sandy could tell things had changed between her and both her parents. Did they now consider her a *zoyne*? A whore? A strumpet? Yes, if they had to admit it. Did they still love her? No question. For years, Sandy often wondered if she should've never admitted to her father that she had been spending Friday nights with a boy. She had thought by telling only a half-lie she wouldn't feel as bad about being dishonest and that God wouldn't punish her too badly.

Every time Sandy walked into theory class, some students would look at her knowingly with a wry smile, an excited nod. Others would send her nasty, disapproving gazes. Such as the '50s, the latter were mostly female, the former, male. As much as they tried to keep it secret, apparently, their affair was obvious to the whole class.

This day was no different as she entered, bouncing as she did, and took her seat. She got the normal looks, which she was used to by now.

It took practice, but she had learned, while in class, not to look at him a loving way. She thought it through one evening at home; she would take that loving feeling and morph it into academic admiration instead.

Burt was engaged in his usual musical stroll, moving slowly between the aisles of desks as Tchaikovsky's *Symphony #2 in C minor* played on the classroom phonograph. As he passed Sandy, he dropped a tiny note onto her desk. She covered it quickly with her hand.

He had done that once before. The first time, the note said she should see him after class after all the other students had left. When she did, he asked her on a date.

Today, this note said the same thing. Her curiosity was piqued. What did he need to speak to her about? Maybe he just wanted a lock-the-door, quick tryst. They'd never done that before. Or maybe he just wanted to hear her voice. Whatever it was, it was perfect timing to tell him about the conversation she had had with her dad. They would have to find another way to see each other. Maybe she would move out and move in with Burt. She was eighteen after all. She wasn't worried. Love would find a way. It always did.

When class finally ended, Sandy gathered her books slowly, watching until every last student was out of the room. She went and closed the classroom door, then, smiling, approached Burt who was sitting at his desk.

The moment their eyes met, her smile vanished. She'd never seen him so somber.

She sat on the edge of the desk. "What's wrong?" she asked.

He was about to speak, then stopped, dropping his head.

"This is very difficult," he whispered.

Sandy understood immediately. She went limp, her body weakened as if someone pulled the skeleton right out of her skin.

"What's difficult?" she said quietly, putting a hand on his desk to steady herself.

Burt turned his gaze out the cracked open window. "Sandy, we can't continue to--"

"No, no, no," Sandy interrupted, as if stopping him would change his mind.

"I'm so sorry, dear. I really am," Burt said over Sandy's continued, mantra-like dissention. He stood, looking her in the eyes now. "It has nothing to do with us. It's the other students. They know. Eventually, the school will find out and fire me. I can't risk losing my job. It's all I have."

"You have me! And we love each other!" she yelled, the tears rushing down her cheeks now.

"Shhhh! Please dear," he said, trying to lower her volume with his hand.

"I won't shush! You can't do this! Please Burt! Please!" Her crying was chaotic now, coming in retching bursts. "I can't ... I can't live without you!"

"I know it feels this way now. I do love you, dear. But I guarantee you, you can live without me. And you will. I'm sure of it. I'm sure of it."

Sandy grabbed his arm. "We'll run away together."

"Well, that doesn't make much sense."

"We'll go to London! Everyone knows you. I'm sure you could get a job there!"

"I couldn't," he said, flatly.

"Why not?"

"Because I destroyed my reputation!"

Sandy suddenly went silent, pulling back. She had never seen any anger from him before, and it frightened her.

Finding his composure, Burt continued, "You see, dear, I did the same thing at Guildhall. I fell in with a beautiful student, but there, I got released. Fired, as you would say. I just can't make that same mistake. Do you understand? I've been an idiot - again. And it's my fault."

Sandy was hyperventilating. Fell in? Fell in? What did that mean? He wasn't in love with her after all? He just *fell in* with her? As he does with different girls, at different schools, around the world? Part of her wanted to ask for clarification, but she was afraid she couldn't take the answer. The betrayal was dizzying. If they were several floors up, she might've jumped out the window.

But Sandy had a strength she wasn't completely aware of. Instead of letting the fear and confusion win, she used them. Subconsciously perhaps, but together, that day, they gave birth to rage. It was a first for Sandy and she welcomed it. Fury would prove to be her best partner in life, helping her make it through some of the worst days.

That next second, she detonated, sweeping up her three textbooks, screaming - part shriek, part roar - and throwing them right at Burt, hitting him square in the face.

Burt grunted and fell back a few steps, stunned, now bleeding from the nose. Before he could say anything, Sandy ran out of the classroom, her uncontrollable weeping taking over once again.

THE GREAT EXODUS

IT WAS EARLY JUNE, A STEAMY, STICKY DAY. I SAT ON THE stoop of our building, holding my Anne Frank book, pushing my glasses up my sweaty nose, and staring numbly at the dozen suitcases sitting awkwardly on the sidewalk.

The moving company had come and gone, and I had just gotten back from saying goodbye to Micah and Mitchell. I saved them for last.

The whole family was coming outside now. It was a slow, sullen march, full of trepidation.

"Bye Yos," Lynn said, standing next to me, her arms outstretched for a hug.

"You're leaving now?" I asked, looking up.

"Give me a hug," she said quickly, anxiously. The sooner this was over, the better.

I stood up and hugged her tight.

"Love you," she said, "No more nightmares, okay?"

I nodded, not thinking for a minute that would actually be the case. We separated and Lynn walked the few steps down to the sidewalk. I followed her as she approached Mom.

"Bye, Mom," Lynn said, giving connection one last shot.

Mom turned to her, damp-eyed. They fell into an embrace.

"It's not too late," Mom said meekly, a likely affectation.

"Maybe we'll come down for the high holidays," Lynn said, hugging her tighter.

Mom was the one to separate.

Lynn moved on to Dad, Gram, and finally Gramps. All long, tight embraces. When she got to her little sister, Susan gave her the limpest of hugs. Still no words.

Lynn was crying quietly as she grabbed her suitcase and took off running down the street.

I always thought that odd – why was she running? Why didn't she ask Jacob to come get her? It would've made things easier. Instead, she disappeared around the corner, headed for the subway I assumed. All six of us were staring after her, in shock, like we were witnessing her death.

I turned away quickly. When I did, I noticed, across the street, a short, Puerto Rican boy, looked about seventeen. He was on the sidewalk, looking over at us, and clearly agitated.

"Why's that kid staring at us?" I asked Gram who was standing next to me.

"Oh, shit," Susan said under her breath, then ran across the street.

"Susan! What are you doing?" Mom screamed after her.

"I'll be right back!" Susan yelled over her shoulder.

We couldn't hear what they were saying, but they definitely knew each other. He was very upset and kept putting his hand on her arm, and she kept pushing him off. Who was this goyim kid?

After a few minutes, he walked away, his shoulders slumped. I think he was crying. Susan ran back to us, her face faux-bright, big smile.

"It's fine! Everything's fine. His name's Eduardo. I was tutoring him in science and he's not happy I'm moving. I left him a message at school. I guess he just got it."

She nodded, her mouth clenched. There were some *mehs,* some *humphs,* and one *oy* - mine. It was a pretty good explanation, hard to poke holes in, but it sure seemed like a lie to me.

Right then, two Lincoln Continentals pulled up - thanks to Dad's new company. For a second, I felt like a movie star. But soon enough, the reality of leaving became all-consuming. Gramps, Dad, and Susan were in the back of one of the cars. Gram, Mom and I were in the other.

As we headed down the Nassau Expressway, I rolled down the window and took one last, long smell of New York City. It was glorious.

Mom noticed. "What are you smelling?" she asked.

I smiled broadly, closed my eyes. "Garbage," I answered.

⁂

The day was strange and long. There were delays at JFK. Gramps was forced to remove his belt before going through the metal detector, and our plane seats weren't all together, something Dad had thought he'd arranged. That caused major *tsures* – primarily created by Mom. Gram and Susan ended up in the back of the plane, separately. We had to go through Atlanta, and there were delays there as well. Mom made sure to remark on the fact that we had to connect in Atlanta because Oak Ridge was too hillbilly, therefore too unknown to have a direct flight from New York. It was actually Knoxville's McGee-Tyson airport that didn't have any direct flights to New York. Oak Ridge, 25 miles west of Knoxville, didn't have an airport at all. So Mom was wrong and she was right, as was often the case.

To make matters worse, Dad was a tortured flyer. In 1960, his parents were killed when a flight headed for LaGuardia had a mid-air crash and came down on the apartment they were in. Consequently, he was crippled with a kind of twisted logic that he, too, would die in a plane crash, even though they didn't exactly die in the plane.

It was close to 11pm when Dad weaved our rented Chrysler station wagon down Newell Lane. The neighborhood was newish, upper middle class with a mix of split-level and ranch style homes, all big, with heavily treed front yards that stretched to the curb. Between each house, tall, arching streetlamps cast an eerie, grayish light, beckoning the bats and moths and flying beetles.

"They forgot to put in the sidewalks," I mumbled aloud, as we got closer to our new home. It all looked odd enough, but add the summer symphony of insects, and we might as well have been on another planet.

"And in summer," Nancy the realtor had said to Dad, "there's frogs, cicadas, crickets – it's a real nature party!" After his two interviews, Dad had come back down to find a house. I guess to break the tension of our final descent he recalled Nancy's selling story with a horrific rendition of her Southern accent. Unbeknownst to her, Dad was not a fan of nature. Or parties. It was probably a good thing for her she didn't mention the snakes or scorpions.

Our house was at the bottom of the hill. 131 Newell Lane, one of the split-level monstrosities, heather gray with maroon shutters. I was impressed, surprised actually. Didn't seem to be any barefoot, corn cob smoking hillbillies 'round here.

We pulled into the driveway, parked, and began to pile out, the warm, stickiness smacking us all in the face. At least that was the same.

"It's so loud," Mom said. Gram nodded. Gramps didn't seem to notice. Or didn't care.

Suddenly, a strange, cracking sound filled the air.

Everyone froze, and our eyes met.

Was that what we all thought it was?

A gunshot?

There was no one among us who hadn't heard one before – we did live in New York City. But this was different. We were standing, vulnerable, in a dark jungle, surrounded by the unknown. True, no whistling bullet went by, but it didn't seem far off.

Crack! There it was again. Yep. Definitely a gunshot.

"Run!" Dad screamed as he took Gram's arm.

"*Oy gevalt!*" Gram screeched as Dad helped her walk/run toward the front door of the house.

Mom grabbed her dad's arm and helped him. Susan and I ran like bandits and reached the door first.

"Go up the stairs and lay belly down in the living room!" Dad yelled.

"Belly down!" Mom emphasized.

We entered the foyer landing, hiked up the short staircase, and made our way into what we assumed was the living room. We dropped, as instructed. It was pitch black, so we had no idea if we were even in the living room. Hopefully, it was the right house.

Another shot went off as the rest of the family stumbled in, made their way up the stairs, and joined us on the carpet.

We were all in a line like an oversized can of sardines, New York style.

Welcome to Tennessee!

Mom was squirming, trying to find a comfortable position. "What kind of rug is this?"

"Shhhhhhh!" Dad said loudly. Then whispered to Mom, "I tried to show you the photos - you weren't interested."

"Shhhhhhh!" Mom reprimanded.

"It's carpeting," Susan added, keeping her voice low. "It's not a rug."

"Shhhhhhh!" That one was me.

Somebody was panic breathing, I think Dad, maybe Gram. Whomever it was, combined with the crickets and cicadas, it made for a bizarre concert as we waited for the gunman to enter the house.

I'm not sure how long we stayed down there. I'd say about an hour. When asked about it later, everyone had different memories. Revisionist history and all that. Also, Gramps fell asleep. Living in New York City for so many years, he'd heard the most gunshots, so it wasn't really a big deal for him.

Turns out, no one was shooting at the new Jews. Pretty sure it was just somebody hunting squirrel or rabbit. In fact, quite possibly someone I grew to know quite well.

※※※

The next morning, I awoke groggy and disoriented. My head hurt. My back was sore. My bed had become oddly uncomfortable and springy.

I reached down to grab my ruler and flashlight, but as my eyes fully opened, I gasped, remembering where I was. Or more aptly, where I wasn't.

All around me was weirdness. Wall-to-wall, green and yellow shag carpet. Two tall windows with thick, blue drapes. Wood-paneled, forest green walls, because, apparently, there wasn't enough forest outside. My bed was a rented twin that I could only assume was recycled from a prison cell. And that was it.

I had estimated the movers were somewhere in Virginia at the moment, so we'd have to wait a day or so for any semblance of normalcy.

I decided it best to leave my deformity of a bedroom and check out the rest of the house.

The bedrooms looked exactly the same. Three of them were clustered upstairs on one side of the house: mine, Gram and Gramps', and Mom and Dad's. A big, extremely yellow bathroom was across from my room, with a linen closet next to it.

On the other side of the second floor was an expansive kitchen with new appliances and an orangey linoleum floor, a dining nook, and a formal dining room with more yellow and green shag carpet and, shockingly, white walls. Opposite the kitchen was the living room, the piece de resistance - a fireplace that we never used, not even once.

A foyer was in the middle of the split staircase. It featured a stone-filled planter with a dying plant, a blue, vinyl floor, and a thick dark wood, double front door. Dad had already affixed a mezuzah to the doorway, likely a sweaty, panicked reaction to the previous night's attempted bloodbath.

The second half-staircase led to the laundry room, another yellow bathroom, Susan's room, and an empty room where Lynn would live - you know, when she finally came to her senses.

Finally, the rec room. Partially underground because of the split level, it had the loathsome carpet and the requisite wood-paneled walls, but also, a bar that jutted up against a small, marble dance floor, specially lit from above. I couldn't even speculate on what the builders were thinking. In that era, most Tennessee parties were more Merle Haggard and line dancing than Gladys Knight and The Pips. Or maybe they thought we were all going to get blasted and dance the Hora every single night. There's no telling.

My little self-guided tour over now, I opened the sliding glass door that led to the backyard, walked onto the cement porch, stared out into the dense woods, and shivered in the 85-degree heat.

⁂

A summer wind shook the half dozen giant, bushy oak trees as the six of us stood outside the little house on the prairie, also known as Temple Beth El, our new synagogue.

"What denominations?" Gramps asked the man hovering above us.

Rabbi Brenner stretched his long neck down toward us like some kind of giddy giraffe. He was a good seven-feet-tall and un-bearded with one of those sophisticated, Old South accents, the kind that might make you seasick if you closed your eyes.

"Mostly reform, couple Conservative," he said.

"No Orthodox?" Dad asked, nervously.

"No, not around here, really," the Rabbi said.

"Wait ... " Gram said, worried, pulling her freshly bandaged hand to her breast. "No real Jews?" She had asked Dad several times before we moved, and he assured her there were definitely a few Orthodox Jews in Oak Ridge.

Mom looked angrily at Dad. "Murray?"

"Murray..." Gram repeated, as if who else, but of course Murray.

Dad shuffled his feet. "I thought there were," he lied. "I'm sorry!"

"Well, actually," the Rabbi interjected, smiling, "we do have six new Orthodox members."

"Ah, there we go," Gram said, smacking Mom playfully on the arm. "What are their names?"

The Rabbi just smirked.

Susan rolled her eyes. "The Bambergers, Gram. He's talking about us."

95

Dad and the Rabbi laughed. Mom and Gram found no humor in it.

"Let's go in," the Rabbi said, leading the way.

It wasn't until decades after we moved that I learned Gram and Gramps had seriously considered not coming with us. Like all of us, they feared their Jewish traditions would not be tenable in a small Tennessee town. (Spoiler alert! Dad lied about there being spinach log, too.) The difference was, of course, their age - the elderly being less likely to acclimate. Apparently, they consulted with Rabbi Berkwitz about it. (He thought they should stay.) And they had several arguments with my folks. Mom fought hard - as she's known to do – because she couldn't imagine being separate from her parents. She had never been apart and wasn't planning on it until both of them were dead. Or she was.

Apparently, right after Gram's accident, in the recovery room, her and Gramps decided they would tell the family they were staying.

But, that night, Lynn beat them to it.

That changed everything. They decided they couldn't fracture the family even more. Besides, Gramps reasoned, they mostly only left the house in Brooklyn to go to Shul; why would it be any different in Oak Ridge? So, what, they'd stare out at trees instead of fire escapes? Fine.

As we entered the shul, the first thing I noticed was there were no tallits up front, but there was a bin full of yarmulkes. That was odd; who doesn't have their own yarmulke? The place was about a third the size of Ahavath, with a complete lack of beauty, or grandiosity. No velvety red carpet. No stained glass windows. Just beat up tan carpet, regular windows, a blasé bimah with two splintery, wooden Jewish stars on the wall, and no sex-separating partition.

I'm supposed to have my Bar Mitzvah in this hillbilly hut?!

The Rabbi was walking us slowly, painfully slowly, between the pews, toward the ark. My attention was going in and out, vacillating between curiosity and terror.

"Rabbi, how many in the congregation?" Mom asked.

"Thirty-two members," he said, "plus y'all would be thirty-eight. No ... wait ... sorry, thirty-seven. I forgot, Gary died."

Thirty-seven?!

Thirty-seven?!

Even if Gary had survived, that is one small congregation. I looked over at Dad, but he just smiled, as if thirty-seven had become a big number overnight. That was how Dad was going to be now: Mr. Justification. No matter what the atrocity, the shock, the barbarity, he was going to act like it was all completely normal. Denial gets you through the day.

As the Rabbi continued the tour, I whispered to Susan, "I can't have my Bar Mitzvah here, look at this place."

She whispered back, "Don't care, Putz."

"Most of the Jewish families in Oak Ridge came here in the '40s," the Rabbi said, "to help build the Atomic Bomb."

"That's fascinating, Rabbi," Dad interjected, kissing ass.

"Of course, many scientists and engineers are Jewish, so it all makes sense, right?"

"It does," Dad said.

"You're an engineer, right, Murray?"

"I most certainly am."

He most certainly is an engineer who got fired! In New York!

As we reached the front, the Rabbi stopped, turned, and looked at me, "Yosef, right?"

I nodded slightly, unhappy he was engaging me directly.

"I understand you've got a Bar Mitzvah coming up," he said with that goofy, giraffey smile.

No offense, sir, but you understand nothing.

"Yes, Rabbi!" Mom said suddenly, loudly, symbolically smacking me with her voice. "He does, and he can't wait!"

"Fantastic," the Rabbi said, "you'll be working with Cantor David. He's a wonderful man, and he is so very excited to study with you."

I smiled. Okay, half smiled. Okay, it might have been more of a sneer. It was all coming at me so fast.

Mercifully, it was time to go. We said our goodbyes to the Rabbi, piled into the car, and rode back to the house, silently.

I had wanted to, at least, stay in Brooklyn over the summer, then move when school started in the fall. But I wasn't making the decisions. Dad started his job right away, so the powers-that-be decided we should move sooner than later.

Or as Mom had said, "Just get it over with."

The added benefit would be that Susan and I could take the summer to acclimate before school started.

Turns out, for me, with the exception of going to our shitty synagogue every Friday night, I stayed in mostly - intermittently wailing into my pillow, rearranging my room, popping Maalox tablets due to my new digestive problems, and reading.

I devoured books on Jewish history, New York history, engineering, astronomy, boxing, the Holocaust, and tons of Hardy Boys books. Dad had a really cool book about old movies, too. I enjoyed that.

Then, of course, there was TV: *M*A*S*H, Kojak, The Six Million Dollar Man, Brady Bunch*. Susan would join me for the latter. She connected with Jan.

And then there were the phone calls. My jaw-clenching, anxiety-riddled conversations with the beloved people I missed so desperately. When I did manage to get the two meshuggeners on the phone, it was always short, as they had a summer to enjoy. They would jabber at me simultaneously and I could barely understand them. It didn't really matter because all I could think about was how bad I wanted to be there. I also spoke to Lynn a couple of times. I would talk too fast about some fascinating person I was reading about, and she would tell me to slow down, but I wouldn't, because I knew Mom was about grab the phone from me. Lynn had to say hello to everyone, and then she'd get tired and want to hang up. Who could blame her?

Me! Hand raised! Over here! Abandoned brother! Right here!

So, there it was. My summer of '73. While outside, the heat deep-fried Oak Ridge to a crispy brown, I became an introvert. Busy as an indoor beaver, doing my damndest to deny past, present, and future.

SEAFOOD MURRAY

STANDING THERE, GAZING AT HIS NEW PLACE OF WORK, Murray felt that he might be in some sort of alternate universe. He had been here for the interviews, of course. But now he was really here. Working here. He had moved most of his family. How did this happen? Maybe there was a mix-up. He would have to speak with God on Friday, if only to understand.

The Gaseous Diffusion Plant, known as K-25, was a mile long and four concrete stories high, surrounded by thousands of white-lined parking spots and grassy hills lacking in any majesty. Architecture certainly wasn't a concern of the builders, Murray thought, but this wasn't New York. And he didn't care, anyway. He was making money again.

Murray brushed off his sky-blue suit jacket, then secured the bobby pins into his matching yarmulke. He took a deep breath, tried, unsuccessfully, to pull in his belly, then started toward the entrance. He shouldn't be late for his first day.

There were two security check points, both with apathetic, aged security guards barely eyeing his badge. He smiled and nodded each time. This would be an everyday event, so he figured he'd be pleasant to them, even if they weren't to him.

Murray walked briskly down the seemingly endless, white linoleum hallway. It reminded him of the famous Hollywood *Hitchcock shot*, where the camera is physically pulled back while the lens zooms in. Hitch had first used it in the movie *Vertigo*. It's meant to cause disorientation.

Murray was sure his bosses didn't have the same intention, but it was certainly taking a long time. At least he was on the ground floor and didn't have to deal with elevators or stairs.

He passed two computer rooms, a coffee room, and the bathrooms, before finally arriving at his office. A secretarial pool worked away across the hall.

His office was yet more linoleum floor, with cream-colored walls pocked with a dozen nail holes from the previous occupant. His desk was small, metal. As was his chair. Considering his girth, this would be a daily battle. Also, no window. At least they had set him up with plenty of paper and drafting tools. And a coat rack.

Murray put his briefcase on the desk and squeezed into his chair.

Hollywood still on his mind, he couldn't help but think how this was the antithesis to the movie business. Their offices were poolside; every chaise lounge covered in movie stars, producers, and screenwriters with typewriters on their laps. The creativity was non-stop, bursting out everywhere as Playboy bunnies bent over to deliver boob views and strong martinis (I'll just have a Tab, thank you.). Of course, no one's impressed because everyone's impressive.

Murray opened the top drawer to his desk. And something stopped him.

What is that?

"Murray!" Roger Carlsmith said loudly as he walked in.

Short hair parted in the middle, with a sarcastic demeanor and a licorice black mustache, Murray's boss came at him like a firehose. He reminded Murray of Groucho Marx.

"Welcome!" Roger said, offering his hand.

Murray stood, shook his boss's hand vigorously.

"Roger, how are you?"

"Better than most," he laughed. "Getting settled in?" Roger didn't have a Southern accent. That was refreshing, Murray thought. But also not East coast. Maybe Midwestern. Or Californian maybe.

"I am, thank you. Everything's fine," Murray said, grinning.

"Great. You let me know if you need anything. We're working on getting you a secretary. Meeting in 15 minutes, my office. The whole Deep Base team'll be there - I'll introduce you. We'll get you oriented. Sound good?"

"Fantastic," Murray answered.

Roger winked and walked out. Murray stood another moment, waiting to make sure Roger didn't return for some reason. His professional manners were good that way.

Murray was actually excited to work on Deep Basing. He couldn't remember one time in his engineering career when he looked forward to a project. It was always a grind. Always a chore, like, when as a kid, he had to bucket out the rainwater from the family's flooded basement. No, Deep Basing was a worthwhile endeavor. It was eliminating something that could kill people. He was doing good and that pleased him.

Murray had forgotten about the thing that caught his eye in his desk drawer, but now once again he fixed his attention on it.

The drawer was still open, and as he stared at it, he realized what it was now.

His body went limp.

It was a crab. Dead, thank God, but still, a crab.

About the size of a danish. How on Earth did it get in there?

Kosher Jews don't eat shellfish, so ... did some bigot actually put it in there for Murray to find? Madness. Who would do something like that? Was this anti-Semitism, Tennessee style? Covert? An silent, angry growl behind a toothless smile?

He had never experienced anything like this, and as hard as he tried, he couldn't come up with a better answer.

Murray tore a piece of paper off one of his pads, and cringing, wrapped it around the crustacean and pulled it out. He could feel the sweat building under his arms and around his forehead, and he could smell it now too. He didn't know what to do with it, but knew he needed to think fast. Simply tossing it in his office trashcan wouldn't suffice. The stink would only get worse. He finally came up with a solution.

Murray walked into the restroom and checked the stalls. Empty. He threw the paper-wrapped crab in the wastebasket, then washed his hands for a long time.

A nice potted plant would have been a more welcome welcome gift, he thought, trying to lighten the situation.

After giving it a few more seconds of thought, he decided it was best to forget about it.

ROUND JEW IN A SQUARE HOLE

SINCE I WAS STILL IN JUNIOR HIGH AND SUSAN WAS IN HIGH school, we took different buses that year. I begged Dad to take me that first day, but he said I needed to get used to the walk and the bus, the sooner the better.

Thank you so much, lazy Dad. I was only completely dreading every, single moment.

Before I left, I checked and double-checked to make sure I had everything.

Bus ticket: Check.

Textbooks: Check.

Kosher bagged lunch: Check.

Gym clothes: Check.

Bulky brown bottle of Maalox in front pocket: Check.

I was as ready as I was going to be. I said goodbye to Mom and the grand folks, then headed out of the house and up Newell Lane.

I was dripping immediately, as it was probably 100-degrees already.

About twenty yards up, I noticed I was the only one walking to the bus stop. I had seen a few kids playing in our neighborhood, but they were nowhere to be seen that morning. Maybe their fathers were kinder. The absence of other children was simultaneously comforting and distressing. Maybe I wasn't headed in the right direction. What if I had the time wrong and I missed the bus? Should I go home and tell Mom? Or maybe I should just act like I went to school. Like father, like son.

Suddenly, something caught my attention and I froze.

On the road, about four yards in front of me, was a thick, writhing snake. It was the color of cardboard, speckled with darker brown, quilt-like patterns. It was about three-feet-long, just casually crossing the road. I was fascinated. The only snakes I had come across were of the goyim lawyer species. They could be deadly.

It didn't seem to notice me, but I decided to give it a wide berth, regardless. Survival instincts, I guess, since I had no idea what kind of snake it was, or if it was even venomous. Later I would learn it was a copperhead, the most common East Tennessee snake. That would be a *yes* on the venomous question.

As I passed it, I wondered how one might wrangle a copperhead and sneak it into his father's brand new, white, 1973 Ford Maverick for a surprise fang party; a skin piercer on said father's neck that might finally convince him to reconsider an insane move to redneckville. Just curious. Never got an answer on that.

Moist and short of breath, I finally reached the top of the hill, the corner of Newell Lane and Normandy Road where the school bus was supposed to arrive. Still no other students. No bus either. 8:10, right on time.

I stood and waited, gazing down at my clothes, which turned into a whole thing the night before as we dined on the kitchen countertops - our furniture having not arrived yet.

"Everyone's gonna call you a schmuck, you okay with that?" Susan said, as she shoved some boiled potato into her mouth.

"No!" I shouted.

"No reason for that language, young lady!" Mom said. "He'll be fine."

"All I'm tellin' you is that you'll be known as the putz from New York City with the bogus clothes," Susan argued, defending me while calling me an idiot. "I already have cool clothes."

"No one around here says shmuck or putz," Gramps interjected.

"Mom, how come I have to wear dress up clothes to school?" I asked, getting more upset.

"Because it's school," she said, trying to shut down the argument.

"But it's different here," I whined.

"What do you know?" Mom asked rhetorically.

"Mom! Please!" I howled.

She sighed loudly, making sure everyone heard her. "This is what we'll do. You'll go to your first week of school, in your dress up clothes, but you'll see what the other boys are wearing. If they're in *shmatas*, fine. If they're not, you'll wear your nice clothes."

"Darn it!" I screamed.

"Watch your mouth," Mom reprimanded.

I wasn't happy with the conclusion, but it was better than nothing.

So there I stood in my Hebrew school clothes, new yarmulke firmly attached to head. I looked up, through the leafy, early September trees. Dark clouds were slowly taking over the sky and I wondered if it would rain - not that I cared about getting wet.

Then I heard it. That sad, old coughing and rumbling of the orange school bus.

It stopped in front of me, the door opened, and I got on. When I handed the driver my red bus ticket, he rolled his eyes and pointed to a little basket by the steering wheel. I put the ticket in.

Then, like a weak little hatchling, falling out of his nest, I turned and began walking down the aisle. It was a full bus, probably thirty kids, and every single one of them was staring at me. Then came the taunting in those Southern accents, some with lengthening vowels, some shorter and melodic, all mean.

"Weirdo!"

"Freakazoid!"

"What in the Sam Hill?!"

"Chucklehead!"

"Dunderhead!"

"Ignoramus!"

"Boy, don't know whether to check his ass or scratch his watch!"

No one said shmuck, which, believe me, I would've been okay with.

As I sat in the back, by myself, I prayed, and I prayed hard, all the way to school, that every day would not be like this.

❧❧❧

Secular school was odd, missing something.

Religion! That was it. Also, culture. East coast Jewish culture. My culture.

I did sense it would be scholastically easy, so there was one consolation. I got to each of my classes early so I could sit in the back, as unnoticed as possible. First was Algebra - that was a breeze.

Second, English, which I found ironic, given I didn't think the teacher had a good handle on the language. Although there were several different accents in Oak Ridge, I would come to realize the East Tennessee accent, at its strongest, was an unintelligible, fat-tongued drawl, developed over years. Of course, they probably said the same thing about my heavy Brooklyn brogue. Fuhgedaboutit.

Science was next. I always enjoyed science, but that year, we would be dissecting a frog. Unfortunately, they didn't have an opt-out option back then. I know, I checked.

Next up, lunch.

I entered the cafeteria, found a seat alone, sitting down and digging into my leftover lamb chop. As hard as I tried not to attract attention, it was mostly a repeat of the bus. Ridicule. Sneers. Giggling. Someone made monkey noises. Was I the only Jewish person in this school? I was confused, as that didn't exactly match with what the Rabbi said.

One oversized kid, sitting across from me at another table, was holding court with a half dozen other boys. As he caught my eye, he put his napkin on his head and did an imitation of me like I was special needs; sad, weepy, flailing arms. His buds loved it, whooping and hollering, pounding the table, sending food trays skyward. One of the boys even stood up and did some kind of stupid dance. Either that, or he somehow caught fire.

At first, I couldn't figure out why the napkin, then realized it was meant to mimic my yarmulke. It hadn't occurred to me as I had worn it every day of my life. Apparently, though, in Oak Ridge, Tennessee, it was like a spotlight following me from class to class, shining on my clueless little Jew head. Look! Over here! I'm Jewish! I might as well have had Spock ears and spiders coming out my nose. I ripped the kippah off my head and shoved it in my pocket.

My brand new, shiny blue yarmulke that I loved, I now hated.

My stomach seized. I pulled my Maalox bottle from my pocket, and keeping it under the table out of view, opened it, then popped a couple in my mouth.

I looked up. Thank God, the boys were on to some other nonsense.

All I had left was gym, Social Studies, Spanish, another bus ride, and then, finally, home.

131 Newell Lane, that is.

⁂

The gym floor had blurred. Tear-filled eyes will do that to a boy's view. I had just had a ridiculous, religious argument with Calvin Macafee, the napkin boy from lunch.

And now, I was bent over, my head not a foot away from the floor with both hands covering my genitals and waiting for Big Bertha. Big Bertha, also known as God's wrath upon my sweet, innocent Semitic cheeks.

Some spiritualists believe that when you die violently, your soul separates from your body the moment before the violence occurs. Why go through the pain and anguish? Makes sense.

But that signals a forgiving God, a sympathetic God.

No, I was still alive in my body, present and accounted for.

I couldn't decide whether to close my eyes or not, so I shut them, then opened them, then shut them again. The suspense was excruciating.

I heard the Coach's voice again:

"Now repeat after me: I will not …"

"I will not ..." I said, stumbling over the words.

"Take the Lord's name ..."

"Take the Lord's name ... "

"In vain," he finished.

Maybe, just maybe, if I didn't say that last part, he wouldn't hit me. *In vain*, the necessary end of his twisted, little declaration. Like *amen* (pronounced ah-mein). You can't eat Seder dinner till you say it. Yep, without that last utterance, he'd be forced to send ol' Big Bertha packin', y'all. Clearly, this little Jewish boy was cleverer than he thought. Besides, I didn't use Jesus's name in the vicinity of a curse word - he was wrong about that. I only proclaimed my innocence as regards to his murder.

"I said," the Coach said, losing patience, "in vain."

Uh-huh. I heard you. What are you going to do about it?

"If you don't say this last part," he went on, "I'm gonna smack you five times instead of three."

"In vain!"

I shouted it, and the next thing I heard was a collective gasp from the boys, my audience. It was the sound you make when you see a giant wooden paddle just before it turns skin to flame.

Ladies and gentlemen, may I present to you the shrieking stylings of yours truly, little Yosef, not Joseph, Bamberger. An ass attack of dizzying proportion, it felt like a dozen, angry, stinging jellyfish, combined with several loads of Double X Magnum buckshot, with a thousand wasps thrown in for good measure. I'd never felt such searing pain before, nor have I since.

After it was over, I stood up and came close to fainting. Luckily, I was of sound enough mind to pull my shorts up quickly, so no one could get a look at my lack-o'-johnson.

Wiping my eyes with both fists, I staggered back to the group, and sat - on my knees - as far from Calvin as possible.

The boys were silent as the coach pontificated. "Boys, any type of cursing, or taking the Lord's name in vain, will not be tolerated in my gym. Y'all understand?"

"Yes, Coach," we all said in military unison.

"Now," he continued, "if you have an older brother or sister who went to school here, you know this, but if you don't - we take showers at the end of class."

And the humiliation continues.

"I know most of you never showered with a bunch of other boys before, but you'll get used to it," he said as several kids snickered quietly. "First, let's run some laps."

We all stood up and ran laps around the gym floor, circling the basketball hoops on each side. I lagged behind, of course, partly because of my sore butt, partly because there was no lap-running in Hebrew school. Although, what I was mostly thinking about was having to shower with a couple dozen boys who were almost certainly already endowed down below.

When class was over, we all retreated to the locker room. Most of the kids knew each other, so there was now a loud, constant chatter. Once at my locker, I heard the showers turn on and a giant lump formed in my throat. Maybe I could suddenly start choking violently, and because no one there knew the Heimlich Maneuver, they'd have to call an ambulance. No group shower for me.

Boys around me were shedding their gym clothes and walking awkwardly toward the showers. I knew if I didn't comply I'd have another encounter with Big Bertha. Pass, thanks. Somehow, I managed to go on autopilot, tore my clothes off, and told my legs to start moving.

I almost expected two prison guards to join me on either side yelling, "Dead Jew walking!" As I made it to the shower stall, I figured if I just got wet and ran back out, that would suffice. But the coach was standing at the entrance, making sure everyone was following orders. Although I moved quickly - grabbing the soap, dragging it across my body in a one fell swoop - I could hear the hee-hawing and cackling. I had two things going against me, my tiny unit *and* my ruby-red buttocks. It was mortifying - the kind of shame and embarrassment that soars far beyond a confederacy of naked, little rednecks.

⚜

Somehow, I managed to get through my last two classes without having a nervous breakdown or heart attack.

Of course, the bus ride home was awful, and isolating, and horrible, and hostile, and unfriendly, and crippling.

Now, walking down Newell Lane with the crickets and katydids in full opera, I was just happy to be out of that place they called school.

It was hot, the air thick with moisture. Four other kids got off my bus and were walking in front of me. I made sure of that. I did make it through the day - devastated, walking funny, and in pain, but alive. For now, anyway.

Once home, I dashed upstairs, ignoring the how-was-your-first-day questions, and ran into my room. After slamming the door, I ripped off my school clothes, and put on a white T-shirt, my no-name sneakers, and a pair of dreary, brown slacks with the weird pockets in the front. They were only a year old, and I was already outgrowing them.

I managed to slip into the kitchen unnoticed, had a couple spoonfuls of peanut butter, then went out to explore the woods behind the house.

It was a whole acre of trees, more trees, and a few more trees. Our property merged with our neighbors' on every side, and there were no lines of separation. So I could've easily been on someone else's property, but I didn't care. I needed to clear my head of the disastrous day.

As I navigated the Red Oaks and *viney kudzu*, I imagined them as slow tourists in New York, and I had to maneuver past to get where I was going. Perhaps it wasn't so different here. Also, there was that shooting the night we arrived. Plenty of shooting in New York, too. Maybe I could actually get used to this.

When I heard the crack of the gun and the bullet swooshing past me, for a second, I thought I had imagined that, as well.

Nope! That was real.

Suddenly paralyzed with fear, I looked about twenty yards into the woods, and saw none other than Calvin Macafee, aiming a gun, a long rifle - right at me.

He shot again: crack, whoosh!

"*Oy gevalt!*" I screamed, hitting the forest floor, hyperventilating. That one seemed closer.

My face flush with the ground, I was inhaling whatever fungus and animal dung might be present. Of all the gin joints, or something like that ... my main nemesis in my backyard?! I killed Jesus, so Calvin's going to kill me?!

"I see ya down there!" Calvin yelled.

I stayed motionless, praying I might turn into a Leafy Sea Dragon and blend into my surroundings.

"Hamburger! I seeeeeeeee youuuuuuuu!" His voice was closer now, and I could hear the crunching sticks and leaves beneath his feet.

It was fight or flight. I'd never had to do either, but I couldn't just lay there and get shot. Although, being excused from school the next day was an attractive thought. It's tough to run laps dead.

Then, directly in my eyeline - a pair of beaten, once-white Converse high tops. I froze and held my breath.

"Shit, man, stand up," he said, laughing that cackly, gurgly throat thing he did. "I ain't gonna shoot ya."

I stood slowly, inches now from the freckled giant in the red flannel shirt and Levi's.

"You just tried," I said, shaking with anger.

"Tried what?"

"You just tried to shoot me!"

"You got a weird voice, man."

"I have a New York accent!"

"Well, I guess New York people dumb as a box of rocks," he said, jerking his head up at a big Oak beside us. "I ain't shootin' at you, I's shootin' squirrel. You's just in the way."

Indeed, there was a squirrel high up on a skinny branch, looking down, laughing at us. "It's a pellet gun, anyway. Ain't gonna hurt you much - less you're a bird or somethin'."

Calvin turned his gaze up into the tree. The squirrel had already climbed higher. Not his first rodeo.

"Where you go, you little fucker?" Calvin whispered.

I winced at the curse word. We heard it plenty, but we didn't use it.

"I think he doesn't want to get shot, either," I said, trying to calm things.

Calvin looked back down at me, smiled, then suddenly pointed the gun skyward - crack!

"Whoo-hoo!" he screamed.

I jerked. The squirrel hopped over to another tree as several leaves floated down around us. Calvin laughed, as he did at most things.

"Anyone ever call you four-eyes?" he asked.

"Yeah," I answered, pushing my glasses up my nose as if to say it didn't bother me.

"Come on," he said, turning and heading further into the woods.

"What?" I asked, confused.

Suddenly, this kid was fine fraternizing with a Jesus killer?

"I said, come on," he repeated, not stopping. "Instead of layin' like a dumbass in the dirt, I'll teach ya how to shoot some squirrel."

I stayed put, but I was torn. I had zero interest in learning how to hunt, if that was really why he wanted me to come. He hadn't exactly gained my trust. Of course, he would've killed me already if he truly wanted to. He didn't seem like a murderer - more like a goofy, gun-slinging Alfred E. Neuman.

Still, it felt risky, but I decided to take my chances. I knew minimizing the threat of an enemy would be a smart move, and it's not like I had anyone else to hang out with.

I took a deep breath and caught up to him. Just to be safe, I stayed a couple feet behind. That way, I wasn't in the line of fire.

A few moments later, I remained un-shot and laying on my belly next to Calvin on the upside of a creek. He was, yet again, aiming the gun up at one of the thousands of trees.

Crack! The pellet soared through the branches and smacked into something - bark, I think.

"Damn!" Calvin said, pulling the gun's eyepiece away from his face. "You try." He held the rifle out to me.

I hesitated … again … I didn't want to hurt that cute, little squirrel. But I knew if I didn't take the gun, I'd never live it down. Calvin would mock me endlessly.

So I took hold of it … and something happened. I felt in charge for the first time in a long time. Like an outlaw. The Jew, the bad, and the ugly, now ready to exact my fury - on a defenseless little rodent.

"How do I do it?" I asked Calvin.

"Put one hand here, your trigger hand in here, then stick your eyeball through here," Calvin instructed.

I did as he said, and it felt good. I had no idea a pellet rifle was practically a toy compared to a serious firearm, but it mattered not. I aimed up at the trees. There were several squirrels jumping about, foraging for food.

"Put one of those little fuckers right in the crosshairs," Calvin said.

I smiled and pulled the trigger … crack! It jolted me backward as the pellet shot up into the air. Missed the squirrel, every tree, I was lucky I hit sky. "Cool!" I screamed, anyway.

Calvin looked at me with a weird look. "You missed, dumbass. Big time!"

I shrugged. He didn't understand. That was okay.

He took the gun from me and took aim once again … crack!

I heard a thunk, then watched as a squirrel fell from high atop the tree, his furry tail wagging in the wind, like it was waving goodbye.

"Shit yeah!" Calvin yelled as he got up and ran to retrieve it.

"*Oy gevalt,*" I muttered as I joined him.

There was a small, bloody hole in the animal's side. I felt another jolt, a sadness for the little thing. Actually, he looked pretty pissed off. I would've been.

Calvin picked up the carcass by the tail.

"You get to take the first bite," he said, swinging it in front of my face.

I backed up. "Uh, no thanks," I said, laughing and becoming nauseous.

"I'm serious, man," he said, inching toward me as I kept moving backward. "We eat squirrel around here."

"Really?"

"Hell, yeah! What's wrong? You chicken? Chicken to eat squirrel?" he cackled.

"No!" I protested. "It's just --

"Youuuu're chicken," he said sing-songy. "Bawwwk!"

Apparently, friendly teacher Calvin was short-lived, and we were back to asshole Calvin. Or maybe this was part of the plan all along - tough to say.

"I can't eat it cause it's not kosher!" I shouted, still walking backward.

"What the hell's that?!"

"Kosher, duh," I argued, trying desperately to make *him* look like the idiot.

"How do you know it ain't ... kosher, whatever the fuck that is?"

"I know! Jewish people know!" I started firing off a list I'd memorized long ago: "Mammals have to have split hooves and chew their cud. Fish have to have fins and removable scales. Only a few birds are kosher, like chicken. They can't be predatory. Pork, rabbits, squirrels, eagles, owls, catfish, sturgeon, shellfish, reptiles, and insects, are all non-kosher!"

I took a big breath as Calvin ripped into that loud, horrible Muttley laugh.

"Damn, you Jews is so fuckin' weird!" At that, he stopped and pulled his dead squirrel-throwing arm way back, aiming at me, of course. I turned quickly and took off running back to my house.

I ran so fast I'm not even sure he ever threw it. If he did, it didn't hit me. But it didn't matter. I was the weird one, and I would have to be okay with that.

Or somehow - become less weird.

YOUNG MURRAY WRITES

MURRAY STARED AT THE LAST LINE OF DIALOGUE AS THE
paper rested in the typewriter, choking from the unmoving roller. Maybe
he could think of something better, something more dramatic. Or maybe it
was okay the way it was written.

He was at his parents' small Manhattan apartment, in his old bedroom; not that you'd know it by the decor. The week he left home, his
mother boxed up his childhood and turned the space into a guest room.
Gone were his Yankees posters and movie magazines. Now, cheap water-
color paintings, Hanukkah snow globes, and other pointless tchotchkes
consumed the room like weeds.

Not exactly the perfect writing environment, but it would have to do.

He was home from college for the High Holidays, and in-between
family gatherings and services, he figured he'd work on his screenplay. *This
Little Piggy* would be his film noir opus. Eventually, it would get him out of
M.I.T., or if it took longer, release him from whatever engineering job he
was stuck in. Not that he didn't have a feel for engineering - he did, and was
making decent grades, but it was always meant to be a stopgap.

He knew that being a Hollywood screenwriter was his true destiny.
And the reason he knew was because of how lost he would become when
he wrote. He became his characters, had sex with their partners, celebrated
their triumphs, and suffered their fatal flaws. Even when they died, he felt
it to some extent. Hours and hours would go by unnoticed. On several

occasions, working late into the night, a light would hit Murray in the face, and he would think it was car headlights. Instead, it was the sun rising.

It had been two years. He had the whole script written, but he needed to make sure it was the best it could be. So he'd go in, at random places, and try some new dialogue or a new location for a scene. Usually, though, when he'd go at it again, he'd fall into a rewriting maze, not knowing how to get out of it or where he was in the narrative. He had read somewhere that when that happens you should stop for the night and pick it up again the next day. That tended to work for him, but then it would happen again. It was a vicious cycle.

Unfortunately, he couldn't talk about it with anyone since everyone thought he was going to be an engineer. That was hard for him. He hadn't told his friends, his parents, no one, but he did have a plan.

A secret weapon by the name of Herb Greenberg. Herb was Murray's twenty-year-old second cousin and already a Hollywood big shot. The plan was, when Murray felt the script was ready, he would send it to Herb out in Los Angeles, then Herb would share it with all the brilliant filmmakers, studios, and Hollywood agents. It wouldn't be long before Murray's film writing career would be in full bloom. He could tell everyone, and he could let go of engineering for good.

When they were kids, Murray and Herb had spent several summers together on Long Island. Their parents shared a rental home on Montauk, and there they'd spend long, sweltering days on the beach in their tight-belted, bathing trunks, swimming, laughing, and crabbing.

They both loved movies and movie stars and would talk about them constantly. One year, when they were ten, they argued incessantly about which of them was better suited to be Ingrid Bergman's husband, believing incorrectly, as ten-year-old boys can sometimes do, that she was single and available. The debate was also based on the assumption that she was Jewish (due to her name) which, although there's been some question of Jewish ancestry, she never identified as such.

One morning, they managed to steal two bottles of Schlitz from the house fridge then took off for the beach. No one saw them, but they ran anyway, Murray trailing behind as he was a bit heavier than skinny Herb.

They knew of this one sand dune where they could hide among the high grass, and they planted themselves there, laughing and catching their breath.

Herb had been the instigator, even making sure he had a bottle opener, but Murray was excited to taste beer for the first time. Herb opened his and took the first sip; he swallowed, cringing and shivering. When it was Murray's turn, his reaction took a more violent turn, coughing and spitting it out. Herb gave him grief about it, so Murray quickly took another swig and kept it down this time. He took another and kept it down, too. Herb killed his whole beer. Finally, Murray was able to do the same, and they belched themselves silly before eventually throwing their bottles into the ocean.

Then, someone had to bring up Ingrid.

Two drunk, Jewish ten-year-olds arguing about who's going to marry a Swedish movie star. It was not a scenario that would end well. As both were fairly inebriated, this particular disagreement became more impassioned than previous ones.

First, they hurled insults.

Then sand.

Then rocks and shells, plus a couple dead sea creatures that had floated ashore.

Finally, fists.

Neither had ever been in a fist fight, so although there was a lot of swinging, the only damage was bruised egos and pulled shoulder muscles from too many missed punches. The fight ended a few minutes in, with both boys running back to their respective parents, crying and screaming that the other beat him up.

They continued to get together for several summers thereafter, and even saw each other at Bar Mitzvahs and funerals, but things between them were never quite the same. They had shared something ridiculous and humiliating. And neither could reconcile how incredibly inept they were at achieving anything close to machismo.

To make matters worse, Ingrid would divorce in 1950, turn around rather immediately, and marry someone else, neither Murray Bamberger or Herb Greenberg.

Now, ten years later, Murray had let all that go. It was childhood nonsense, of course. They were adult cousins now, and he needed Herb.

But, there was a kink in his plan that he needed to consider. His father had told him that Herb and his folks were going to be in New York during the High Holidays. Wouldn't it be nice if they could all get together? Maybe go to Carnegie Deli for dinner. Murray wondered - should he wait to send Herb the script as planned, when he knew it was ready, or was it actually ready now and giving it to him in person would be better. This could be a real opportunity, and he came to see it that way.

Suddenly, the door flew open. Murray's mother, Ruth, partial to dyed black hair and dangling pearl necklaces, poked her head in, smiling.

"Yes?" Murray said smiling back.

"What are you writing?" she asked, looking over at the typewriter.

"Oh, just something for school."

"I have a girl for you," Ruth said, her smile growing wider. "Her name's Sandy Solomon. She goes to the shul."

"Mother, I live in Boston. Remember?" Since Murray's plan was to move to California sooner than later, he hadn't been very aggressive at meeting college girls, much less girls from his hometown.

"You're moving back here when you get your degree," his mother said, smirking. "She'll wait."

Murray laughed, nodded, and figured why not. "Sounds grand."

"Here's the phone number," Ruth said, handing him a piece of paper. "Make sure you speak to her father first."

"Okay, Mother. Thank you."

"Dinner in a few minutes," she said, winking, then closing the door.

Murray stared for a moment at the space where his mother was, thinking about everything that seemed to be coming his way. A date might be nice. What the hell.

He looked back down at his unfinished screenplay, took a deep breath in and out, then thought, *okay ... what now?*

⁂

"I thought it got a little boring!" Murray yelled from his perch at the counter, looking dandy, but anxious in his tight, new haircut, light brown suit and matching yarmulke. The diner was New York noisy: snarky waitresses, clattering dishes, everyone trying to talk louder than the next guy. He had no choice but to raise his voice.

"The plot started to drag about, I don't know, midway, I suppose. I mean, the set-ups were all good, the characters were really interesting, especially Stanwyk's character. She was really something, wasn't she? But you take Sterling Hayden in *Asphalt Jungle* and compare him to his character in this film, and you can see he felt like he probably had a lot more to work with in the *Jungle. Kansas City Confidential, The Hitchhiker,* what was that one, *The Big Heat,* yeah, all better movies. Maybe I just like the classics better. Sometimes it's hard to enjoy something new, you know?!"

Sandy was sitting next to him, looking lovely, he thought, in her soaring, black bouffant, yellow poodle skirt, and red kitten heels. Murray could tell by her fashion choices that she, like himself and his family, were in that growing American mix of Jews - Orthodox and less Orthodox, but still Orthodox. Some traditions like formal dress were becoming unnecessary and outdated.

Beyond her good looks, though, so far, she wasn't especially interesting. She seemed melancholy, and Murray couldn't tell if it was due to her date, or something else. Maybe this was her normal manner. They had just seen *Crime of Passion,* where a woman takes control of her husband's career and ends up being a cold-blooded murderer. Maybe she preferred lighter fare.

"I'm sorry, I'm talking too much!" Murray conceded, shaking his head and diverting his eyes toward the menu. He wasn't hungry, and as more silent moments passed, he thought it might be a good idea to wrap up the date.

He had had exactly one date in high school and one in college, with both ending badly. At twenty, he was as horny as the next guy, but the idea of rejection terrified him too much to make the first move.

Consequently, he was still a virgin.

This girl didn't seem attracted to him in the least, and that was fine. He didn't care. At this point, he just wanted to go home.

"It did get a little *farkakteh*!" Sandy shouted.

Murray looked at her, surprised and happy that she finally engaged. He leaned toward her so they didn't have to yell quite as much.

"*Farkakteh*?" he asked.

"Yes," she answered, smiling.

"Right," Murray said, nodding, trying his damndest not to head into another long-winded, obviously for her, boring, diatribe about 1950s film noir. "What did you think of Stanwyk's character?"

"Well," Sandy started, "she was a strong girl, took control of things. I like that. You don't see that often."

"That's true," Murray said, "Someone you could relate to?" he asked carefully.

"Sure. Especially when she murdered that man."

They shared a laugh.

"You're funny," Murray said, surprised.

"Sometimes," Sandy agreed. "So, you're at M.I.T.?"

"Yes," Murray said. "Studying to be an engineer - chemical and nuclear mostly."

"Impressive," Sandy said.

"Oh, I don't know about that. Your father said you studied voice?"

Sandy's face suddenly went flat, and she turned to her menu.

"It was just for a little while," she answered quietly.

There was that sadness again, Murray thought. Part of him figured he should move onto another subject, but besides Judaism, the performing arts was the only thing he felt they had in common. He decided to press on.

"Where did you study?" Murray said.

Sandy shook her head. "Doesn't matter."

"I've never heard of that place. Is it a good school?"

Murray laughed at his joke, managing to get a smile out of his date.

"Julliard - School of Music?" she answered.

"Oh, sure!"

"I work at Mansoura's Bakery," Sandy said. "Do you know it?"

"Who doesn't know Mansoura's? They're the best. Period." Murray smiled.

"I don't bake," Sandy said, focusing on her menu again. "I just help out, sweep the floors, that type of thing."

"Do you enjoy listening to female singers?" Murray asked, changing the subject back. "I do very much. Ella Fitzgerald, Billie Holiday, ooh - Patsy Cline."

Sandy nodded, then started gazing over Murray's shoulder. "I wonder if anyone's ever going to take our order?"

Murray turned and raised his arm, trying to get someone's attention. When it didn't work, he turned back to Sandy.

"I bet you have a beautiful voice," he said.

Sandy looked at him. This time more annoyed than anything.

"I'm sorry," Murray stammered, "I didn't ... I didn't mean to offend you."

She paused a moment, then said, "Forget it."

Murray leaned in, not sure why he was coming clean with this stranger, maybe because she *was* a stranger. Maybe because, even with all her *tsures*, he felt they were finally connecting.

"I like to write movies," he whispered, as if the two of them were in cahoots in a great crime of arts against humanity.

Sandy looked into his eyes, nodding approvingly. "What kind of movies?"

⁂

It was quite a trick bringing a one-hundred-twenty page screenplay to Carnegie Deli for a family celebration without anyone noticing. To begin with, Murray had to figure out how to carry it. He decided shoving it down the back of his pants would be the best way. His jacket would cover any part that stuck out at the top, and he could (hopefully) sit on it somewhat comfortably. First, he had to deal with the cab ride with him and his folks sardined in the back. Then, upon arrival, the greeting and hugging at the door. Then, at one of those Henry the VIII long tables, he would have to sit through the noshing segment, followed by the actual eating: the bowls of matzo ball soup and the leaning towers of chopped liver and pastrami. Finally, there was the task of finding just the right moment to pull the script from his ass cheeks and hand it to cousin Herb - still without anyone noticing.

It was a fitful two hours, forty-six minutes, and nineteen seconds for Murray.

But he did it.

Later that week, he came up with a much less stressful plan he wished he'd thought of earlier. He should've put the screenplay in his knapsack and told his parents that after dinner he was meeting a classmate who was also in New York for the High Holidays. He would tell them the knapsack was filled with schoolwork when it actually held the screenplay.

Herb had greeted Murray with a simple handshake and a smile. No winking knowingness. No hug. No *yeah, boy did we have some laughs!* Herb didn't even sit near him. He sat four seats down. At least he was on the other side of the table, so Murray could make occasional eye contact.

Herb was certainly the star they had all heard about. He had a commanding, big and beautiful presence and a roaring laugh to match. Everything out of his mouth was a boast, but that was A-okay with

Murray; it simply meant he was the right guy to know if you wanted to be a Hollywood screenwriter.

Towards the end of the dinner, Murray was getting nervous he wasn't going to be able to approach Herb one on one.

Then, luck struck.

Herb got up to go to the restroom. Murray knew this was his shot. He waited, took a bite of pickle, chewed ... then another bite ...

Finally, Herb exited the men's room, and Murray shot up from his seat.

"Herb," Murray said, greeting him in the bathroom hallway.

"Murray, it's great to see you," Herb said, not stopping.

Murray put his hand on his old bud's shoulder. Herb stopped and turned.

"Listen," Murray started, reaching deep down for the little self-confidence he had. "I know you get this all the time. I have a fantastic screenplay. It's about a serial cop killer. It's called *This Little Piggy*."

"Great title," Herb said, smiling.

Murray nodded, thrilled for the positive feedback. "Thanks! I think so. It's really perfect for Billy Wilder or someone like him. I thought you should read it. Maybe on the plane home."

"Of course, Cuz!" Herb said. Then added quickly, "Cheesecake!" he laughed and put an arm around Murray. "Come on," he said and led him back to the table.

Murray was ecstatic. It was a lot easier than he thought it would be.

Finally, after cheesecake, and after the departing embraces, out on the sidewalk, Murray handed Herb his one-hundred-twenty page screenplay about a serial cop killer.

Herb took it. They shook hands.

And now, all Murray could do was wait.

Before Murray gave his script to Herb, he had the forethought to put his Boston phone number and address on the script cover. He contemplated putting his New York information on it, but thought better of it, since he still wasn't ready to share any of this with his parents. They were, after all, paying for his expensive education.

He had gone back to school after the holidays but getting his head into his studies proved almost impossible. All Murray could think about was which studio would produce his movie, who they might get to star in it, and what it would feel like to actually watch it in a theatre. Every night, after doing the minimum amount of homework necessary, he'd take a quick cab to the Capitol Theatre in Arlington and watch whatever movie was playing.

After a few weeks went by without any word from Herb, Murray started to wonder if maybe, he had called his folks' house or sent a note to that address. One Saturday morning, after suffering a long wait for the dorm hallway phone, Murray called his mother. After asking how everyone was doing, he casually asked if Herb had called.

No.

He then asked for Herb's mother's number and later called her, asking for Herb's Los Angeles number and address.

He called straight away. No answer.

Maybe Herb had lost the script. Maybe he had left it on the airplane by accident. Murray was becoming despondent, not sleeping, and his grades began to suffer. In the ensuing week, he sent Herb several letters and called him every day or night, at different times, each time unsuccessfully.

Finally, one Friday evening after a grueling week of exams, and continued, constant attempts at communication with Herb, a letter arrived. Murray sat on the edge of his dorm room bed and tore open the envelope. It read:

Cuz,

I read your script. Sorry to be crass, but I just don't see it as a movie.

Good luck with everything.

Herb

Murray was catatonic. He read the letter several more times, a couple of times out loud, just to make sure he read it right. Each time he did, he wondered something new.

I just don't see it as a movie.

How is it not a movie?

Was there something he could do to make it more of a movie?

Were the characters undeveloped?

Did it need a better ending?

A better beginning?

He could keep rewriting!

Murray crumpled the note in his fist and held it tightly. Maybe he could suffocate it out of existence. Who does this guy think he is, anyway? They're the same age, they come from the same place, for God's sake.

Gritting his teeth, Murray let his head drop onto his shoulders and stared up at the ceiling, tears now flowing steadily past his temples. The pain was excruciating. If he had had a gun, he would've put it in his mouth that instant. He had worked so hard, so intently, for two whole years.

Turns out, this knowingness Murray had - it was a hoax. A flimflam. A self-con.

❦

Murray stared down, past his green loafers, and into the black. It was barely fall, yet he was cold, shivering from the incessant winds. Maybe it was due to the fact that he was coatless, wearing only a T-shirt and slacks. Or maybe he was shaking in fear.

No matter. He was ready for relief.

Somehow, he found his way onto the railing of the Tobin Memorial Bridge, hundreds of feet above the Mystic River. He was steadying himself with one hand on a rusty, green-painted steel girder. He had lost sense of time, but he knew it must be very late as the only vehicle that passed was a mac truck, and that was a few minutes ago.

Over the past few weeks, Murray had hoped the pain would subside, but instead, it went the other way and became too much for him. He was doing poorly in school, speaking to no one, and often going to bed before eight. Sleep was release. There were no nightmares, but the second he awoke, the depression would come rushing back.

Often in class, attempting to drive the torment away, he would think about an engineering career and what that would look like, what it would feel like. He'd have a fancy job in Manhattan and be a big shot nuclear engineer. He would develop better energy systems and make good money doing it. He would also think about a wife and a family and how that might feel: the love, the tenderness, the dedication. They would go to Shul, pray and celebrate the glory of Judaism and family.

There were molecules of solace in those thoughts, but it was never enough. Within minutes, the searing despair would return; he would never create stories that brought viewers to tears, laughter, or contemplation. He would never hobnob with the likes of Gary Cooper or Grace Kelly on movie sets as they showered him with praise. He would never sit in one of those velvety red chairs in the Hollywood Pantages Theatre, squirming with excitment as they called his name for the Best Screenplay Oscar. No, he would never be put up on that pedestal. He simply wasn't talented enough.

I just don't see it as a movie.

As the days dragged on, Murray realized that thinking about suicide was the only thing that made him feel better. He could get through the next second as long as he knew he had a way out. But even that didn't last. He needed to take the next step.

So here he was - somehow - about to jump, anxious and excited for the pain to finally end.

As he loosened his hand from the steel, he jerked, tightening his grip again.

A black and white movie scene had suddenly begun playing in his mind.

Over soaring Israeli music, we open on a Manhattan living room where RUTH BAMBERGER bursts into tears. Her husband DANIEL BAMBERGER hugs her, tries to console her.

Cut to a Manhattan synagogue where a funeral is underway. The place is packed. Everyone is emotional while the Rabbi speaks with great passion.

Cut to a burial site as family and friends of the deceased solemnly throws rocks on the coffin, as is Jewish tradition.

Cut to New York's Carnegie Deli where Ruth, Daniel, cousin HERB GREENBERG and other relatives have dinner. The mood is dark, the music continues to play.

Camera moves in for a close up of Herb. He turns to look into the lens, and with a slight smile ... he winks.

Over the following days, it became clear to Murray that his vision was what saved him. It hit him hard: he simply couldn't give Herb the pleasure of thinking he had won. Period.

What's more, he relished in the irony: Herb actually saved him from killing himself.

As Murray focused on his studies and the new girl he had met in New York, the pain did eventually, finally, begin to subside. That, Herb had nothing to do with. It was something Murray created himself. A different narrative, a new Murray story, where it simply didn't happen. He never had a passion for anything but engineering. He never wanted to pursue a career in the movies. He never wrote a screenplay. Simple. Done. It just didn't happen.

As the years passed, Murray would occasionally see Herb at funerals, the High Holidays, and Bat Mitzvahs. And they would successfully avoid each other. Once, at a family event in 1971, where Herb was not in attendance, Murray was speaking with an uncle, and Herb came up in conversation. Murray wondered aloud which films he had been involved with, and the uncle's response was a shock and a delight: *Movies? What movies?* Apparently, Herb had been an intern at MGM for a month back in 1958 before he was fired. He was never the big shot he liked to make everyone think he was.

Unless you call a manager at Corky's restaurant in Sherman Oaks, a big shot.

GOY GEVALT

IN THE SPAN OF ABOUT THIRTY MINUTES, I HAD DEVELOPED A love-hate relationship with this guy, Moses. Moses - what kind of name is that? I wondered - did anyone ever call him Mo? Seemed an appropriate nickname.

Okay, I suppose my dysfunctional and dichotomous relationship was not with him, per se, but with his five books - the Torah.

In Brooklyn, I was all-in with everything it stood for: morals, values, honesty, compassion. But now, all that was fading. All I could think about were my friends, my neighborhood, my school. Those things were me. I missed me.

Instead, I had to sit through irksome Bar Mitzvah classes with Cantor David. A *zaftig* man with short, raven black hair and beard, and blindingly white teeth. He sang like Pavarotti, smelled like sautéed onions.

Stuffed in his small, musty office, we sat across from each other as he sang the part first:

"*Haggadol hazzeh. Mi haraq et-ha anasim ha elleh.*"

"*Haggadol hazzeh,*" I sang back with low energy. "*Mi haraq et-ha anasim ha elleh.*"

"Okay," he said, "next part. Give me more umph."

"*Yasabau betok ha-ir welo halakau.*"

"More emotion," he said, "like this: *Yasabau betok ha-ir welo halakau!*"

I over-emoted, just to be an asshole. "Yasabau betok ha-ir welo halakau!"

Showing me the appropriate tone - somewhere in the middle - he sang it again, "*Yasabau betok ha-ir welo* ... " then suddenly stopped himself.

"You know what, I think we're done for the day." The Cantor leaned back in his squeaky desk chair and pursed his lips. It was jarring, unnatural to hear him could go from operatic serenading to that drawl-y dialect.

"I could stop," I agreed easily.

"Alrighty then. Not a bad start. You just need to give it a little more gusto, but you sure do know a lot already."

"I know," I answered gruffly.

"Look, Yosef, I realize it's hard. I mean, moving and all. I get it."

I nodded as I gathered my schoolbooks.

"I bet New York synagogues are pretty different."

"Bigger."

"Well, that makes sense, doesn't it?" he said, nodding, laughing.

I got up and opened the office door.

"See you Thursday then," he said.

"Bye," I said, closing the door behind me.

God, it was good to get out.

Now in the thin, wood-paneled hallway, I passed a boy going the other way. I didn't acknowledge him, but he looked at me. A few feet past, I heard him stop. He didn't say anything, just watched me walk away I guess. Weird.

I stopped and turned to him. He just stood there staring at me like a Jew in headlights. Skinny as a Hanukkah candle, dumb smile, flying saucer eyes too big for his head, shock of black hair.

"Hey!" he blurted out with multiple syllables, one of the heaviest accents I'd heard yet. You'd think I was a long-lost friend, or maybe I'd kidnapped his little sister and he had to be really nice to me in order to get her back.

"Hi," I responded calmly.

"What's your name?!" he asked, same intensity.

"Yosef."

"Oh, wow. That's a real Jewish name," he said, still way too excited. "I'm Devin."

"Okay," I said, "see you around."

"You in 7th grade? I haven't seen you in school. You go to Jefferson?"

"Robertsville."

"Ah, shoot. I go to Jefferson. You studying for your Bar Mitzvah?"

"Yeah. You?"

"Yeah, man, it's cool, right? I love it. It's gonna be so darn great!"

"Well, see you around," I said again, now trying to escape.

"We should hang out, man! We could study together."

I stopped but didn't know how to respond. I disliked him before I even met him. But my damaged, compromised ego said maybe we could be friends as long as no one else on the planet ever found out. "Maybe. I have to go," I said, moving fast down the hall now.

"Cool, man! See ya later!"

It wasn't clear to me at the time, but my discomfort that afternoon wasn't due to the Cantor or even Devin Levit and his loud, whelpy puppy dog desperation. The idea of a Jewish Southerner was simply an oxymoron to me. Like nails on a chalkboard, incongruent, contradictory elements that simply didn't belong together. Like deafening silence, Liz Taylor and Richard Burton, or laughing at a funeral. I couldn't get past it.

I rushed out into the parking lot, and the now cool, fall weather. I looked up at the tall trees. They seemed to lord over everything. The leaves were turning shades of yellow, orange, and red, which we had less of up north. Red leaves. Rednecks. Red states. Makes sense.

"Hey, man," a voice said, pulling me out of my gaze. I looked over to see Calvin, a few feet away, sitting on a rusty orange, Schwinn bicycle.

I immediately turned to go back inside.

"Wait!" he yelled.

I opened the door and got about halfway in when he shouted again. "I'm sorry!"

That stopped me. I turned toward him, still holding the door open. I wanted to believe him, but, come on - how does one go from raging douchebag to contrite hillbilly in a matter of days?

I don't know exactly what it was; maybe that goofy I-know-I'm-a-dick grin, or his lax body language, but I decided to hold off on retreating. If he did suddenly give chase, I could always run to the cantor's office. There, he'd suffer death by body odor, and I wouldn't have to worry about Calvin Macafee ever again.

"Really, man," he said, "I'm sorry 'bout your ass-whoopin' ... and the squirrel thing."

I stared at him a few moments, giving him a chance to show any ulterior motives. But he just smiled.

I came back out slowly, closing the door behind me. "How'd you know I was here?"

"Followed you. Itty bitty town, you know."

"You followed me here to say you're sorry?"

"Yep," he said, riding over.

Part of me wanted to talk about it, lament the humiliation, the pain, the anger, to make him feel bad about it. But, I figured I better not push it. His apology did seem authentic.

Stopping a few feet in front of me, he stood, balancing the bike between his legs.

"My mom's coming to pick me up any second," I said, grabbing the door handle again, just in case.

"You like your mama?"

"You like yours?" I asked, sarcastically.

"Ain't got one."

"Everyone has a mother," I said, rolling my eyes.

"She died, okay?"

"Oh," I said, more shocked than sympathetic.

Calvin head-nodded toward the synagogue. "So, you pray in there?"

"Of course."

"Cool. Hey, what's that 'oh vey' thing you say?"

"Oy vey, not oh vey."

"What's it mean?"

"It's like 'oh shit.'"

Calvin laughed, "Oy vey - oh shit. Why don't you just say oh shit?!"

"Because it's Yiddish!"

"Is that like skittish?"

"No!" I screamed. "It's a language? Used to be a German dialect?"

"Here's one for you," Calvin said, smiling, "you're 'bout as wily as a wart hog at a sock hop!"

In a horrific, combo Brooklyn/Southern dialect I gave it a shot. "You're about as wily as a wart hog at a sock hop." It came out like a vocal freak of nature, and we both erupted into laughter.

"That sucked, man!"

"I know!" I shouted, still laughing.

We calmed a couple moments later, and I leaned against the door.

"So, you have a church you go to?" I asked.

"Oak Ridge Southern Baptist!" he yelled it like a battle cry. "Daddy said I can be baptized again, if I want."

"What's baptized?"

Calvin shook his head slowly. "Damn, man, you got a lot to learn."

"Well, you didn't know what Yiddish was."

"I still don't!"

We blew up laughing again.

Then his expression suddenly changed, his eyes now squinting, scrutinizing. "Hey, you want to know somethin' really messed up?" he asked.

"What?"

"You can't tell no one else. Seriously."

I nodded firmly.

Just as he was about to spill it, we heard a long, loud honk. It was Mom, sitting in the blue, Dodge Dart that Dad had bought her. The day after he got himself the Ford Maverick to get to work, she asked how she was supposed to get around. This idea that we only needed one car was a New York miscalculation. So, he bought her a used '68. She had zero knowledge of model years and probably would've been happy with an Edsel.

We looked over. Calvin waved. She didn't wave back.

"I got to go," I said.

Calvin bent in closer, whispering just loud enough for me to hear, "Some bullshit story goin' round that my daddy killed somebody."

I burst into laughter, yet again.

But this time, he didn't. "I ain't shittin' ya," he said, keeping his voice low.

Honk!

I didn't know how to react and was acutely aware that, if Mom heard any of this, she'd handcuff me to the downstairs toilet till college.

"Yosef!" she screamed.

"I'm coming!"

Calvin whispered again, "I'll come get you at your house Sunday mornin', tell you all about it."

I didn't nod, didn't say yes or no. I just got in the car, more than a little discombobulated.

As we took off, Mom gave Calvin a suspicious look while he smiled and waved again.

"Who was that?" she asked, alarmed. "He doesn't look Jewish."

"Just a kid from school," I said, then promptly changed the subject, "so the Cantor is nice."

"Well, good. Good, good, good."

I nodded and scratched the top of my head. As I did, I felt something odd, a bump of some sort. I took my hand away and looked at my fingers to see if there was any blood, or anything else. There was nothing.

"What? What's wrong?" Mom asked.

"I don't know. Some kind of bump."

"A bump?!"

"Yeah, it's round and soft," I said, feeling it again, moving my fingers over the surface.

Mom's expression turned to concerned disgust, and she hit the gas.

Then she took her foot off the gas.

Then she accelerated, hard.

Then, she decelerated again.

You see, both her and Dad were New York drivers, regardless of the state they were driving in. The style was herky-jerky, having learned from being in the back of so many New York cabs dealing with the stop-and-go of city traffic. On the rare occasions they'd actually drive in the city, the head-snapping style would make me dizzy (which is why I loved the subways). But now, with zero traffic and the urgency of some kind of terrible bump on her son's head, the decelerations were short, and the accelerations were long and full throttle.

I dropped more than a few Maalox that afternoon.

❄❄❄

But, we made it. This time. I always figured one day, we wouldn't.

Mom rushed me into the upstairs bathroom, sat me down on the toilet, and ripped off my glasses.

Gram and Gramps joined us from the living room.

"What is it? What's wrong?" Gram asked.

"We don't know! Some kind of scalp bump!" Mom screamed.

"*Du Zol Nicht Vissen Frum Tsores*," Gram said, on cue.

"Is it a tumor?" Gramps asked.

"No!" I screamed.

Mom started separating my thick black strands, searching for the non-tumor.

"Oy!" she said loudly, sickened by whatever she was looking at.

"What is it?!" I screamed, now completely freaking out.

"What is it?" Gram asked, just in case no one heard me.

"What is it?" Gramps asked, in case Mom knew, but wasn't planning on sharing.

"I don't know!" Mom yelled. "Everyone, calm down!

I could feel her pulling on it, whatever *it* was.

"Ow, ow, ow," I whimpered.

Mom was focused. "Sorry … give me … a minute here …"

It detached with a slightly weird sucking sound and Mom threw it quickly into the sink. The four of us stared down at it, horrified, but curious. It was a light green insect of some sort. Fat for a bug, it was about the size of a large pea. It had landed on its back, so its body was squirming, its little legs jerking.

"What is it?" Gramps wondered.

"A bug," Mom answered, grimacing.

It was actually a tick. A wood tick that had found a temporary new home in the black curlies of one Yosef Bamberger. Originally black, the tick had turned green because it was now full of blood. The good news: it's color probably made it easier to find. Why he or she chose my head instead of the vast Tennessee woods, I'll never understand.

"Get up, Yosef," Mom instructed.

As I did, she lifted the toilet seat, grabbed some toilet paper, picked up the bug once again, and flushed it.

"Where on Earth did you get that?" Mom asked me, as if I knew.

"I don't know!"

"Tonight, you wash your hair really, really good," she said, air-jabbing her finger at me. "Understand?! Really, really good!"

"Okay," I said, as I headed out, exhausted but happy I didn't have a tumor.

As I walked into my bedroom, I noticed no one had followed me out, so I went back to see why. There was the three of them, still jammed in the bathroom, checking each other's hair like grooming monkeys. It was the beginning of a new ritual.

Some bullshit story.

The words kept repeating in my head.

Maybe. Maybe not. Some rumors aren't rumors. I never met the guy, so it was impossible to make a judgement. Either way, it seemed like a good idea to stay away from any kid whose Dad might've killed someone. Then again, he did seem to want to be friends, this from a guy with a whole slew of friends. And he did apologize. I figured if he showed up at the house in the morning, I could decide then.

It took me at least an hour to get to sleep, albeit fitful and unsettling with one long dream where everyone in my family, including Lynn, were four-legged animals, foraging in the woods for kosher treats.

Ka-dink!

Startled out of sleep, I sat up in bed and looked at the clock: 4:55am.

I listened for a repeat of whatever the weird and loud sound was. Several seconds went by and I started to lay back down, when ...

Ka-dink-dink!

It was something on my window. A bird, or lizard maybe? I got out of bed and drew the curtain back, slowly, like a first grader revealing the first scene of his class play.

Apparently, come get you at your house Sunday morning meant come get you at 5am Sunday morning because, standing right below my window, was Calvin, holding a handful of tiny rocks.

He was grinning and laughing. "Come on!" he loud-whispered, gesturing for me to come out.

"Shhhh!" I loud-whispered back, as I opened the window. "What are you doing here? It's five in the morning."

"I know what damn time it is. Come on!"

"I can't," I said, shaking my head in disbelief. "My parents would kill me."

"They ain't gonna find out. You'll be back before they even wake up."

I stared at him, considering it. I had never snuck out, or really done anything against my parents. I was no Lynn. Goody Jew-shoes, that was me.

"Why don't you come back around ten?" I asked.

"Aw, man, forget it," he said, hanging his head. "I thought you was gonna be fun."

As Calvin turned to go, I suddenly felt like I was watching my only chance at a friend walk away. I went into rationalization overdrive. 1) He was one of the cool kids and he wanted to hang out with me. 2) If I blew this, I was sure to see the return of the Great Tennessee Tormentor - didn't think I could handle that. And 3) Even if his dad did kill someone, it's not like it was Calvin who pulled the trigger. I might've had some murderers in my family tree somewhere. Everyone probably does.

"Wait," I said, breathlessly.

He turned back and smiled.

"Be right there." I closed the window and stood up. This wasn't going to be easy.

I went to my bedroom door, opened it as slowly as I could ... then realized I was still in my pajamas.

After changing quickly into slacks and a sweatshirt, I slipped on my sneaks and tip-toed down the carpeted hallway. At first, I was doing my damndest to miss the creaking spots in the floor, then remembered there weren't any. Thank you, new house.

I creeped down the short staircase to the foyer, reached the front door, and opened it ever so slowly, hoping slow meant quiet. It squeaked just a bit, but all the bedrooms were too far away for anyone to hear.

I made it outside and pulled the door closed.

Success!

Calvin was in the front yard grass, straddling his bike. "Cool, man. Get on."

Once again, I hesitated.

Five in the morning.

One giant hillbilly boy.

One smallish Jewy boy.

And one mode of transportation.

The wrath I would have to face if Mom caught me? Was I nuts? Apparently.

"You sit on the seat. I'll pedal."

"Where do I put my hands?" I asked as I got on.

"My shoulders," he said, having obviously done this with other passengers. I did as instructed. Calvin grabbed the ram horn handlebars, and we made our way up to the street.

We were heading uphill so we didn't have a lot of speed, but Calvin was a strappin' boy - as they say - so we kept it at a good clip. Somehow I managed to hold on.

Five houses up the hill, he stopped. I jumped off, and he laid his bike against the no-sidewalk curb.

"Come on," he said for the umpteenth time that morning and led me to a huge oak tree that stood between two houses. He threw his arms around it and started to climb.

"What are you doing?" I asked.

"What does it look like, dumbass?"

"I've never—" I stopped myself. "I mean, I don't ..." I had nothing.

He stopped and looked down at me. "Shit, man. You don't know how to climb a tree?"

"I do," I lied.

"No, you don't," he said, letting go and dropping back down. "I forgot, you's from New York. Like *All in The Family*. Archie Bunker and shit."

I laughed. "Yeah. Kinda, I guess."

Calvin focused back on the tree and said, "Come on, I'll push you up."

"Why do we have to climb the tree?"

"You'll find out. Come on."

I'd never been higher than my front porch without four walls surrounding me, but at this point, I couldn't exactly back out.

As I stood closer to the tree, Calvin put his meaty hands under my butt and pushed me up slowly until I could grab a branch.

It was a thick one, but I managed to take hold if it and pull myself up. Happy with myself, and out of breath, I looked down at him, smiling. "Not so hard."

"Now, just keep grabbing branches as you go up. Duh."

A sliver of sunlight laid on the horizon, lighting us just barely as I ascended the tree. Slowly, carefully, my glasses steadily slipping down my nose.

My satisfaction was short-lived, as a growing trepidation turned to anxiety, which turned to fear, which turned to terror. I looked down and saw Calvin just below me, moving much faster. That was a mistake. A jolt of vertigo hit me and I stopped, holding on for dear life.

"How far?" I squeaked.

"That big branch right up 'ere," he said, pointing to a nearby limb.

Thank you, Hashem!

I was only an inch or so away and was able to take hold of it, and finally, lean against it.

Calvin joined, just opposite me. We were probably 25 feet up or so. The branch was wide and secure, so my panic level did lower just a bit.

Fortunately, I hadn't wondered how we were going to get down.

Settling in, Calvin pulled a medium-sized *Head & Shoulders* shampoo bottle from his jacket. This seemed like an odd time to wash our hair, but then he opened the bottle, turned it up, and drank.

"Ick!" I said, a little too loudly for 5am.

Calvin laughed and handed me the bottle. "Go ahead."

"No, thanks."

"It's not shampoo, dumbass," he said, still holding it out for me. "It's moonshine. I got a buddy who gets me all kinds of shit."

I nodded as if I knew what that was. Well, as long as it wasn't shampoo.

I took the bottle and took a swig, hoping for a taste like water or maybe chocolate milk; they were both shiny.

If you've ever swallowed a sword … covered with flaming lava … while trying not to fall out of a tree, you know exactly what I went through in that moment. It was the most startling, searing pain I'd ever felt. Twice. Because the second it went down, it came back up: half cough, half vomit.

To this day, I don't think Calvin has laughed as hard. And I've heard him laugh a lot.

He took the bottle and slapped me on the back several times as I struggled to recover, all while keeping my balance.

After what felt like several days, and at least a dozen more gasps and gurgling hacks, I cried out, "What is that?!"

"I told ya. Moonshine," he said, still laughing and taking another hit.

As I continued to recover, Calvin suddenly erupted into song, an off-key, soaked in whiskey version of Lynyrd Skynyrd's *Freebird*.

"*Won't you flyyyyyy myyyyyy freebird, yeeeeeah!*" Then came the air guitar. His fingers flicked wildly, as he sang the lead guitar notes, his face contorting and curling with emotion. A perfect display of daft pre-teenary.

I laughed and applauded.

His last note played, Calvin calmed some and shoved the bottle in my face. "Wanna try it again?"

"No, thanks," I said, recoiling.

Calvin chuckled, took another swig for himself, then shoved the empty bottle back into his pocket. He leaned back against the branch and took a deep breath.

"'Member that thing I's gonna tell you about my dad?"

"Oh, yeah," I said, pretending I'd forgotten.

"So, I's at the hardware store couple days ago, right, buying a new ax, and this girl, well, woman, at the counter, she got a weird look on her face when she saw me. So I said, 'Why you looking at me like that?' and she said 'you're Boone Macafee's boy, right?' And I said, 'What of it?' And she got all quiet and said, 'You know he killed someone, right?' I shook my head, no way. Then she says, 'Everybody knows, but you.' I think I laughed or something, paid for the ax and left. But when I's walking out, I turned back to look at her and she was starin' at me, boy, not smilin'. Not jokin'."

He paused a moment, thinking, then said, "I mean, he's mean sometimes, but that's some bullshit. He ain't no killer."

I was creeped out, but I could tell sympathy and camaraderie is what Calvin needed right now. "What does she know?" I said. "She's just some woman at a store."

"I reckon, but she said, 'everybody knows.' That's fucked up."

"Did you tell your dad what she said?"

"What?! Hell naw! He'd whip the skin right off my back! Just for even bringin' it up!"

"Okay. Bad idea. Sorry."

Tearing skin off a human body, yes. Murder, no. Got it.

As Calvin took another hit of shine, I thought about how I might ingratiate myself with a potential friend.

"You ever see that program, *The Fugitive*?" I asked.

Calvin shook his head no.

"Well, this guy is accused of murdering his wife, but he didn't do it, so he has to find the real killer. To clear his name."

Calvin squinted at me, slowly getting my point. "Find the real killer. Whoa. Okay. How the hell we do that?"

We?

"I don't know," I said, suddenly wishing I hadn't brought it up. "That was just a TV show."

The birds were beginning their morning serenade - in spite of their uninvited guests. Calvin seemed to be considering my idea, when suddenly his face lit up, and he pointed at the house to the left of us.

"That's why we're here!" he said whisper-screaming.

I looked over to see - in a bathroom window - a young, blond-haired girl in her pajamas, turning on the shower. Oh wow.

"Every Sunday morning before church, good ol' Becky Baker takes a shower."

This was excellent. But there was a slight problem: Like the tall guy with high hair sitting in front of you at the theatre, I wasn't in the best position to see. I would have to adjust.

Unfortunately, in my excitable fixation, I may have rushed said adjustment, forgetting my present altitude …

… and I slipped …

Shrieking at full volume and flailing like a drunken octopus, the fall probably lasted a solid five or six seconds. My glasses flew off at some point and landed on the grass ahead of me. I hit the ground like a hammer, landing on my left arm, causing my humerus to make an audible snap. Flashes of me and Susan cracking the chicken wishbone flitted through my mind.

Then came the pain.

⁂

As I ran back home, tears turning the dirt on my face to mud, a pulsing pain was shooting through my arm like a Roman candle. I was in panic mode - no idea what I was going to do once I got home. I was sure my arm was broken, but I couldn't be honest about what happened. I'd have to concoct some kind of story. But I was the good son, parental deception was foreign to me.

As I opened the front door and entered the foyer, I figured if I could just get to my room without anyone hearing me, I could do my concocting in private. It was still early and doubtful anyone was awake yet, so it seemed like a good plan.

Wrong.

From the foyer, one could see down the split staircase and into Susan's room, and right at that moment, she decided to open her door.

I froze, wondering if I should shoot quickly upstairs, or if I did that, would she hear me? She was in her underwear (gross) … and kissing a boy.

He was tall, with bell-bottomed jeans, a shiny, designy shirt, a wide-brimmed hat and … dark skin.

Dark as in *schvartze*, an African-American person.

I must have gasped because, when I saw them, they saw me, pulling quickly from their embrace. The boy took off into the rec room, and I'm assuming out the back sliding glass door.

I'd never seen Susan quite like that before: caught, frightened, hostile, and half-naked. It was a nasty combo. Her eyes ablaze, she ran up the stairs to where I was on the foyer.

"Yo-yo," she loud-whispered, "if you say one word ... "

I stood still, still shocked, still holding my arm in pain.

She waited for a response, but then noticed my predicament.

"What happened to you? Why were you out?"

I had nothing. "I was up in a tree, trying to spy on a girl taking her clothes off. I didn't see anything, but I fell. I think I broke my arm. It really hurts."

"Jesus," she muttered, shaking her head.

"I won't tell if you don't," I said, squirming in pain.

She thought about that a moment, then nodded. "Tell Mom and Dad you fell in the shower and broke it that way."

"I was taking a shower at six o'clock in the morning?"

"Got something better?"

I did not, and a minute later, I was shutting the bathroom door and taking off my clothes; something, by the way, that's impossible to do with a broken arm and not experience insane pain. I don't recommend it.

Now naked, I turned on the water, waited for it to warm up, got in and sat down in the tub.

Then, I screamed as loud as I could, making sure to wake up the whole house.

❧❦❧

They had all come rushing in, naturally assuming I had a heart attack or a stroke or I was attacked by sharpies (New York thugs from Gramps' era). I told my story, and within minutes, me, Mom, Dad, Gram and Gramps all piled into the Dart, and headed to the ER.

A new hospital, this time.

Now, on the Oak Ridge Turnpike, with zero traffic, Dad's spasmodic driving was worse than normal; I'm assuming because he was taking his eyes off the road every few seconds to study a sprawling, gas station map. We were lost.

Sitting next to Dad was Gram, half hidden under the map blanket. Next to her was Gramps, in his championship belt, of course. Mom was in the back seat with me.

"Is this the main road? We should be on the main road," Gramps said.

"Yes, Jack. It's called the Oak Ridge Turnpike," Dad said.

"I don't think you know where you're going."

"Partly true, Jack," Dad said with his signature patience. "I've never been to the Oak Ridge Hospital before, but I know we're headed in the right direction."

"Unless we're going in the *wrong* direction," Gramps countered.

"*Mishegoss*. Breaking your arm in the shower," Gram said to me, accusingly.

"I put those flower sticky things down," Mom said. "I don't understand. That's the whole point of them - to keep you from slipping and falling and hurting yourself. How would you fall? How could you fall?"

"I don't know, it was still slippery," I said, my liar-in-training demeanor in full display. "It hurts! Really bad!"

"I'll tell you what hurts," Mom said, shaking her head, "my son, my mother's grandson, lying to us."

"Did you call before we left, Murray?" Gramps asked.

"Call who, the hospital?"

"Yes, the hospital."

"Who calls the hospital before you go?" Mom asked, oddly sticking up for Dad.

"They could've given you directions," Gramps argued. "If we had directions, we'd be there by now."

"I'm not lying!" I screamed to Mom.

"Go ahead. Lie to your only mother who holds you in your time of pain."

"Dad, hurry. It really hurts."

"I'm going as fast as I can, Zees. It won't be long now," Dad said as he spent a little too much time staring at the map, gliding into the opposite lane.

There was no traffic or honking horns, but we all screamed anyway, and Dad corrected quickly.

"Maybe I should drive!" Mom shouted.

"It's fine," Dad said, "I'm fine."

"That swerving didn't feel fine to me," Gramps said.

"Are we on the right road?" Gram asked. "I don't think we're on the right road. Jack, I think you're right."

"We're on the right road," Dad said.

Not only were we on the right road, we were on *the* road the hospital was on. That's what they do in small towns; they put the hospital on the main road.

⁂

There was no blur or confusion this time. Just me in a sea of orange seats. Row E, seat 8, surrounded by thousands of other fans. McGraw was on the mound, looking toward first base to eye a possible steal. Focused on the batter again, he reared his arm back and threw a curve ball. Ball 2. As the catcher tossed it back, the crowd around me was suddenly gone.

Everyone just disappeared.

I shot up in bed, gasping for breath. For a moment, I thought, hoped, I was still in Brooklyn. I remembered once I looked down at my chalky white arm cast.

I checked the time - 3:44 am, then got up and started the ritual.

Barefoot in a pair of drab, yellow PJs, I walked down the hall to my parents' room, opening their door an inch. It was too dark to see them, so I opened it further to let some of the hall light in. That worked - both there.

I moved onto Gram and Gramps's room next door and did the same.

Next was down the stairs to Susan's room. She was alone (thank God) and sleeping.

All present and accounted for.

When I reached the top of the landing to head back to bed, I stopped suddenly, looking down the hall, then into the kitchen, then toward the living room. I was looking for Lynn, as if she might casually walk out of the kitchen munching on a late-night matzo snack. I was stuck, terrified. Of what, I had no idea. Life without her? A baseball nightmare that meant nothing?

Maybe it was some kind of momentary clairvoyance of what was to come.

Whatever it was, it lasted less than a minute. I got an idea and managed to mobilize, making my way back down the hall to the linen closet between Mom and Dad's and Gram and Gramps's room.

I opened the door and saw, at the bottom, a couple blankets. Perfect. With some tricky maneuvering, made more difficult due to my cast, I managed to pull myself into the fetal position and pull the door within an inch of being closed, just enough to let some light in. It was a tight fit, but it was safe.

And the beginning of a new ritual.

After every baseball nightmare, I would end up there, then hours later, manage to get up before everyone else did and return to my room until it was time to face the day.

***

Fucking dumbass!

That's what Calvin wrote on my cast the next day at school. We were in the hall, between classes, when he asked a kid he knew if he could borrow a pen. The kid only had a couple pencils and a thick, black Magic Marker. Calvin said the latter would do, and using giant strokes, wrote the aforementioned words, covering most of my cast.

My feelings were mixed on that. It was so big there was no room for anyone else to sign it, but since I had no friends, that was fine. On the other hand, it was so big, I had to cover it with my other hand when I was around my family - except Susan who thought it ranked among one of the funniest things she'd ever seen.

I asked Calvin if Becky saw or heard us. He didn't think so but wasn't sure. He did feel, since the show was so abruptly cancelled, that we should try again.

The good news, my broken arm was a battle wound I could use for sympathy and evidence of some badly needed badassery. When the Magic Marker kid asked how it happened, Calvin told him I was up in a tree trying to rescue my cat from a snarling, hungry raccoon. When it viciously attacked me, I dislodged from the tree and broke my arm. Fortunately, it was not my dominant arm. Unfortunately, the cat did not survive, which was the favored ending since we didn't have a cat. I must have repeated that story a dozen times throughout the day.

Now, home from school and standing on the foyer, one hand covering Calvin's creativity, I stared up at Mom. She was at the top of the stairs, still in her nightgown at 4pm.

"You shouldn't go back out. You've been injured. You need to rest."

"Mom, I'm fine. I got through school all day without any problem."

"What about homework?" she pushed.

"Did it on the bus," I answered, truthfully.

"Bar Mitzvah studies?"

I was impatient and knew Calvin was outside waiting for me. I also knew that, if I got too riled up, it would motivate Mom to keep pushing. "Mom, I'm way ahead of where I need to be. The Cantor said so himself."

"There's harm in studying extra hard for your Bar Mitzvah?"

"Of course not. It's just ... I'm doing really good. Can I just go?"

"Where? What are you in such a hurry for? It's very dangerous out there," she said.

"*Du Zol Nicht Vissen Frum Tsores!*" Gram shouted from the living room.

"It's not dangerous! I mean, it's different, yeah, but it's not dangerous."

Mom looked at me with those suspicious eyes. "You didn't answer me."

"What?"

"I asked you where you were going."

"Why are you being such a noodge?"

"I'm your mother?"

I shuffled my feet. I wasn't sure whether to tell her. She already didn't trust Calvin, but I didn't want to lie again.

Gram joined Mom at the top of the stairs.

"I'm just hanging out with a friend."

"That boy from the shul parking lot?" Mom asked.

"His name is Calvin Macafee. He's a very nice person. Can I go please?"

"He doesn't look Jewish," she said, her finger wagging.

"You said that before."

"I can't say things more than once?"

They were both shaking their heads in Semitic disapproval; Mom with her hands on her face. (Palms to cheeks meant extra discontent.)

I don't know what got into me, maybe it was some of that Southern fire from Calvin, but I decided it was time to go. "I won't be long. Bye!" I opened the door, shot out, and slammed it behind me before I could hear more rebuttal.

I didn't make it far.

Before I could get off the front porch, I ran into a wall of white - sauce-stained and wrinkled. I stopped about an inch away, and looked up to see a massive, Earth-sized man in his 50s, wearing a dirty apron and an enormous smile.

"Hey, hi you doin'?" His accent caught me off guard; sounded New York.

"Hi," I said, question-like, thinking I might be hallucinating.

"I'm Pete. I own Pizza Pete's restaurant, downtown."

"Oh, hi. I'm Yosef."

"Look, I just came by to welcome your family to Oak Ridge. Rough start, eh?" He asked, eyeing my arm cast.

"Oh, yeah, it's nothing."

Pete nodded. "I hear y'all are from New York."

"Yeah. Brooklyn."

"I'm from Staten Island, way back, long time ago. You know Staten Island?"

"Of course!"

"Heh, that's great," he said, handing me a coupon. "Listen, that's for a free, large pepperoni. Y'all come in soon, Ok?"

Calvin rode up on his bike. "Hey Pete. What are you doin' here?"

Pete turned. "Welcoming committee. How you doin', Calvin?"

"Doin' all right."

"Okay, I got to get outta here. Look," Pete said, pointing a beefy finger at me, "I want to see you and the family soon."

"Ok, cool. Thanks."

Pete nodded, turned, and walked back up the lawn toward his dark, green Camaro.

"See ya, Pete!" Calvin yelled after him. Then to me: "Used to play for the Miami Dolphins."

"Really? That's cool."

"Yeah, don't want to mess with him," Calvin said, smirking.

As we watched Pete squeeze into his car and take off, I pocketed the coupon, then hopped onto the back of Calvin's bike and we rode off.

A few minutes later, we were off the bike and deep in the woods. Although we entered from my backyard, I could no longer see the back of the houses on my block, as the browning leaves had only begun to fall.

"You know what it is?" Calvin asked, staring down at a plant about a foot high.

It was gorgeous. Big, dark, green leaves with graceful ridges on each. Fuzzy buds and seeds in the middle of the most mature ones. I answered with a headshake.

"Pot, man!" Cavin said, excitedly, his eyebrows jumping up and down.

My sisters had smoked plenty of weed back in Brooklyn - I found out years later - but I was too young to even know what it was. "Pot?" I asked.

Calvin slapped his hand against his forehead. "Oh man! Reefer? Mary Jane? Tennessee homegrown, man!"

Calvin pulled a joint from his pocket, held it up for me to see. "This is called a joint. It's like tobbaca, but it's whacky tobbacky! It gets you high like shine, but it's different."

"Different how?" I asked, praying to my pal Yahweh I wouldn't have the same reaction I had with the moonshine.

"Hell, I don't know. Just different." Calvin thought a moment, then said slowly, "It's like it makes everything buzzy and high and shit. I don't know. It's cool, is all."

Buzzy and high and shit. Got it.

Calvin sat in the mulch, crossed legged. Then, pulled a pack of matches from his pocket and lit the joint. I liked the smell immediately. It reminded me of certain Brooklyn alleys where hippies would hang out. I was adamant with myself that I would not barf this time.

Calvin took the first hit, long and slow.

He blew it out, then said, "So I's thinking about, you know, what you said about *The Fugitive,* and all. Findin' the real killer. How you think we can do that? You're smart."

Not smart enough to know I shouldn't be coming up with danger-ously, stupid ideas around Calvin.

"Maybe it's not a good idea," I said, shaking my head. "We're just kids. What do we know?"

"I know you're chicken, that's what."

"I'm not chicken."

It looked like old Calvin was back, but then he surprised me.

"Naw, man, you're right. It's stupid. Forget it."

I was relieved - for about 3 seconds. Right behind us, a male voice suddenly interrupted our little party. "What the Hell?"

It was a deep Southern drawl, hard to understand, like maybe the guy only talked while chewing rocks. Calvin erupted into a coughing fit. I jumped a city block high as I turned to see a man in his late thirties, fashion-backward in a filthy T-shirt, and '50s style, cuffed jeans. He was six feet and change, maybe half that wide, an overbearing presence with tight, rusty red hair, a leathery face, and a mouth missing more than a few teeth. I never took the time to count exactly.

Calvin quickly snubbed the joint into the ground as we both stood to face him.

"Daddy! What are you doin' here?" Calvin asked, shaking.

A high-pitched gasp shot from my mouth. I might have also farted. Yes, I could see how that rumor might be true. He couldn't have been the Woody Allen type?

"Who's this one?" he asked, head pointing at me.

"Yosef," Calvin answered. "I told you 'bout him. 'Member?"

"Who's drugs is that?"

Calvin and I looked at each other. If I couldn't understand his words exactly, I knew the gist of the inquiry. The woods became quiet, like all the frogs, crickets, and birds were eavesdropping. Boone was wearing his resting hick face, waiting for an answer.

"Not mine," Calvin and I said in unison. I couldn't believe it! Of course I *should* believe it! This was Calvin after all.

"Right," Boone said. "Calvin, pull me a switch off 'at tree."

Calvin's shaking got worse, and his ears turned red. "No, Daddy, please, I--

"Don't be pitchin' no hissy fit! Just do it!" Boone boomed.

Calvin walked over to a nearby tree, cracked off a thin branch, and handed it to his dad.

"Go on, you know the drill."

Calvin dropped his pants and underwear, leaned against the tree and started to cry.

I hadn't noticed until that point, but I had been slowly, walking backward. And now that Boone was preoccupied, I considered running. But I was too scared he would chase after me. Recently, in gym, I clocked a very lame, thirty-second fifty yard dash. Add a bulky arm cast to that equation, and I'd be as easy to catch as a cold in daycare. It might also make him angrier.

I tried something else. "Is it okay if I go?"

"Don't move, boy!" Boone barked back at me.

Got it. Sorry. Not moving.

Boone pulled the switch back ... I closed my eyes and scrunched up my face, waiting for the crack of the whip ... and ...

Nothing.

Weird.

I opened my eyes to see Boone had lowered the branch and was now stretching his head, squinting his eyes to get a better look at Calvin's butt.

"Wait a dang second," he said.

"What?" Calvin sputtered.

"Is that a ... is that a dingleberry?"

"What?" Calvin asked again, trying to look back at his own ass.

"I said, is that a damn dingleberry hangin' from your butt cheeks?"

I turned away, not wanting to look that close. I had never heard the term dingleberry before, but considering the circumstances, it wasn't hard to figure out what he was referring to.

"I can't see from here, Daddy," Calvin answered, confused.

Boone suddenly burst into laughter. Muttley, but with more bass. Like father like son.

"I had you both! Suckers!" Boone screamed, tossing the branch at me, playfully.

Shocked, Calvin turned to see his pop's demeanor had turned oddly relaxed and jovial. I wasn't quite trusting the abrupt change in attitude myself but did manage a forced laugh.

"I's just messin' with y'all!" Boone screamed, laughing even harder.

"No whupping, then?" Calvin asked, hopeful.

"Hell no, boy," Boone said as he plopped down onto the dirt. "Pull up them britches. Go on, light up that marijuana joint again."

Needless to say, I was relieved as well. It appeared we weren't in danger. Of course, a burning red ass for Calvin would've been some epic payback. And I guess grown-ups in Tennessee were okay with their kids smoking pot?

Calvin pulled his pants up and we joined his dad on the ground.

"Go on," Boone said to Calvin. "You can smoke it. I'm serious."

Calvin hesitated, then looked over at me. I shrugged. Don't ask me, he's your dad.

Calvin sighed heavily, then lit the joint, taking a hit.

"So y'all settlin' in nice?" Boone asked me.

"Yeah, I guess."

"Daddy, you want a hit?" Calvin asked slowly, cautiously.

"Naw, you boys go for it," he said. "Just make sure you don't get caught."

Calvin was almost giddy that, except for not smoking it himself, his dad did appear to be suddenly pro-weed.

Calvin handed me the joint. I took it gingerly as not to burn myself. I'd never held a cigarette, much less a marijuana cigarette. I drew in ... just a little ... and predictably, coughed it right back out. Both Macafees howled in laughter. This time, I laughed along, and it felt good. Joining in made it hard to feel ostracized.

After the hit, my head hurt and my lungs felt like I had just inhaled the sun. What was it with Calvin and his love for scorching his insides? What was next - lightning bolts dipped in tabasco?

"Well, takes time," Boone said, bringing the subject back to the move. "New place. New people. Now, you spend as much time with us as you want, all right?"

"Really? Thanks."

Boone turned to his son, "You be a good friend to Yosef now, y'hear?"

Calvin smiled, nodded.

"So, how'd you break your arm, anyway?" Boone asked.

"Oh, well, this rabid raccoon grabbed my cat and took it up in this tree, so I went up there, then fell trying to save it. It died."

"Damn liar!" Calvin screamed suddenly, now clearly buzzy and high and shit. "There was no cat! Daddy, we was gonna watch Becky Baker take a shower ... Yosef goofed it all up by fallin."

Boone laughed. "Well, she fine as frog hair split four ways, that's fer sure. I could see why you'd fall. Hey, Yosef," he said, changing the subject, "could you come to dinner tomorrow night?"

"Oh," I was taken aback. "Sure, I guess. Just have to ask my mom and dad."

"Good deal. You let us know, a'right?"

With that, Boone patted me on the back, stood up and headed off. "Come on, boy."

Calvin jammed the rest of the joint into the ground and shot up, "See ya, man."

"Bye," I said as I watched the two of them disappear into the woods, Boone leading, Calvin, pushing his bike, staying about a foot behind.

Well, that didn't end badly. Things were actually looking up. And how about that Boone? He certainly looked like he could've been a murderer, and sounded like he could've been a murderer, but also seemed quite nice for a murderer.

Turns out, actually, good ol' Boone had a reason for being so agreeable down by the pot plant. And in case you were wondering, I didn't get high that day; it was just one tiny hit.

JACK AND GERTRUDE

BATTLING SOLOMON SAT ON A SHORT STOOL, TRYING TO catch his breath. His mouth was throbbing in pain and he could taste the blood - it was warm and chalky. He dragged his fingers through the clump of wavy, black hair atop his head, a pointless attempt to clear the non-stop sweat.

Jack had started boxing only a year ago, not long after he turned 32, and he took off quickly. In boxing terms, a thirty-two-year-old start was considered late. Maybe that was why he fought his fights slow, plodding, strategizing - then striking like a cobra at just the right moment. And right now, the match was moving too quickly for him. He needed this break desperately, and thanked God for the end of the round.

Sure didn't seem to be the case for his opponent, Bushy Graham. Bushy was just as scrappy and ripped as Jack, but he was wilder, less focused, Jack thought. Right now, he was already back up and hopping around like a crazed kangaroo.

With only two more rounds to go, they were about a half hour into it, but to Jack, it seemed like hardly a minute since he'd been in the back-room, lacing up his shoes, as Sam, his stalwart trainer, pumped him up. Time always disappeared when he was in the ring. He had read somewhere that, when you get lost in that way, it meant you were doing what you were supposed to be doing. That made some sense to him.

But never in his wildest imagination, even during those late-night alley brawls, did Jack think he'd be in this fight. Jack Solomon, a short-statured, Jewish schlub from nowhere, fighting for the 1926 World Bantamweight title in Madison Square Garden? Unbelievable.

He had trained hard the past few weeks, pretty much the only thing he did. Spar, run, jump rope, do pull-ups, push-ups, spar some more, vomit, start again. Sam had told him to act like the training was no different than the fight itself: it was all part of one long win. Sam had hoped that thinking would minimize Jack's anxiety. It didn't work.

Jack had been as nervous as he ever was; this was for the title, after all. The winning purse would translate to an easier life, and hopefully, a nice girl.

Not that he didn't already receive some attention from females, but Jack was religious and was strictly interested in Jewish women. Unfortunately, for the Semitic woman of the day, *boxer* wasn't exactly at the top of the list of occupational preferences. More typical were doctors, lawyers, businessmen. It was all about the cabbage, see?

Due to his violent and - so far - low paying profession, he knew Jewish women looked at him like he was some kind of rageful, low class gangster.

But that wasn't true. He was a sweet, gentle Jewish man who happened to grow up in the brutal Lower East Side. It was during the age of gang warfare, and since he had always been a small kid, being efficient at connecting an oft-needed blow to the kisser was a worthwhile endeavor. From the first punch he threw as a scared, unripe eleven-year-old, he knew he had something when he knocked out an unsuspecting Irish lad, twice his size.

His punch was an endowment, and he was smart enough to use it.

So, Jack figured, if he could just win this title, the money would be the bait that hooks the fish.

The Garden was packed, boisterous, full of drab, loose suits and suffocating cigar smoke. Right now, it seemed everyone was screaming at him, including Sam, of course. Dizziness was doing its damndest to take over, so Jack shook his head, hoping that would eliminate it, rather than make it worse.

Thank God, it worked.

The bell rang and Jack popped up from the stool, started matching hops with his opponent, making fun of him in hopes of throwing him off. Bushy smiled, revealing blackness where most of his teeth used to be. He knew what Jack was attempting, and as far as he was concerned, it wasn't going to work.

As the two met mid-ring, Jack started feeling better, ignoring the pain, focusing on moving, protecting, and where to pop Bushy next.

Sam knew the science of boxing and taught it to Jack, who loved every bit of it. But, in the end, he just did what came naturally. Don't get too cocky or take wild, unnecessary punches. When it felt right, just ... Boom! Jack threw a left jab to the mouth. Bushy fell back an inch.

The crowd roared. "Solomon! Solomon!"

Jack came on with another; this one to the body, a surprise to Bushy. He flailed back again, and Jack came at him with a rear uppercut, again to the jaw.

Bushy banged against the ropes, his knees buckling slightly. Jack stepped into him again, but Bushy was up and swung wildly at Jack's face.

Missed. Bushy swung recklessly again. And again. Each time, Jack avoided contact.

His opponent weakened and frustrated now, Jack came at him in his calculated way, peppering him with consistent, well-timed hits.

"Solomon! Solomon!"

Left, right, left, right, all to the face. Bushy's blood was splattering everywhere, but Jack was unrelenting.

"Solomon! Solomon!"

Finally, with Bushy seconds from checking out, the ref stepped in and pushed Jack away, stopping the fight.

He raised his arm, shouting, "The new World Bantamweight Boxing champion! The Battling Solomooooooooooooooon!"

The crowd thundered. Sam was jumping around in circles, crying.

Jack was in a daze, a pain and pleasure dream state. Eventually, Sam led him off the platform and through the booming, adoring crowd. Everyone was screaming his name over and over, and those who could reach, patted him on the back. He'd never experienced anything so extreme. It didn't suit him.

An hour later, there was a celebration at the Casa Blanca speakeasy; Jack, now dressed in a brown suit and stylish bowtie, accompanied by Sam, a few reps from the National Boxing Association, and a slew of goyim groupies, each of which Jack was, of course, completely uninterested in.

Jack didn't drink, but he enjoyed watching everyone else imbibe - for a while, anyway. Not a half hour into it and still with that half-beaten muddled head, Jack slipped out to go home and get into bed.

He wouldn't completely realize he won until the next morning around 2am when he woke up suddenly, aching all over, and wanting to call Bushy to see if he was all right. But he didn't even know the guy, so he thought better of it.

Instead, he called someone else.

✻❀✻

Gertrude was trying to get comfortable in her tiny, wooden chair. She tucked her short, brown curls behind her ears to control the sweating, loosening her dress around her bottom and slipping off her dark blue, button strap shoes.

Nothing was working.

This was her new reality - one of a hundred suffocating women wearing white dresses, making white shirtwaists, elbow to elbow, in a noisy, unsanitary, and uncomfortable factory.

Also known as a sweatshop.

At only seventeen, Gertrude was younger and thinner than most of her co-workers. And taller at 5'10. A tall *tomata,* as her boss remarked more than once. About half the women there were Yiddish-speaking Jews: Lithuanian, Russian, German, and Polish, like Gertrude. The commonality was nice. Most of them were friendly too, and some even talkative. Unfortunately, there were also a few who appeared to be jealous. Gertrude could tell by the *farkakteh* looks they'd give her. Why the envy, she had no idea. She never considered herself a real dish or anything. Certainly not a *mieskeit*, just unremarkable.

Then, there were the *schvartzes*. There were a lot of them, and they made her nervous. She found them unpleasant and distrustful. The other day during a five-minute break, one of them tried to speak to her. Gertrude shook her head, made it clear that she spoke no English, and went back to work. This was a lie; she could understand and speak English just fine, but most of the time, she chose not to. In this case, it served her well.

As she continued to struggle in her seat, Gertrude reminded herself that, not long ago, the factory conditions were even worse. So much so, that a few years back, the women's labor union went on strike. In the end, they won several concessions, and she was grateful for that. But her feelings were mixed with guilt because, not long after the strike, the great Triangle Shirtwaist Fire erupted, taking the lives of hundreds of women. Grandmothers, mothers, wives, it pained her to think about it. *Du Zol Nicht Vissen Frum Tsores*, as her mother would say.

She'd only been there a week so far, but she couldn't help wonder how long she would have to endure it. Six months? Six years? A lifetime? Her mother, father, and younger brother, Yosef, were also in the garment industry, but worked out of the family residence, a tiny tenement apartment. Gertrude and her brother had been going to school, but when most of her father's clients were wrested away by a low-balling competitor, the kids were pulled from school in order to work.

Truth was, she didn't miss school at all. All her courses were homemaking, yet her mother had taught her how to cook, clean, sew, and do the wash. So what was the point in getting an education?

The goal now was to find a nice, young Jewish man who could give her children and a comfortable home. Gertrude's parents had recently begun to inquire at their shul for potential husbands, and she was excited about that. She made sure that, when she was there, she was coquettish and tried not to appear too tall. Apparently, there were no takers yet, but they'd just begun looking. She was optimistic.

She knew of some goyim girls, a few of them even flappers, who would go to meet men at speakeasies and dance halls. But Orthodox Jewish girls didn't do that type of thing. Alcohol was illegal, of course, and rather than marriage, from what she heard, debauchery was the more common outcome.

That bothered Gertrude - this indulgence and depravity. She couldn't understand why young people would choose to live that way. She had even heard of several people brutally murdered at these clubs, for what she could only imagine. Clearly, God was not on their side.

That said, Gertrude wasn't completely innocent.

She did have one guilty pleasure; at least, that's how she perceived it.

A few months ago, on a Wednesday while their parents were at the market, Yosef had turned on the radio for a live broadcast. It was from Harlem's Cotton Club. Up until then, the only music Gertrude was acquainted with was of the spiritual, Jewish kind, like Klezmer. To her, music was always reflective of Judaism, appropriate only when expressing religious joy or mourning a death.

She was preparing dinner when that big band sound first played, full of static, blaring through their dome-shaped radio. She didn't care for it and told her brother as much. But Yosef began hooting and hollering and clapping along, and he wouldn't stop - even after several minutes of Gertrude telling him to turn it off.

But, every Wednesday when their folks were out, Yosef would turn on the show, and slowly, Gertrude began to appreciate what she was hearing. They called it jazz: horns, piano, drums. The music made her feel vibrant, happy, hopeful. Eventually, she even began to dance, right there in the kitchen, as she fell in love with the likes of Duke Ellington, Cab Calloway, and Fats Waller. It became a weekly event. She looked forward to it, and it was always jubilant. But she also knew it was wrong and made Yosef promise not to ever speak of it. As far as she knew, he never did.

Finally, settling in her ridiculous seat, Gertrude realized she was going to be uncomfortable and there was nothing she could do about it. This had been the case all week. Why would it be any different today?

And so she began to sew, the clickety clacks of her Singer sewing machine now in full concert with the rest.

✻✼✻

Jack trudged up the dark, filthy New York street. He'd walked through the Garment District probably a thousand times, usually having to avoid the shoppers and the rack men pushing their fashions down the sidewalk. Not this time. It was late, close to 11pm now, so that was nice. It was a clear shot home.

A warm wind picked up and he steadied his hat, one of those cream-colored, short-crowned ones. Jack couldn't wait to get some sleep. His body was starting to feel the fight.

As he increased his speed, someone suddenly shot out of a building he was passing and started walking in front of him, at about the same speed, in the same direction. It was one of those odd only in New York circumstances that happens when you suddenly find yourself walking too close to someone.

And at this hour, that someone's likely to get nervous.

Before leaving work that night, Gertrude had heard of another strike being planned and how her boss had hired some local gangsters to muscle up some of the union leaders, maybe talk them into not striking at all. Give 'em a good scare. No one gets hurt kind of thing. Gertrude was a union member, of course, but far from a union leader.

But now, as she walked home at this late hour, she couldn't help wonder if this person tailing her was about to attack. If she was about to be jumped, she didn't have much time to consider her options, so she figured she better deal with it. And now.

She turned around quickly and threw a wild punch at him. Since she was a good four inches taller, she hit him right in the hat, sending it several inches off his head and into the street.

Jack reared back with a surprised laugh, "Hey, now!"

Gertrude kept her dukes up, growling in Yiddish, "I'll give you another, maybe you won't be so lucky this time!"

If he understood the Yiddish, great. If not, English would do.

"It's okay. I'm harmless. I'm a mensch." Jack spoke in Yiddish, smiling and putting his hands up in surrender.

Gertrude shot back, "Why are you following me?"

"My apologies. I wasn't intending to," Jack said, his voice trailing off as her enormous, brown eyes caught his attention. This was some tall, gorgeous, feisty girl. She had him at the first punch.

Gertrude kept her fighting stance, not trusting this man; sure he was Jewish, but so what. He looked like a real brute with that beaten face.

"What happened?" she asked, motioning to his face.

"What do you mean?"

"Your face."

Jack laughed. He was so used to being bloodied and bruised it hadn't occurred to him it might be threatening.

"I'm a professional boxer."

"A Jewish boxer?"

"I'm one of a few."

"By the looks of it, not a very good one," Gertrude said grinning, finally relaxing her arms.

"Well, I did just win the Bantamweight World Championship."

"Mazel Tov. What is it?"

"Bantam is a weight class: one-hundred-fifteen to one-hundred-eighteen pounds. It's a boxing award. Best in the world, so they say."

Gertrude nodded skeptically.

"I'm being honest. You know, they got a championship belt they're sending me, being delivered in a couple of weeks. They're going to take pictures of me posing in it. Maybe I can show them to you."

"I'll take your word for it."

"You know, it came with a fat purse, too," Jack said, smiling and relaxing his arms behind his back like a man with money might do.

"I should really be getting home," Gertrude said, not moving. There was something about him. His kindness. His grace. Their height difference didn't even seem to bother him - that kind of self-esteem appealed to her.

"What's your name?" Jack asked.

"Why do you want to know?"

"Any girl who punches me in the hat, I always like to get her name."

Gertrude smiled, winked those brown eyes. "A lot of girls take swings at you?"

"You're the first."

"I'm Gertrude."

"Jack. Jack Solomon."

She nodded, waiting now.

"I wonder if ..." Jack stammered. This happened when it came time to make a move. He steeled himself for the rejection.

"I wonder if you might join me for a cup of coffee."

"I'm seventeen," she said, just to make sure he was aware.

"How old you think I am?" Jack asked.

"Hard to tell with that face," Gertrude said, twisting up her lip to make it seem like a difficult decision.

Finally, she said, "It's too late for coffee. But, you may come calling at my home tomorrow. You can meet my parents and my brother. I'll cook dinner. I'm a good cook."

"I would be delighted," Jack said, trying his absolute damndest not to appear too excited.

Gertrude gave him her address. He relegated it to memory. And at that, she walked out into the street, retrieved Jack's favorite hat, and handed it back to him.

"I have an idea," Jack said. "You walk ahead for a bit before I start again. That way it won't seem like I'm tailing you."

"That will work. *Shoylem*," she said.

"*Shoylem*."

Gertrude turned and headed back down the sidewalk. She'd be surprised if he came calling, but she hoped he would.

Jack stayed put - as he promised - and watched her every step. From this point on, for the rest of his life, he would not go a day without thinking about her.

JEWS FOR JESUS

I COULDN'T HELP WONDER WHAT THE OTHER TWO MESHUG-geners would think. Would they tell me I was all *farkakteh* and disown me? Would they go screaming about it to Rabbi Berkwitz and tell the whole congregation? Would they call my parents and tell them that I was sitting at a dinner table where the main conversation was about Jesus?

Some of that, yes ... if they knew.

Well, they weren't going to hear it from me.

So I had a plan. Since I knew Mom wouldn't let me have dinner with the Macafees, on the day of, I would tell her that the Rabbi needed some help around the shul, so she needed to pick me up a couple hours after Bar Mitzvah studies. Instead, Calvin would pick me around the back of the synagogue, we'd have dinner, and then get me back to the shul in time for Mom to come get me.

I thought it was foolproof.

That is, until Calvin the fool rode us, on his bike, into my neighbor-hood and down through the grass between my house and my neighbor's! What the Hell?! Okay, no one saw us, but they could have. I screamed at him, angry with his carelessness. He said it was the fastest way, so I let it go.

If I had been more clear-headed (and not twelve), I would've seen this as a good indication of Calvin's lack of foresight and disregard for potential consequences. He certainly was raw and original. But crafty without craft will get you every time.

We rode through the woods, dodging trees and splashing through the shallow creek.

Within a few minutes, we came up on another row of backyards. It was the nature version of the other side of the tracks, as these homes couldn't have been more different than mine. They were dilapidated, single-floor, ranch-style houses with peeling paint, and prison cell-sized backyards, with rusty car skeletons parked on *see-ment* blocks.

In 1942, when they first created Oak Ridge for the Manhattan Project, the government brought in highly educated scientists and engineers to help build the bomb. They also brought in blue collar folk from surrounding areas, Tennesseans for generations, to run the services: gas stations, restaurants, a bowling alley. After the war, with the infrastructure in place, new government projects continued, attracting new scientists and engineers.

Cue the Bambergers.

So, in some ways there were two Oak Ridges, but there was comingling: in schools, shopping centers, restaurants, churches. It had been this way for years.

Most often, it went without conflict.

We pulled up into Calvin's yard, hopped off the bike, and walked across the uncut lawn toward his bedroom window. Calvin opened it, moved aside the sheet he had hanging in lieu of curtains, and climbed in first.

Our home in Brooklyn was small, but this place was sad small. Calvin's bedroom was claustrophobic and musty with a bent twin bed, a desk Thomas Jefferson might have used, and a dull, blue chest of drawers with a GI Joe and a dust-covered Lite Brite on top.

The rest of the house, what there was of it, was comprised of wobbly wood floors, dismal, 1950s furniture, bathroom tile long emptied of caulk, and a miniature dining area, half of it in the kitchen.

Oh, and a shotgun sitting upright just to the inside of the front door - not exactly a surprising feature of the Macafee household.

Boone was putting some food on a small folding table as we entered from Calvin's room.

"Hey, Daddy, look who I got here," Calvin said, smiling.

"Welcome, Yosef," Boone said, sitting down. "Go on, sit."

I sat in a folding chair and immediately grabbed a chicken wing, taking a giant bite.

"Hold up, boy," Boone said, admonishing me.

I froze, nodded, the bird meat halfway down my throat.

"We say Grace before we eat."

I had no idea what he was talking about. I looked to Calvin, who closed his eyes and took my right hand.

Holding hands at dinner? Weird.

I debated whether to swallow the rest of my chicken or hack it up. As I chose swallowing, Boone took my other hand. It felt more paw than hand, King Kongish, scratchy, and coarse like black pepper. Understandable, since Boone had a business pulling stubborn tree stumps. I suppose when he wasn't doing that, he was smacking helicopters out of the sky.

"Lord," Boone started, his eyes closed, "we are so grateful for the food that you have set before us. We know not everyone has what we do, and we thank you for everything you have given to us. We also want to take this time to pray for the poor and hungry who are in lack. Please be with them and sustain them. And finally, please be with and comfort Calvin's dear mother in heaven. In the name of Jesus, we pray."

They opened their eyes and together said, "Amen."

I knew that one, but came in late with it, said it differently too: "Ah-main."

Luckily, Boone nodded approvingly anyway. I had kept my eyes open during the prayer, studying the other items on the table. Besides the wings, I was clueless.

"Dig in!" Boone screamed.

Calvin jammed a pile of something into his mouth and I, again, went for my wing.

Boone must have been reading my mind.

He pointed, as he spoke slowly, "Okay, so these are chicken wings, right here's pig's feet, this is collard greens."

"Thanks," I said, smiling and nodding, appreciating the tutorial, but thinking I might just stick with the chicken.

So we ate and nobody spoke. I certainly wasn't going to initiate anything. As far as I knew, you weren't supposed to talk at all while eating.

Everything was going fine, but when I reached for my glass of milk, something suddenly stopped me: Chicken. Pig. Milk.

Not kosher, Yosef!

What was I thinking? This was madness. If God catches me mixing meat and dairy, he's sure to strike me down.

But then, something occurred to me. Boone and Calvin looked perfectly healthy, totally unstruck. As a matter of fact, they look as though they'd *never* been struck down. They're not Jewish, one might argue. But how does God know? How does God know *I'm* Jewish? Okay, he knows. He knows everything. He's God, damn it. But maybe I can hold off on being Jewish - just this one meal. He'll let me slide. He's cool like that.

"What's wrong?" Boone said. Twice he said, it, I realized. I didn't hear the first time.

"Nothing," I answered. "Everything's good."

I was so thirsty. I decided to go for it, to take my chances, to risk my short, Semitic life. I reached for the white poison, slowly wrapping my hand around the plastic cup.

I held it there a moment - still alive.

Keep going. Again, as slowly as I could move, I brought the cup to my mouth, tipping it ever so carefully up.

That's when I saw both Macafees staring at me, their eyes squinty.

"It's just milk, you know," Calvin said, confused.

It was now or never.

I closed my eyes, took a deep breath, and like I was standing on the edge of the highest building in Manhattan, ready to jump, I went for it.

Gulp, gulp, gulp, gulp, gulp.

Done, I lowered the cup, satisfied and ready to die.

"You okay, man?" Calvin asked.

I nodded, waiting.

Boone and Calvin shrugged, then went back to their dinner.

Nothing was happening!

Thank you, Yahweh!

It'll be just this once, I promise!

I celebrated with a couple more wings.

"So, y'all find a church you like?" Boone asked.

"Pardon?" I said, not quite understanding.

"I apologize," Boone said, "my mouth was full. Here I am always tellin' Calvin here not to speak with his mouth full all the time, and here I am doin' it!"

Everyone laughed.

"Anywho, what do y'all call that Jewish church?"

"Shul, synagogue?"

"Synagogue, right, right."

"There's only one here," I said, sadly.

Boone nodded, smiled. "Did you know Jesus was Jewish?"

"I did," Calvin said, wanting in on the conversation.

"I know you did, boy," Boone said sharply. "I'm talkin' to Yosef."

Calvin shrunk, clamping down on some fresh piggy toes.

"Yes, sir," I spoke haltingly, "we consider Jesus a great Jewish teacher, but not--"

"Oh yeah!" Boone said loudly, nodding intensely. "A great teacher cause he is the Messiah, the son of God! Our savior!"

I smiled and tried some collard greens. Two things had occurred to me regarding what Boone had just said. First, I didn't think God had any kids, so that was news. Second, I was familiar with the term *messiah*, but for Jews, the messiah wasn't Jesus, rather a future Jewish king who's expected to save the Jewish nation during the Messianic Age, hence the name.

Save us from what exactly, I wasn't clear. Maybe collard greens. That'd be good.

"We got more in common than you think, Yosef." Boone said, standing up. "Be right back." He disappeared into his bedroom.

There was just enough time for Calvin and I to exchange goofy looks before Boone returned, now holding a book. Not just any book, I would soon learn. It was stuffed with clumsily torn notebook paper bookmarks Boone was now flipping through.

He remained standing as he made a selection and read it with a completely different voice than his speaking one. It was big and expressive, with rumbling bass sounds, and feverish, pregnant pauses.

"And when it is full, the fishermen haul it ashore; then, sitting down, they collect the good ones in baskets and throw away the others! This is how it will be at the end of time; the angels will appear and separate the wicked from the upright, to throw them into the blazing furnace, where there will be weeping and grinding of teeth!"

That last part shook me, as I assumed the wicked would not have access to a good dentist. Of course, my terror had a lot to do with the messenger. When a Rabbi reads religious text, it's typically calm and convincing. When a preacher does it, it's full of passion and fire. But when a possible murderer does it, it tends to come off more criminally insane.

The fear must have been all over my face because Boone was looking at me with a huge smile on his face. "Here," he said, handing me the book. "Read us a passage. Just turn to any page there."

I took the book and saw the title for the first time: *Holy Bible. King James Version*. I'd obviously read from many a Jewish text, but I'd never seen a Christian bible, much less read from one. I didn't mind - as long as every paragraph wasn't about everlasting torment.

"Any part?" I asked.

"It's all the Lord's word," Boone said.

I took the good book with my good arm, balanced it with my casted one and, randomly, stopped at a page. I cleared my throat and read, "In all truth I tell you, no one can enter the kingdom of God or truly experience salvation without being born through water and the Spirit. Mike 3:5-8."

"Jesus is our savior!" Boone thundered.

"Jesus is our Lord!" Calvin screamed.

"What does it mean?" I asked, wanting to be part of the excitement.

"Means you'll only go to Heaven if you're reborn through our lord Jesus Christ," Boone said. "It's all about being saved! We all got to be saved. Hell's too scary a place!" Boone leaned back, happy to help connect me with the good book.

I still wasn't quite understanding what we needed to be saved from, but ... I was happy they were happy.

"Hey, Daddy," Calvin said, leaning in.

"What?"

"I know where Hell is," Calvin said.

"Oh yeah? Where is it?" Boone asked, genuinely curious what his son thought.

"It's down the back of Yosef's underpants."

We all burst into laughter.

When things calmed a bit, I offered Boone the Bible back.

He leaned toward me, flashing a big, toothless smile. "You go on and take it. Learn all about the Lord. He's the one true way."

I looked down at the book. I would have to hide it. Then again, it's just a Bible that my new Southern Baptist friends gave me. No big. I'm Jewish. I'm always going to be Jewish. Besides, the Bible had some real interesting things in it. I found it intriguing, and educational. How could it hurt?

"Thank you," I said.

"You know what, Yosef, we's real happy to have you in our lives." He then looked over at Calvin, then at me again and said, "Sure hope we can keep it that way."

I understood what Boone was getting at. If you're going to be pals with Calvin, you're also going to be pals with Jesus.

Quid pro quo. Strings attached.

And let me tell you, those were some complicated, tumultuous strings.

❦

Calvin and I became closer over the weeks and months, hanging out between classes and at lunch. He had released his little band of blowhards. They weren't happy about it, but he tossed them off pretty easily. Good ol' Junior high, a place to find new forever friends, or shed the ones who no longer serve you. I was now Calvin's right hand man: Tennille to his Captain, Robin to his Batman, Agnew to his Nixon.

No one was making fun of me anymore.

He would talk to girls, of course, Becky included. I would stand by, listen and laugh at the appropriate times, and act like I wasn't 100% terrified of females.

So, there I was, halfway into 7th grade in my new school, my *dumbass* arm cast was finally off, and I even convinced Mom to buy me some white Converse high tops and a couple pairs of bell bottom jeans. I wasn't so much *the new Jew* anymore. I was one of the cool kids.

After school, for Bible study, we'd go to his house or by the pot plant. Calvin would smoke. I'd pretend to. Boone would join us at some point. One of us would read a passage and we'd discuss what it meant, and what we needed to do to make sure we stayed good with Jesus.

I even added my own private study time to my morning ritual. Once awake, I'd grab my flashlight and ruler, check my package for growth, then pull out my Bible, which had replaced the Anne Frank book. I had already read all of Boone's bookmarked pages and had dog-eared the ones that interested me. There were some fascinating things that I felt the Talmud didn't focus on much, if at all.

The fear material, for one. Fear was something that I understood quite well. Moses was chalk full of it. Caleb, a spy, was also a bigtime scaredy-cat. Hell, Jesus himself freaked out more than once.

Then there was the whole sinning deal, and the fact that Jesus will save you, regardless.

Get a peek at Becky's boobs? Saved!

Getting high? Saved!

Lie to your Jewish parents and grandparents? Saved!

Seemed like a no-brainer. All you had to do was take him into your heart, and when it's your time to die, He'll take you to Heaven and keep you out of Hell. Bada-bing. Bada-boom.

Of course, I was also studying for my Bar Mitzvah, even though I barely had to. Some days, I'd be Southern Baptist in the morning and Jewish in the afternoon. Other days, Southern Baptist in the morning and afternoon, then Jewish at night. Still other days, Southern Baptist morning, noon and night, but Jewish late at night - if I woke up to have some midnight gefilte fish with Gramps.

⚜

Come December, on our street, there was no question which house the Jews lived in. Just look for the only one without Christmas lights. No big, bright blue, red, and green bulbs adding colorful, wintery cheer to the block.

Nope, just darkness.

I hated it.

At least this first year, Christmas Eve and the first night of Hanukkah landed on the same night, a religious convergence that only happened every 15 years. It made me feel a little better. Even though this was the year I happened to be cheating on God.

Mom, Dad, Susan, Gram, and Gramps were all sitting at the table when I came bursting up the stairs and into the dining area, sweating and panting.

"I thought you went to the bathroom," Mom said, confused about my appearance.

"I did," I said, sitting down and fabricating as I spoke. "I just ran back really fast. I didn't want to miss anything."

"You look like you're having a heart attack," Mom said, worried.

"He's not having a heart attack. He's twelve, for God's sakes," Dad said.

"Oh, so you're a doctor now?" Mom snapped back. "We should be so lucky."

"You don't have to be a doctor to know he's not having a heart attack," Susan said.

Mom kept her focus on Dad. "If you were a doctor, we'd still be in Brooklyn," she said.

"Who's the champ?" Gramps asked me.

"I am, Gramps," I answered.

"Go ahead, Yosef. Light the candle," Gram said, pointing at our gorgeous, antique brass menorah. It was a family heirloom.

I nodded, took the servant candle from the middle, lit it with a match, then as I lit the first candle, chanted: "*Baruch atah, Adonai Eloheinu, Melelch haolam, asher kid'shanu b'mitzvotaz v'tisvanu l'hadlik ner shel ... oy gevalt*! I have to go to the bathroom again!"

Screwing up the blessing, I bolted out of the dining room once again and back downstairs.

If there's one thing Jews have understood for centuries, it's diarrhea.

As I descended the stairs, I could hear everyone's oohs and aahs, feeling bad for me.

And then there was Susan. "You have to use *my* bathroom?! Gross!"

"He can use whatever bathroom he wants, young lady!"

I could almost hear Susan's eye roll.

Once I got downstairs, I pulled the bathroom door shut from the outside, passed through the rec room, and slipped quietly out the sliding glass backdoor.

It was like I was in a 1950s comedy film where the bumbling bachelor has two dates on the same night, and he's running between rooms of his NYC apartment where each unsuspecting girl awaits his return.

Except I was running through acres of woods, at night, without a light, in winter.

There was a thick layer of frost on the ground, and every footfall I made crunched like matzo. This, I hoped, would alert any small animals to get out of my way, but there was no guarantee. I didn't have a coat, as that would've blown my cover, so frostbite seemed like a real possibility. There was one thing on my side. There were no leaves on the trees, so I could see house lights - Christmas and otherwise - and they helped me navigate.

A couple days ago, I had accepted Boone's Christmas dinner invitation, knowing it was mandatory. I assumed they had no idea Christmas Eve was also the first night of Hanukkah, especially since it was doubtful they knew what Hanukkah was in the first place.

The first time I left the Macs to run back home, I had told them I forgot to take the trash out. But this time, I had no plan. The diarrhea scam wouldn't fly here because their only bathroom was right next to the dining area. Crap.

About seven minutes later, I arrived back, out of breath, cold-sweating, and seriously stressed. After we said Grace, we dug into our black-eyed peas and hamhocks with red-eye gravy. This was Christmas dinner at the Macafees and didn't seem real different than regular dinner at the Macafees. I was starving as I guess I worked off my partially-eaten brisket, kugel, and latkes (sour cream and applesauce on the side).

My eye on the radio alarm clock in the living room, I ate as fast as I could while formulating my next departure. That was when Boone interrupted the meal. He wanted to recite a Christmas prayer he had memorized.

Naturally, he did it in his big, booming preacher persona.

"Yosef, Calvin, may you both be filled with the wonder of Mary, the obedience of Joseph, the joy of the angels, the eagerness of the shepherds, the determination of the magi, and the peace of the Christ child! Almighty God, Father, Son, and Holy Spirit bless you both, now and forever!"

"The gifts!" I screamed, staring at the towering, tinsel-covered Christmas fir in the living room.

Calvin and Boone both looked at me oddly.

"I forgot to bring your gifts!"

"It's all right, son," Boone said, "finish your supper, first."

I jumped out of my seat, ran to the front door, and opened it before he could protest.

"Be right back!"

"Yosef!" Calvin shouted.

I kept moving, slamming the door behind me, and taking off around the back of the house.

It took me a while longer to get home this time. Besides being exhausted, cold and anxiety-ridden, now I was also nauseous. As I snuck back in, I wondered what would happen if I barfed hamhocks all over my Orthodox grandparents.

Before going back upstairs, I went into the bathroom, wiped the sweat from my brow, pulled out my trusty bottle of Maalox, and popped a couple in hopes of calming the nausea.

A few minutes later, I felt a bit better, and was back in the dining room where everyone was still at the table, now exchanging presents. It was tradition for Dad to give me a few bucks to buy everyone Hanukkah gifts. This year was no different, except I needed to spread it out to include the Macafees. Covertly, of course.

"Oh, Yosef, how are you feeling?" Mom asked.

"Meh," I said, sickly.

"Sit down, Zees," Dad said. "Happy Hanukkah."

As I sat, he handed me a gift - a tube, about two-feet-long, gift-wrapped in blue Hanukkah paper with big Jewish stars. I ripped off the wrapping paper, revealing a rolled-up wall poster.

"Cool. What is it?"

"Unroll it, show everybody."

I unfurled the poster, holding it up for everyone to see. It was a photograph of a small Hasidic man in a Superman outfit, but with the traditional black hat, beard, and *payot* (side curls). Also, instead of the "S" on his chest, there was the Hebrew letter, *shin*. There were no words, just the image.

Faster than a speeding dreidel! More powerful than Jesus on Sunday. Able to practice two religions in a single evening! It's Super Yosef!

"Thanks Dad," I said, smiling. "It's really funny. Can't wait to put it up."

"You're welcome. Enjoy," he said, getting up to clear some dishes.

Gram was squinting at the poster. "I don't understand," she said.

Susan answered, "It's a joke, Gram. Just not a very funny one."

"It's funny," Dad protested.

"*Schmegegge*," Mom said with a hand pass.

"Wait, you agree with me?!" Susan said with overblown shock.

"I'll pick the presents from now on," Mom said, taking yet another jab at Dad.

Dad raised his voice from the kitchen. "You didn't want to get a present because you're not comfortable driving here yet. So I offered, and what happens? I'm a putz."

It was time to implement another diarrhea attack when … something I was eating, obviously too fast, got stuck in my throat. Chewed food, meet extreme stress. I froze, my eyes bulging. I stood up, panicking.

"I'm choking!"

Everyone but Susan stood up and surrounded me.

"Who knows the hindlick?!" Mom shouted.

Dad started smacking my back with his palm.

"That's not the hindlick!"

"*Du Zol Nicht Vissen Frum Tsores!*"

"Cough it out, champ! Cough it out!"

The lump in my throat started to pulse like a bullfrog, mid-croak.

"It hurts!" I yelled, crying now and pacing around the table.

Everyone was screaming.

This would be a terrible way to die, but at least I was surrounded by family.

"Yo-yo!" Susan screamed, still in her chair. "If you're talking, you're not choking."

"Shut your mouth, young lady!" Mom roared back at her.

"What?! It's true! It's probably just stuck. Drink some water."

I grabbed a glass of somebody's water and guzzled it.

At first, it hurt, but then slowly, the liquid started moving down whatever was lodged. Finished, I put the glass down. Everyone was staring at me.

"I'm okay now," I said, sheepishly, sitting back down.

"*Oy gevalt*," said Mom, Dad, Gram, and Gramps in unison, all shaking their heads.

"Sorry," I added.

"Like I said," Susan said with her signature eyeroll.

"Ooh!" Mom yelled. "I forgot! I have a letter from Lynn."

She took off into another room as everyone else sat back down. I knew I had to get going again, but I really wanted to hear what Lynn had to say.

Mom came back in, ripping open the letter.

"You didn't open it yet?" Gram asked surprised.

"It's addressed to the Bambergers, not Sandy Bamberger. It's like a gift. I wanted to wait for Hanukkah."

Lynn did not come down for September's High Holidays. Instead, it was a quick phone call saying how busy she was, but don't worry, she'd be sure to write. I wasn't home at the time.

Mom read from the letter:

"'Hello family! I hope everyone is settling in nicely in Tennessee. I'm sorry I wasn't able to come down for the High Holidays. I became very busy, and I promise I'll use the airplane ticket soon. Thanks Dad. Gram, I hope your hand is healing well. Gramps, I hope you haven't punched anyone who didn't deserve it. Dad, I hope you are getting along well at your new job. Mom, make sure you use plenty of mosquito repellant. I hear they're bigger than Carnegie Deli pastrami sandwiches down there. Susan, please try not to get into too much trouble. And Yosef, I hope your nightmares aren't too upsetting these days.'"

Mom stopped, looked up at me. "What nightmares?" Thanks Lynn.

"They're nothing," I said, "what else she say?"

Everyone was staring at me, waiting for a better answer.

"They're nothing! Really! Come on, read."

Mom took a deep breath and continued,

"That's it. Just ... 'Love, Lynn. P.S. I dropped out of NYU ...' "

Shocked, Mom's reading slowed. "'broke up with Jacob and left New York. I'm now living in Detroit, Michigan?! ... And working as a waitress at a ...'"

She barely got out the last three words. "'Thai food restaurant.'"

Mom's grip loosened and the letter floated to the floor. Every Bamberger mouth was agape as the rhetorical questions shot around the table like a summer hailstorm.

Dad: "She dropped out?"

Susan: "She broke up with Jacob?"

Mom: "Michigan?"

Gram: "What is tie food?"

Gramps: "Who can I knock out?"

Me: "She left New York ... and didn't come here?"

I was furious. The kind of angry you get when you've been rejected by someone you've spent your whole life loving. It burns like a deep con, making you feel trivial, weak. That was a pathos I was used to by now, and we all could've had a mutual *kvetch* about Lynn's newest *shanda*, but I had somewhere I needed to be.

Making sure it was dramatic, I jumped out of my chair holding my stomach, almost knocking over the menorah, and bolted out of the dining room without a word.

I had hidden the Macafee's gift bag under the sofa in the rec room. I grabbed it and took off once again.

Ten minutes later, Boone was ripping open his present. The wrapping paper was covered with Jewish stars and dreidels. He either didn't notice or didn't care.

"I love it!" Boone yelled, holding up a cheap corncob pipe.

I had thought long and hard about what to get him and couldn't come up with anything. When it hit me, it felt like I struck gold. The two meshuggeners had given it to me as a parting gift, half joke, half *you're going to need this*.

Yep, I was regifting before regifting was even a thing.

"Thank you, Yosef," Boone said, smiling and patting me on the back as we all sat around the Christmas tree.

"My turn!" Calvin screamed as he tore open my gift. It was an 8-track tape. He read the cover. "Lynard Skynard! Oh man! I love it, Yosef! Freeeee-biiiiiird yeah!"

Boone and I cracked up. Calvin was easy to buy for.

Boone grabbed a gift from under the tree and handed it to me.

I tore open the Rudolph the red-nosed wrapping paper to find a small, rectangular box. Inside was a four-inch wooden cross with pointy ends. It was beautiful, star-like.

"It's a Southern Baptist cross," Boone said.

"Beautiful symbol of Jesus," Calvin added, looking for that ever-scarce fatherly approval.

Boone nodded. "Just so you know, it's different than regular Baptist or Catholic."

I took it out of the box and turned it around several times, admiring it. "Thank you. I like the wood. It's very nice."

"Merry Christmas," Boone said.

Thinking we'd have a laugh, I held it at arm's length, pointed at Calvin and screamed, "Out Satan, out! The power of Christ compels you!"

Calvin reared back in mock fear, thinking it just as hysterical as I did.

"Yosef!" Boone screamed, tearing the cross out of my hand and pulling it to his heart. "What in Jesus's name was that?!"

I went numb, stammered, couldn't find words; my head was heating up like a furnace.

"Explain yourself, boy!"

Finally, I sputtered, "I was just imitating this movie, *The Exorcist*. My sister told me about it. I didn't even see it! I'm sorry! I'm really sorry!"

Boone stood up and started pacing. I glimpsed over at Calvin for a clue of how to deal with it. Calvin answered by shaking his head violently, meaning, *Just shut up. Don't say anything else.*

"Mr. Macafee, I'm sorry. I didn't know."

Boone stopped suddenly and whirled around, glaring at me with dragon-like eyes.

"Ain't no Satan in this house! You get me?!"

"Yes, sir. I'm sorry. I didn't know, I mean I didn't mean anything. I'm sorry."

Boone grabbed his Bible from the coffee table, turned to a page quickly, and thrusted it at me.

"Read," he said.

"Timothy 1:15-17," I said, quivering. "'Christ Jesus came into the world to save sinners—of whom I am the worst. But for that very reason I was shown mercy so that in me, the worst of sinners, Christ Jesus might display his immense patience as an example of those ... I mean ... for those who would believe in him and receive eternal life. Now to the King eternal, immortal, invisible, the only God, be honor and glory forever and ever. Amen.'"

"Amen," both Macafees said.

I looked down and waited. I could see through the corner of my eye that Calvin was doing some nervous, twitchy thing with his face. Hadn't seen that before.

Boone sat on the torn sofa and crossed his legs. He was trying to calm down.

"I'll never do that again," I said, standing up. "I promise."

Boone nodded with his eyes closed.

I was about to leave when he handed the cross back to me.

"Thanks," I said, putting it in my pocket. "I better go home now."

I walked to the front door, stopped and turned. "Merry Christmas."

"Merry Christmas, Yosef," Calvin said.

I waited, glanced over at Boone.

"Merry Christmas, then," he said, quietly, still stewing.

Back for good now, I trudged back up the stairs.

Everyone had retired for the evening, but Mom, who was in the kitchen, doing dishes quietly, had her back to me. I stood at the doorway, bothered by something at first that I couldn't put my finger on.

Until I realized … it was the absence of her singing. I hadn't heard her sing once since the move. The sadness hit me hard, mine and hers. My eyes started to water.

"Hey, Mom. I'm going to bed. Happy Hanukkah."

"How's your stomach?" she asked, without turning. "You need some Alka-Seltzer?"

"No, it's getting better, thanks. I just need to go to bed."

"Are you doing drugs down there?"

"What?!" That came out of nowhere. "No! I had diarrhea. It was really bad, just kept coming."

"Right," she said, still not turning around, and clearly not believing me. I waited another few seconds, just to make sure there wasn't another accusation I needed to deny.

"Happy Hanukkah," I said, again.

She turned to me now, her eyes narrowing, like she might see into my soul for the truth.

"Happy Hanukkah, then," she said.

With that, I turned down the hall toward my room.

I was so tired I felt I might sleep for a year.

That might not have been a bad idea.

⁂

One cold, January afternoon, while sitting in bed reading Matthew 5:44 about loving your enemies, my bedroom door flew open.

"Mom!" I yelled. "You scared me. You're supposed to knock!"

She stood a few feet from me, furious with her hands on her hips, and her face as red as a Bald Uakari monkey.

I laid my Bible on the bed, my hand casually covering the title.

"What?" I asked, impatiently, doing my damndest to stay calm.

She remained silent, her eyes blinking and darting around the room. It was clear I was in trouble ... for something. I started equal opportunity praying: Yahweh, Jesus, Muhammad - whoever had a minute. The suspense was killing me.

Finally, she spoke. "I'm going to ask you a question." Long, dramatic pause. "If you lie to me, it's going to make things much, much, much worse for you. Understand?"

I kept eye contact, trying to prove my innocence. "What is it?"

"How did you break your arm?"

Well, that threw me. I repeated it just to make sure. "How did I break my arm?"

She nodded. It was obvious she knew, but I was still new in my role as demon liar, so I kept up the ruse.

"I told you when it happened. In the bathtub. In the shower."

She glared at me now, burning invisible lasers into my eyes.

When I remained silent, she sighed heavily, and spilled it, slowly, like she was just learning English. "Mrs. Baker, up the street, she just called me, said her daughter, Maggie — "

"Becky."

"Whatever! Becky just told her that last Fall, she saw you fall out of a tree! Says you were spying on her in the bathroom!"

I could feel my eyes widen, and my mouth starting to move, but I had no words.

"That's how you really broke your arm, isn't it?!"

"Fine! Yes! I'm sorry, okay?!"

"Oy gevalt! My son, the peeping tom! Do you know how humiliating that is?!"

Becky saw me? Count me as humiliated, too.

"You can go to jail for that!"

"No, you can't."

Mom grunted, shaking her head from side to side. "Yosef. Yosef, Yosef, Yosef. Your father and I raised you better than that."

"I know. I'm sorry."

She was finally quiet. I was hoping it was over, and she would turn and leave, slamming the door.

"You were with that hillybilly boy, weren't you?"

"His name is Calvin and there's no such thing as a hillybilly! It's *hillbilly!*"

"I'll take that as a yes!"

"It wasn't his fault!"

"He's a bad influence!"

"No, he's not!"

"Yosef," she said, snorting like a bull before the attack, "you are not to see that boy ever again! Do you understand?!"

"What?! He's my only friend!" And here come the tears.

She moved closer to me. "I do not care. You can cry all you want. You are not to see him. Do you understand?"

"I understand," I said with contempt. Apparently, it was non-negotiable. I decided not to push it since there was no way I was obeying the order anyway.

She turned, stomped out, and slammed the door.

I sat there, still crying, surprised she didn't ground me or levy some other punishment. Then again, I figured she knew that ending my relationship with Calvin was a steep enough penalty.

Suddenly, she burst back in and walked over to my tall, double windows.

"What are you doing?" I asked, confused.

She grabbed hold of the curtains and yanked them, violently, off their rods.

"Mom!" I shouted, as the spinning, wooden rings made a weird clicking sound before finally stopping.

"Now *you* can get undressed with people staring at *you* naked."

She draped the drapes across her arm and walked out again.

Then, she walked back in again.

"One more thing. Thursday, you're going to play with Devin from shul."

I shot out of bed. There was no choice but to confront her. "Mom! No! I can't stand him! He's such a spaz!"

"He's Jewish," she said, as if all Jews were spazzes.

"Mom, please! He's so uncool. I can't hang out with him."

"Well, his mother tells me he wants to be friends. And you need Jewish friends. Part of the deal, young man. Dinner is soon. Goodbye." And with that, she left for what I prayed was the last time.

I yelled after her, "And just so you know, almost thirteen-year-olds don't *play* with other thirteen-year-olds!"

I fell back onto my bed, crumpling into the fetus position and wishing I was actually still a fetus, but within a different womb.

After a few moments, I grabbed my Bible. It opened naturally to the same part I was reading before my conversion was so rudely interrupted. The *loving your enemies* section.

I put it back down.

⁂

Our first six months or so, Mom, Dad, Gram, and Gramps scoured all the grocery stores looking for our beloved food: lox, spinach log, and rugelach. Most managers were clueless, but the Kroger did have gefilte fish. We bought them out every week.

There were also a dozen, awkward, post-synagogue introductions and uncomfortable lunches at people's homes. These were educated families, with the patriarch working at one of the plants, but none were from

New York. Sitting in their living rooms, we'd talk about the Yankees, graffi-tied subways, and the new World Trade Center.

They'd talk about high school football, Chevrolet cars, and the new One Hour Martinizing.

Then Gram would tell a horrific Holocaust story halting all conversation.

But the problem wasn't only cultural.

They were also much less Jewish than we were. (My clandestine affair with Christ notwithstanding.) Apparently, Rabbi Giraffe wasn't being com-pletely truthful with us. The congregation wasn't mostly Conservative; they were mostly Reform. Forget about not working on Shabbat. Yes, there was the occasional Bar Mitzvah, but rarely a Bat or Bas Mitzvah. No mezu-zah kissing. No yarmulke wearing outside shul. At least we weren't Hasidic with big, black hats, and *payot* where it's nothing but Judaism, all day, every day. I can't imagine how they'd have reacted to that.

At first, my parents and grandparents did what they could to make connections at shul, but they soon began praying at home more often, and eventually figured out that staying to themselves was the best way to hold on to their Jewishness, religious and cultural. It was fear-based. They were worried that, if not careful, they could be sucked into that Tennessee Reform Jew abyss.

Bottom line: To them, Oak Ridge Jews weren't Jewish.

For me, it went beyond that. I saw them as outcasts, the ridi-culed minority.

Devin.

He was the me I was fighting against: the desperate, prepubescent, Jewish twerp. My God, except for my glasses, we even looked similar. It was as if Jefferson Junior High was a mirror image of Robertson, and Devin and I were the same Jewish humans living in Oak Ridge, each in our own opposite school. The difference was, he lived in ostracism and loneliness, and I chose not to.

A few days after the big Mom confrontation, Devin and I had our little playdate, and it was as horrible as I imagined. We played Go Fish and Gin Rummy. After that, Devin pulled out his Ouija board; something I'd never seen before. He asked his dead great uncle if he could hear us and then moved the planchette from letter to letter.

The answer spelled out: N-O-O-D-L-E.

The afternoon wasn't completely lost.

I left soon after that. It wasn't easy getting out of there. It was still early, and Devin didn't want me to go, but I had some new wheels, so I could leave when I wanted. Dad had bought me an old, used Schwinn bicycle similar to Calvin's, but yellow. Mom was angry since I was supposed to be in punishment mode, but the bike wasn't a gift. It was a way to keep her from having to schlep me around. The real reason: she was sick of constantly getting lost.

Little did they know that the bike was actually facilitating my relationship with Calvin and Boone. I realized that if I could stand Devin for short periods of time, I could leave early and spend time with Calvin, all while Mom and Dad thought I was still at Devin's. Sure, they could call his mom or dad, but would they? Calculated risks were becoming a specialty of mine.

MAYBE-MURDERER #1

THE NEXT MORNING AT SCHOOL, BEFORE CLASS, I WALKED quickly down the hall looking for Calvin. I had a lot to tell him. Amongst the glob of kids, I spotted him from a distance. He saw me at the same time, and we rushed toward each other. He appeared to have something to tell me, as well, and we erupted into a ping pong match of different agendas.

I managed to go first. "Did Becky's mom call your dad?!"

"What? No! Listen, man, I got an idea!"

"Her mom called my mom! Becky saw me fall out of the tree!"

"Ah, man. That's crazy. Listen, I got an idea."

"I guess she didn't see *you*."

"Well, I reckon you made too much noise for her to notice me."

"I guess."

"Anyway, listen, Yosef, I got an idea ..."

"My mom knows you were with me. I'm not supposed to hang out anymore, but I don't care. Just don't come to my house, I'll come there."

"Fine! You want to hear my idea or not?!"

"Fine! What?" I finally shut up and listened.

Calvin slowed down and lowered his voice. "When them detectives on TV are tryin' to find killers, they's askin' everybody questions, right?"

It irritated me that this was still on his mind. I didn't have enough to worry about?

"Yeah, right," I agreed.

He counted on his fingers, "McMillan & Wife, all them folks."

191

I nodded, eyeing the hallway clock. Biology in five minutes.

Calvin continued, "The more info you got on a case, the more your chances of solvin' it! So I's thinkin' we go back to the hardware store and ask that woman some questions. We don't know who was killed, why, nothin'!"

Generally speaking, it's good to know if one's sharing grits and the Gospel of John with a cold-blooded killer. But, a big part of me didn't want to know. I couldn't really see the upside.

Then again, what could asking a few questions really hurt? Maybe, if we were lucky, this woman could help put this thing to rest.

"Sure," I said, "let's do it."

❧❦

The hardware store was downtown - an odd descriptor, I thought, for a U-shaped construct made of squat, architecturally insignificant buildings.

No, *downtown* was the majestic, cast-iron Gunther building, the gawking tourists, the blood-stained sidewalks of Little Italy.

Not … this.

We were both bundled up in fleece-insulated jean jackets and black toboggan hats. No gloves. (They were for wussies.) Of course, for me, it wasn't cold. Mid-February in Tennessee was typically far north of freezing. I only wore the jacket and hat to fit in.

Shocking, I know.

We dropped our bikes in front of the hardware store and went in, and as we entered, a bell above the door went *ding*. I had never been in a hardware store since neither Dad, nor Gramps, were good with a hammer. In Brooklyn, our Scottish handyman, Mr. Erskine, took care of maintenance.

The store was a small, warm place, smelling of motor oil, and cramped with ceiling high shelving with baskets of nails and bathroom fixtures. Behind the counter, a bald, gray-bearded man was doing paperwork.

"Shit," Calvin said under his breath.

"She could be here somewhere," I said. "Ask him."

We approached the counter. "Help ya?" the man asked, without looking up.

"Hi, sir," Calvin started awkwardly. "There's a lady up here sometimes. She here somewheres?"

He looked up, curiously. "Patty?"

"I don't know her name," Calvin answered.

"What d'you need with her?"

"Oh, we just wanted to ask her a question."

"You can ask me," he said, getting annoyed.

"We have to ask her," Calvin said.

"Why?" he persisted.

I stepped in. "It's a personal issue, sir."

The man's face wrinkled up like he just stepped in a pile of dog crap. Not a fan of the Brooklyn accent, I guess.

"A personal issue," he repeated, suspiciously.

Calvin and I nodded, smiling.

"Fine." He yelled to the back, "Patty! Some boys need you up 'ere."

A couple seconds later, a middle-aged woman appeared from the stacks. She was wide with high, yellow hair, and Dolly Parton boobs. The second she spotted Calvin, she bristled and stopped about six feet from us.

"What do you want?" she asked.

"Ma'am," Calvin said, his voice hesitant now. "You 'member when I's in here before?"

She nodded, just barely.

"Well, you said there's a rumor about my daddy, and we was just wondering, you know, if we could, I mean, if you could tell us more, maybe?"

He was no Mannix, that's for sure. Patty was irritated, glaring. Finally, with a head jerk, she said, "Come over here."

We followed her to a corner, away from the other clerk.

"What d'you want to know?" she asked, impatiently.

"Well, uh, do you know who was killed?" Calvin asked. "Or when, or why or anything?"

Patty's agitation morphed to anger. She looked around to make sure no one else was listening. "It was a young, nigger boy was killed, okay?"

Calvin and I gasped at the same time. His ears turned immediately red, and his mouth hung open like a creepy carnival clown.

Patty went on, "They say your daddy did it and your Great-Uncle Muir, he was part of it. But there was some kind of cover-up, so they got away with it."

Calvin uttered a couple false-start sentences, before finally saying, "You got proof?!"

"I told you what I know."

"Wait a minute. When was this boy killed, now?" Calvin asked.

"I don't know."

This was suddenly very real. I was feeling hot and weak. I needed to get the hell out of there. Calvin was trying to digest the information, as well as, I think, doing his damndest not to slug Patty in the face.

"Y'all go on, get out of here, now." And with that, she turned and disappeared, back through the stacks.

Moments later, we were back outside, straddling our bikes. Calvin was fuming. My stomach was churning, so I popped a couple Maalox. What had I gotten us into? I didn't know what to believe, but it sure didn't seem like a rumor, not the way she told it.

"That's some crazy shit, man!" Calvin spewed. "She ain't got no proof."

"Right. I think we should just forget it."

"Naw, man! We got to find out what the hell's going on. We need to clear Daddy's name! You said it yourself."

Actually, that was my schmuck twin.

I could've rode away, right then and there. Thanks for the memories. Farewell, good, freckled sir, and good luck in your endeavor.

Then I realized something.

There was only one thing that could truly cause me to walk away. A gun barrel shoved down my throat. Or a long, serrated knife poking me in the gut. Or being tied to a Middle Ages rack and stretched into two: Yo and sef.

Okay, that's three things, but you get the gist. No, I wasn't going anywhere. I was Calvin's right-hand boy, and clearly, he was not going to let this go. I had to stay involved. The good news is there was a cover-up, which meant we probably wouldn't find out anything anyway, no matter how much we snooped. I just needed to expedite a quick investigation, eventually we'd come to a dead end, and Calvin would have to forget it.

"All right," I said. "I'm in."

"Yeah! Give me skin!" Calvin shouted, putting both his hands out. I slapped them back as was the tradition.

"Okay," I said, "so at this point, if we were McMillan & Wife, we'd follow the leads."

"Right. Good," Calvin said, hunching over his handlebars.

We both thought a moment, then Calvin said, "Now she mentioned my Great-Uncle Muir, that he was part of it, whatever that means. Is that a lead?"

"Could be," I said. "Where is he?"

"Six feet under."

"Oh. Did you know him very well?"

"Naw, not really. He took care of Daddy when Grandpappy was killed."

"How was Grandpappy killed?" I asked, recoiling.

"WW II."

I nodded in relief. *Legal* murder, thank God.

"Wait a minute!" Calvin shouted, straightening, excited. "Maybe it was Great-Uncle Muir who did it, but they blamed it on Daddy! Daddy always said he was a real shithead."

I nodded, thinking. "Yeah, maybe. When'd he die?"

"While back. I don't 'member."

"Is he buried around here?"

"Yeah, been there with Daddy couple times."

"Can we get there by bike?" I asked.

"Hell yeah," Calvin said, "let's go. Oh, and by the way, I'm McMillan, you're wife."

We laughed and took off. Next stop: the cemetery.

It was getting dark as we biked our way up and down Oak Ridge's wide, curvy backroads. This was more downtrodden Macafee country, than affluent Bamberger country. And speaking of Bambergers, I was getting worried I wouldn't be home for dinner. How would I explain that?

Sorry, I'm late. Trying to figure out who killed this schvartze boy, and traffic back from the boneyard was a beast! Pass the hallah!

It was dusk when Calvin finally led us onto a gravel road that took us into the woods. The smell of mulchy leaves and far away fireplaces filled my nose as we headed into the darkening backcountry.

It was too hard to ride our bikes on the small stones, so we got off and pushed. Our tires made a steady, grinding sound as we went. It was the only noise, as it was February, and that meant the frogs were wintering at the bottom of a pond somewhere and the crickets were as dead as Uncle Muir.

It was almost completely dark when we finally came to an opening on the side of the road, a small hill dotted with two dozen headstones covered with moss and tall, dead grass. At least there was no eerie, sooty fog or howling werewolves.

We laid our bikes down and headed up the hill.

Passing several graves, I noticed some were ancient with crumbling, unreadable stones, while some were more recent. I could feel the weight of the place. It was full of lives not celebrated with proud, granite monuments, but tiny markers instead, as if the poor were more dead and gone than the rich.

About midway up, we stopped.

"This is it," Calvin said, looking down at one of the newer-looking graves. Muir's headstone was about a foot tall, arched, no swirly designs, just words.

Calvin read it: "Here lies Muir Macafee. Born 1902. Died 1965."

"Okay," I said, "so let's just say he did have something to do with it, it would had to have been before 1965. That was nine years ago."

Calvin nodded, trying to figure out where I was going with this.

"He wouldn't have been involved in any kind of murder probably, till at least, I don't know, eighteen-years-old?"

"Sure, I guess," Calvin agreed.

"So he was eighteen in 1920. That means it probably happened anywhere from 1920 to 1965 when he died."

"That's forty-five years," Calvin said, frustrated.

"Yeah, that's a lot of years..." I stopped myself. "Wait a sec ... there has to have been a police investigation, right?"

Calvin nodded.

"Well, if any of the police chiefs during that time are still alive, we could ask them about the case. We just have to find out who they are."

"Shit, man, that's pretty smart."

As I smiled, a cold breeze came out of nowhere, tossing our hair. The ghost of a pissed off Great-Uncle Muir? Fine by me. I was hoping, if we did find out anything else, it would be that he was the perpetrator. I like my murderers dead.

"Hey, Calvin?"

"What?"

I hesitated a moment, then blurted out a question I'd had on my mind for a while: "How'd your mom die?"

It startled him, but in my defense, we were in a cemetery. A cemetery where he had family.

It took a second, but I did get an answer. "Car crash. Come on, let's get out of here."

Never have I heard two words that said so much. Clearly, if she was buried there, we would not be paying a visit.

We rode home as fast as we could. Calvin had to show me how to get to my house, of course.

Two flaming legs later, I arrived home just as dinner was starting, took my seat, and dug into Mom's burnt brisket.

Gram still wasn't cooking, even though her finger had healed.

It was mostly an uneventful dinner. Mom tried to get Susan to talk about her day. Susan, instead, presented her normal but sporadic and crappy quips. Gramps tried to explain the sound his nose made when it was broken for the second time. I explained why I was late - Devin and I were soooooooooooo involved with Jewish studies. And Dad told us about a new, classified project he wasn't supposed to be telling us about. Deep Base nuclear waste disposal. He explained how a nuclear reactor leaves behind radioactive waste and that he was partly responsible for figuring out what to do with it. The idea was to bury it, but how deep, and encased in what? I think he broke the rules because of me. I was clearly fascinated. After all, I was going to be an engineer like him.

⁕⁂⁕

The next day after Bar Mitzvah practice, Calvin and I met in the temple parking lot and, from there, went to the police station.

The building was like most in Oak Ridge - uninspired, tan-bricked blocks.

The inside was as predictable as the outside. White cinderblock. White tile floors. The only real color in the place was blue, and that was worn by the police officers. Although something smelled buttery. They might have had a popcorn machine somewhere.

We approached the front where a mustached, young officer was sitting behind a wooden, semi-circle counter.

"Fellas," he said with a drawl, straight-faced and waiting for a problem.

"Hi," I said as friendly as possible, "my friend and I were wondering if you could give us some information. We were wondering who the police chiefs were from 1920 to 1965."

The officer glared at me, his eyelids thinning with suspicion. He looked at Calvin, who smiled quickly, then averted his gaze.

We had agreed I would do the talking for this leg of our adventure. Calvin wasn't real comfortable around the police, seeing as his extra-curricular activities usually involved some type of law he was breaking. Weed, moonshine, voyeurism, who knows what else.

"Why?" the cop asked, clearly knowing something wasn't kosher.

"School project." I was prepared.

"School project," Calvin added unnecessarily.

The officer smiled arrogantly, then asked, "You really expect me to believe that?"

"It's true," I said, "why else would we want information like that?"

"I don't know what game you're playin'," he said, "but I'm busy. Y'all need to get out of here."

"It's not a game, sir--"

"Not another word," he interrupted. "Out. Now."

Calvin nodded nervously and turned to go. Disappointed, I turned to follow, but then stopped when I recalled seeing something down the hall when we entered.

"I'm sorry, can I just use your restroom before we leave?"

The cop took a deep, annoyed breath. "What?"

"I need a restroom. Please."

He pointed down the hall. "On the left. Hurry."

I turned and was going to signal Calvin, but he was outside already.

I hurried down the hallway, a wide corridor with ceiling fluorescents blinding all who dared past. What I had noticed before, but didn't think much of at the time, was a long row of framed pictures, all perfectly spaced on one side of the wall.

I did not have to drain the lizard (more like inch-worm), and as I moved by the pics, I realized I was right. They were all headshots of Oak Ridge cops. Maybe, just maybe our guys were up there.

I looked over toward the desk officer; luckily, I was far enough down where his eyeline was blocked by the wall. I would have to work fast, though. Turning my attention to the portraits, I saw each had a plaque underneath with some kind of identification.

The writing was small and they were hung fairly high, so I had to get up close and stretch on my tippy-toes to read them. I moved down the hall, reading one after another, intermittently checking to make sure our friend at the front wasn't coming to find me. I was sweating, my heart was beating heavy metal fast, and now I really did have to pee. A lot of the pics were officers killed on duty, cops retired.

Finally, I came to one that stopped me. It was a picture of a smiling, bald, long-headed man with a mustache hanging too far over his top lip.

The plaque read: *Chief Theodore Kitchens, 1944 - 1967, retired.*

Score!

Maybe. We were missing a few years, but it was something.

I reversed my direction and headed out, a bit calmer now. The desk cop eyed me all the way out of the station.

Chief Theodore Kitchens, I kept saying to myself. Chief Theodore Kitchens.

MURRAY FINDS OUT

HE'D BEEN IN THERE A HUNDRED TIMES. THE BIG CONFER-
ence room, the one with the twelve-foot cherry wood table, high back
leather chairs, and bulletin boards covered with computer printouts and
prospective blueprints.

But he wasn't in there now.

Murray had just walked by the open door to see the room filled with
colleagues. It was only a glance; regardless, a quick chill shot through his
body, like he'd just walked under an air-conditioning unit that suddenly
went on.

The avalanche of questions soon followed: Was that a deep basing
meeting? It looked like the whole team in there, except him. Did he miss
the memo? If not, why wasn't he invited? Had he been pulled off the project? That wouldn't make any sense. He was integral and had done a lot of
work on it. Of course, he knew, in the workplace, dedication was never a
determinant of loyalty. But if he was removed, wouldn't someone have told
him? And shouldn't he be reassigned? Or were they about to show him
the door?

Or was this because of Friday?

When Murray was first interviewing with Roger, he intentionally
omitted the fact that normally, he didn't work on the Sabbath. He needed
the job too badly and had a feeling that would be a deal killer. He had
reminded Sandy that he was in no position to be making demands, so he
would have to work all five days of the week. But he had a solution. He'd

leave early on Fridays - plenty of Jews did that - then, as time went by, he'd gradually take Fridays off completely. Eventually Roger and the team would get used to it.

That was the plan.

It didn't go quite as smoothly as Murray had hoped.

The first Monday morning after he started, just as Murray was settling in his office, Roger had walked in. His manner was short, unusually subjugating for Roger.

"Good morning, Roger," Murray said smiling nervously, knowing what his boss wanted to discuss.

"You left early Friday," Roger said.

"Yes. Friday is the Sabbath," Murray answered as he opened his briefcase to take out some reports.

"You didn't say anything."

"I should of mentioned it. I apologize."

"Is this going to be every Friday?" Roger asked briskly.

"Well ... yes," Murray said, smiling bigger now, doing his best to diffuse the tension.

Roger looked like he was about to say something else, but decided against it, nodded, and walked out.

Murray took a deep breath, leaning back in his chair, his eyelids fluttering with tension. The good news was that even in tiny little Oak Ridge, Tennessee, in the early 1970s, there was a certain religious freedom afforded employees. Even Jews. So said the 1st and 14th amendments of the United States Constitution, as well as the more recent Title VII of the Civil Rights Act. So he coudn't be fired for it. He'd done his research.

But clearly, even leaving early wasn't okay with Roger.

Murray decided he'd walk by the conference room - going the other direction now - just to make sure he wasn't imagining the whole thing.

This time, though, the door was closed, which might have actually said more than his first pass. He stopped at a secretary's desk just outside the conference room. The desk belonged to Tammy, with the airy, bleached blonde coiffure, fake eyelashes, and lying smile.

"Hello. Murray Bamberger."

"Mr. Bamberger. What can I do for you?"

"Do you know what meeting … is, uh … happening in the conference room?"

"Deep Basing," she said matter-of-factly. "Anything else you need?"

Murray didn't hear the last thing she said. Somehow, he moved one foot in front of the other, wobbled back to his office, hurried in, and shut the door.

His heart was pounding so hard, he could feel it in his head. Or was it his head that was pounding? Likely both.

His mind raced. More questions. Could this be due to his weight? That's ridiculous, he thought. He may not have been pretty to look at, but he didn't let it get in the way of work.

No, it had to be the Sabbath issue.

Unless it was that good ol', Southern-style, anti-Semitism seeping into the upper management.

The fact is, there were several more covert, seafood offenses Murray was forced to endure: a different, dead crustacean on each Jewish holiday. After the initial welcome crab, it was shrimp for Rosh Hashanah, and later, lobster for Pesach.

It's not as if he put a mezuzah at his office door or spoke any Yiddish. He wasn't even the only Jew in the place; Barsky, Fineman and Levitt were of the tribe, though they were Reform, of course. Also known as secular, in Murray's opinion.

One recent day, during lunch, without telling them exactly what had been happening, Murray asked the three of them if they had encountered any type of anti-Semitism. Not only had they not, they very much did not want to discuss the subject.

Also, Barsky, Fineman, and Levitt worked all day Friday.

Murray did his damndest to ignore the odd, surreptitious assaults over the months, but instead, he found himself suspiciously eyeing almost everyone he came into contact with, as if he could stare them into admitting it was him (or her) who was filled with this misdirected hate.

It tormented him, the not knowing who despised him for no reason. Many times, he considered speaking to Roger about it, or someone in Personnel, but he felt he wouldn't be taken seriously or he'd be considered a troublemaker. And those things could lead to his dismissal.

Somewhere in the back of his mind, Murray was also aware of something else: the whole situation diminished his interest for his work in general. If an organization as large as this could let this type of bigotry occur, did he want to put his all into his job?

Could he put his all into his job?

MAYBE-MURDERER #2

WE FOUND CHIEF KITCHENS' ADDRESS IN AN OLD PHONE-book at the Oak Ridge Library, yet another stubbornly gray hunk of cement, just west of downtown.

482 Westover Drive. Calvin knew the area and we headed in that direction, riding the shoulder of the Turnpike as cars whizzed by.

"All riiiiiiiight," Calvin suddenly said-sang loudly, in a low, Southern tone.

I smiled, knowing what was coming - Black Oak Arkansas's *Hot Rod*. We heard it on the radio about 20 times a day. It started with a spoken intro, then ripped into one of the finest boogie woogie redneck romps ever recorded. Naturally, Calvin memorized it.

"'Right here's a song for you men. And you women. You listen to the words of this song. I'm gonna sing it for the men. You men imagine now, you just getting' off on Friday afternoon, you done worked a hard week, and you getting' off and you ready to go out shinin'! You got in your car; it's all cleaned up. You get out and you get on the straight highway. You press your foot feet down to the floor and it's rollin' down the highway! You feel it good cause you got a lot of motor under your wheels. You headin' to see your woman, yeah, when you get there to see your woman, you screech up in the driveway and walk out and you go up to her and you tell her one thing: You say mama ... '"

I joined in for the last line. "I got a hot ... raaaaaaaaaahhhhhhhhhhh-d!"

I lost it laughing as Calvin exploded into wild, spitty drum sounds, and his signature air guitar (Look ma, no hands!).

Kitchens' house was in a nice area, not far from mine. It was a two-story blocky thing, painted blue, with a winter brown lawn and latent flower beds under the front yard trees.

We stopped our bikes in front and straddled them before disembarking.

"Okay, let me hear it one more time," Calvin asked.

I cleared my throat. "Hello, Chief Kitchens. My name is Yosef, this is my friend Calvin. I'm doing a school report on murders in the South, and there's a special case I was interested in. It involved a man named Muir Macafee and a boy who was killed. Were you, by any chance, on that case? We'd sure appreciate any information you could give us."

"That's pretty good, man," Calvin said, smiling.

"I think it's going to work this time," I said.

We saw her at the same time.

A woman wearing filthy overalls was standing on the lawn, about ten feet away. She looked to be in her 40s with a beer belly and pale, blotchy skin.

"Boys," she said with a high, nasally, Southern accent.

"Oh, hi," I stammered.

"You know, I heard every word you just said," the woman said with a smirk that turned into a laugh.

Calvin and I chuckled along.

"Everything?" I asked.

"Come on," she said as she turned back toward the house. Calvin and I looked at each other, shrugged and followed.

Her front porch was pleasant, with two cushiony chairs and a porch swing in need of a good sanding. Calvin and I sat in the chairs.

"Y'all want something to drink?" she asked, hovering above us.

"No, thanks," Calvin and I said in unison.

She sat on the porch swing, gave a kick, and started swinging.

"I'm Kate Kitchens. Chief Kitchens is my dad, I mean, was. He transitioned."

Transitioned was, and still is, how many Southerners refer to the deceased.

"Ah, man," Calvin said, disappointed.

I'm not sure what the look on my face said, but I wasn't unhappy to hear the news. No offense, Chief. It's just that, that meant we had hit a roadblock with the investigation, and we could let it go now. We didn't solve it, so they wouldn't be adding *Calvin & Yosef* to the *NBC Sunday Night Mystery Movie* line-up anytime soon, but we did survive it. And that was good enough for me.

"So," Kate said, "I'm gonna assume you're not doing a school report?"

"No ma'am," I said. "We apologize."

"Don't worry about it," she said, with a hand wave. "Makes no difference to me. I will tell you, though, I do remember that name - Macafee."

"You do?" Calvin asked, suddenly interested again.

"Yes sir," she said, "but not Muir Macafee, Boone, Boone Macafee."

Calvin and I exchanged glances. Oh shit. What does that mean?

"Boy, did I hear that name, more than a few times," she said, keeping her swing going with one foot. "The Lewis Hall murder. Daddy talked about that case for years. He was obsessed. Boy was only thirteen-years-old, lynched." She paused, shaking her head. "These days, you know, folks tend to kill Black people much slower. You know, keep 'em from gettin' educations, buyin' houses, that type of thing. They live in poverty, die early, mission accomplished - just takes a little longer. So horrible."

"But why was he talking about Boone so much?" Calvin asked, impatiently.

"Oh, sounds like you know this Boone character."

Calvin and I caught each other's eye again. He was about to answer, with what I don't know, but I broke in, "No, ma'am, we just, we were, you know, interested in the case, that's all."

She nodded, not buying it, then spoke directly and slowly to Calvin. "Daddy was absolutely certain Boone Macafee committed the murder. I guess there was some evidence, but not enough. Hearsay maybe?

Witnesses? I don't really know. But he was always lookin'. Always investiga-tin', even when the case went cold."

There it was again, that creeping, burning feeling inside, combined with sudden muscle atrophy. The body prematurely reacting to some, unknown future disaster. But this time, it wasn't only me. I could tell Calvin was experiencing something like it as well.

Now we knew: It wasn't just some store clerk spewing rumors.

Kate was staring at us, concerned. "Sure y'all don't want somethin' to drink?"

Calvin could only stare down at the porch. I managed a head shake and a mumbly answer. "No, thanks."

"All right, well, hope that was some help to you," Kate said, standing up. "I got to get back to work. Y'all head on home, now," she said as she walked down the steps and around the back of the house.

Calvin was breathing erratically, trying to keep tears from falling from those blue eyes he shared with his father. Neither of us were ready to go yet. Our states of shock were still in control.

But a few minutes later, we somehow succeeded in pulling ourselves up from our chairs, down the steps, and across the lawn.

As we got on our bikes, I said, "Cops are wrong all the time, you know."

Calvin nodded once, brusquely. We rode home without another word that day. I didn't just say that to make him feel better. I held it. Made myself believe, that in this case, it was true. I had to. Neither Boone, nor I, were going anywhere, and I couldn't exactly be in a state of terror every moment I was around him. As for Calvin, he'd bring up the murder only once more, and that would be months later.

CAUGHT

SPRING IN OAK RIDGE CAN BLOW YOU BACK A FEW FEET - even when you're consumed with two religions, as well as the incessant tingle of impending manhood. I imagine it's like Dorothy felt when she walked out of that drab, black and white shack into the suddenly vibrant land of Oz. It was sublime; the royal purpling of so many suburban crocus gardens; the apricot tree blossoms, red and white like peppermint candy; the bright, white shock of an endless row of Dogwood trees.

Toto, I've got a feeling we're not in Brooklyn anymore.

Of course, not everyone saw it that way, if they saw it at all. Mom was hibernating in her room more and more. Dad still delivered his kisses and goodbyes to everyone before he left for work, but when he came home, he'd keep mostly to himself. Susan was much too consumed with her secret relationship and keeping it hidden. Gram and Gramps ate and napped, ate and napped, ate and napped. Calvin's moods were in constant flux. One minute, we were laughing and playing air guitar, being stupid in the lunchroom. The next, he was smoking weed in the woods, brooding silently; I could only assume it was about his father's likely torrid past.

Not surprisingly, the Macafees took Easter as seriously as they did Christmas. Lots of praying. Lots of Bible. Lots of church. Easter dinner. All, sans bunnies. Thank God, there wasn't a replay of the Christmas/Hanukkah stress fest. Easter dinner did not fall on either of the two nights of Passover, aka Seder. I was easily able to celebrate both the rising of Jesus, as well as the Jews' escape from Egypt.

My Bar Mitzvah was about a month away. Saturday, May 5th, to be exact. The day before my actual birthday. I had been practicing with the smelly Cantor, but not on my own like I told him I was. I had more Christian things to do.

Truth is, I didn't really need to practice that much. I knew my stuff a year ago, and I wasn't exactly overflowing with anticipation. I was excited to see my old friends, of course. Me, Gram and Mom had sent out a hundred invitations, mostly to people in New York. We even sent one to Teddy from the laundromat and Jerry from the deli, and of course, to our cherished Rabbi Berkwitz. We had gotten RSVPs from everyone except the two meshuggeners. They would have to miss school that Friday to make it down by Saturday morning, so they weren't sure yet.

A week after Easter, I was at the Macafees, back from church and Pizza Pete's. (We used the non-kosher coupon meant for the Bamberger clan.) Full of Jesus and cheese, we were just starting to relax when Boone looked at the clock and suddenly bolted up.

"We got somewhere to be, boys," he said, excitedly.

Calvin and I popped up off the floor. "Where, Daddy?" Calvin asked.

"You'll see. Come on," he said, grabbing his keys and heading out.

I took the middle as we all piled into the front seat of Boone's rusty, brown Ford F-150. I never knew the year, but it was so old, it had the gears on the steering wheel and some of the side panel metal was disintegrating. This thing creaked standing still.

"Come on Daddy, tell us where we're goin'," Calvin pleaded.

Boone backed out of the driveway, turned on the radio, and took off. Jim Stafford's ode to young love, *Spiders and Snakes,* had just started, and we all started moving to it. Strictly country music in this vehicle. The dial sat at 107.7, WIVK. Move it and suffer the consequences.

We hit the Oak Ridge Turnpike and rolled down the windows. It was obvious Boone wasn't sharing our destination, so Calvin and I just leaned back and let the wind and music take us away.

There's a point on the Turnpike where it goes from four lanes to two, and just a little past that, there's a small section of Melton Hill Lake that laps onto a grassy knoll. As we approached, Boone slowed down and parked half on the grass, half on the street. There were a dozen other cars and trucks parked exactly the same way. It's how you had to do it in that part of town. When I first saw the lake, I figured we were going swimming. Odd, since none of us had our swimsuits. And it wasn't exactly hot yet.

Boone looked over at us and smiled. I had never been this physically close to him. The black gaps between his remaining teeth looked like stuck licorice, and he smelled like leaves. I was comforted by him, but at the same time, discomforted. It was a peculiar feeling, but that's how my relationship with Boone was building. When I was at my most vulnerable, this was a man who took me into his home, his family. Yet, there was this hostility impossible to ignore. It was complicated, as they say.

Boone pointed toward the edge of the water. There was a small group of 10 people, all dressed in their Sunday finest. One man was standing in the water, about three feet deep, dressed in a black gown that was floating up around him like an oil spill.

Calvin looked at the scene, then back at his dad. "Who's gettin' baptized?"

Boone shouted, "You, dumbass!"

"But I's already baptized," Calvin said, confused.

"I know that," Boone drawled, "I think Yosef would appreciate seein' one, is all. It's part of his learnin'."

"Well, hell yeah, then!" Calvin blurted out. "It'll be twice as nice."

We all laughed, jumped out of the truck, and headed down the short hill to the water.

Boone was not wrong about that. I had read a lot about baptisms but seeing one in real life was a whole other thing. I thought it especially interesting that there were stark similarities to Tvilah, the Jewish water purification ritual. It made me wonder if all the ancient religions of the world weren't invented by the same guy with the same ideas.

But back to baptisms - apparently, they could be based on any combination of repentance, purification, and initiation into the Church. The first baptism was performed by disciple John on none other than Mr. Jesus Christ himself. I wonder how that went down. One sunny Nazareth day, were the two of them just hanging out at their mud brick house, shootin' the shit, when John suddenly got a wild hair?

"Hey, Jesus, want me to dunk your head in the water?"

"What for?"

"I don't know - repentance and purification?"

Jesus paused, thinking that it was a pretty hot day anyway. "Why not," he said.

As we reached the water's edge, the man standing in the lake came better into focus. A short, pasty creature with more than his share of chins, he was smiling, and oddly, I thought at the time, looking up.

"Pastor Loy," Boone said loudly as he stood between me and Calvin and put an arm around each of us.

"Boone, welcome!" the pastor responded with a lilting Southern accent, his eyes still affixed above. That's when I realized he was blind. I would later see him in Church where he would preach from a huge Braille bible.

"Pastor, this is Yosef here. You know Calvin, of course," Boone said.

"Hello boys," Loy said, his arms out now.

Boone nudged Calvin forward. "Calvin's coming to you!"

Calvin pulled off his Chucks, and his knee-high striped socks and waded out into the murky, brown water. Reaching the pastor, he stopped, his body half immersed.

One of the church people shouted, "Praise Jesus!"

"Praise Jesus," Boone said, looking at me.

"Praise Jesus!" I shouted. This was fun.

Calvin stood next to the pastor as they both turned to face us. I stuck my tongue out at Calvin. Either he didn't see or he ignored me.

"The Lord your God will set you high above all nations of the Earth!" the pastor preached. "In front of the eyes and ears of these witnesses, I baptize you, Calvin Macafee, in the name of the Father, of the Son, and of the Holy Ghost …" He paused.

"Amen!" the crowd shouted.

Calvin closed his eyes as the pastor put his right hand on Calvin's back and his left arm in front, which Calvin grabbed a hold of while he took a deep breath in. The pastor splashed Calvin backward into the water, causing small waves to ripple out toward the half-dozen speed boaters, further away, enjoying a different part of the lake.

The pastor finished, "… And in the name of Jesus Christ!"

"Hallelujah!" the crowd screamed.

Pastor Loy pulled Calvin up out of the water. And with as much spiritual gravitas as a silly, pot-smoking kid can muster, Calvin yelled, "Hallelujah! Thank you, Lord! Thank you, Jesus!"

I half-expected him to rip into some Molly Hatchett, but no.

Calvin walked, dripping, back up to the shore. I put a congratulatory arm around him. "Cool, man!" I said, honestly excited for him. He was beaming.

Boone looked down at me, smiled, and whispered, "So whatyathink?"

"It was really cool. Thanks for showing me," I answered.

"That's not what I mean. You ready to get baptized?"

My internal Jew-wrench turned hard to the right, squeezing my stomach, an obvious and painful signal that this was definitely not something I should be doing. Maybe it was a cellular-level, genetic reaction. Maybe it was my Holocaust ancestor spirits punching me in the gut. Or maybe it was too much Pete's.

Whatever it was, this was wrong. Very wrong.

Then, amidst my psychosomatic cramping, I remembered what Boone had said months ago at the dinner table: *Sure hope we can keep it that way.*

Just eight simple words, but I always knew what he meant.

SANDY PANICS

EVERY MORNING AS SANDY WOKE UP, SHE REMEMBERED where she was before she opened her eyes. And every time, she deliberated whether to open them at all. Keep them closed and maybe they would think she was dead. They'd have a nice funeral for her - back in Brooklyn of course - then bury her. And since she wasn't really gone, but six feet under, she'd eventually suffocate and that would be that. It would be painful but easier than say, putting a steak knife in her throat, or gulping down a bottle of pills, or taking a toaster bath.

Alternately, she could open her eyes and fix her gaze while she jumped out of bed with her purple-green floral moo-moo flowing behind her, screaming that she had lost her sight while asleep. She couldn't be blind, as well as the matriarch of a Jewish household, so they'd have to move back home.

Or she could do what she did every day: lay there for who knows how long, eyes still sealed shut, and obsess about everything and everyone. It usually started with her physical self-hatred; how she had let herself go. She had put on a couple pounds. Maybe a few. Maybe a couple and a few. It was hard to say since she never weighed herself.

Also, apparently, Sandy's male hormones had decided now would be an ideal time for a light mustache. That combined with her red, patchy skin and purple-black circles made for quite the *mieskeit*. She'd never seen herself that way before. It was startling but apropos, she thought, in that she was becoming as ugly as this little town she was being forced to live in. These days, she wasn't even bothering to change out of her moo. For months, it was the same routine. After finally getting out of bed, making her parents something to eat, then loading her own plate, she'd often come back to bed. There was a small color TV in their room now. She'd watch *General Hospital, Phil Donahue,* sometimes *Let's Make A Deal.* Great escapes, all of them. Even the news about the Vietnam war although she would worry what would happen to Yosef if the war dragged until he was old enough for the draft.

Sometimes she'd gaze at the TV with tunnel vision, fantasizing that she was watching from the living room in Brooklyn. The fantasy didn't last long as it was usually interrupted by a local commercial: some hick selling cars or stereo speakers or twenty-five cent grape slushies.

Her resentment toward Murray followed soon after. As scary as the thought was, more and more, Sandy wondered if she ever truly loved him. Sure, at first, they had things in common. Religion, cultural comforts. They both had artistic interests: her with singing, Murry with film. Murray loved the old noir movies they used to see in the theatres when they were courting. They also both wanted a Jewish family, falling in line, of course, with the mantra developed after the Holocaust: *Keep the Jewish family alive.* Unfortunately, the little fire they did have was extinguished early and completely with his work and her caring for the children. Maybe they should've been friends. Maybe they mistook having similarities with being in love.

Sandy knew what love was. Two words: Burt Zimmerman.

So much her senior, so deliciously English, he came to her mind now, more and more. She knew why. It was because a few days before the move, Sandy thought it wise to look him up. She had taken the subway to his old apartment, not really expecting anything, maybe just curious if he stayed in New York or moved back to London. She had stood across the street and looked in the windows - maybe she'd see him milling around. Or perhaps recognize some tchotchke on a shelf that would tell her if he was still there. In those few moments standing on the sidewalk in her Joe Namath Pumas, their past intimacy flooded her mind. She remembered his woodsy-citrus smell. (Chanel Pour Monsieur cologne, he told her one day, in case she wanted to buy him some.) She thought of his silky soft palms holding her shoulders when he had something serious to say or was telling a joke. She remembered his tender way of lovemaking as if he was holding a just-blown, champagne glass and he might break her if he wasn't careful. Finally, after ten minutes or so, she decided to head back to the subway. What was she thinking? If she did see him, what would she do? Would she scream out and jump into his arms so many years later? Would he remember the love they shared? Would he remember her at all? He had to have had countless young women since her.

That's when she saw him. Thank God he was across the street. He looked to be walking home. Grayer naturally, slightly bent, but still Burt. The Burt she was mad about. She turtled immediately, New York style, running and hiding, down into a stinky trash cubby. He never saw her, at least she didn't think he did.

Regardless of past love or wedded non-bliss, ultimately, Sandy considered her commitment to family unbreakable. Having children protected the sanctity of marriage like a bank vault protected cash. And divorce? It was simply not something religious Jews did.

No, she would never abandon her family. Of course, though, her daughters definitely abandoned her. She knew she was a good mother and certainly didn't deserve being left out in the cold. But that didn't stop Lynn or Susan. One recent evening, after a dinner of trying everything she could to get Susan to share her life, Sandy wondered if she blamed *her* for the move, instead of her father like everyone else. Susan was always quiet. Even as a baby, she cried the least between the three. But the move silenced her even more. When she did bother to communicate, it was typically argumentative and borderline hostile. Sandy craved feedback from her second child. What was high school like? How about boys? Has your period been heavy? Even a conversation about how much she hated her mother would've sufficed.

Sandy couldn't imagine deserting her own mother, especially since she could no longer cook or, to be more honest, refused to. Over the years, their relationship had grown from challenging to a constant, one-sided, faultfinding critique. But deserting her? Never. Who does that to their own mother?

What she could imagine, though, was revealing her mother's secret to Yosef. Since he was still young, he was the only one left who didn't know. This capability gave Sandy some power over her mother, not that she ever discussed it with her. But it made Sandy feel good, even if it never seemed to be worth the chaos it would create. Several years ago, she spoke to Jack about it, but he was in so much denial, or so much in love with his wife, he responded as if Sandy asked him which train she should take to Queens. *The E to the F or the E and then walk - depending on where in Queens you're going.* The sad and obvious diversion didn't sit well with Sandy, but she knew she needed to let it go. Not so much for her mother's sake, but for her dad's. He had done so much for her, supporting her in every endeavor, from her singing to her marriage. Sometimes, when she thought about how much she loved him, a silly grin would appear on her face and she'd burst into tears. She was also jealous of him - he seemed to be the only one who really didn't care about the move. It made sense. All he did these days was go to shul, eat, nap, and fart. He didn't need New York for those things.

But Yosef ... she knew he was hurting. The look on his face when Murray told the family about the move - the absolute devastation. She felt his pain as much as her own. The fact that he was being robbed of a Brooklyn Bar Mitzvah, surrounded by all that love was, at times, unbearable for Sandy.

She had made a decision.

Regardless of her depression, she would make his Tennessee Bar Mitzvah the best damn Tennessee Bar Mitzvah any Jewish boy from Brooklyn could have. Her and her mother had already sent out all the invitations and planned the after-party. If any guest said they couldn't afford to fly down, she would send them a bus ticket - they were pretty inexpensive.

Whatever she had to do. The celebration would be so perfect, in fact, that laying on his death bed, it would be the last story Yosef told his grandkids before he died. All the planning had been a much-needed respite from her spiraling, dark thoughts. The time and energy for sadness was less. Being Jewish and doing Jewish things was always of incalculable comfort to her.

Unfortunately, soon, the work that went into it, and the celebration, and the Brooklyn love would all come to an end. And she'd still be there. Then what?

There was no question, those Tennessee mornings were excruciating for Sandy. But, eventually, at some point, her mind shit would finally begin to fade and she'd realize she had only one real choice: Curse herself out of bed, take two Valium and two Darvon and just get ... through ... the ... fucking ... day. That's what she'd been doing since they'd moved to this Godforsaken joke they call a city. The *city* of Oak Ridge - *mishegoss*!

And so she did finally manage to open those reluctant, miserable eyes, and get up. It was Sunday, which meant Murray was already out of bed, and probably at the grocery store by now.

First stop for Sandy: the medicine cabinet.

Next stop: Yosef's room.

The night before, as she was walking past his room, she was appalled at how filthy it was. He was laying on his bed when she told him to clean it. He nodded, but she knew he wouldn't. That was fine. It would give her something to do the next day.

He wasn't there when she walked in. She picked up several pairs of shorts, T-shirts, and socks, throwing them all in the clothes hamper. As she leaned down to grab a sneaker protruding from under his bed, something else caught her eye.

Three things actually: a flashlight, a ruler, and a book. Odd combination.

Was he measuring something ... in the book ... in the dark?

She pulled them all out.

As one might expect, it was only one of those things that slugged her in the face:

The Holy Bible.

Sandy squeezed her eyes shut, yet again, but for just for a second this time, hoping when she reopened them, the book title would instead be *Franny and Zoey* or *Are You My Mother?*

Anything but ... nope ... still the Holy Bible.

Sandy had never opened a bible before. But she had to be sure what she was seeing was real. After all, the drugs could make her groggy sometimes. As a cold sweat slowly creeped across her skin, she opened it to a random page and read to herself. As she did, her face slowly turned to disgust, like she was smelling a dead animal.

She read a few words again, aloud this time, just to be sure:

"Neither height nor depth, nor anything else in all creation, will be able to separate us from the love of God that is in..." She paused as her pupils inflated, her tone now rageful, ending the passage as a question...

"...Christ Jesus our Lord?!"

"Yosef!" she screamed, breathing hard. She knew how he got it. It's not like he picked it up at the bookstore.

"Yoseeeeeeef!"

"Yoseeeeeeeeeeeeeef!"

Full-on shaking now, Sandy bolted out of the room, still holding the book.

Running into the kitchen, she saw her parents sitting, waiting at the breakfast nook.

"Where's Yosef?!"

"What's wrong?" her mother asked.

"He's probably there right now!" Sandy roared, as she went to the sink and turned on the garbage disposal.

"Who's where right now?" Jack asked, confused. "What are you doing?"

As the disposal grinded away at nothing, Sandy tried to jam the bible in, grunting and twisting and pushing. Too fat. She finally stopped. Then tried to tear it in two - maybe it'd go in if it was smaller ...

No.

"Sandy! Turn that off!" Gert demanded, cringing at the loud commotion.

Sandy turned off the disposal, then went to the counter where the yellow Princess phone and phonebook laid. She put down the bible and opened the phonebook to the "M's" and, with a jittery finger, started going down the page.

"Who are you looking for? Sweetie, calm down!"

Sandy found the Macafees in the phonebook. All 14 of them. "Crap!" she yelled.

"What, crap?" her mother asked, irritated. "Sandy, we've got bupkes here. We're hungry. You know I can't cook anymore."

Grabbing the bible again, and now her purse from the counter, Sandy shot out without a word.

Jack looked at Gert. "I'm starving."

"That's what happens when you don't eat," Gert said.

"I think we have some leftovers," Jack said, standing up slowly, "I'll get it."

"What is wrong with her?" Gert asked.

"I think it might be about Yosef again," he answered as he poked his head in the fridge.

"What again?" Gert asked.

"You know, the thing with the girl and the tree and the arm," he said.

"*Oy gevalt.* You couldn't let me forget?" Gert asked, shaking her head.

Jack brought a few Tupperware containers to the table, sat down, and started opening them.

Gram stared at him and said, "No plates? Silverware? What are we, wild dogs?"

Sandy was in her car, already halfway up the block, when she slammed on the brakes in front of the Baker's house, got out, ran up the lawn, and knocked hard on the front door.

When Becky's mom answered, Sandy asked if she knew the Macafee's address.

Luckily, she did, and about 5 minutes later, Sandy was back in the car, driving erratically, and stealing glances at the beat up, half-torn Oak Ridge map sprawled out in the passenger seat.

She was lost.

"Crap! Craaaaap!" she yelled, pounding on the steering wheel.

Then, she suddenly let out a cry, "Ah!"

Spotting the Macafee's street, she took a sharp right, the Dart's screaming tires attracting the glance of a middle-aged neighbor sitting on his front porch.

Finding the house number, Sandy pulled to the curb and threw the car into park. She grabbed the Bible, jumped out, and slammed the door behind her. Suddenly, something pulled her backward.

Her moo-moo. It was caught in the door. "Crap," she said under her breath.

She opened the door, released the garment, then turned again, now stomping through the weedy grass toward the front door.

Her head was pounding, and she matched it with five hard knocks.

No answer.

She knocked again, this time beating the door with the bottom of her fist. That same neighbor was locked in now, watching and waiting like he was enjoying a movie.

Still no answer, Sandy stumbled around the back of the house, scowling and cursing as she stepped over a rusty muffler and a mattress spring.

She stopped at the kitchen window and peered in.

"*Oy gevalt*," she said, disgusted by the decaying interior. Clearly no woman lived there, she thought. She knocked hard on the window.

So hard, it cracked.

"Crap!" she yelled, surprised.

OY LORD

JUST AS I WAS ABOUT TO ANSWER BOONE, A WIDE GRIN SUD-
denly stretched across his face.

"I"s just messin' with you, Yosef! You ain't nowhere near ready to be
baptized," he said, putting a hand on my back and laughing. "Nowhere near!"

"You ain't ready!" Calvin screamed.

My anxiety diminished, but I was immediately disappointed. I
wouldn't have to hide this blasphemy from my family, but what do you
mean - *nowhere near ready*? Am I *farkakteh*?! It's a good thing I wasn't
ready! But what could I do to *be* ready? Yosef Bamberger, the poster boy for
mixed feelings. Maybe, when my family abandoned me, poster sales could
be a steady source of income.

As Preacher Loy plunged another pure believer, the three of us
headed back to the truck and loaded in.

It had been a fun morning. As the wind swirled around the truck's
cabin, Boone sang badly to Gamble Folk's *Dear Jesus*. Calvin popped his
head up and down. And I had an epiphany.

If Jesus died for our sins, and my sin was straddling the religious,
splintering fence, then I would be forgiven of that sin. It wasn't more complicated than that.

We arrived back at their house a few minutes later. And as we made
our way to the front door, from the corner of my eye, I saw a shrieking,
purple banshee coming at us from the street. Or maybe it was an atomic
bomb exploding. Tough to say, but then I heard it screaming my name.

"Yoseeeeeeef!! Yoseeeeeeef!"

Mom was fast-walking toward us in her ballooning moo-moo, more desperate and shattered than I'd ever seen her. We stopped, the Macs trying to make sense of what was happening. I was gobsmacked, frozen as a confederate statue.

The jig was up.

"You!" she cry-screamed at Boone, holding high my bible and shaking it like a fire and brimstone preacher, "You leave my son alone! Goddamn you! He's Jewish!" She turned it into a short chant, "Jew-ish! Jew-ish! Jew-ish!"

"Praise Jesus!" Boone yelled, unwavering, and oddly happy to see my mother.

She stopped about ten feet away and threw the scriptures at him, the pages flapping wildly as it fell at my feet.

Boone picked it up and held it to his chest. "Jesus is the real and only Lord, our God!" Boone hollered.

"Shut up! I'll have you arrested for kidnapping!" Mom screamed at him.

"Jesus is the real and only Lord, our God!" Boone repeated, unfazed.

Calvin joined in. "Jesus is the real and only Lord, our God!"

"Come here, Yosef!" Mom thundered, her fists clenched.

Bursting suddenly into tears, I went to her. It was instinct. At my dozen years, I was still conditioned to think she was my only shot at survival. A little older and I may not have budged so easily.

When I reached her, she wrapped her protective, suffocating arms around me and quickly started pulling me across the yard to the car.

"Come back real soon!" Calvin yelled, trying to lighten the catastrophic mood.

Boone smacked him so hard on the back of the head, Calvin fell forward onto his knees.

"Daddy!" Calvin cried. Upset, he got up quickly and ran inside the house. I was stunned and wanted to go in after him. Of course, that wasn't happening.

Mom flung one last icy stare at Boone as we got in the car.

And Boone yelled one last thing at her. "Woman, you should know: Yosef has rejected Satan as his master! Praise Jesus!"

She hit the gas hard enough to break her foot, and as the back tires spun, I could hear the tiny street rocks denting the parked car behind us. I had never been in this kind of trouble before, nor had I ever seen Mom quite this unhinged, this frightened. I was feeling every emotion but happy, crying so hard the bottom of my glasses was flooding.

Neither of us spoke as we rocketed down the turnpike, Mom doing that nauseating, on-off gas pedal thing - more on, this trip. I squeezed my armrest, fleetingly thinking it might be best if a car crash killed us both. The rest of the family would never know the backstory.

And I was angry at Boone. He didn't exactly make the situation better.

"That Maccabee was pretty happy with himself!" Mom shouted suddenly, bitterly.

"Maca*fee*," I corrected.

"I don't care!"

"Mom, all I was doing was educating myself about, you know, another religion!"

"*Schmegegge!*" she screamed at me, drops of spittle landing on my cheek.

"Mom, slow down! Please!"

"Pages were dog-eared, Yosef! Don't tell me *educating*! Such a *shanda*! How could you do this to me? How?" Her voice was turning whimpery. "I asked you a question!"

"I don't know!"

"You are so selfish. How could you do this to me and your father and your grandparents?!"

"I didn't think it was a big deal, okay! It's just a book!"

"Just a book?! Just a book?! You didn't think it was a big deal? You didn't think it was a big deal! How exactly is studying Jesus Christ, when you're Jewish, not a big deal?! In case you didn't know, Jewish people don't read the bible, Yosef! No, they don't! They read the Torah! They read the Talmud!" She burst into uncontrollable crying now, squeezing in her last thought amid the blubbering. "Maybe, just maybe, they read *Friday the Rabbi Slept Late,* but not the bible!"

She was referring to the *Rabbi Small* murder books by Harry Kemelman. I read the whole series much later in life. Great stuff.

"You are never to see those Maccabees again!"

"It's Maca*fees!* Ma-ca-*fees!*"

"I will pick you up from school every day and take you to Bar Mitzvah practice. After practice, you will help that Rabbi clean and do whatever he needs! I will be waiting in the parking lot until you're done. Every day! Then I will bring you home and you are not allowed to go out until school the next day! Do you understand me?!"

My tears turned to ones of pure fury now.

"Do you understand me?!"

"I heard you!" I shouted.

A minute later we swerved into our driveway and Mom threw the car violently into park. She made some kind of grunting sound, as I grabbed the door handle--

"Wait," she said, grabbing my left arm.

I froze, mid-exit, directing my gaze onto the floorboard.

"We are going to forget this ever happened," she said quietly. "If your grandparents found out about this, they would die. Right there. On the spot. And your father? What would he think? He works so hard every day, a new job, in this very weird place! All for you and your sisters. The idea that you would do this ... this ..." She was searching.

Blasphemy, I thought, recalling Mark 7:22-23.

Unable to think of the word she was looking for, she changed the subject slightly. "Just ... tell me one thing, Yosef. Why? Why?"

The surface answer might have been obvious, but she needed to rule out what she feared most. That by reading the bible and hanging out with the Macafees, I was choosing not to be Jewish; that I would decide not to go to shul anymore, or pray anymore, not to have my Bar Mitzvah, or to celebrate any more high holidays. To my mother, if this was the case, it was a repudiation and disownment of the family.

Of her.

I knew my answer wouldn't satisfy her, so I remained silent.

She sighed loudly, full of frustration. "Fine. Just remember, this never happened."

With that, she got out and slammed the door behind her. I was about to follow, but something told me I needed to sit in the quiet for a while.

The next few days, I played the obedient son. Mom drove me to school, picked me up, took me to Bar Mitzvah practice, waited till I was done, then took me home. I did my homework, helped with dinner, and watched TV with my grandparents.

It was boring. And nerve-racking.

Although I was able to hang with Calvin at school, I worried that Boone would forbid him to see me if I didn't, at least, make an appearance at bible study.

But then, Mom suddenly announced she had to go to New York for a week. To see relatives and *just be in New York,* she said.

The be-in-New-York part I got. But seeing relatives was odd, as most were coming down for my Bar Mitzvah in just a couple of weeks. Was someone dying? Something to do with Lynn? Where will you stay?

No one is dying! I'm staying with Cousin Michael! Stop the inquisition!

We never really got an answer. Not a truthful one, anyway.

The next afternoon, Mom and Dad both picked me up from school, and we went straight to the Knoxville airport. There was very little conversation on the way, which made me even more suspicious. Mom was anxious, but not in her normal, kvetchy way. She was quiet, alternating between agitated and sleepy.

After a quick curb drop-off, two cheek kisses and as many hugs, Mom was off, suitcase in hand.

Dad and I didn't have a lot of conversations, especially those days. We were both busy with our new lives, but as we headed back to the Ridge, I tried to get at the real reason for Mom's sudden departure. Either he knew and wasn't telling me, or he truly didn't know.

With Mom gone ... I know this will come as a shock, but ... I took the opportunity to reconnect with Calvin and Boone. It was easy peasy. The grand folks were busy doing their nothing. Susan kept so hidden she could've joined the Coast Guard and been kidnapped by pirates and we wouldn't have known. Dad, of course, was consumed with work.

Neither Calvin, nor I, mentioned what happened with Mom, and Boone's subsequent attack. Both parental freak-outs were easy to ignore. What are you gonna do? Just parents being assholes. Nothing to see here. Keep moving.

So it was back to bellbottoms, Baptists, and boobs.

These were the Gilligan years, that period when boys would ask other boys if they were more a *Marianne* guy or a *Ginger* guy. When I was asked, I would always add Becky Baker to the options. Heavenly Becky, close to fourteen, long, straight, just-brushed blonde hair, satin skin, soothing drawl, breasts just aching for release. Proverbs 5:18-19 put it perfectly: *Let your fountain be blessed, and rejoice in the wife of your youth, a lovely deer, a graceful doe.* My feelings about Rachel didn't come close to how I felt about Becky. This, this was different.

One afternoon, Becky, Calvin, and myself were all sitting on a fallen tree in the woods. The goddess was in the middle, playing with a Nerf Ball, while Calvin passed around a joint and his moonshine shampoo bottle.

Becky's eyes were red, veiny, and half-shut, as she waxed bombastic about Pink Floyd's new album.

"It's called *The Dark Side of the Moon*. Each side is a ... it's a ... a non-stop piece of music. Right? The songs have titles but there actually ... aren't any, you know, songs!"

"Cool," I said, nodding, becoming an immediate Floyd fan, regardless of what they sounded like.

Calvin jumped onto the log, started air-guitaring and singing country-rock.

"Gross, Calvin! You and your Southern rock," Becky shouted, handing me the weed and the bottle. "There's other, better music you know." She threw the Nerf ball at him and it bounced off his chest. I don't think he noticed.

As she bent to pick it up, I put the joint to my lips and blew out, forced a little cough. Then I raised the bottle to my mouth and pretended to take a swig. Mmm, that's some tasty air.

I had been faking it for months. Drugs and alcohol scared the crap out of me. Even before my initial moonshine episode up in the tree, back in Brooklyn, Lynn had told me how some of her favorite musicians died from drugs. Hiding my disimbibing from Calvin, and now Becky - a couple of extremely stoned children - wasn't particularly difficult.

Then I noticed Becky staring at me.

"What?" I asked, figuring I was caught.

"I can't believe you climbed that tree to watch me take a shower. Gross!" My turn to get hit with the Nerf.

"S-s-s-sorry," I stammered, looking down, considering telling her that she could come by and look in my curtain-less room if she wanted.

"Hell, I was there, too!" Calvin said, jumping down from the log and punching Becky on the shoulder.

"What?!" she said, standing up. "Gross! Both of you?!"

"We're men, Beck! Can't be sorry for that," Calvin said, bursting into laughter.

Becky suddenly pushed Calvin hard, and he tumbled backward over the log, landing with a thump. We all roared with laughter.

Becky grabbed the Nerf again as Calvin got up and things settled a bit.

"So, what's it like being Jewish?" she asked.

"Yeah, Yosef, what's it like?" Calvin chimed in with his shit-eating grin.

"I don't mean anything by it," she said sweetly. "I just don't know any. Least I don't think."

"What religion are you?" I asked.

"Baptist," she said matter-of-factly, like I should know. And she was right. "Y'all Jews believe in God?"

"We're monotheists," I said, nodding.

"What's that?" she asked.

"The belief in one God. Actually, a long time ago, Jews believed every nation had their own God."

They both laughed.

"That's funny!" Calvin said, mid-guffaw. "Like Tennessee has a God. Alabama has a God. Kentucky has a God." He took a long whiskey swig.

"Those are states, dumbass," Becky said, "not nations."

"Far out!" Calvin shouted.

"You know," I said, "Jewish people and Southern Baptists aren't all that different. I've been reading the bible a lot with Calvin and his dad. They have lots of things in common."

Becky took that in, along with another hit off the joint.

Then, blowing out the smoke, she asked, "Do all y'all Jews talk funny?"

"*I* talk funny?!" I nudged her shoulder.

We all had a good laugh at that one. We all talked funny.

"Beck!" Calvin screamed at her. "Show us your boobs! Come on! We been waitin'!"

I shot Calvin a look; he was going to screw up the whole afternoon.

Instead, my life suddenly became infinitely more satisfying. Because as Becky scowled in disgust at both Calvin and myself, she also lifted her shirt and bra.

"Fine!" she yelled.

And there they were. The most beautiful breasts I had ever seen. Granted, I had only seen one other pair before them, and I was an infant at the time, so I don't remember them - thank God.

But Becky's boobs? There was nothing on God's lascivious Earth more breathtaking. They were the eighth and ninth wonders of the world and I wanted, needed, to be with them.

I sat there on that log, drooling like a lecherous camel. In a way I could've never expected, Becky's mammories had become my catalyst. Not unlike Moses parting the Red Sea, they parted the dark clouds of my childhood, revealing the blue skies of manhood.

That moment ... was my first horny.

Also, Calvin fell backward over the log again.

⚜

Urinals are weird, especially when you're a little squirt and you're peeing at the low baby ones, with redwood-sized men next to you releasing their firehoses.

And especially if all that's happening while you're trying to get back to the baseball game going on outside the restroom, down the long corridor, down hundreds of steps, and out on the field.

And especially, during all this, you end up peeing mostly on yourself because anxiety, terror, stranger danger, so on and so forth.

Especially if you're having another fucking nightmare!

My eyes flew open like an old school window shade.

I jumped out of bed and did my thing - checked to see that everyone was okay.

Mom wasn't in bed with Dad, and I panicked for a moment, before I remembered she was in New York.

Everyone else checked out.

I squeezed into the bottom of the linen closet and squirmed for quite a while, trying unsuccessfully to get comfortable. After five minutes of turning from side to side and pushing on walls that wouldn't move, I went back to my bigger bed, the more appropriate resting place for a growing boy.

It was 5:45am. Later than I thought. I closed my eyes and tried to fall asleep again, but the mind shit wouldn't stop: Those crazy baseball nightmares were getting worse. My Bar Mitzvah was only a few days away. People were coming. Was I as ready as I thought I was? Most importantly, would I ever see Becky's boobs again? And if I did, would she let me touch them? I assumed Jesus would forgive me for that.

I gave up on sleeping and reached under my bed for my ruler and flashlight. They weren't exactly where I left them, and at first, thought that odd ... but then remembered ... Mom must have shuffled them around when she found my bible. I wondered if she guessed what the flashlight and ruler were for. If so, that would be embarrassing beyond repair.

I pulled down my PJs and underwear.

Flashlight: On.

Measuring ...

Wait ... is that right?

Is that right?!

I craned my neck, painfully, getting as close as possible to the little ruler notches that were next to my penis.

Yep! 3 inches, all right!

Previously 2.5! I grew a half inch!

!!!!!

And then I noticed something else: fine hairs growing around the base, as well as on my testicles!

By the time I realized I was screaming loudly with joy, I heard two doors opening down the hall. I quickly flipped my flashlight off and pulled my head out from under the covers just as Dad threw my door open. He was panting, frightened ... and naked.

"What's wrong?!" he shouted. "Are you okay?!"

Like a magnet, my eyes were pulled to his fully-realized package. This was what I had to look forward to. Girth. Length. Nicely-forested.

Forcing myself to look him in the face, I tried to calm him. "I'm okay, I'm okay! It was just a nightmare!"

Gram and Gramps arrived and were immediately assaulted by Dad's rear view. Both cringed and quickly looked away.

"What is it?!" Gram asked, panicked. "Tell me it's not a heart attack. *Du Zol Nicht Vissen Frum Tsores!*"

"It's not a heart attack, Gram," I said. "Just a nightmare. Everybody go back to bed."

Dad nodded, raising his hands. "Okay, good. It's nothing. Just a nightmare. That's good! Period!"

"You sure you're okay, Champ?" Gramps asked.

"I'm really fine, Gramps," I said, smiling, wanting badly to tell him.

"Okay, goodnight, Zees," Dad said, closing my door.

I could hear everyone mumbling as I laid there, still, waiting.

A minute later, things were quiet again ... and I went ballistic. This time, silently. I ripped off my PJs and underwear and jumped out of bed. Silently screaming with my mouth stretched open, I punched the air, strutting around the room in a marching band circle.

Exhausted after a dozen rounds, I collapsed onto the carpet, and laid on my back, catching my breath. My head was perfectly positioned to see out my unadorned window. The sky was brightening, and I couldn't wait to take on the day.

As a new man.

***

At school the next day, everything was different. I felt taller, smarter, sexier. I was intoxicated, under the influence of half an inch. Each period, as the afternoon encroached, all I could think about was one class: Gym.

When it finally came time, I joined in more willingly than I ever had, for the first time able to enjoy the sweaty camaraderie of growing boys. I ran faster. Took more shots in basketball (missed them all). I even listened more intently to the Coach pontificate about pulled muscles.

Yes, sir, I was gymin' like a boss.

It was the last exercise of the day, and Calvin and I were standing in line, waiting for our turn to climb the rope. Rope climbing - good training for those of us who would pursue careers in mountain climbing.

"Why you so damn happy?" Calvin asked me as we moved up.

"What do you mean?" I asked back, knowing full well what he was referring to.

"I don't know. You just seem happy," he said. "You comin' round the house tonight? Daddy has some new verses he wants us to go over. Wants to give you your bible back, too."

"Yeah, I'll come over. Mom's not back for a couple more days."

"Hey, ain't your, what you call it, your Bar Mitzvah comin' up?"

It had become more than obvious that I needed to keep Calvin and Boone separate from my Jewish life. I didn't think it would be that hard, but oddly, Calvin remembered the big event. I didn't want to lie to him; he was my best friend.

"Yeah, it's coming up," I said.

"When?"

"It's this Saturday, but you don't want to come," I said, grimacing like I just ate a bitter herb. "It's really boring."

"Course I want to come! I never even been inside a Jew church."

"I want you to come, but my mom definitely doesn't. Know what I mean? Remember the other day?"

Calvin laughed that crazy laugh of his. "Your mama's wild as a wart hog at a sock hop, man!"

"That's true," I said, smiling, then changing the subject, "all I know is I got two words for you ..."

"Yeah?"

"Becky's ... titties."

"How great was that?!" Calvin exploded into laughter again, this time causing the coach to look over. Their eyes met and Calvin quickly shut up.

Finally, we made it to the front of the line where two ropes hung from the ceiling.

"Next!" Coach Lee shouted at us.

Calvin and I each grabbed a rope and started to climb. He shot up, hand over hand, heading easily to the top.

Me, it would be a while before I had any upper body strength.

I'm lying. I would never have any upper body strength.

I made it about 5 inches up and dropped, all puckered out. Lee looked at me with his hands on his hips, his mustache flitting in the wind of his disappointed sigh. But I didn't care. I had some nudity to attend to.

Moments later, I was moving slowly through the corridor toward the showers. Full on swagger, peacockin' all the way. I could not have been groovier.

Once in the shower, I lingered there, lathering up, in no hurry, making sure anyone who wanted to take a gaze, could help themselves. Yes, it was a glorious 10 minutes. I could've stayed naked all day and night.

BAD MITZVAH

MAY 5TH HAD FINALLY ARRIVED. BY THE END OF THE DAY, I would be a Bar Mitzvah. And the day after, thirteen-years-old. A man, yet a teenager, one of Judaism's great paradoxes.

Mom had come back a couple days ago, and the minute she came in, she went straight to bed. And stayed there. I assumed she needed to rest up for the big celebration, but for two days? It didn't matter because, today, she was up and getting ready early. Anxiety can be a powerful stimulant, I suppose.

I was still in bed.

After being disappointed due to the lack of more johnson growth, I felt a stomachache and a headache coming on. Early male menopause being unlikely, I figured it was stress. Like mother, like son. As Maalox didn't help the head, I had to bring out the big guns: Alka-Seltzer.

I started to feel a little better physically but was still ping-ponging between fear and apathy, until I heard a certain someone come in the front door.

I bolted from my room, ran down the hall and down the stairs onto the landing, pulling Lynn into one of the longest, tightest hugs we've ever had. Neither of us wanted to let go. I was fighting back tears. She was too, I think. She looked different. More hippie, with flowery and wrinkled clothes, a daisy in her unkempt hair. And there was something freer about her. As we ascended the stairs to the living room, I noticed she had an actual bounce to her step. She practically floated. Maybe because she had been out from the confines of the Bamberger clan. Or maybe it was Detroit. Or drugs. Or the fact, that we would find out later, she stopped eating meat. Whatever it was, she was joyful and brighter than I'd ever seen her. I'll have what she's having.

Within minutes of Lynn's arrival, everyone started showing up, a Semitic cluster unlike them parts had ever seen. Dad had picked up some of them from the airport. Some rented cars. Some took Checker taxis, a disappointing revelation if they were expecting anything resembling an actual taxi. As instructed by Mom, I stood at the living room entrance, taking on a battery of awkward hugs and premature mazel tovs. I hardly knew these people anymore (if ever).

By 11am, we were one-hundred deep: aunts, uncles, first cousins, first cousins twice-removed, second cousins, the Cohens from the Bronx, the Rosenbergs from Shul, and the Caplans from Ridgewood. Even Rabbi Berkwitz made it down. No Mitchell and Micah yet. They were supposed to be there. I would never let them know this, but a part of me didn't want them to show up. Getting back in with them, albeit temporarily, would only confuse the new me. Two religions were fine, but three BFFs?

Most guests were in the living room and kitchen. Some had bled into the hallway while others self-toured the house, marveling at all the space we had. If they were appalled by the carpet, no one said anything.

Mom was buzzing around like a giant, spastic bee, pollinating each guest with Kroger cold cuts and hallah bread she had brought back from New York.

Dad parked himself by the TV, being cordial, smiley, having short conversations with people, always ending with how grateful he was they were able to come.

Susan was wallflowering in a corner, only in the vicinity because she would have to deal with a tyrannical Mom if she wasn't. She looked nice, having brought her Cybil Shepherd savoir-faire to Tennessee. That was one of the few good things about the Oak Ridge synagogue: they were pretty lax when it came to dress code.

Gram and Gramps were dressed in their traditional Orthodox wear, sitting together as they spoke with old friends about the Holocaust and other terrible things, like broken noses and severed fingers.

How's your finger, Gert?

Gone.

Most guests having showed up, there was a break in the blitzkrieg, and I slipped away, back to my room.

I shut the door behind me, sat on my bed, and stared out the window.

Just as I was relaxing a bit, there was a knock on the door. Exasperated, I plopped backward on my bed.

"Come in," I said.

The two meshuggeners threw the door open, both beaming with their arms outstretched. "Does Yosef Bamberger live here?!" asked Mitchell.

I shot out of bed like a runaway subway car. We crushed into a three-some hug I can still feel to this day. My brothers. The trepidation of seeing them again vanished as I remembered this feeling. Unconditional acceptance. So far out.

"Mazel tov, Spaz!" Micah said as we came slowly out of the hug.

"Thanks! I'm so glad you guys are here," I said. "You're both so tall!"

"You are too," Mitchell said.

We were both right. We had all grown to some degree, physically anyway. Mitchell's voice had even changed. Think Telly Savalas, sans lollipop.

We planted our butts on the carpet, talking over each other, laughing loudly and often. I told them about my weird, secular school and how easy all the subjects were, and about Becky's boobs and how they were better than Nino's pizza in Bay Ridge. I even told them about Calvin and Boone, leaving out the Jesus part, of course.

They told me about Brooklyn and how nothing had changed, except that it was weird with me gone. I immediately made some stupid joke I don't remember now, just to make sure I had an excuse to break into laughter instead of the opposite.

If Mom hadn't stormed in telling us it was time to go, we might've spent the next week right there, on that shag carpet, not eating, sleeping, or pooping, just talking, connecting, loving.

❦

Dad drove me, Micah, Mitchell, Mitchell's dad, Mom, and Gram who was half in Micah's lap. That made for more than a few adolescent giggles.

We got there an hour early so I could settle in. I bid my pals good-bye and went to Cantor David's office. He was sitting at his desk when I appeared at his door.

"Yosef!" he yelled when he saw me. "Come in, come in."

I came in and sat down in my regular chair.

"How you feeing? Good? You ready?"

"I think so," I said, a bit tentatively.

"You were ready the day I met you," he said, smiling, flashing those giant white teeth.

I nodded, remembering the day I asked Rabbi Berkwitz if I could break every Jewish law and get Bar Mitzvahed a year early.

"Anything you'd like to discuss?" the cantor asked.

"No."

"Okay, then ... good luck! You're gonna do great!"

"Thanks," I said, standing up.

"See ya out there," he said, as I walked out in the hall and closed his door behind me.

As I stood there, unmoving, two thoughts occurred to me. First of all, do *well*, I'm going to do *well*. Second, why do I need luck if I'm going to do well? Maybe the good luck part was because he knew I needed it? It was true. I hadn't really been focusing on my Bar Mitzvah studies. Okay, fine, I was ignoring them. I had all my justifications, of course. Sure, I may have known everything a year ago, but now ... it was hard to tell.

A second later, a raging panic attack came on me like an angry poltergeist. Palms sticky like Elmer's glue, desert mouth, shriveled sack. Heart beating at the speed of light.

There were over a hundred people out there! All for me!

I needed some air.

I moved quickly down the hall, into the lobby, and out into the parking lot.

Ah, fresh air. It was warm, not muggy yet, and there was a bit of a breeze. I inhaled deeply.

Out of nowhere, Calvin rode up on his bike and did that slidey, braking thing that I loved.

"Hey man!" he yelled.

I was so happy to see him. And I wasn't.

"What are you doing here?! I told you not to come," I said, looking around to make sure Mom wasn't in sight.

"Relax, man. Just came by to wish you good luck," he said.

"Thanks. I'm actually … I'm kind of nervous."

Suddenly, I had a brilliant idea.

"Do you have any moonshine with you? Or pot?" I was desperate for something, anything that could take me down a few notches on the heebie-jeebie ladder.

Muttley laughed loud and hard.

"What's so funny?!" I shouted.

"You been fakin' it all this time, now you want some?!"

"What do you mean?!"

"Forget it, man," he said, still laughing. "I ain't got anything on me."

"Oh," I said, disappointed. "Well, I better get inside."

"Sorry, man, good luck."

I thanked him and turned to go.

"Wait!" Calvin yelled, leaning in.

"What?" I said, turning back.

He was reaching into the front pocket of his jeans. "I just remembered, my buddy gave me a few of these pills. They been in my pocket for a damn week, ha!"

He pulled out a small, scrunched up piece of tin foil, opened it and held up a tiny yellow tablet. "Wanna try it?"

I grabbed it and looked it over - as if by doing that, I could make an educated decision.

"What does it do to you?" I asked.

"He didn't say. I reckon it's like pot. Relaxes you." Calvin shrugged with a cockeyed smile. "Why not, right?"

I'd seen Calvin, and Becky now too, both pretty high. The last thing they seemed was anxious. It was small enough to swallow without water so I popped it in my mouth.

"Hope it helps," I said with not a tiny bit of desperation in my voice. "How long you think it'll take to start working?"

"Shit, I don't know. Never done one. All right, man, well, good luck."

"Thanks. By the way, you're supposed to say mazel tov," I said, relaxing already.

"How you say it again?"

"Ma ... zel ... tov."

"Mazel tov!" Calvin screamed as he started off on his bike. "Mazel Tov!"

I think he liked the sound of it because he shouted it over and over, until I saw him shrink into a tiny, hillbilly microdot on the horizon.

❧❦

The good news: the panic attacks were gone.

The bad news: I was high as fuck.

It was a packed house. Bambergers in the front. New Yorkers scattered everywhere. Even Devin was there. I was sitting between Mom and Dad, giggling uncontrollably, as Rabbi Brenner gave his derasha.

Mom bent down, whispered, "What's wrong?"

I answered in my drawliest Southern accent, an accent I apparently decided to premiere that very moment. "Not a thang, man. Not ... a ... thang."

Under normal circumstances, the furious, disgusted look on her face would've shut me up for hours, but in that moment, every goddamn thing was funny, the kind of hysterical that could only be disrupted by something deadly, like the 1931 China floods, or a penis that stops growing at three inches.

"Shhhhhh," I said to Mom, mid-giggle, thinking her facial response was a vocal one.

Right then, for some reason - maybe something the rabbi said, maybe because, you know, narcotics - I shot up out of my seat and began to head up front.

"Yosef!" Mom yell-whispered. "Not yet! Come back!"

Dad said something - I can't remember.

As I managed to climb the short steps up to the bimah (the stage), the Rabbi stopped the sermon, laughing. "Looks like we have an impatient Bar Mitzvah boy, here."

The congregation laughed along as I made my way across the bimah.

Cantor David was right beside me. "Yosef, it's not time yet ... are you okay? You don't look well."

Really? What gave it away? My planet-sized pupils, or my general fuck-all attitude?

Doing my damndest to hold in the laughter, I grabbed the Torah, and brought it forward to the pulpit.

The cantor and rabbi flanked me as the latter addressed the congregation, "Okay, folks, we're going to go ahead, let Yosef begin. We're easy here." Then, quietly to me, "Take a few breaths. Calm down. You're going to do fine."

I opened the Torah and started to sing, a Hebrew Bar Mitzvah readings to the tune of *99 Bottles Of Beer On The Wall.*

"*Yaledaa ha issah yeladim rabbim weyapimo ... Lo rapal ehad mehanna-arim ...*" I stopped suddenly, bursting into laughter. "Wait, wait, let me try it again!"

I guess I couldn't get the tune out of my head. because the next time was exactly the same. "*Yaledaa ha issah yeladim rabbim weyapimo ... Lo rapal ehad mehanna-arim ...*"

"Yosef," the rabbi said, bending down to me, "what's wrong?"

"Nothin'," I said, matter-of-factly, looking up at him.

His expression shifted to shock and revulsion. "What ... are you on drugs?"

I exploded into laughter, yet again.

"I think we should delay this," the rabbi said to the cantor.

"Absolutely," the cantor agreed.

The rabbi took a hold of my arm and began to gently pull me away from the pulpit.

"Stop it," I yelled, yanking my arm back, looking out at the congregation. "You believe these guys?!" I asked, appalled they would attempt to stop my Bar Mitzvah. *My Bar Mitzvah,* the thing I'd been waiting for, for so long!

Dismay played across every face in the place. Mom was up on her devastated feet and heading up to the bimah. There were at least three dozen people with their hands on their faces, mouths wide enough for Amtrak. Lynn and Susan were both shaking their heads uncontrollably, silently mouthing *stop.*

"Yosef, please, come on," the cantor said, taking a hold of my other arm.

"Let go of me!" I shouted, throwing an unintentional elbow into the cantor's chin.

He screamed out, falling backward a few steps.

"*Li repl ehod,*" I sang, "*nehanna-arimmmm!*" This time, it was just a mutterey mess.

Mom joined the cantor and rabbi, the three of them now putting some muscle into getting me out of there.

I segued into *Sweet Home Alabama.*

"Singing songs about the Southland! Lord, I'm coming home to you! Southern man don't need you around, anyhow!"

"Stop it, Yosef," Mom barked.

"You know something?!" I screamed, struggling unsuccessfully to break free, "Jesus saves all good Christians! I think that's pretty Goddamn cool!"

Huge gasps filled the room.

"Shut up! Shut up!" Mom shouted.

"Answer me this," I continued as they pushed and pulled me down the aisle. "How come us Jews don't have anyone to save us?! Noooooooo! We had to go and kill the guy who wanted to do it! Jesus! Son a' God! That's right. You and me, we killed him! We're murderers! Jews, the killers!"

At that point, I'm pretty sure everybody was screaming at me. That was when I felt someone grab me from behind, locking my arms back and pushing me, forcefully, forward and out.

It was Dad. I guess he couldn't sit idly by anymore. Wonder what it was: the shout out to my main man Jesus, or the murder accusations?

❧❦

Dad had dragged me out to the parking lot, put me in the car, and rushed me home. I don't remember him saying anything, probably because I still couldn't control the incessant laughter.

The minute we got home, I realized I had to pee very badly. I ran to the upstairs bathroom. And that's when the howling laughing turned to just howling.

There I was, just standing at the toilet doing my business when, like a fight scene in *Batman,* the room suddenly turned sideways. Terrified, I started screaming and ran the - what seemed like a thousand yards - to the bathroom door.

When I finally managed to get into the hallway, everything was still crooked. I ran, shrieking loudly, down the hall, down both flights of stairs, and into Susan's empty room. Confused and dizzy, I backed into a corner by her bed, like I was being chased by something evil. I started to cry, praying for whatever was happening to me to stop. I could see the stairs from where I was. Dad was sitting on them and had turned into a statue. *The Thinker*, perfectly solid, silent.

There was some kind of time jump because the next thing I remember was Mom running downstairs, screaming at me, but with the volume turned off. As she barreled into the room, she turned into the *Wicked Witch Of The West,* complete with tar black hair, and hook nose with a massive wart on top. She was putting several spells on me although, since there was no sound, I have no recollection of what they were. Probably a good thing.

Finally, I recognized someone who could save me. Lynn was walking into the room, and as she did, I bolted from my cowering position and pulled her into a hug, begging her to do something.

"Okay, John-Boy," she said, her voice echoing. "It's gonna be all right. Calm down, just calm down."

I nodded, breathing erratically.

"Did you take some kind of pill or something?"

I had actually forgotten. "Oh ... I think ... maybe I did."

"Yep. I think you might have taken a hit of acid. It's all groovy. It wears off. It's gonna be all right. I'm here."

She helped me to Susan's bed and laid me down.

"See if you can fall asleep," she said as she rubbed my back.

Unfortunately, slumber wasn't part of the immediate program. The next several hours were punctuated with various, lunatic bouts of panic, leaving my body multiple times (destination unknown), and watching Susan's head shapeshift into the size of a triangular pea. I also have a vague memory of the Romper Room woman looking through the magic mirror and calling out my name. "I see Yosef ... mother fucker's tripping his freakin' balls off."

Funny now. Petrifying then.

Eventually, mercifully, I did fall asleep.

So, yeah, it turns out, Calvin's little gift wasn't just some little pill that would relax me. It was Yellow Microdot. Also known as LSD. No gateway drug for me. I rammed the gate and bolted straight for the main attraction.

⁂

I didn't wake up the next day until 1pm. Sitting up slowly in bed, I was still dazed and confused. I knew something heinous and sickening happened, but it took me a few moments to remember.

The memories rushed in like Pamplona bulls, starting with the faces of all the people I offended: my parents, grandparents, Cantor David. Then there were the fuzzy recollections of Skynard and Jesus and the giant rabbi.

And what about the two meshuggeners?

And Rabbi Berkwitz?

What were their reactions? Where were they now? Would they ever talk to me again? I couldn't imagine confronting any one of them.

I was quickly coming to the conclusion that I would be better off dead. Since I couldn't stand the thought of seeing anyone, I would just lay there until I starved to death.

My bedroom door opened an inch. Gram peeked in.

"Hi," I said, surprised it was her I would have to see first.

She came in silently, closed the door behind her, then sat on the edge of my bed. Staring at me with wet, bewildered eyes, I imagine she was wondering if this was her grandson or some incarnation of Satan that she previously didn't believe in.

"I'm sorry," I muttered.

She dropped her head in her hands. I was waiting for some Yiddish, at least a short *What a shanda!*, but there was none of that. What I did was so wrong, so sacrilegious, so inexplicable that apparently there were no words. Not even a Yiddish exclamation of sorrow and catastrophe.

"Yosef," she finally said sadly, looking at me.

She had a couple false starts, her wrinkled mouth opening one moment, then closing again when she couldn't think of the right thing to say.

Finally, she said, "There is nothing that you can do, or say, that destroys your Judaism. It is who you are. The Nazisci, they wanted to destroy us. Yes?"

I nodded.

"Yes, they tried. In the camps, every day." She paused, deciding whether to continue. "I don't think I ever told you this story. One night, late, I was walking back to the bunk, by myself. I had been doing some cleaning for one of the officers. I was only a few yards away when one of the Nazis grabbed me from behind and threw me on the ground. He pinned my arms, and sat on top of me. I was terrified I would be raped. He didn't say anything, just bent down close to my face ... and spit. Twice."

Gram closed her eyes a moment, then opened them again.

"He let me up and I went back to the bunk. Every day it was these types of things, but I remained who I was - a proud, Jewish woman. It's true, there were some of us, some who forgot who they were, but in the end, God wins, one way or another. Even today, when it comes to Yosef Bamberger. God is with you. And you will try again. Your Bar Mitzvah. Okay? Understand what I'm telling you?"

I was moved, and grateful. I hadn't thought about trying again. "I do," I answered. "I will."

She patted my knee, nodded, stood up slowly and headed toward the door.

"Gram ..."

She stopped and turned back toward me.

"How's Mom and Dad? Are they...I guess they're pretty mad, huh?"

"Mad? Hmm...not a word I would choose."

And not what I wanted to hear. "What about everyone else? Are they still here? Did they go back to New York?"

Gram moved again to the door. "Some left last night. Some today. What am I? Your schedule keeper?"

I half-smiled as she left and closed the door behind her.

I closed my eyes, then the door opened again. It was Susan.

I bristled as she walked in, a new pair of elephant bell bottoms flapping around her ankles. She stood by the window, crossed her arms, and looked out.

"Wow, Yo-yo. Just … what is wrong with you?"

"How's Mom and Dad?"

"Dad's been quiet, no shock there. Seems really sad, though. Mom spent the whole day yesterday apologizing for you."

"What about Micah and Mitchell?"

"I think they left yesterday, not sure. My boyfriend picked me up around seven last night, so ... I don't really know."

"Still dating that same guy?" Anything to change the subject.

"Don't change the subject. No, different guy."

"Is he Black, too?"

"It doesn't matter," she said, annoyed. "What the hell was all that Jesus crap?"

"It's not crap! Judaism isn't the only religion, you know?"

Susan's eyes rolled so far back in her head I thought she might topple backwards.

"Okay, Yo-yo, whatever you say. If you want to keep ruining your family's life, go ahead."

"I'm sorry!"

"Calvin Macafee selling you this shit?"

"He's my friend!"

"Your *friend* gives you drugs?!"

"No!"

"Then where'd you get it?"

"None of your beeswax!"

"God, you even sound like him!"

247

"You never even met him!"

"Everybody here sounds like that!"

She was right. Apparently, my new Southern accent had not been fleeting. Like racism and bigotry, it wasn't going anywhere.

"At least I don't hang out with *shvartzes*!" I shouted.

She turned to look at me, her heavy blue eye shadow glistening in the sunlight.

"Newsflash, moron: my new boyfriend is not Black. Go ahead, though, tell Mom and Dad all about how you caught me. They won't believe you, not after you embarrassed the whole family."

"I wasn't going to say anything," I said, honestly.

That seemed to calm her down. "Good. I gotta go. Look, Yo-yo, you'll try it again. As long as you do it right, at some point, they'll forget all this other *mishegoss*."

"I hope so."

Susan nodded and walked out.

That rare vote of confidence sat with me a good four minutes or so, before I started to cry again.

A few minutes later, Lynn came in and gave me a big hug. Just love. No attacks.

"Happy birthday," she said, as she left.

I completely forgot. It was my birthday. And to this day, the worst birthday I've ever had.

Welcome to thirteen, you blasphemous, ungrateful, adolescent shithead.

I expected the parade to continue with Gramps, Mom, Dad, maybe one or both of my rabbis. But there was no one else that day.

Around 8pm or so, I managed to sneak into the kitchen without anyone spotting me, taking some leftover salami and cheese back to my room.

Monday morning finally came, and I couldn't wait to get back to school. Partly, just to get the hell out of my suffocating house, partly to tell Calvin what happened. I figured I'd stick to the highlights: peeing sideways, Susan's shrunken head, Mom's silent incantations. I could hear him laughing about it all, and I could see how a few chuckles might even help me see beyond the horror of it all.

But none of that happened.

I was just about to get out of bed when Dad came into my room, like he did every morning. But this morning, he was dragging and sullen, grieving. He closed the door behind him but didn't move much past that. It was good to see him, and not. I wanted desperately to get past all of it. The day before, I had rehearsed a thousand times what I was going to say. But when I saw him, it came out like vomit.

"Dad, I'm sorry, about, you know, all of it. I took this drug. I didn't know what it was, what it would do to me, but I shouldn't have taken it. I'm sorry about all that crazy Jesus stuff. It was wrong. I didn't mean anything. I was thinking I could try my Bar Mitzvah again, I don't know, sometime, you know, later, in the future."

He had no reaction. He had prepared a speech of his own.

"Your mother and I have talked. I know you're aware of our devastation. I know you wish none of it happened. But it did. You practically killed your mother."

Eyes widening to keep the tears at bay, he turned his gaze out the window.

I started crying again.

"Are you a drug addict?"

"What?! No! Dad! No! It was one tablet thingie. It was a mistake!"

Thanks Lynn. Apparently, she told everybody.

"Did you get it from that boy, that boy you've been spending time with?"

"No. It wasn't him. Dad, it doesn't matter. Believe me, I would never do anything like that again! It was really scary!"

He nodded in agreement, then took a deep breath and turned back to me.

"So, here it is: Rabbi Berkwitz is willing to speak with you about what you can do for forgiveness. You will listen carefully and do exactly as he says. Furthermore, you will not be going back to school this year. It's only a few more weeks. You will finish your schoolwork here at home. We've already spoken to your teachers. You will be grounded that whole time, absolutely no trips outside of the house, unless accompanied by one of us. When school is over, you will go to summer camp at Camp Ramah in the Berkshires. It's an Orthodox camp. There, with God's help … we can fix you."

Relieved he got it all out, he nodded once, opened the door and left.

I felt like I was just blasted in the face with a flamethrower. I didn't move, couldn't move, just sat there on the edge of my bed, staring at the closed door. It took me a while to process everything he said.

Eventually, it entered my callow little brain in spurts.

No back to school.

No outside.

No Becky boobs.

No Jesus.

No Boone.

No Calvin.

Days later, I was still in a daze. My punishment was clearly severe, but my anger never stayed focused for long; one second I blamed Calvin, the next Boone, then Dad, Mom, God, Jesus, the microdot. And just as quickly, the anger would go away entirely, often replaced with embarrassment, confusion, or both. What I wouldn't understand till later was that I was in shock, *Psychological Shock*, being the technical term. In no small part, due to the LSD; it can be responsible for all kinds of brain mischief. Bottom line: there was a lot going on in that mangled, little noggin of mine.

Rabbi Berkwitz was calm and pointed. There was no outrage, or judgements, or reprimands - not that any of that surprised me. He asked me if I regretted my actions and I told him I did. The remedy was simply to pray a lot, and God would forgive me. Apparently, it wasn't more complicated than that. I was relieved.

Mom still wasn't speaking to me, so I told Dad what the Rabbi had said. He told Mom, then reported back to me. Apparently, she wasn't happy with the Rabbi's response. Allergic to easy solutions, as always. Honestly, what could I do except what the Rabbi suggested, anyway? They already had me spending a ridiculous amount of time at that bad Jewish joke of a synagogue. What, maybe I should eat twelve jars of gefilte fish in one sitting? Grow my hair hasidically? Give Mom a Jewish grandchild, a future doctor or lawyer, by way of an otherwise unwanted teenage pregnancy?

Just like Gram, to Rabbi Berkwitz, I was Jewish no matter what I did. I was born Jewish. I would stay Jewish. And there was nothing that could change that.

❧❧❧

Ka-dink!

I shot up in bed.

It had been a few days since my sentencing. I'd been focusing on my schoolwork and watching TV with the grandparents. No room-destroying tantrums or endless pillow-screaming, suppose I was getting too old for that nonsense. Maybe it was the tiniest bit of maturity, whispering that I needed to take responsibility.

Mom still hadn't said a word to me. The silent treatment isn't difficult if you imagine you never had a son in the first place. I did notice her and Susan were actually talking more, often peacefully and even with a few laughs. As they say, when God closes one door …

I had fucked up so comprehensively, I didn't expect Mom to forgive me anytime soon. If ever. But it still hurt. A mother's abandonment stays with you for a lifetime.

I had decided it best not to complain about my punishment. There was no way I was changing their minds. But there was a bigger reason: part of me was actually looking forward to camp - anything to get away from the tension. I just had to keep my head down, do my work and get through these couple of weeks.

Ka-dink-dink!

I looked at my clock: 2:46 am. I got out of bed, went to the window, and opened it slowly. Calvin was standing over his bike, wearing a grin so wide, it practically stretched off his face in each direction.

He loud-whispered, "Hey man, where you been?!"

"I'm grounded. Can't go to school. Can't go anywhere."

"Aw, that sucks!"

"Nothing I can do about it."

"Hell, everybody at school's talkin' 'bout you."

"What do you mean?"

"Your crazy damn Bar-whatever."

I hadn't thought about it, but it did make sense that a boy tripping his way into manhood might make for lively conversation in the halls of Robertsville Junior High school.

"That pill you gave me? It made me see things. I hallucinated," I said, one-third warning him, one-third blaming him, and one-third thinking it was cool.

Calvin chuckled. "Really? That's wild, man. I heard you was singin' Skynard and praisin' Jesus! Man, I wish I's there!"

"Yeah," I said smiling, hiding the true terror of it. "Well, I better get back in."

"Hold your horses!" he screamed.

"Shhhhh!"

"D'you know your folks came to my house?"

"What?!"

"Yeah, man, your mama, your papa, and your granddaddy. Daddy answered the door. Man, they's madder than a wet hen! Your mama starts sayin' that your granddaddy was the 1927 heavyweight champ --"

"Bantamweight, 1926."

"Yeah, right. You told me all about it. Anyway, she was saying how he was gonna pop Daddy in the mouth and that he needs to 'stay away from my son!'" Calvin couldn't stop laughing.

Me? I was mortified.

"She said they's goin' to the police, too!"

"What?! What did Boone say to that?"

"Shit, man, he just laughed."

"Sorry, man," I said.

"Ah, man, it's cool. It was pretty damn funny."

I rubbed my eyes. "I better go."

"Naw man! Come on out. Let's get up in that tree again. Becky boobs await!"

This was intensely hard and painful for me. I had had a thought the day prior that, if I got caught screwing up again, Mom would disown me for good and send me to Israel to live out my years.

"I don't want to get in anymore trouble," I said.

"You won't! Come on!"

In the months I'd known Calvin, I don't think I said no to him once. It's like getting a colonoscopy when you turn 50; you need to do it, but you put it off, and put it off, but eventually, you have to do it.

"Sorry. I'll see you later," I said, forcing a smile.

As I closed the window, his shoulders slumped and that fabulous grin fell away like an Apollo rocket booster. He rode off shaking his head slightly, as if to say, 'forget him.' And I felt that, acutely.

I wanted to tell him I wouldn't see him, or Boone, till September. But I couldn't. As I climbed back into bed, the frustration kept me tossing and turning. When I did finally drop off to sleep, it was fitful and upsetting, unrestful because I felt like I had something to solve.

By the way, Susan told me that Mom did go to the police. They said they couldn't do anything unless Boone had done something illegal. Apparently, trying to convert your Jewish son to Southern Baptist wasn't against the law.

❧❧❧

I woke with a high-pitched wail. It was short and loud, like the call of a loon, or one of those abrupt honks ambulances make when some asshole's not pulling over. For several seconds, I couldn't tell where I was. I wasn't in my bed, or the linen closet, or as I realized eventually, not even Oak Ridge.

What I did know was that nagging, terrorizing nightmare of mine had finally unfolded completely. It was the 7th inning stretch, also known to many as the 7th inning pee. In order to beat the onslaught, we had left our seats a bit early. I had saddled up to the low-standing urinal and started doing my business when I was besieged by hundreds of drunk and boisterous males, fellow urinators to the sides of me, with uncomfortable, got-to-go fans at my back.

I stared at the cold, wet porcelain, pushing, pushing, wanting desperately to finish and escape the swarm. I could feel someone's breath on the back of my neck and made the mistake of looking behind me. It was just a momentary glance, a blur, but it caused me to start peeing on my right shoe, a now-soaked Thom McAn standard brown.

It was time to leave. My goal unaccomplished, I stopped the flow, tucked myself in, and squeezed between the legions until I reached the corridor.

But then I stopped. Dad was nowhere to be seen. He said he'd meet me right outside the bathroom. Panicking, I swung my head in every direction.

Dad? Dad?!

There were so many people, so many strangers, everyone taller and wider than me. It made me dizzy.

I figured he must've gone back to our seats, so I ran toward the bleachers and entered the massive stadium area. Of course, being the myopic, little cherub I was, I had no idea where our seats were. So I sat in the first empty one I could find.

The 7th inning had begun, and every few seconds, I would take my eyes off the game and look for Dad, knowing I shouldn't move since, eventually, he'd return.

My level of anxiety crept up with each out, each run, each inning, and by the 9th, Dad still hadn't showed. Why wasn't he there? Where could he be? Was he getting peanuts or something to drink? I was about to explode with fear and confusion.

The Mets lost, and I watched as all the dour spectators started piling out, and eventually, I was alone. I looked out on the field, hoping that at least, the Mets hadn't abandoned me. But they had. There was no one. That was when the sobbing began.

And when I stopped remembering.

We were passing through Roanoke on Interstate 81, driving the twelve hours to Camp Ramah. Seventy miles an hour, open road, just me and my dad. I had begged him to let me fly, the last thing I felt I could handle was being in a car for so many hours, with only him. It was too expensive he said and too complicated. I'd have to fly into LaGuardia, get picked up, blah, blah, blah. At least Mom wasn't there.

We had spent the first couple hours mostly in silence, a bit of small talk here and there. It was awkward at first, then we both got used to it. Then I fell asleep.

Now, Dad's eyes were darting back and forth between me and the road. "You okay?" he asked.

I nodded ever so slightly, picking up and folding the road map that had landed on the floorboard in front of me.

"I had a nightmare," I said quietly, maybe even a little accusingly.

"Sorry to hear that."

I stared at the side of his head a good while, still making the connection. Dreams sure can be pushy when they want to be.

"We're making good time so far," he said.

"D'you ever take me to a baseball game?" It came out fast and jumbled.

But he understood. As a matter of fact, he flinched, like I shot him in the neck with a blow dart. His reaction alone turned my nightmare to a memory.

"Once," he answered, struggling to stay focused on the road. "You remember that?"

I couldn't look at him anymore and stared out my window at the millions of passing trees. "I think so," I said, "how old was I?"

Dad rolled his shoulders a couple of times. "Five," he said. "What exactly do you remember?"

"Being in the bathroom by myself and being really scared, then running out and wondering where you were. I watched the rest of the game by myself, waiting for you to come back ... you never did."

Dad pulled into the far-right lane and slowed down. Clearly, a big part of him didn't want to have this conversation, but like a nine-year bout of nausea, I imagine it was going to feel good to finally throw up. You know what they say: sometimes it takes a twelve-hour drive after an acid trip Bar Mitzvah to motivate a good catharsis.

"I was waiting for you outside the bathroom," he said, still shaky. "It was very crowded. I ... I lost you, looked everywhere. I got the security guards to help look. I went back to our seats, you weren't there, not that you would've been able to find them at five-years-old."

He looked over at me; it was just a moment. I could see the terror in his eyes. He was now reliving it, just as I had been for so many years.

"I've never been so frightened, Yosef. I thought you'd been kidnapped."

"How did it ... how did you ... how did we get back together?" I asked.

"At the end of the game, you were sitting alone in the bleachers. Crying. I hugged you and apologized, and ... I don't know, about halfway through the train ride home, you seemed to have forgotten already."

I nodded, then asked angrily, "Why didn't you ever talk about it?"

"I didn't see the point."

"Ever?"

"I didn't think you remembered."

"I didn't! I mean, I kind of did."

He slowed down even more, causing cars behind us to honk and swerve around to the faster lanes. I'm not even sure he noticed.

"I'm sorry," he said, quietly. "I don't know what else to say."

I nodded again, not accepting his apology and looking back out my window.

"You ever tell Mom?"

He paused, then said, "Why cause pain for no reason?"

He wasn't referring to the pain it would cause her. He was talking about the pain she would inflict on him.

What she doesn't know won't hurt him.

Ten hours to go. I opened my window to let the wind drown out the encroaching silence. Dad turned on the radio and it would stay on the rest of the way, the stations, some only static, coming and going with the miles. We talked about directions, traffic, where we might get food. How much time was left in our journey.

Our damaged relationship improved a small fraction on that trip - funny thing about full transparency. Maybe, just maybe, the revelation was a bit of compensation for the great New York extrication.

But for me, it was mostly about clarification, and release. Later, I did find sympathy (and empathy) for him. He had been harboring great guilt for what happened, a grand failure in fatherhood that he thought about often, while hoping I'd forgotten. And while we never spoke of it again, I would come to forgive him.

As far as the nightmares, I still have them to this day. They're less frightening and less frequent, but just as vivid, and always prodding, forcing me to look at the psychology underneath. The subconscious mind, always the sneaky co-conspirator.

MURRAY PAYS

MURRAY WAS A MUDDLE OF EMOTIONS: EXCITED, HOPEFUL, trepidatious. This last interview sealed the deal. He would start his new job in a matter of weeks. He had a good feeling for deep basing, so it was easy selling his new boss on his nuclear engineering chops.

The icing on the cake? (Jewish Apple, please). He could finally stop worrying about money.

But as these things go in Murray's life, all he really did was exchange one worry for another. How was he supposed to convince his family that moving to a strange, suffocating, almost certainly bigoted small town in Tennessee was a good idea? And how would they react? Would they throw him off the nearest, tall building? Would they simply refuse to go? Would they hate him for the rest of their lives?

Sandy would be the biggest challenge, of course. He would have to be strong, hold to his guns. He searched his memory, trying to find a time he stood up to Sandy for something he wanted and she didn't...

He came up short. Fine. She might run the household, and make most of the important decisions, but he was the one who brought home the bagels.

It all came down to money.

Regardless, he knew he'd have to trump up the town's positive attributes. No gun violence. No pollution. No crowding. No filthy subways filled with graffiti gangs and screaming hobos. Of course, there was also no Zabars, no H&H, no Statue of Liberty, United Nations, or museums, or buzz, or energy, or … most importantly, Jews. Or better put, he thought, no New York Jews. Murray was well-educated on all types of Jewish people: Algerian, Chinese, even the Lemba people of Malawi. But he had trouble imagining hillbilly Jews. They must have been some kind of amalgamation, mutants. A mistake.

He practiced his pitch:

"Yes! There are Jewish people there, and we will certainly become friends with them! Of course there's a synagogue! Yes! There are grocery stores with all kinds of kosher food!"

Murray shook his head. He didn't think he sounded very convincing. But once everyone understood that they were out of money, they'd realize there wasn't really a choice. Maybe his in-laws could stay in New York; where, he didn't know. He loved them dearly but being relieved of their food and board wouldn't be the worst thing in the world. Lynn could enroll in the University of Tennessee in Knoxville next year. And Susan and Yosef would acclimate. They were young enough. How bad could it get? There was a synagogue - what else did the family really need?

Murray looked at his watch and gasped, *"Oy gevalt."*

His flight was in a little over an hour and he wasn't entirely sure where he was, somewhere on Route 170, hopefully going in the right direction. So many trees. Everywhere.

Living in a city with some of the best mass-trans in the world, Murray had rarely driven. He had a driver's license, but it was mostly for ID. Driving was for hard-edged taxi hacks and the fresher-smelling limo drivers. When he lost his job a few months ago, Murray thought if he couldn't land a decent engineering job soon, he might have to become one of those hacks. So for days, while he pretended to be at work, he studied for his special taxi-driving license. The Oak Ridge interview came up before he had to pursue it. Thank God.

Murray lifted his yarmulke, swept his fingers through his short, sweaty hair, then placed it back. He could feel the sweat building in his underarms, as well. Early May, and it was already hot and humid down South. To make matters worse, for some reason, he couldn't get the car's air-conditioning to work. Of course, his snowballing weight didn't help.

In recent months, Murray had become the fat guy. For some reason, butter had become his new weakness. A thick slab of the creamy yellowness went so beautifully with, well, everything. It melted nicely in a bowl of matzo ball soup, just as it did on a crispy slice of rye toast or a sugary danish. Even already buttery things like cakes, cupcakes, rugalach and cranberry cream cheese babka were better with more butter.

At least four times a day, from a standing position, Murray would gaze down at his growing mid-section, just to make sure he could still see his feet. Another few weeks and the answer would be no. He didn't seem to have any control over it, but perhaps now that he was once again employed, he'd be too busy to eat.

Murray accelerated, keeping his eye out for signs to the airport, as well as trying to read a wide and uncooperative map spread out on the passenger seat. He didn't have time to stop. He also had to return the rental car; that would add time. And just in case all this wasn't enough stress, it was Yosef's birthday. If he missed his flight, he wouldn't get home till late. He'd have hell to pay just for that, much less for planning on moving his family to Dixieland.

"Ah," he said, spotting the old, peeling Elza Gate outpost. During the war, Elza was the main security gate at the border of the then-closed city of Oak Ridge. He didn't know if this meant he was going in the right direction or wrong, but at least the gate would be on the map somewhere. He tried to find it, looking closer, one eye on the map, one on the road. There weren't many cars, so that was helpful ...

"Ahhhhhhhhh!" Murray suddenly screamed, slamming on his brakes. His tires screeched and burned into the pavement as he careened toward the back end of an old, dark green Pontiac sedan.

He braced for the crash … and … bump.

He hit it, but just barely. Thank God. Hardly even heard the impact.

Murray sat there a moment, breathing, relieved, staring at the stopped car in front of him.

He looked to his right and saw, between heavy brush, a dirt road the car must've pulled out from. No street signs, no markers of any kind. Could happen to anyone.

He knew no one would be hurt, but he thought he should check just to make sure. It was his fault, after all. What's more, these people would soon be his new neighbors.

As he stepped out, the folks from the Pontiac were doing the same.

Joe and Paula Vaughn, a scrappy middle-aged couple in overalls and sour moods, walked toward the rear of their car.

Murray joined them there. "Hello," he said, smiling, making nice. "Everyone okay?"

"Suppose so," Joe said with a deep drawl, looking Murray up and down.

Paula kneeled, investigating the impact site.

"Oh, good," Murray said. "I didn't see you pull out. Very sorry."

Joe nodded, his grizzled face contorting as he looked down at his bumper. There were no dents. But since the Pontiac had to be close to 20 years old, and unkempt, there were scratches and rust everywhere.

"Well, I'm in a bit of a rush. Doesn't look like there's any damage, so I'm going to get going. Again, my apologies." Murray turned to go.

Paula stood up. "You blind?"

Murray stopped, his body immediately weakening. This happened to him any time he was being threatened. It was like his skeleton was summarily ripped out of his skin - right when he might need it the most.

"Sorry. What's the problem?" he asked nicely, turning back toward them.

Joe stepped closer to Murray. "Way I see it, you came up on me too fast."

"Well, yes--"

"I'm talkin'," Joe said, cutting Murray off.

Murray nodded, half-smiling. He was starting to shake.

"As I's sayin', you came up on me too fast and definitely caused some damage here."

Murray bent down, looking closer at the dent-free bumpers.

"Where you from, man?" Joe asked, suspiciously.

"Oh, Brooklyn. But we're moving here. Me and my family. Got a big family," Murray said, smiling big, in hopes of creating a more neighborly environment.

"Well, Mr. Brooklyn," Joe said, cracking a smile, "whether you see it or not, we do have some damage here, and we agree it was your fault, so … how much cash you got?"

Murray looked at Joe, then Paula. Both were smiling as if they just asked him how his day was going. Shitty, thank you. He was drenched in sweat now; and more emasculated than a moment ago, if that was possible.

He'd been robbed before. Walking home from visiting a friend late one night, a man jumped out from between some trashcans and jammed a gun into his side. Overcome with fragility, Murray put his hands up without even being instructed to do so. The thief took his wallet and ran off. Murray must have stood there for at least five minutes afterwards: frozen. terrified. The guy was probably home, cozy, sleeping in his bed by the time Murray lowered his arms.

But this, this was different. In the light of day, only a hint at violence, almost polite. Maybe this was what they meant by southern hospitality.

"You can check your wallet, or we can check your wallet," Paula said. "Either way."

He wanted so badly to find his strength, some pluck, some ballsiness, then rear back and slug these two right in the face. He had prayed for it that night he was mugged, too.

Instead, Murray reached around to his back pocket, took out his wallet, opened it, and handed Joe what he had.

Forty bucks. "It's all I have," Murray said.

"Well, thank you kindly," Joe said, taking the money.

Murray ran back to his car, jumped in, and took off. As he did, he realized he was hyperventilating and tried to calm down, even as he accelerated around the Vaughns and their decrepit, undented vehicle. Making sure they weren't following him, he looked once in his rearview mirror. They were laughing.

Humiliation washed over him, as he realized he would miss his flight home, at least partially due to fear. Murray promised himself he would never let that happen again.

HELLO MUDDAH, HELLO FADDUH

WEARING A PLAIN WHITE T-SHIRT AND BLUE BERMUDA
shorts, Michael Perelstein periodically brushed mosquitos off his arms and
legs, being careful not to kill them. Thirtyish, balding, bespectacled, and
bucktoothed, the Rabbi/counselor stood on the brown grass, the ginor-
mous Lake Ellis and rolling, arboreal hills behind him.

He yelled jubilantly, "Shalom and welcome to Camp Ramah!"

A celebratory roar rose up from the crowd surrounding me: several
hundred, over-excited red-faced Jewish kids, all sitting cross-legged on
the grass.

The camp was started in Wisconsin, just after WWII. Amid the
aftermath of the Holocaust, Ramah's founders felt Jewish life was going to
need some reinforcing, a shoring up of the Jewish ranks and values, with
a renewed connection to Israel where Hebrew would be taught between
feeding farm animals, swimming, and playing giant Jenga.

Camp Ramah in the Berkshires wouldn't show up until 1964. But just
an hour and half from New York City, it soon became a juvenile microcosm
of the East coast Jewish people, Conservative mostly, but some Reform and
some Orthodox. If you went there one year, you went the next. And the
next and the next. Until you became counselor age and you did that. Your
sisters and your brothers did the same, as did your cousins and your second cousins. Once you married and had kids, they spent their summers
there. A never-ending cycle, if all went as planned.

I stared at the cement docks that stretched out like long tarmacs into the lake. After his initial welcome, I stopped listening to the Rabbi.

I was confused. I wasn't sure how I felt being there. In many ways, it was comforting. The people felt like home with their East coast accents, expressive mannerisms, and general Jewishness. I was already missing Mom and Dad, so that part felt good.

But I also missed Calvin and Boone, Becky, and my new life.

I also still might have been stoned.

After the rabbi introduced the summer's other dozen counselors, they told us our bunk building numbers, how to find them (for the newbies), and to go on and get settled. As we all stood, several kids smiled at me, said Shalom and patted me on the back. I smiled back. It wasn't awful. I could handle this, whatever it was going to be.

Besides the dozens of bunks, there were five main structures: the arts and crafts building, the Shul, the cafeteria, the auditorium, and the gym, complete with a basketball court. There were also several covered, bench areas for religious study, conversations, Jews hangin' with Jews. Closer to the lake there was a vegetable garden and a massive play area with rappelling walls, the aforementioned giant Jenga, and tetherball. Finally, scattered around the whole area, were two-feet-high log stools - for random sitting, I suppose.

The bunk exteriors were unremarkable: square, green and tan painted cabins. Boys on one side of the camp. Girls on the other. They broke us up alphabetically, so I was in Bunk #2.

Dusty, musty, and tediously wooden, the inside wasn't much bigger than your typical rubber room. And no shag carpeting. Two bunk beds were pushed up against one wall. Two fossilized dresser drawers were on the opposite wall. Not only had I never lived with boys my age, none of us had ever *been* our age before, so every single thing was new.

I took a bottom bunk. Above me was Samuel Blumenkrantz, a creepy, chubby fourteen-year-old from the Bronx, complete with *payot* and a high likelihood of becoming the very first Hasidic serial killer.

In the other bunk, on the bottom, was Frederick Ben-Zvi, a tiny, frightened thirteen-year-old from Philadelphia. He was mute by choice and might have been a jellyfish; we never knew for sure.

Finally, on the top bunk was Louis Brickner from Woodcliff Lakes, New Jersey, a tic-y kid with Tourette's Syndrome and an unnatural obsession with Bottle Caps, *the soda pop candy*.

There it was. Welcome to Camp Ramah, Bunk #2. A smelly, acned cluster of high- and low-pitched Jewish weirdness and inexperience.

I was unpacking my things when I heard a deep, rushed voice not more than an inch behind me.

"I'm Samuel."

Taken aback, I turned quickly. He was, indeed, right behind me, wearing that Jack-o-Lantern smile that I would never get used to. We were both about five feet, so he wasn't as terrifying as he might have been. I stepped to the side a tad, giving us some space.

"Hi," I answered. "I'm Yosef."

Louis came over. "Shalom," he said, his right eye blinking. "I'm Louis. I have Tourette's Syndrome. It's no *tsuris*, just a mild case; I don't curse or anything. I used to do psychoanalysis, now I take Haldol. It's a drug and it makes me sleepy and sometimes it doesn't work. I have these facial tics."

I nodded and smiled. "I'm Yosef."

"Hi, Yosef."

"I'm Samuel."

"I'm Louis."

"I know, I heard you," Samuel said, unnecessarily.

Neither Samuel, nor I, had heard of Tourette's, but I knew what a syndrome was, and looking at him, I was immediately glad I didn't suffer from it.

We all looked up at Frederick, our fourth. He was laying on his back, staring at the ceiling.

"Hi," I said, in his general direction.

"Hi," Samuel and Louis added.

Frederick waved a jittery hello and rolled onto his side, facing the wall.

The three of us shrugged and went back to unpacking.

"Camp Ramah! The best thing since sliced hallah!"

We all turned toward the door to see the Rabbi standing there with his arms outstretched. This, I would find out, was his go-to Jewish joke.

"How is everyone?!" he shouted.

"Good," I answered.

"Okay," said Louis.

The Rabbi walked in, grabbed each of our hands, and shook them vigorously.

"Shalom!"

"Shalom!"

"Shalom!"

Frederick had shot up when he heard the Rabbi come in and offered his hand for the shaking.

We said our Shaloms back as the Rabbi gazed at us like a proud, weepy father seeing his newborns for the first time. Now, up close, I could see he was covered in mosquito bites.

"What's your name, son?" he asked, his friendly eyes on me.

"Yosef Bamberger."

"Yosef," he repeated, smiling. "Meaning *he will add*, as in multiply, as in have babies, eventually, or in some interpretations, *adding* to people's lives."

"Yes," I said, remembering. I hadn't thought about any of that in a while.

"Yosef, did you bring your yarmulke?" the rabbi asked.

Whoops! Ever since that day at school when I yanked it off, thanks to Calvin, I had only worn it when I absolutely had to. Naturally, Dad and Gramps still wore theirs constantly, and Dad had tried to get me to wear mine more so over the last year. Instead, I wore it briefly so they could see, then I'd take it off again.

Not going to fly at Camp Ramah. The good news? I did have it. I turned around quickly, dug through my suitcase, found it, and put it on.

"Sorry."

"A beautiful blue," he said as he scratched a mosquito bite on his leg. "You boys get settled now. We'll see you later, okay?!"

As Rabbi Perelstein bounded out, Frederick jumped back into his bunk.

Samuel made a weird humph noise. "Why is he so young?"

"What do you mean?" Louis asked.

Samuel stared at him, like returning his question with another question was the most ridiculous response. "He's young for a Rabbi."

"I guess. I don't know," Louis said, shrugging and turning quickly back to his suitcase to hide his twitching mouth.

Samuel turned his attention to me. "Is your Rabbi back home young or old?"

"Old. Sorta." I was thinking of Rabbi Berkwitz, who was in his 40s; old to a thirteen-year-old.

"My rabbi is Rabbi Solomon. He's old," Samuel said in Louis's direction. "See what I mean?"

I turned back to unpack. We each had three drawers, which was fine. I didn't have much: one pair of brown pants, three white T-shirts, a white button-down for shul, a pair of swimming trunks, a full bottle of Maalox, and a pair of cut-off jeans shorts that were uneven, one side about an inch longer than the other. I could see Mom wildly, wielding a pair of scissors, furious and disappointed with her only son, maybe even cutting them lopsided on purpose.

I started thinking about Calvin and Boone and how they were probably wondering what happened to me. I would deal with that in the fall; maybe I'll say I was kidnapped and escaped just in time for school to start. Even though I missed our time together and studying the gospel of Jesus, I wondered if maybe this would be a good break from everything. Who knew? Either way, Jesus would wait. He was that kind of a guy. Oooh, mosquito spray! Yay! I guess Mom did still love me.

❧❧❧

The Shul reminded me of our synagogue back home - with the exception of walls. The camp synagogue was more of a giant carport with benches, with one large partition at the front featuring a wooden Jewish star, Jewish texts and a mural of the Israeli flag. No separation of sexes either, which was fine by me.

It was Friday night Shabbas and the place was jam-packed. Me and my three roommates were sitting in a row, each of us wearing our yarmulkes and now tallits as well. The Rabbi was leading us in singing a Hebrew hymn.

I can't recall the exact hymn now. And there's a good reason for that. Because, about mid-paean or so, my attention was taken by a girl sitting two rows in front of me, just to the right. She was hypnotic: jade green eyes, ski slope nose, lips like thick strips of pink pillows, wavy brown hair that floated past her elbows, and an adorable set of freckles on her left shoulder forming something close to the Little Dipper, a hint at her obvious celestial origins.

In that instant, I understood what they meant by love at first sight.

I also understood what it meant to have a boner.

Recent science tells us that boys can develop erections while still in the womb, which means I could've had my inaugural hard-on ... inside my mother. Considering the Oedipal implications of that, I like to think this one was my first. Of course, I had to have mine in a house of worship. A Jesus-laden acid trip wasn't enough; I could now add towering inferno of throbbing manliness to my growing list of things that should be avoided in synagogue. The good news was, I could tell it was big, which, considering my past penile frustrations, made me very, very happy.

I figured if I focused on the service, the engorgement would subside. But I couldn't keep my eyes off her. I was afraid if I did look away she might

269

disappear. It wouldn't be the first time a mirage appeared as a mythological siren. Also, it was possible I was hallucinating, having an acid flashback. Just as I had imagined my mother a witch, this was the antithesis.

Then, something else did catch my attention. Out of the corner of my eye, I saw Louis looking at me. Uh-oh.

"What?" I mouthed, perturbed.

"You stopped singing," he mouthed back, then started singing again himself.

Silly Louis. It wasn't possible to sing and be in love at the same time.

The service lasted another excruciating 30 minutes, of which I spent thinking about how to approach this goddess. And I prayed, oh God did I pray that, whenever I did finally say hello, my excitement would not be so obvious.

❧❦

The cafeteria was barn-like, but painted white, with A-frame rafters atop wood-planked walls and floors.

Holding my tray, I walked slowly among the hundreds of loud, ravenous children sitting at picnic tables covered with ugly, dark blue tablecloths. I had let my roomies go before me, so they'd already be seated when I arrived. That way, I could sit where I wanted. And, of course, that was wherever *she* was sitting.

Mercifully, I had finally become flaccid. Apparently, whitefish salad and Jell-O are not aphrodisiacs. The bad news: my hands were trembling, as was evidenced by my quivering dessert. I had to get Jell-O. I'd never been so nervous and motivated at the same time. There I go again, me and my dichotomous ways.

Suddenly, there she was sitting at a table surrounded by girls and other crushing boys sitting opposite. Undeterred, I approached the male side of the table, smiling, and trying to hide my intentions.

"Hey, y'all. Can I squeeze in?"

Unlike the students at Robertsville Junior High, Ramah campers were known for their convivial, inclusive reputation. Two older boys smiled back and moved apart as best they could as I jammed myself between them.

"Thanks," I said. They nodded, smiled back.

She was even more of a stunner close up. I tried to keep my composure and dug into my salad. There was a lot of chatter and stuffing of faces and I tried to look as nonchalant as possible. But I had a plan. If I could catch her eye, I would not avert my gaze, or even smile, I would look her right in those hypnotic eyes and introduce myself.

A half a salad later, I still had no opening. The table was getting louder, she was laughing at lot with the other kids, and worse, I could see she had, at the most, two more bites of her brownie.

"I'm Yosef!" I said suddenly, bits of chopped dill shooting from my mouth. They landed back in my salad, thank God. If anyone noticed, they didn't say anything. Several kids introduced themselves, only one of which I heard.

"Sarah," she said, her melodious voice matching every single, other mind-blowing thing about her.

"Hi, Sarah," I said, jittery.

She gifted me a short smile and resumed talking with her friends.

Okay, well that was something - a baby step. Far, far from enough.

Then it came to me. Maybe, if I listened in on her conversation, I could add something, or at the least, pick up something useful to use later. She was chatting with one girl in particular, Felice, I think her name was: a matzo ball shaped girl, with John Lennon glasses and enough pimples for all of us.

"I thought we were going to play volleyball after Hebrew," whined Felice.

"We can play volleyball tomorrow," Sarah assured her.

Hebrew, volleyball - noted. Hmm, interesting dialect. It had the Jewish East coast lilt, but I hadn't heard it before.

"It's so hot," Sarah said. "I just want to be in the lake ... all day."

"I guess so," Felice said, disappointed.

"Oooh!" Sarah shouted, suddenly excited.

"What?!"

"I think they're doing West Side Story this year."

"I thought we only did Jewish plays," Felice said confused.

"It's a mix."

"What's Western Story?"

"West Side Story," Sarah corrected.

"Oh. What's that?"

"You don't know what West Side Story is?!" Sarah asked, shocked.

"No." Felice lowered her head, embarrassed.

I know! I know! It's a movie musical about gangs, starring Natalie Wood, but she didn't really sing, someone sang for her! It happens to be one of my favorites. Absolute favorites!

Sarah didn't mean to upset her friend and answered nicely, "Oh, it's a movie, a musical. I want to try out for it."

"Oh, okay," Felice said. "Yeah, I guess I might've heard of it. When is it?"

"Sunday at seven, after dinner and prayers."

West Side Story auditions, 7pm. Noted.

"I'm not a good singer," Felice muttered under her breath.

"Okay. I'm going to do it," Sarah said, finishing her brownie and standing up. "Shalom, everybody!"

Upright, her body came into full view for the first time. She was one stone fox: tall, taller than me anyway, and thin, wearing a frilly, blue and white blouse over denim jeans shorts, patterned with colorful, geometric cherries. If cuteness could kill, I'd have keeled over that moment.

A minute later, everyone was gone but me. I had just begun my Jell-O. Eavesdropping is hard work and time-consuming, one can't gnaw on salad when trying to decipher important intel.

"Sarah," I said out loud. "Sarah," I repeated with a different pronunciation of the "a", exploring the beauty of it. I knew a lot of Sarahs back home. In Hebrew, it means a woman of high rank, a princess. Indeed.

⁕⁕⁕

I stood on the dark and scratched wood stage reading from a playbook, thank God, erectionless.

I was in my crooked shorts, T-shirt, and Converse, singing solo, my off-pitch voice sounding like something between whining and a poorly played violin.

"Don't waste your pucker on some all-day sucker!" I sang. "And don't try a toffee or cream. If you seek perfection in sugar confection, well there's something new on the scene. A mouth full of cheer, a sweet without peer. A musical morsel supreme! Toot sweets! Toot sweets! The candies you whistle, the whistles you eat. Toot sweets! Toot sweets! The eatable, tweetable treats!"

I lowered the book, smiling in relief, ecstatic I had gotten through it. I had given it my everything, if not more. Only because I was, thank God, auditioning opposite Sarah.

We hadn't spoken beforehand. Our names were called, and we went up on stage for our dual number. I couldn't have played it better. It was easy; I found her name on the sign-up sheet outside the auditorium. I signed up for the same time slot, same scene. Thankfully, only one Sarah was auditioning, as I didn't know her last name at that point.

Gorgeous in a knee-length tan dress and matching sandals, she stood straight and belted out her part. It was much shorter than mine.

"Toot sweets! Toot Sweets! The toot of a flute with the flavor of fruit! Toot sweets! Toot sweets! No longer need candy be mute!"

Wow. Mellifluous, beautiful, the delicate sounds of a siren. To me.

In reality, she probably sounded closer to a dying parakeet.

Hopeful, Sarah looked out to the director sitting in the front row, a lively - and we would soon find out - dishonest counselor.

"That was great, you two!" she shouted. "Thank you! We'll let you know!"

I smiled at Sarah. She shrugged.

"Thank you," I shouted back to the counselor and started off stage. Sarah followed.

As we walked up the aisle, I slowed down so we were side by side. I was so nervous I could've shat myself. There were no distractions now, Felice, whitefish salad, or otherwise. It was just her and I.

"You think we got it?" I asked.

"*Oy gevalt*! I don't think so! I sounded horrible!" she said loudly in that curious dialect, following with a high-pitched, machine gun giggle.

"I sounded horrible, too. I mean ... I don't mean ... I don't mean I think *you* were horrible. Sorry."

"No, it's fine. I think we were both pretty bad. I thought it was supposed to be West Side Story."

"So did I," I said.

"You did?"

"Uh, yeah. I ... think I read it somewhere."

"I read it somewhere too! I don't remember where."

We reached the exit and walked out. It was around 8pm, hot and humid as is the standard. Most of the kids were still out, playing, hanging out, talking.

I looked out, squinting past the water, toward the hills. Every evening around this time, if there were no clouds, the sunset would create a blinding shimmer off the lake.

Using her hand to shade her eyes from the glare, Sarah sighed. "I was not prepared for Chitty Chitty Bang Bang."

I chuckled. "Yeah, I think I like West Side Story better. The gangs, Bernardo, all those guys. It's pretty boss."

"Yeah, it's a groovy movie. Hey, that rhymes," she said, breaking into that giggle again.

Uh-oh. Here comes that hardened criminal again. Mr. Penis - always showing up at the most inopportune times.

"Hey, did you know Natalie Wood didn't even sing her parts?" she asked.

"Yeah. Her name was Marni Nixon."

"Wow, I can't believe you know that," she said, nodding, her gorgeous hair bouncing in rhythm with the pounding of my loins. "Yosef, right?"

She remembered!

"Yeah. What's your name, again?"

"Sarah Miller," she said.

I nodded, smiling, knowing my excitement would not stay invisible for long. Naturally, stopping the conversation was the last thing I wanted to do.

This was a whole new kind of stress. I had to think fast.

"Hey" I said, "do you, maybe, want to go swimming or something? It's so hot."

Sarah looked out at the lake, then back at me. "Sure."

"Cool. We'll change into our suits - meet on the dock in five minutes?"

"Cool," she said, then took off.

Success! So far.

My bunk wasn't far from the auditorium. I decided to run, hoping that might cool me off some.

I got there in a minute, ran in, bent over and put my hands on my knees, trying to catch my breath.

All three roommates were there, staring at me.

"Hey y'all," I said, walking quickly over to my drawers, trying to keep my protuberance hidden.

"Shalom," Louis and Samuel said at the same time, the former with his signature eye twitch. Frederick gave me a lame courtesy wave. If they noticed, they didn't let on.

I found my Maalox, took a couple tablets - just in case - then grabbed my swimsuit.

"What's doin'?" Samuel asked.

"Nothin'," I answered curtly, heading into the bathroom. The last thing I needed was one of these bozos to screw things up.

I shut the door and locked it, then stripped naked.

Looking down at my swollen self, I panicked, wondering how I was going to get rid of this thing before the big swim. Only a month ago, I was begging God and Jesus for growth, yet here I was today, begging for the opposite. Of course, the irony completely escaped me, as irony does for blossoming, little boys. Frustrated, and clearly unaware of any penile physiology, I tried pushing it down. Repeatedly.

That didn't work.

But it did enlighten me to something … touching it over and over felt pretty good.

Suddenly, a memory shot through my mind: I was seven and Mom was telling me about sex, and how when you're on top of a woman, something different than pee comes out of your penis. It's called sperm and looks like the inside of a cheese blintz, but helps make babies. She went on to explain how Dad should've been telling me all this, but she knew he wouldn't, so she had to, and I shouldn't blame her one day if she leaves out something important. It was a lesson on the birds, the bees, and the asshole (Dad).

A minute later, I had masturbated. Although a sticky milestone in every young boy's life, that first time was simply a means to an end. It wasn't particularly euphoric, more of a delightful spasm, a short tryst with a new friend.

I knew Sarah was probably waiting so I hurried and put on my suit. I looked around on the floor quickly, but couldn't find anything resembling ricotta cheese, or farmer's for that matter. Odd. Maybe Mom was wrong about that part - or I just didn't look close enough.

Sarah was already in the lake when I showed up. I ran down the long dock, my awkward, newly-pubescent body barely passing for thirteen. In the past few months, I hadn't grown taller as much as stretched. Apparently my skin didn't get the memo. My ribs were more pronounced, my neck longer, my knees knobbier. Any manly muscles I would see were still years away.

Also, I was partially blind, as I left my glasses back at the bunk. Like drinking and driving, swimming and glasses don't mix.

She waved as I got closer. "Yosef! Over here!" she shouted.

"I'm coming!" I shouted as I jumped in the six feet deep, murky water. I hit with a good splash - right in her face.

"Hey!" she screamed in delight, splashing me back.

"Hey back!" I screamed, also in delight, splashing her even harder.

This went on for a bit, until we eventually calmed down, floating and treading water a couple feet from each other.

"Where do you live?" she asked.

"Brooklyn, New York."

"Oh, I've heard of Brooklyn," she said, then cocked her head curiously.

"What?" I asked.

"Is that a Brooklyn accent?"

She wasn't just beautiful, she was perceptive. I hadn't given my newly acquired Southern accent a second thought. But she caught it.

"Yeah, it's Brooklyn. Canarsie, though," I said, with as Brooklyn an accent as I could muster. "Ever heard of Canarsie?"

She shook her head. "What's your synagogue called?"

"Ahavath."

"Oh, that's beautiful. It means love."

"I know," I nodded.

"Is it Orthodox?"

"Definitely," I answered.

"That's good," she said.

"Where do you live?" I asked.

"Boston," she said. "Ever heard of it?"

"Duh!" I screamed. We had a good chuckle.

"Our synagogue is called Young Israel of Brookline."

"That's a good name."

"I love it. Do you love your synagogue?"

"Oh, yeah, it's great. Got lots of friends there. The Rabbi's far out."

"How old are you?" she asked.

"Thirteen. Are you thirteen?"

"Fourteen," she said proudly.

"Oh," I said with some fear in my voice, hoping it wouldn't be a deal killer.

"I just turned fourteen," she said, as if she knew what I was thinking.

"Cool." I was getting winded from treading water, so I turned over and started floating on my back.

"Oh, that's a good idea," she said, and did the same. "You like it here so far?"

"Yeah, a lot," I said. "I mean I just got here, but it seems great."

"This is my second summer. It is wonderful, isn't it?"

"Very wonderful."

"It's kinda nice ..." She stopped, hesitating, but then went for it. "It's kinda nice getting away from my parents for a little bit. I mean, I love my parents, but we're, you know, we're pretty Orthodox, and that's really important to me, but it's also kinda nice to, you know, be somewhere not so religious."

"Sure," I agreed.

"My mom and I had a fight last winter. She wanted me to go to Israel this summer, but I wanted to come back here. I won, but I had to promise I would go next summer."

"Israel's cool," I said. "I mean, I've never been, but I'd like to go some time."

"Definitely," she nodded, then suddenly dove down into the water. This time, it was my turn to follow. We swam around in silence for a bit. And for a minute, I worried our relationship might be over. There was nothing stopping her from swimming off and hooking up with Felice, or whoever, on the other side of the dock.

"Boo!" she shouted, popping her head up right next to me.

"Ahh!" I shouted, shocked.

We continued to giggle gleefully and splash each other. It was repetitious, and immature, and never got old.

"Want to sit on the dock for awhile?" she asked.

"Sure," I said, grateful she got tired before I did.

We swam the fifteen feet or so to the dock, pulled ourselves up, and landed sitting barely an inch apart. Naturally, I started to feel that stirring down below again. I could thank her skin-tight, yellow one-piece for that. It showed off her just-arrived curves quite nicely.

Trying to stay calm, I gazed out at the wooded area on the far side of the lake.

"You know, last night," she said, turning toward me, "I was thinking about what the Rabbi said at services Saturday."

"What part?" I asked.

Sarah swung her legs, barely skimming the lake water with her perfect toes as she put her thoughts together.

"The part where he said that we're all created in the image of God, but also, we're supposed to be acting like God to other humans, in, you know, how we treat them, whether they're Jewish or not." She paused, tilted her head as she continued to remember slowly. "And then he said, you know, how we're supposed to be responsible for them, our fellow human beings, and respect them too; how it's all part of our relationship with God."

I let that soak in as the sun disappeared behind the tree line, casting a purplish blue to the sky and water, a muted twilight that added spellbinding to Sarah's many adjectives.

She was waiting for a response.

"Well, yeah ... what it means to be Jewish - it's not just about Jewish people; it's about all people."

Even though I essentially repeated what she said, and she repeated what the Rabbi said, the smile that appeared on that *punim* - I can still see it to this day.

If I thought Rachel from Brooklyn was beautiful, and I thought Becky's boobs were worth breaking body parts for, this girl, I realized now, without a doubt, would be the centerpiece of the Yosef Bamberger story.

She would be the mother of our children and the grandmother of our grandchildren.

And when I was ready for the great nothingness, she would hold my hand and stroke my face until I departed. Then she would lay her body next to mine and leave as well, for she was simply waiting for me to go first, her selflessness shining through until the very last moment.

⁂

After our God talk, Sarah had stood up abruptly, patted me oddly on the head, said Shalom, and ran off. I watched her until she folded into the dark, hoping she might suddenly run back to me, and we could talk and laugh till dawn.

Of course, that was forbidden at Camp Ramah, so I trudged back to my bunk. My roommates appeared to be asleep, so I slipped into my bed as quietly as I could.

I laid in bed, mindlessly scratching a dozen mosquito bites (the spray never worked for me), and replaying every moment of that evening in my head. She said this, then I said that, then she said this, and we laughed. I said this and that made her smile. I didn't miss a detail. A new erection was rearing its beautiful head, and I again, considered taking care of it in the bathroom. But I didn't want to wake anyone by getting up.

Remembering Mom had said the man laid on top of the woman, I turned onto my stomach and began making love to my gorgeous Sarah in absentia. Staring lovingly at my pillow and close to eruption, I sensed something, someone. There was no way I was stopping, so still in action, I managed to turn, and saw a head, an upside-down head, silhouetted above me. Frederick, the silent sea creature, was hanging over the bunk, staring at me. Apparently, I'd been shaking the bed more than I realized.

Turning quickly back to my pillow, with my mind's eye now toggling between Sarah's face and Frederick's, I had the second, and most ambiguous, orgasm of my life. And I wasn't quiet about it either. I half-expected the whole bunk to be staring at me in disgust.

But, I looked again, and there was no one. Still, knowing Frederick knew, I was embarrassed, terrifyingly so. The good news - I ejaculated.

Welcome to Yosef's creamery, soaking bedsheets since 1974.

Apparently, I was normal - physiologically, anyway - so I was relieved. I knew getting out of bed would certainly cause a stir, so I looked around for something to clean up with. Fortunately, my socks were right by the bed; my filthy, not-quite-white gym socks with the red and blue horizontal stripes. One of those would do just fine. Socks can be laundered. It's like it never happened.

As I commenced clean-up, I noticed the top bunk was shaking; I'd say maybe a 2.2 on the meat-beating scale. A minute later, I heard the first and only sound out of Frederick's mouth: a short, squeaky grunt.

The next morning as we were all getting up for morning prayer, I wondered if Frederick had gotten into it because I had excited him, or he was doing it in a kind of bonding brotherhood so I wouldn't be embarrassed. We never did become friendly, but I certainly had a new respect for him.

***

Rabbi Perelstein walked slowly between the packed pews, smiling as he sermonized Friday services.

"In the scheme of things, some of our Sabbath celebrations, and their origins, are really not that old. About 400 years ago - give or take - a mystic, named Solomon ben Moses Halevi Alkabets lived in a small Israeli town called Safed. Now, in the Talmud, the Sabbath is characterized not only as a time of prayer and celebration, but as a bride. Yes, a bride."

As we did during every service now, me and Sarah sat thigh to thigh. At the Rabbi's second mention of *bride*, I gave her the side eye, hoping to connect, but she was in deep, her gaze locked on our grand teacher of halacha.

That was fine. We were connecting plenty. What's more, over the several days since our lake date, I was getting used to being around her, so my groin was learning when and when not to be aroused.

"On Friday nights," the rabbi continued, "Alkabets would dress in the traditional white of the bridegroom and dance in the fields to greet the Sabbath! Now, besides being a mystic, this great man was also a musical person, and he created an ode to the Sabbath bride, Lekhah Dodi. We all know Lekhah Dodi, don't we?!"

A singular "Yes!" swelled up from the congregation, myself included. We all sung in Hebrew, not a one in the house needing the text.

Let us go, my beloved, to meet the bride, and let us welcome the presence of Shabbat.

Safeguard and remember in a single utterance, we were made to hear by the unified God,

God is one and God's Name is one. In fame and splendor and praiseful song...

It's not a short hymn, nine verses in all. And I remembered every of them. As I sang with volume and gusto, I felt a tinge of homesickness, missing my family as they had been my physical connection to this world of comfort. But with Sarah, with all my camp brothers and sisters, I felt safe, like I was floating in a massive bowl of warm matzo ball soup that Gram made before chopping her finger off.

I was feeling part of something bigger. Part of that giant Jewish love.

I finally managed to catch Sarah's eye, my one-day bride, and she gifted me with that knowing smile, a wink to our future where we'd create so many deep, spiritual, and romantic secrets.

Finally, at the last verse, the congregation rose and faced west toward the setting sun, to greet our Sabbath Bride.

Come in peace, crown of her husband, both in happiness and in jubi-
lation. Amidst the faithful of the treasured nation. Come O Bride! Come
O Bride!

⁂

"Tell me about your Bar Mitzvah."

Sarah and I were, once again, sitting on the dock at sunset, as we had so many evenings for weeks now. A few other kids were playing in the water, but we were mostly alone. Except for sleeping, there wasn't a lot of time we weren't together. Volleyball. Kosher chow time. Rappelling off a giant wooden scaffolding. It was terrifying but, if she did it, I had to. Vegetable gardening. Helping prepare the food in the kitchen. Basketball, singing, art classes, baking. And, of course, all services, Israeli history, and dancing the Hora.

Unfortunately, Samuel was sublimely jealous. He'd rotate insults throughout the day.

"You're one lucky putz."

"You're one lucky shmuck."

"You're one lucky schlemiel."

After schlemiel, he'd start again with putz, and so on. Considering his already odd demeanor, his drooling with envy wasn't exactly a shock, even if it wasn't a popular trait among the highly religious.

Louis wasn't as vocal, but every once in a while, he would insert a *yeah* in support of Samuel. As usual, Frederick kept quiet and I followed his lead, refusing to respond. I knew if I talked about it, the whole thing might disappear: Sarah, camp, my jealous roomies, all of it. That happens with dreams, and I wasn't sure this wasn't one, so I wasn't taking that chance.

This was the happiest I'd ever been.

Until this latest, lakeside request.

"What do you want to know about it?" I asked.

"Everything," Sarah said, taking my hand in hers.

Melting.

Up until that very moment, the only female hand I'd ever held was my mother's. And Sarah's could not have been more different: sweet and tender, so lacking in *tsures* or judgement. It was an astonishing feeling, exactly what I needed to fuel my dishonesty.

"Sure," I said nervously, "well, we were at my shul, Ahavath Achim Anshei."

"What's it like?" Sarah interrupted.

"Oh, it's very nice. And big. With white bricks."

"Stained-glass windows?"

"Lots."

With her other hand, she flipped her still wet hair out of her face. "What else?"

"Well, red carpet. We have lots of red carpet."

"It sounds beautiful," she said, squeezing my hand in approval.

"Our partition, you know the one separating the men from women, it's actually shelves with plants," I said, laughing.

"Oh, that's lovely!" Another squeeze. "Did a lot of people come?"

"Oh, sure. It was packed. All my relatives were there. All my friends."

"How did you do? Did you make any mistakes?" she asked with a giggle.

"One, I think. It was early in the service. Mostly, I did real good," I said.

"Well," she corrected, "you did well. What was your mistake?"

"Oh ... I don't ... I don't remember."

Oh no, please God, no. Could she tell? Were Skynyrd's lyrics written all over my face? Were there Macafee's Chicken Fried Steak pieces still in my lap? Had I been so astoundingly sacrilegious, she could still hear the echoes of my praising Jesus?

"Try to remember," she said.

I racked my brain. I knew my stuff - at one point, anyway - I just couldn't think of what part would sound like I wasn't lying.

Finally, I said slowly, "Well, it was part of my Haftarah. In the beginning."

She suddenly lowered her head. "I'm sorry."

I didn't say anything at first, unsure of what she was apologizing for.

"For what?" I asked, finally, carefully.

She looked at me again. "I can tell it upsets you to talk about it. I'm sorry. I didn't mean to push."

"Oh. It's okay. It wasn't that bad."

She straightened, joy returning. "Tell me about your party!"

"Oh! Yeah! The party was really groovy. I mean … we sang. And danced. And ate. Get this - my gram was so tired after about an hour, she fell asleep in her chair and fell out of it!"

"Oh no!" Sarah burst into laughter, immediately putting both hands over her mouth. It's not very kind or Jewish-like to laugh at someone else's suffering.

"She was fine," I assured her. "I picked her up and she was fine."

Sarah smiled. "Oy! Thank goodness."

Before I knew what was happening, her lips were on mine, her tongue pushing its way in like a SWAT team battering ram. I opened my mouth, more out of surrender and shock, than passion. She explored the roof of my mouth, then the lower part, around my teeth. It's like she was looking for something.

Then I gagged.

She stopped abruptly and pulled back. "Are you okay?"

"Yeah!" I said, like nothing happened.

"You just gagged," she retorted, her face crumpled like a can of Tab.

"I did? No, I love this! Really. Let's do it some more." Truth is, I did find it strange and intrusive, like she was trying to choke me. I wanted to enjoy it.

"Doesn't seem like you like it," she said, hurt.

"I do!" I said, loudly. "I just … I've never … I've never kissed anyone. I mean, you know, like this."

"Ohhhhhhhh," she said, in that drawn out, understanding way. "Well, I can teach you."

"Oh. That'd be great," I said, relieved.

"Okay. I will be your French kissing teacher for the day. You will call me Miss Miller."

I laughed, sat up straight and held an imaginary pencil. 'Yes, Miss Miller."

"So ... what you do is you close your eyes. Then, you open your mouth, put your lips on mine, then stick your tongue out, onto mine, and then we swish them around together."

"Swish them around?" I asked.

"Yeah. Kind of like little snakes, sliding around each other."

"Sliding snakes – okay," I said, nodding. "Why is it French? Are the snakes French?"

"I don't know. Oh!" She remembered something. "It's really good to imagine a song while you're kissing. It makes it more romantic."

"You mean like, sing a song, but in my head?"

"Yeah!"

I nodded, trying to think of one. "What song do you sing?"

"It changes - depends on who I'm kissing."

My eyes went buggy, and I backed up a little. "How many boys do you kiss?"

"I'm kidding!"

We shared a good laugh, then she said, "Baby I'm-a Want You."

"Oh! I know that song," I said, excited. "I think. Can we do the same song?"

"Definitely. Okay, ready to try again?"

I was a good student; this shouldn't be that hard. This time, I did as she instructed, closed my eyes, met her tongue with mine, and sang in my head, *Baby I'm a Want you, baby I'm a love you*. Her tutelage was excellent, as it didn't take long for me to get the hang of it.

Turns out, by kissing back, the gag reflex becomes dormant, so not only was I getting pretty good at it, I was starting to enjoy it: the sexy curves of her hard palate, her ultra-soft incisors, the stringy pieces of broccoli I was more than happy to jostle loose.

Of course, you-know-who had to show up. My uninvited downstairs roommate, always wanting attention.

A few minutes in, she stopped. "You're doing well," she said, and we went back at it.

Yes, thank you. I thought so too. I don't know how long we made out that night. However long it was, it wasn't long enough. It was pitch black when we departed, I know that. And we both had to sneak back to our bunks.

Once settled into bed, I grabbed one of my socks from the floor (there were always many to choose from), and I had passionate mattress sex with imaginary Sarah. Then Frederick did his thing afterwards. This had become the routine. But that particular night, it took me hours to get to sleep. My mouth and jaw were so sore, I thought I might have lockjaw. It worried me, not because I feared the Tetanus, but that I would never kiss Sarah again.

I was fine the next morning.

I couldn't wait to see her. I couldn't wait to hold her hand, to feel those cotton soft lips on mine. To commence the clash of the titan-tongues for yet another go.

But today, there was something else I had to do first, something part of me did want to do: call home. This was the first of two calls we had planned.

It went all right. Not great. Not horrible. I told Gram about the food; Gramps about the sports; Dad about the Hebrew and Israeli studies; Susan told me how she was pissed at me for leaving her alone with everyone. I did not speak with Mom. I guess she wasn't ready.

When I hung up, a hollow feeling rose up in my gut because of it. Until the next moment, when I thought of Sarah, and the feeling quickly vanished, not unlike doughnuts at an AA meeting.

Finally, it was evening, and Sarah and I commenced our thing - as we had been doing for days, skipping Friday of course, as that was the Sabbath. Yes, this would go down in history as the Frenchiest French kissing any Jewish people had ever engaged in.

And why is this night different from all other nights?

My hand made its way to her swimsuit-covered breast - that's why.

"Not yet," she whispered, as she gently relocated my paw back to my side. I thought of Becky's boobs and the boobs from Dad's dirty magazine, whoever they belonged to. They were my visual references. It was all so heady ...

Wait ... did she say *not yet*? Meaning there would be a time when it *would* be okay?

Yes! Yes, she did!

And I could wait, absolutely, I could wait.

Or could I? Our two months at Camp Ramah were coming to a close. We only had a week and a half left.

A rush of dread suddenly fell over me ... come to think of it, how would we continue our relationship a thousand miles away? We'd figure it out, that's how. We were meant to be together for life; with God's help, we would work it out. For the time being, I decided not to concern myself with it.

＊＊＊

The next day, after morning prayers and breakfast, I was headed back to my cabin. As I approached, I saw the rabbi standing out front. When I got closer, he turned toward me and waited till I got closer.

"Yosef," he said, narrowing his eyes.

"Hi Rabbi Perelstein," I said, stopping.

"Let's talk, you and me."

This couldn't be good. Why would the Rabbi want to speak to me? My head reeled with painful possibilities.

He sat down on one of the nearby log stools. "Sit," he said.

I sat on the stump next to him. He was still squinting at me.

"Is everything okay?" I asked.

He brushed off an annoying mosquito. "You've been returning late to your cabin."

Gulp. "Oh?" I asked, sounding guilty as hell. "I mean, what time is late?"

"9pm is lights out. You know that."

"Right. Sorry."

He glared at me a moment, not angry, but like he was trying to extricate some kind of truth from me.

"Yosef, are you doing drugs?"

"What?!"

"LSD? Something else? Heroin? Marijuana? Be truthful please."

"No! None of it! Rabbi! Why would you think that?!"

I was incensed and weighed telling him the truth - it was a lot better than what he was suggesting.

"Listen," he said, leaning forward, "your father, he told me you had some history with drugs."

"Oh! That?! No, that was ... that was ... a bad decision. It was an accident. It just happened once."

"You know we have a very rigid policy on drug use here. We permit their use only if it's for a legitimate medical reason and they're prescribed by your doctor. Otherwise, they're forbidden."

"I know that, Rabbi."

He nodded, still suspicious, then brushed away yet another bug. "Listen, a heightened state of consciousness is a good thing, but through *God*, and only through God, not through drugs."

"I'm not doing drugs, Rabbi. I swear," This was getting ridiculous.

"Do I need to search your bunk?"

"No! I was late because of Sarah, not drugs, okay?!"

And there it was.

The rabbi leaned back, his demeanor changing: not as accusatory, but just as punitive.

"Sarah Miller," he said, "right. You two have been spending a lot of time together."

"We just like each other. We probably just lost track of time."

"You're not doing drugs with her."

"No!"

"Yosef," he said, tentatively, "you know sex is also forbidden here."

I felt my face blush as I fixed my gaze on the ground. "I know, Rabbi."

Wanting out of the conversation as much as I did, he suddenly slapped his hands on his knees and shouted, "Okay!"

He stood up and pulled me into a bear hug. I hugged him back.

"Go," he said.

"See you later," I said, heading into my cabin to get ready to meet my real addiction.

In bed that night, after another mind-bending make-out session, I thought about my little exchange with the Rabbi. Someone had to have told on me. It was mostly dark by the time Sarah and I would return to our bunks, so the idea that he saw me was unlikely.

Whatever. It didn't matter at that point.

It was time for the grind. I grabbed a sock, put in on the bed, and turned onto my stomach.

As I began, I once again sensed Frederick's head hanging off the top bunk. It was odd because he hadn't done that in weeks. I stopped and looked up at him, expecting him to pop back into bed.

Instead, he jumped down.

Okay, that's super-freaky.

I sat up and pulled my blanket up to cover my nakedness. "What are you doing?" I angry-whispered. "Get back in bed."

He handed me a torn piece of notebook paper, then jumped back up into his bunk.

I figured it was some kind of note, but it was too dark to read, so I pulled up my underpants and went to the bathroom.

Closing the door, I turned on the light and read the pencil scratchings.

Samuel told on you.

"Oh, man," I said to myself, letting it soak in.

My anger building, I went back to bed and immediately started to consider how I would enact my revenge. I could do it this instant; wake up Samuel with a heavy shoulder shake, then punch him right in the nose. Unfortunately, if he ended up punching me back, a fat lip would definitely get in the way of future kissing. So that was out.

I could pull a *camp Luca Brasi*; find a nice, big, slimy bullfrog, cut its head off, and slip it into Samuel's bed. Me and my other roomies would watch him freak out while we laughed and pointed. Finding the frog would be easy; they were plentiful. But catching one and removing its head would be difficult. So that was out.

Since Samuel slept in the nude, I could steal all his clothes. The next day he'd have to either stay in bed or go about his camp activities naked. But that didn't seem fair to everyone else, as no one wanted to see Samuel naked. So that was out.

The last option: I could ignore him the rest of our time there, relaxing in the knowledge that I had the gorgeous girlfriend, and all he possessed was a very painful jealousy he tried to relieve by turning me in. His petty vengeance was a failure anyway, so why not let it go. Yes, this was the smart choice.

It's true sometimes revenge is best served cold, and sometimes, when you're dealing with a future serial killer, it's best not served at all. Not strangely, I learned something else that night. Anger coupled with thoughts of payback does not arouse me. That was the one night at camp I did not have an erection. And I appreciated the break.

The last day had finally arrived. The precious, closing hours of praying, volleyball, gardening, swimming, necking, and German chocolate cake.

Rabbi Perelstein stayed with the theme leading services that centered around eschatology, the Jewish doctrine surrounding the end of days. This involved the coming of a human messiah, a resurrection of the dead, and the belief that Jews and gentiles will unite during this time.

He also led several celebrations that day. There was a lot of singing and hugging, also weeping, mostly the girls, of course. We wept inside.

As you might expect, all I could think about was my end of days with the goddess Sarah. How would I get through the day knowing our tongues would not slow-dance to Bread that evening? How would I concentrate in school without having watched Sarah's adorable little toes endlessly kick the murky, Lake Ellis water? How would I praise Jesus when all I could think about was that half-second I touched her polyester-covered breast?

I had no answers.

As usual, we did everything together that last day. But when swim time came, and we approached each other on the dock, I noticed she wasn't in her suit. I became immediately nauseous, wishing I'd taken some precautionary Maalox. Had the withdrawal already begun?

As we drew closer, I saw she had a smile on her face.

"Meet me in the woods tonight," she whispered with a seductive tone I hadn't heard before. "Seven O'clock."

Before I could answer, she walked right past me and joined a female friend. As they went off giggling, I turned to watch her go.

Wait. What? Meet you in the woods?

Why would the woods suddenly be better than the lake?

Then, like a Three Stooges triple face slap, it struck me.

I could hear it in her voice ... she wants to have sex. With me!!! With me?

Oh my God. What else could it be? Unless she developed a sudden interest in bark rubbings, or the dietary habits of the Eastern Cottontail, this was about sex. We needed to be in the woods because we were going to do something no one should witness.

I sat on the dock so I could think it through, focus on looking like I knew what the fuck I was doing.

Okay, first thing to do was lay her down on the ground and start kissing; maybe make a joke to relax her, something about the man on the moon being a peeping Tom or something. Then slowly, while still kissing, grab both her breasts, and mount her. Then ... wait. How does the penis actually get inside? Does she put it in? Do I? Hope the hole's easy to find.

What if I can't find it?! Panic was setting in, tightening its grip around my throat as I ping-ponged between chills and hot flashes, fearing a slow, humiliating demise when I screwed up. Death by laughter. Hers. I already ruined one coming of age ritual. It was possible this was just the next event in my now predictable, self-sabotaging pattern. Perhaps I just wasn't meant to become a man. I could see it: I would pass my teens, twenties, thirties and into my nineties, with my unchanged voice, pubic fuzz, and half-grown, but always hard penis. My muscles would remain embryonic - I would never *fill out* as they say. Doctors would study me and publish papers with titles like: *Forever Young* and *Stranded on Puberty Island: The Yosef Bamberger Story*. Finally, once I died as a shriveled pubescent, they would stuff and display me at the Mutter Museum of Medical Oddities. And I would feel the shame from the afterlife. If there was one, of course.

Stop it! I suddenly yelled at myself.

Just ... stop.

I knew I had to push the doubt aside. Like Sisyphus, it would be an uphill battle. But unlike the mythological king, I would be victorious. Some mature part of me, way, way, deep down, realized it was the panic that would ruin it. I simply needed to stay calm and follow my instincts. I was going to be fine! I would soon be making sweet, sweet love to my Semitic

enchantress, and yes, it may be a bit awkward, but no, no sir, I would not
… fuck … this … up.

SANDY CONSIDERS

SANDY STOOD IN HER MOO-MOO, STARING OUT THE LIVING
room window, not believing what she was seeing. Panic began to spread
through her body like a restless cancer, hell-bent on debilitating her before
she could act. Any calming effect her medicine had had, certainly disappeared now.

"What are you looking at?" her mother asked.

Sandy only barely heard her mother, like she was speaking to her
from the other side of a tunnel.

"Sandy," Gertrude urged. Still nothing. "Sandy!"

"What?" Sandy finally said, turning around.

"What's so interesting out there?"

"Nothing," Sandy answered as she bolted out of the room and down
the hall.

Gertrude stood up and looked out the window. Couple of cars. Too
many trees. She shrugged.

"What is it?" Jack asked.

"Nothing," Gert said, letting her daughter's weirdness go.

Sandy ran into her bedroom, shut the door, and leaned against it. She
did a quick family overview:

Parents: Living room.

Susan: Her room.

Murray: Rec room.

Yosef: Camp.

Nodding to herself, she ripped off her moo-moo and threw on some jeans and a blouse. She looked at herself in the mirror, quickly brushed her Medusa-like hair, then threw on a bit of rouge, and some pink lipstick.

She decided going out the front door would be the least suspicious, so after slipping on a pair of gold-colored flats, she headed back down the hall toward the staircase.

"Where are you going?" her mother asked.

"Just out for a bit," Sandy answered, not stopping.

"We need milk," Gert said.

"Not going to the store, Mom. Just need some fresh air."

Sandy opened the front door and closed it quickly so she didn't have to hear her mother's response.

Speed-walking across the lawn, she snaked between the dozen or so yellow poplar trees, trying to figure out what she was going to say. It was a hot day so thick with moisture that she was drenched by the time she reached the red, rental sedan parked across the street. He had seen her coming, hard not to, so his window was down, and he was wearing that wry smile she had seen so many times before.

"Sandy," Burt said in that glorious English accent. "Wonderful to see you."

When she spotted him a year ago, it was so fleeting it had been easy to imagine him the way he was when their affair began. But now, up close, Sandy could see the folds and laugh lines in his face. His dimples were now filled with gray stubble, and those luscious black locks of his had thinned to wisps. He even had glasses now, John Lennon round-frames.

"Burt ... what ... what are you doing here?" Sandy asked, incredulous, shaking her head. "How'd you find me?"

"The letter you wrote - it had your return address," he said, chuckling uncomfortably.

When Sandy escaped to New York last spring, she had, again, spent some significant time spying and stalking him. Not that that was the reason she went in the first place - at least that's what she told herself. She didn't end up seeing him that visit, and when she returned, she did, indeed, write him a letter.

Burt turned more of his body toward her. "I wrote you back - several times, but you didn't respond, so ... I'm here."

"Burt, this is crazy. Why would you ... you can't be here!" Sandy said, getting more upset with every passing second, knowing her mother was now watching through the window. Unless she figured out a good cover story, there would be a firing squad of questions.

"Well, darling ... you did write me first," Burt said, smiling, hopeful. Then he quietly said, "It was a love letter, if I'm not mistaken."

"Burt ... I ... I you need to leave. My husband is home."

"Precisely why I didn't knock."

Sandy tried to breathe through her anxiety. "*Oy vey*. Okay, uh, meet me somewhere. Somewhere else. Let's see ... uh ..." Sandy tried to think. Even after all this time, she barely knew the town.

"Bruner's!" she blurted out. "It's uh, a grocery store."

"Like D'Agostino's?"

"Yes. It's just down the Oak Ridge Turnpike. There's not much but trees and fields before it, so it's easy to spot."

"Bruner's. Got it," he said, nodding.

Shake it off, she said to herself. Shake it off.

This is not a good thing.

Driving down the Turnpike, Sandy had this nagging urge to tell Burt everything.

Everything.

How when she dropped out of Julliard, her mother had set her up with Murray, and how he was a mensch, and that was nice, and good marriage material. She wanted to tell him how she always wondered, if she hadn't met Murray, would she have come to her senses and gone back to school to pursue her singing career. She wanted to tell him about living with aging parents, about the dizzying *mishegas* of raising three children, and the indescribable, inseverable attachment she had to each of them. She wanted to tell him about her long list of losses: her first born, her will to sing, her homeland, her only son who botched his entrance to manhood and was nothing less than a *shanda*. She wanted to tell him about all the drugs she was taking and how numbness was not just underrated, but exactly what she needed.

Then again, she thought, maybe she should tell him nothing.

A few minutes ago, she told Murray and her parents she was going to get milk and some other things. As expected, her parents asked who the man in the car was. Sandy said he was a gardener, wanted to cut the grass. They bought it.

She was close to Bruner's and had no clear idea what she going to say. The *tsuris* swirling around in her head was like a jumbled jigsaw puzzle; if she could just put the pieces together, she might have a coherent, convincing speech. Yes, it was her who stalked Burt - twice. It was her who wrote that first letter telling him how she thought of him often and missed what they had so many years ago. But that didn't mean she should take responsibility. It was motivated by the move, obviously, the tearing away from everything and almost everyone she knew. And that blame was, of course, on her husband.

Sandy pulled the Dart into the grocery store parking lot and, after surveying the lot for a minute, finally saw Burt parked around the side of the building. That was perfect. They would be unseen back there.

After parking alongside him, she got out and got into his car.

Turns out, it didn't matter that Sandy was unclear on what her response was going to be because, the second she sat down, Burt pulled her into a kiss. It was like she'd stepped into a time warp; suddenly she was back in New York in 1953. There was no betraying husband, no children to disappoint her, or rednecks to threaten her, just burning romance. At first it was only lips, then, ever-so-slowly, Burt nudged his tongue into her mouth. And she continued to fall. There was no considering no should I or shouldn't I. When a long, missing passion comes suddenly and shockingly back into one's life, heart tells head to fuck off.

After about a minute, they separated and Burt settled back into his seat, grinning. "Well, that was quite nice."

Sandy was in a daze, likely due to a combination of mother's little helper and the time warp that was now so cruelly over. Burt may have been decades older, but he still had those loving, gentle eyes, and that professor smell she loved so dearly. For some reason she never figured out, he always gave her the feeling that she was home, a British man with a British accent, many years her senior, but still.

She rubbed her eyes, trying to extricate herself from his spell and looking for words that had some kind of meaning, something she could say that would either get her out of this mess, or further into it.

"Sandy, darling," Burt said quietly, "I don't know how to say this without sounding like a cheesy romance novel or something, but ... I never stopped being in love with you. It's daft, I know."

Sandy gasped, her mouth trembling. She felt herself ready to explode into tears, but she stayed in control. She already felt weak enough.

"I guess I just pushed it down," he said. "You were so much younger than me. My job was on the line ... anyway."

Sandy nodded slightly.

"When I received your letter, I was so delighted. Hopeful. Of course, I realized by your lack of responses afterward, you had probably changed your mind. I figured, maybe a road trip to see you would ... I don't know." He paused and looked out the window at the white-painted brick wall. "Do you think it's too late?"

Sandy looked away as well, down into her lap. She hadn't said a word since she entered the car. Unusual for her, to say the least. Then, suddenly, finally, in an instant, she realized what she had to do.

She grabbed his head with both hands, and pulled him into another, more intense kiss; this one, all of her own making.

SKIN ON SKIN

IT WAS YET ANOTHER WARM, SOUPY EVENING, THE KIND where the moisture's so thick it slows travel. Of course, nothing could stop me from my rendezvous that evening.

Around 8pm, in my cockeyed cutoffs, white T-shirt, and yarmulke, I headed across camp. At Camp Ramah, there was a lot of what most would call *the woods*, but there was only one *the woods* that campers actually called *the woods*. And that was behind the auditorium, the very same building where I met Sarah, and where Jeremy and Jemima would soon be flying off in a fantastical car to save their grandfather.

I figured getting there early was smart. I could choose the perfect tree to lean against. The perfect patch of mulch to lay her down upon. Also, I would make sure it was far enough up the hill to where no one could see us.

When I reached the auditorium, I nonchalantly walked around the side of the building, as if I was curious what might be there of interest. After making sure no one was watching me, I bolted up into the trees.

I knew I couldn't go too far up or Sarah wouldn't be able to find me, so I stopped about 20 feet in or so, found a tree and a patch that would do, sat, and waited.

I started to wonder if she might not show, but within a few minutes, there she was, trudging up the hill toward me. She was early too! This boded well for consensual sex, I thought. I started flailing my arms around like a car dealer sky dancer.

She laughed, mouthing, "Relax, I can see you."

And there she was right in front of me: pink, flowery blouse, yellow shorts, big smile. Perfect, as always.

"Hi," I said, my presumptuous erection growing in anticipation.

She immediately grabbed my shoulders and started kissing. Not even so much as a hello.

After a few minutes, we plopped our toushees down on the ground, and yes, you guessed it, we kissed some more.

She finally pulled from my lips and gazed at me with those eyes of greeny goodness.

"I'm going to miss you so much," she said.

"Me too. So much," I agreed.

She grabbed my head and started kissing me again, then stopped again.

"We can talk on the phone. And write letters," she said, nodding and agreeing with herself.

"Definitely!" I shouted ... right before my face froze in despair.

I didn't have a New York phone number. Or address. If I gave her our old Brooklyn address, and she wrote, I wouldn't even receive the letters - unless we were still getting forwarded mail. Wait, I guess phone calls could work. I doubt she'd recognize a Tennessee area code vs. a Brooklyn one. Better yet, I could just call *her*, and she'd never even have to call me.

Or ... I could just tell her the truth. I would have to at some point, although probably best to wait till we were engaged.

If I did it now, I could definitely kiss sex goodbye. Man, was I swollen.

"What's wrong?" Sarah asked.

"Oh, nothing. I'm just ... real sad that I won't see you for a while."

"We don't live that far from each other," she said. "I know! We can meet halfway between Boston and New York! Then next summer, we'll be back here!"

Relieved, she grabbed me and we started kissing again.

She stopped again, needing affirmation, I guess. "Right?!"

"Right!" I shouted and started kissing her again.

I stopped this time. "As soon as I graduate high school … it's only five more years, I'll go to college in Boston. MIT's there, right?"

She giggled and nodded.

I continued, "You can go to college in Boston, right?"

"Emerson! I'm going to Emerson."

"Emerson it is!" I screamed. "After college, we'll get married, have a bunch of kids, we can go to your synagogue, and we'll pray a lot, and invite my parents to the High Holidays, and Sukkah, and Hanukkah, and we'll root for the … who's the baseball team?"

"Red Sox, silly!" she screamed, laughing in delight.

"We'll root for the Red Sox!" I screamed back, pulling her into yet, another kiss.

Our tongues darted in and out of each other's mouths with renewed vigor, and it dawned on me: She didn't flinch when I said we'd get married and have kids. She really did feel the way I felt.

This was unmistakable, unarguable, God-level love.

Suddenly, something made me jump. Either some creepy forest creature was squeezing my crotch or - it was Sarah.

"It's okay," she mumbled, still kissing me.

I grunted something unintelligible back.

Then, reaching over with both hands, she opened my pants and started massaging me. I wanted to keep kissing her, but my head fell backward, and my eyelids started fluttering like a blissed-out hummingbird. It was a true moment of sexual, sensual Zen. Nothing else existed.

It was one of those things that can never be explained, like how Andre The Giant could've been 6'3" and 240 pounds at twelve-years-old. Or how Pablo Escobar thought it prudent to spend $2500 per month on the rubber bands that wrapped his money. Or that light from stars can be older than the human race. This was simply her skin on my penis, yet it was one of the most, mind-bending feelings I've ever felt. To this day. Was the inside of her hand so different than the inside of mine? Was it simply because I was having sex with someone other than myself? Or was it because it was my first love?

Whatever it was, it was over quickly.

Afterward, she smiled, kissed me once on the lips - no tongue - and got up.

"Shalom, Yosef," she said, sweetly. And with that, she walked back down the wooded hill and vanished around the side of the auditorium.

I knew I didn't have to rush back to my cabin as it was the last night, and the rabbi wouldn't care since another summer was done. I don't recall how long I stayed up on that hill, my pants moist with happiness, but I soon began to realize something profound: Sarah was my new connection to God. My God. My Jewish God. She was my obvious destiny. I would have to tell Calvin and Boone I was no longer interested in being a Southern Baptist - I was Jewish again and my Jewish girlfriend (fiancé) and I were going to make a Jewish home in Boston. It was only a matter of time.

I couldn't let go.

But I had to. There were hundreds of Jewish kids screaming their goodbyes. Not to mention several of them snickering at us, Samuel being one, of course. I took an inexhaustible amount of pleasure having had sex - knowing Sammy the Snake had not, and probably would not for many years. And I would surmise, due to our longer than normal hug, he knew.

Sarah pulled out of it first. I almost told her I loved her, right then and there. But something stopped me. Maybe it was due to the fact that was I was an imposter and expressing my true feelings would come out hollow. Or maybe it was because I feared she wouldn't return the sentiment.

As she turned to get on her bus, a wave of sadness almost knocked me into the Berkshire dirt. How would I get through the day without seeing or talking to her? How would I concentrate on schoolwork? How would I not talk about her so incessantly that whoever was listening wouldn't want to kick me in my obsessed, lovestruck balls?

I said goodbye to Louis, Frederick, and Rabbi Perelstein. Only hand-shakes, like men. I said goodbye to Camp Ramah, thanking her for the memories, and promising I'd see her the following year. And Dad was there to pick me up.

I dropped into the passenger seat with a big smile and jubilant energy. Dad smiled back, excited.

"There he is," he said lovingly, kissing me on my forehead.

"Hey, Dad," I said, settling in.

"You look good. Happy," he said, driving off.

That's when I realized this whole thing ended up a win-win-win-win-win-win-win. Mom, Dad, Gram, Gramps, Rabbi Berkwitz, the two meshuggeners, they all got what they wanted. They got their sweet, funny, very Jewish Yosef back. And it was fine by me. It's true, I was back, and I was delighted to be. It felt right.

I talked non-stop for about an hour. I told him about Israeli studies, the mostly outdoors shul, the mosquito-loving rabbi, the lake, the tree stump chairs, and *Chitty Chitty Bang Bang. Oh, and by the way, I met a girl named Sarah, from Boston.* Considering Dad's penchant for booby magazines, he might have appreciated if I had included my favorite thirty-four seconds of the summer, but it didn't really seem appropriate amongst the Judaic subject matter. My judgement was improving.

I could tell he was pleased by his incessant smiling.

I went on to tell him about my plan. A plan I had developed only minutes ago while I was waving goodbye to my significant other.

Once returning home, I would write apology letters to every single person who attended my Bar Mayhem. Then, with him and Mom and Rabbi Giraffe, we'd schedule a day to try it again. If the people who came the first time see it in their hearts to forgive me, and attend again, I would be eternally grateful.

He told me Mom would be ecstatic to hear all this. No shit, Schlemiel.

WHO LICKED THE RED OFF YOUR CANDY?

ANCIENT RABBIS BELIEVED THAT, WHEN IT CAME TO SIN, there was a debt to pay and only the sinner could instigate that payment. It's known as *teshuvah* (Hebrew for repentance). Meanwhile, the person who was sinned upon was required to waive that payment: forgiveness, or *Kaphar* in Hebrew. Those ancient Jews, they sure had it all figured out.

Although Dad seemed good with my repentance plan, Mom might be another story.

And since we didn't talk when I called from camp either time, I really had no idea what to expect.

When Dad and I got home, Mom was standing at the top of the split staircase, the queen of the hill: hands on hips, imposing breasts, intolerable, half-shut eyes, moo-moo.

"We're home!" Dad shouted.

As we walked up the stairs to the living room, Gram, Gramps, and Susan joined Mom on the landing. I decided to hug Mom last, just in case she was still furious. She wasn't exactly known for letting things go, and I figured keeping any maternal abandonment at the end might make me feel, oh, I don't know, less abandoned.

Susan was first. It came with a whisper in my ear. "Thanks a lot for leaving me alone with these dorks all summer." I guess she forgot she already gave me shit for that.

I whispered back, "My pleasure."

Gram hugged my face, kissed me on the lips. Gramps and I threw a couple pulled punches, then fell into a hug.

Before I could get to Mom, Dad said, "Zees, tell everyone what you told me in the car earlier. You know ... about the future." He was smiling, nodding with a head slant, not wanting to steal my thunder - or light drizzle, depending on how it was perceived.

I hadn't planned on telling everyone right that second, but it made sense to say it before I went in for the Mom hug. I was nervous, but these were my people. Even with all the *tsures*, there was love in the room.

"Okay. Well, I uh, I want to apologize ... and I want to ask everyone to forgive me, please, for what happened. I, uh, I'm going to send letters, sorry letters, letters to everyone that came to my Bar Mitzvah, and also, uh, ask them if they might come when I try it again. I want to make a date to, you know ... try it again."

Susan burst out in shocked laughter.

All eyes were shocked and locked on me. Not because of what I said, but *how* I said it. You see, those last three words - *try it again* - they cracked like an Oak branch after an ice storm, loud and cringey, one of the many grotesque by-products of adolescence.

Yes, apparently, my voice was, starting today, headed toward the lower pitches of men, never to be the same again. As the echo of it floated in the air, no one said anything for a few moments, like they were waiting for the sound to fade. At least the slight Southern accent I had acquired had dissipated with my camp experience. I don't think anyone could've handled both.

"Yosef," Gram said, "of course, we forgive you. Family always forgives."

"Look who's turning into a man right before our eyes!" Gramps added, acknowledging the elephant in the room.

"It's fine, Yo-yo," Susan said, laughing again, as she headed downstairs.

Mom moved closer, put her arm around me, and smiled for the first time I'd seen in a long, long time. "I'll help you write the letters."

My first day of 8th grade, I strutted into the lunchroom with a bigger swagger than Abdullah the Butcher in a Brioni pinstripe. I was a few inches taller, my voice was getting lower every day, my penis continued to grow, and most importantly, I was now fully unvirginized.

I was different. I knew the place. I knew the people. Sure, I heard a couple of them whisper a shitty thing or two, due to the fact that I was wearing my yarmulke again. But I didn't care. I wasn't embarrassed to be Jewish. Why would I be when the most beautiful Jewess on the planet was my girlfriend.

It had been a week since I'd returned. I had tried calling Sarah several times over the past weekend, but she was unavailable. We'd only been home a little while, so I figured she was just settling back into her routine. So was I. It was fine.

I was happy to be out of my morning classes, as they had gone in slow motion: Homeroom, Science, Algebra, Spanish. Now, with my bag lunch in hand, I stood, surveying the place for Calvin. I didn't see him and assumed he was on his way. I had a vague idea of what I was going to tell him, but every time I started to think it through, Sarah would pop into my mind, and the Calvin/Boone storyline would evaporate.

"Hey, dumbass!" He was right behind me.

I turned to him with the gummy grin of a boy who no longer sees himself as a boy.

There he was with his sneering smile, post-summer skin peeling from sunburn, and even bigger body, as if he had to grow some so I wouldn't catch up to him.

"Hey, man." It was good to see him, but there was some fear attached to that warm feeling - aka the Boone component. I still wanted desperately to continue our friendship, but Calvin would have to accept me for who I was: a Jew. A Jew in love.

"Your voice! Ah man! Hahah!" he screamed. "Where the fuckin' hell you been, anyway?!"

"Let's sit down. I'll tell you," I said laughing.

As we did, I opened my kosher lunch; salami on white bread with mustard. Calvin started gnawing on his cafeteria burger.

"You fuckin' disappeared, man! Me and Daddy figured they done sent you off to military school or jail or some shit."

"Jail?! Why would I go to jail?"

"I don't know. Breaking some damn Jew laws or somethin'?"

"Ha!" I screamed. Of course, he was right to some extent.

"We didn't know what happened, man. I went to your house, like, three times. Threw rocks on your window. I even called. Your mama wouldn't tell me nothin'. Just told me to quit callin'."

"Sorry," I said, shaking my head, embarrassed.

"So where the Hell were you, man?"

"Summer camp. In the Berkshires."

"Where the Hell's that?"

"Doesn't matter," I said, then lowering my voice, "I had sex."

Calvin jerked his head back, slamming his cheeseburger onto his plate, splashing ketchup everywhere. "You did not!"

I lost it laughing. "I did! I had sex. We're in love. Her name's Sarah. She's so beautiful. You should see her. We're going to get married."

We looked like a murder scene. Ketchup everywhere. Calvin's jaws and eyes frozen open, like rigor mortis was setting in.

"I know, it's wild, right?"

"No shit?" he asked, unrhetorically.

"No shit."

Suddenly, Calvin jumped up out of his seat and put his hands out, palms up. "Well, give me some damn skin, man!"

I jumped up and slapped his hands as hard as I could. "Yeah!" I shouted.

"All right!" he screamed back.

Students looked over, wondering what was so fantastic. I just smiled at them. They didn't need to know, but if they found out later, that was fine with me.

As we sat back down, Calvin leaned in. "So, what kind of, you know, what kind of sex? I mean, you know, what, she suck ya? You stick it in her?"

"I'm not telling you any of that!" I laughed, completely loving the fact that I had had sex before he did.

"Ah, shit, man! Fine." Then, clown-like, as if it wasn't a big deal, he said, "Congratulations."

"Thank you," I joked back.

Calvin took a big jealous bite of his burger and chewed angrily. It didn't surprise me, or bother me really. All in all, it was a satisfying acknowledgment of my ever-increasing machismo.

"Shit! Forgot to tell ya," he blurted out suddenly. "I got a motorcycle! I mean, it's not new or anything; it's a Honda 125. Used. Runs good, though. Daddy and I are fixin' it up."

"Wow, that's cool, man," I said.

"Hell, yeah!"

I took a bite of my sandwich.

"Hey, Calvin, is your dad, you know, mad at me? You know, mad that I left?"

"Darn tootin'. When you started not showin' up for bible practice and everything, he lost it. Started throwin' shit around the house, all kinds of crap." A disturbing thought, or memory perhaps, hit Calvin that moment. He chased it off with another bite of food.

"Ah fuck it, man!" Calvin said, excited. "You're back now! We'll get back to bible study and what not. Drinkin' shine. Maybe Becky'll even let us touch her boobs!" he roared.

I nodded, thinking about Boone.

"What?" he said, noticing.

"Sorry. I don't, I don't know what to do. I mean about your dad. I'm … Jewish … again." I pointed to my yarmulke. "I can't do all that Jesus stuff again."

"Sure you can, man," he said, trying to wish away what I just said. "Stupid beanie cap don't mean anything."

"No, really, Calvin. I can't. Sarah wouldn't be okay with it, I know. Can't we just, you know, hang out in the woods? Shoot squirrel. I can watch you smoke pot. We can definitely still hang out with Becky."

"Well, I'll tell ya, Daddy's gonna be pissed off if he knows you're back and we ain't doin' bible study."

"I know. I just … I can't." It was all I could think to say.

Calvin stopped eating and stood up. He gazed down on me, more upset than I think I'd ever seen him.

"Don't do this, man."

I looked up at him. I felt weak, and my stomach lurched. I felt my front pocket for my Maalox. I had forgotten them.

"Jesus is my life, man. If you ain't gonna do that with me and Daddy, then … shit, I don't know what."

He walked off slowly, heading for the food tray conveyor belt. I tried to think of something to say that could fix it, but I had nothing. A foot away and without stopping, Calvin threw his tray on the belt. The plastic plates and silverware banged and clanged, going everywhere. Dozens of students turned to see what the ruckus was. Calvin just kept moving.

I sat, staring after him. It was so unfair that I couldn't have both my Jewishness and Calvin as a buddy. I wanted so badly to run after him and tell him that it was fine, that I'll let Jesus back in my life. We can keep it a secret like before.

But I'd already lied to Sarah about where I lived and my Bar Mitzvah. I couldn't have yet another lie. The biggest lie.

But … Calvin.

But … Sarah.

But … Calvin.

But ... Sarah.

I could feel the rage building up: volcanic, unrestrained. The last time I felt this much wrath was when Dad told us about the move. I destroyed my room that day.

Fortunately, I had to get to class. Otherwise, I might've destroyed the cafeteria and created yet another broken situation for myself.

⁕⁕⁕

Apparently, suppressing my anger turned it to sadness. Through the rest of the day, the only thing keeping my blubbering at bay were my persistent thoughts of the goddess Sarah. Her nose in History. Her feet in Science. Her tongue in Geography. Pieces of Sarah, each getting me through the dragging afternoon.

Naturally, Calvin would tell Boone about my return and my decision. I could see his face. His missing teeth, the thick veins that would rise up in his neck when he got emotional. Would he come after me? Would he hurt me or my family?

No, I decided. I trusted in God, my Jewish God, Elohim, that me and mine would be safe. Because I was doing the right thing.

The big orange bus finally pulled up to my stop, and I jumped off, rushing home to try Sarah yet again.

Once inside the house, I flew past Gram and Gramps in the living room, then ran into the kitchen nook. I grabbed the phone, opened the sliding glass door, stepped out onto the wooden deck, closed the door behind me - gently as not to damage the phone cord - and dialed the number I had, of course, memorized.

This time, she picked up. "Hello?"

I felt better immediately. "Shalom Sarah! It's Yosef."

"Oh, shalom, Yosef!" She sounded happy to hear from me, thank God. "You sound different, your voice."

"Oh, yeah, well, you know ... that happens to men my age." I cleared my throat.

She laughed. "Yes, that's true. How are you?"

"Oh, you know, doing fine. How are you?"

"Doing fine. How's Brooklyn?"

"Boring - without you," I said, trying to drive the conversation elsewhere.

"That's sweet," she said, giggling.

"I really miss you."

"I miss you, too. Great summer, wasn't it?"

I closed my eyes so I could imagine her beside me. "Really great summer," I said dreamily.

There was an awkward pause.

"Are you happy to be back at your Shul?" I asked.

"Oh, yeah! I missed everybody. My rabbi is the best."

"Hey, I'm thinking about growing *payot*," I said, knowing she'd be impressed.

"Really?" she asked, surprised.

"Yeah," I said, surprised she was surprised. "I thought maybe it'd be a good way to increase my commitment to God."

"Well ... that's great, Yosef. You know, I really should get going," she said. "I have a bunch of homework. It was really groovy talking to you."

"I wish I could kiss you goodbye," I whispered.

She giggled and made a kissing sound over the phone. I did it back. The antithesis of Frenching, but still glorious.

"Shalom, Yosef," she said.

"Shalom, Sarah," I replied.

After she hung up, the dial tone shot through my head like a death ray - killing the sound of her. This - this phone thing - was not going to work.

❧❧❧

"Dear so and so,

I'm writing this letter to you in hopes that you can find it in your heart to forgive me for what happened last spring. As

God is my witness, I am so truly sorry. So very, very sorry for what happened. It was a terrible thing and I know it must have been difficult for you to witness and hear. I want you to know that I am studying and practicing very hard in order to try it again. If you can see past that horrific day in May, I would like for you to come back to Oak Ridge for my real Bar Mitzvah. Please join us in a celebration as I, Yosef Bamberger am, once again, called to the Torah as Bar Mitzvah, January 9th, 4pm.

With sincere apologies and gratitude,

Yosef Bamberger"

I put the letter on the kitchen table and sighed. "How does it sound?"

"Perfect," Mom said. Gram and Gramps both nodded in agreement.

You can be sure the reason it was *perfect* was because Mom and Gram rewrote it a few dozen times. My original version was half the length, half as serious and half as apologetic. But it didn't matter what I thought. This wasn't for me.

But it was honest. I had been studying a lot with the rancid Cantor David. I'd been going over everything by myself in my room every night. (Followed, of course, by my regular withdrawals from the Sarah yank bank.). I was definitely ready, even though we were a good seven or so weeks away. The aforementioned *payot* I was growing was even starting to come in nicely.

After each received my letter, both meshuggeners called me to tell me they couldn't make it down this time. I understood. They said they could tell I had taken drugs that day, and they even thought it was kind of funny.

Yes, it was the drug's fault - clearly.

I also spoke to Lynn who was planning on coming. She told me she wouldn't miss it for the world.

I wanted so badly to invite Sarah. One night in bed, I went through it in my head.

"Shalom, my love, It's Yosef."

"Yosef, shalom!! Oh, how I love hearing your voice."

"And me yours, Sarah."

"And I hate being without you."

"Being without you is like matzo without the crunch."

"Like the Mishnah without the Gemara!"

"Sarah, my love, I have something to tell you."

"What is it, love?"

"After I left you at Camp Ramah, we moved from Brooklyn to a small town in Tennessee where I met a hillbilly who made me take LSD right before my Bar Mitzvah. I tripped so hard I ruined the ceremony, all while praising Jesus. But there's good news! I am trying once again this coming January. Will you come? I know the love we share is too deep for anything to wreck it."

Dial tone.

Come to think of it, there's really no reason she had to be there. Once I'd been Bar Mitzvahed, the story I told her at camp wouldn't be so far from the truth.

Honesty is so important in relationships.

The more relevant question was: How will Sarah and I get together again?

Waiting for next summer was not going to work. Neither of us would make it till then. Deprivation from the kind of love we shared could easily kill you.

So, I developed a plan. During the High Holidays in the coming weeks, I would celebrate with everyone in Oak Ridge. We'd go to Shul, and of course, I'd keep practicing for my big day. I'd be an all-around good Jewish boy - as I had been for a while now. Then, when Mom and Dad were in a good mood celebrating the new year, I'd ask them if, on Hanukkah, I could take a bus to Boston to see my future betrothed. Maybe, I'd even surprise Sarah.

The days clicked by. Rosh Hashanah arrived, aka *the day of blasting.* Although it may sound like a day when Jewish miners blow up mountains with dynamite, it's actually the Jewish new year, the word *blasting* invoked in excitement and celebration of that fact. Jews reflect and pray during this time.

As they do on Yom Kippur, the day of atonement and fasting. That day came not long after Rosh Hashanah.

That morning, as we all began our starvation, Mom made sure to remind me I had a lot to atone for. I was about to remark that I could only fast so much. How does someone not eat more than someone else not eat? But, I didn't say a word, remembering I needed to stay well behaved. She was also right.

The next day, for our Yom Kippur break-fast meal, Susan, Mom, and myself made various kosher foods from the things we found at Bruners, our local grocery store. We also still had some frozen, New York bagels Mom had brought back from H&H, the famous bagel joint named for Puerto Rican, goyim business owners Helmer and Hector.

We were about halfway into the meal. Everyone was chewing and chattering. Gram was lamenting the Holocaust. Gramps listened to her, nodding robustly in agreement, always making sure she saw him doing so. Mom and Dad were talking about Lynn and how much they wished she was there. Susan was eating quietly, deep in thought about something that I'm sure had nothing to do with atonement.

It was time to pop the question.

"Mom, Dad, I'd really like to see Sarah."

"You call her fifteen times a day. That's not enough?" Mom asked, her mouth full of potato cheese bake.

"I don't call her fifteen times ... okay, maybe, but the reason I call her so much is she's never there! I've only talked to her, like, once since I've been back. We really want to see each other. Is that such a bad thing?"

"She's pretty, yes?" Gramps asked for the umpteenth time.

"She's beautiful, Gramps," I answered, as I did every time.

Susan rolled her eyes. "You're barely thirteen. How would you see her?"

"I'll take a bus," I said.

"A bus?" literally everyone said, in unison.

"I thought she lived in Boston," Mom said, scowling.

"Yeah, so?" I said, feeling the fight in me growing. "It's only 948.5 miles."

"Zees," Dad said, "we all know how important she is to you, but that's a long trip. Maybe you'll go back to Camp Ramah next summer. I'm sure she'll be there."

"I can't wait that long! We can't wait that long. Come on, Dad. I was thinking around Hanukkah. I can pay for it myself from the Bar Mitzvah money I'll get!"

"Your Bar Mitzvah's *after* Hanukkah," Susan said.

"What thirteen-year-old takes a bus by himself?" Gram asked.

"Susan can go with me!"

"Dream on, Spaz," Susan said, laughing.

"Shut up!" I shouted at her.

"Hey, hey, hey!" Mom yelled, raising her hands. "Yosef, what your father said: We can talk about you going back to Camp Ramah next summer. End of story."

Nothing like a giant helping of desperation, smothered in rage, to break the fast! Enjoy Yosef!

I was about to blow when Dad piped up again.

"Tell you what," he said, looking at Mom for approval, "if your Bar Mitzvah goes well, and you keep your grades up, maybe I'll take you up there around Pesach."

"That's not till April!" I screamed.

"Calm down, please," Mom said, "let's just see how it goes in January. We'll make a decision then."

"We'll make a decision then," Gramps said, nodding and smiling at me.

"I'm done," Mom said, putting her napkin on her plate, pushing her chair back, and disappearing down the hall.

I steamed, breathing hard into whatever was on my plate. Egg salad, probably.

And these people say they love me?!

They don't understand love.

I would have to figure out something else.

❧❦❧

October had made her typical, Southern entrance: timid, with only an inkling of the vibrancy that was to come. Leaf tips of orange, yellow, and purple. Mild temps. The wood warblers gossiping quietly about lesser birds.

Mom was wrong. I was not calling Sarah fifteen times a day. It was two times a day during the week. Three each on Saturdays and Sundays. Four or five on a day I might have been super bored.

But I was still having trouble getting her on the phone. Either there was no answer, or her mother answered and told me Sarah was unavailable. I never quite knew what that meant because she'd hang up before I could get any more information.

Finally, on Halloween, Sarah answered.

"Hello?"

"Sarah," I said relieved, "Shalom! It's been so long. How are you?"

There was silence on the other end. A lump started to form in my throat.

"Sarah?"

"Shalom," she said irritated, like I was some kind of annoying Hadassah fundraiser.

"I've been calling a lot," I said. "Has your mom been telling you?"

"She told me."

"Is something wrong?"

Another pause.

"Yosef ... oh, gosh, this is hard. I don't think ... I don't think we should keep, you know, talking."

"Oh, okay," I said, disappointed. "I can call you tomorrow."

"That's not what I mean," she sighed. "This summer, it was groovy and all, really fun. But, you know, you live so far away."

"No, I don't." I was starting to feel dizzy.

"If you lived in Boston, maybe we could see each other. But Brooklyn is, you know--

"Two hundred and twenty-seven miles. That's nothing."

"It's far."

"No, Sarah, it's no big deal! My dad said I could take a bus over Hanukkah. That's just a few months away."

"I'm sorry, Yosef. You're really cute and all that, but, you know, I'm also older than you."

"By one year!" I shouted.

Again, there was silence.

"Sarah?"

"I'm here."

"I love you. We love each other. Right?"

More toxic silence. The lump in my throat was the size of a matzo ball, New York deli big. I could barely talk. Why wasn't she saying she loved me too? This had to be one of my nightmares.

"What about all the French kissing, and the Chitty Chitty, and the swimming, and you know, that time in the ... in the woods."

"That was wrong," she said, quietly, quickly.

"No, it wasn't!" I screamed, my voice cracking in sync with my breaking heart. "It was amazing! It was love! It is love!"

"I have to go, Yosef. I'm really sorry."

"Don't do this! Please Sarah! I love you! I need you!"

"Maybe we'll see each other next summer."

"I can't wait that long!"

"Shalom, Yosef," she said and hung up.

"I was growing *payot* for you!"

And there it was again, the dial tone death ray, this time, blowing my abandoned brains all over the cedar deck.

I slammed the phone onto the carriage, my tears now pouring like sweet iced tea on a hot southern day. The phone made that clanging, ringing sound, and for an idiotic second, I thought she was calling me back to apologize and make arrangements to get together.

I picked up the phone. "Hello?! Sarah?!"

Of course, there was no one.

Without thinking, I dialed her again.

It rang on the other end. I would plead with her, beg her. Whatever it took.

Ringing. Ringing. Ringing.

No one was going to answer this time. She knew it was me. Her mother knew it was me.

I hung up, quietly this time. It didn't matter. Begging and pleading, the incessant professing of my love - they weren't working anyway. No, I would need to show her how much I loved her, not just say it. When Benjamin Braddock's red Alfa Romeo ran out of gas, he ran on foot, who knows how many miles, to find and hold his love forever. I could do the same. I would run to Boston, start immediately, with no thought of anything or anyone else.

Then the phone rang. Really, this time.

I snatched it up. "Sarah?!"

The voice on the other end was male. "Susan there?"

I slammed the phone down, yet again, and with my back to the sliding glass door, sunk to the deck, ending up in a folded lump, knees holding up my chin.

Even in my anguished, lovelorn daze, I realized the idea of running from Tennessee to Boston was moronic at best, and it disappeared along with my hopes and desires.

Losing your first love. At least half of you has been ripped away. For some, it can be so devastating, they don't make it to their second love. Others fill the vacancy as quickly as possible.

And then others, say those in their first years of teenagery, they react wildly, an illogical, adolescent whiplash, filled with anger, frustration, and revenge.

⁂

It didn't take long for the news of my break-up to spread through the house. In these types of situations, under a minute was commonplace in most Jewish homes. Had I not run into the house, shock-screaming, wailing and throwing myself onto my bed, it might've taken longer. When Mom, Gram, and Gramps all rushed in to see what had happened, I somehow found the words, then told them to get out. They did.

A couple of hours later, as the neighborhood trick-or-treaters were doing their final rounds, I jumped out of bed, ran into the bathroom, and slammed the door shut. Grabbing a pair of scissors, I frantically cut off the little *payot* I had managed to grow.

Note to self: Cutting hair while filling pity pot with tears - bad idea.

Saturday, Dad took me to the barber and I got my head shaved. That was that.

The first few days I seesawed drastically between *Oh God I love her and have to see her right this second!* and *Fuck her stupid ass! I don't need her! I'm sure Becky will show me her boobs again - if I ask nicely.* During the former state, I called Sarah a lot. Over fifteen times a day, in fact. Each time, her mother answered, and each time she told me to stop calling.

I was sliding steadily into a deep depression. And the darker, early November days didn't help. I dragged myself through classes. Calvin was back to making fun of me and I couldn't care less. I spoke very little to anyone. I was always tired and wanting to go to sleep, not to rid myself of the exhaustion, but for sleep's promise of reprieve. But that was yet another false hope. Sarah tormented me in consistent, ugly nightmares made of

320

staccato camp memories and unfulfilled hand jobs. The pain and the emptiness were so overwhelming that I started contemplating how I would kill myself. Just thinking about suicide made me feel better.

My first thought was to somehow get up on the roof and jump to my death, screaming Sarah's name on the way down. Unfortunately, our house was only two stories, and the highest point was directly over the grass where a chipmunk had somehow lost his life, and now lay decaying. I could move the animal, of course. Eeeooooh. But even if I did, it might not be high enough to kill me. The last thing I needed was a broken leg to go with the depression. So, no on that.

Then I thought about stealing Mom's headache pills and overdosing. I only knew about them because I had gone to the pharmacy with Dad a few times to pick them up. At least that would be easier for my family to explain my demise since I had done acid only a few months before. Clearly, young Yosef Bamberger had become a drug addict. Like Morrison, Hendrix, and Joplin before him, a 1970s sad statistic, lost to narcotics. But I didn't really know anything about the pills, or what they were even called. Also, I had heard about a kid at school who had to get his stomach pumped due to an overdose of something called Quaaludes. That sounded terrifying. So, no.

Then I thought about somehow stealing Calvin's gun or maybe Boone had a better gun and that would work better. I could break into their house when I knew they weren't home, grab the firearm, then do it the woods. But as much as I was no longer involved with the Macafees and Jesus and whatnot, I didn't want them to be blamed. Boone was already a suspected murderer in some circles, and Calvin didn't need to follow in his father's footsteps. So, no on that.

I was out of ideas. Maybe something else would occur to me at some point. Regardless, it did feel good to know I had some options.

Meanwhile, my family was trying to make me feel better. Most of them, anyway.

One evening, Gram came into my room and didn't say a word. She just rubbed my back while I laid on my stomach crying into my pillow.

Later the same night, Susan visited, told me that her new boyfriend had broken up with her, so this might be the first thing we ever had in common. Apparently, her break up was due to him going to prison for robbing a liquor store. Seemed like a good reason to end a relationship. She went on to tell me that she was seeing someone else now, and she liked him even more than the ex. I wanted to ask her why we'd never properly met any of her boyfriends, but I decided against it. I knew she was trying to make me feel better. First time for everything.

A couple of days later, Mom made a visit. It was late afternoon, after school, when she practically fell into my room, blustery and off-kilter. She joined me on the bed, hugging me, and kissing me all around my face. She was obviously high. It repulsed and frightened me, this faux love. I wanted to pull away, but our relationship was still shaky, so I let her love on me. Her voice changed octaves up and down, as she mumbled something about plenty of Jewish fishies in the sea.

Although the encounter only lasted a few minutes before she stumbled out, it stayed with me in a lasting and confounding way. It'd be years later before I came to understand that she was over-compensating, not for any lack of love given, but for the potential of it. That would be the only time I'd seen her in that way. And neither of us ever brought it up. She might not have even remembered it.

One evening after Friday night services, it was Gramps' turn. He knocked quietly, opening the door at the same time.

"Hey champ."

"Hi, Gramps," I said, sighing. Unless Lynn had suddenly come home, this would be the last of the parade. Visiting hours are over, people.

He came in and sat on the edge of the bed. I could see his eyes were red-rimmed and damp, that sure sign of old.

"You know how the Jewish people look at violence?" he asked.

Not a question I was expecting. "Uh … it's bad?

"Yes. And no." He wagged a finger at me. "Violence is okay, but only in self-defense."

"All right," I said, wondering where this was going.

"When I was a boxer, you know, I wasn't breaking any Jewish laws. Some might have thought so. But I wasn't. You know why? Because I was defending myself. Even in the times when I was the aggressor. Cause if I didn't punch the crap out of the guy, he would've done it to me! You see?"

"Okay, I guess."

"Yosef, you are in a fight right now. You're being attacked. Attacked by your goddamn feelings! See? If you don't defend yourself, you're going to lose the match. Understand what I'm trying to tell you?"

"Attacked by my feelings," I repeated, his point starting to sink in.

"That's right," he said, "and you have to defend yourself like your life depends on it. Because it does!" Gramps clenched his fists and put them up like I'd seen so many times. "Now put your fists up, and I want you to scream."

I curled my fingers into fists. "Ahhhh," I shouted meekly.

"Louder," he said, calmly.

"Ahhhhhhhhhh!"

"Louder!"

I did it again. "*Ahhhhhhhhhhhhh!*"

"There you go, champ!"

Suddenly, the door flew open and Dad came running in. "What's going on?!"

Gramps and I both laughed. "It's okay, Dad."

"Go," Gramps said to Dad with a hand wave.

Dad stared at us a moment, shook his head, and walked out.

Gramps patted me on the arm, smiled, and stood up. "You'll get there. Keep screaming, keep fighting back. Got it?"

"Got it," I said, starting to really get it now.

Leave it to Gramps to knock some sense into me. As he left, I thought about how right he was. The Sarah thing was beating me to a pulp, and a knock-out was imminent.

But maybe it wasn't too late for a comeback. I could fight back. I needed to get mad.

Of course I had been, but the anger was always soon replaced with despondency. No, I needed a deep, sustaining anger.

And that ... well, that would take blame.

Slimy, heavy, ugly chunks of blame - the subject of which came to me immediately.

Not the flawless Sarah.

Not Lynn for abandoning me.

Not Gramps or Gram, or even Mom or Dad.

Certainly not myself.

Not even Susan who I really wished I could blame for something.

No, I blamed Judaism.

If it wasn't for Jewishness, I wouldn't have had a Bar Mitzvah to screw up in the first place! If it wasn't for Jewishness, there wouldn't be a Camp Ramah! And there wouldn't be a Sarah Miller! And there wouldn't have been love! If it wasn't for Jewishness, there wouldn't be this gnawing, empty black fucking hole in my heart!

And if it wasn't for Jewishness, I wouldn't have lost my best friend.

It was Judaism that I came running back to, only for it to ultimately fail me.

My new thinking was liberating. And it was time for some serious revenge.

❧❧❧

In jeans, a hand-me-down NYU sweatshirt, and no shoes, I walked slowly, but deliberately, down the grassy hill. As I got closer to the water, a cloud that looked like Santa's beard darkened the landscape. Apparently, even the sun didn't want to see this.

I strode past the dozen or so parishioners and, once at the shoreline, waded into the cool lake.

With his flowing robes, Joker grin, and unseeing eyes, Pastor Loy stood just a few feet from the shore, waiting with open arms. In hindsight, it might've been better to walk right past him, just keep going until the water flooded over my head and filled my lungs until I was neither Southern Baptist nor Jewish - just dead.

After last night's epiphany, I had laid in bed concocting a plan. At school, the next morning, I would wait at Calvin's locker and when he showed up, just blurt it out, and see what his reaction was. I had a feeling it would be positive, but those days, I didn't feel I could count on anything.

So, after first period, there I stood in the hall, holding my books, nervous, waiting.

He was a good ten yards away when he saw me. He stopped and frowned, then strutted the rest of the way to his locker. He ignored me and started to turn the numbered dial.

"I want to get baptized," I blurted out.

He stopped dialing and turned his head slowly toward me, squinting, teeth protruding.

"Say what?"

"I want to go the lake and get baptized. Like you did that day."

"Ah, man. You're so full of shit, your eyes are brown."

"Calvin, I'm serious, really."

"Don't fuck with me, man," he said finishing his combination and opening his locker. "I'll kick your ass."

"I'm not messing around. I really want to do it."

Calvin exchanged a couple of books, shut his locker, and looked at me with a mix of confusion and suspicion.

"All right," he said, challenging me, "if you're serious, then come to the house Sunday morning. I'll tell Daddy, we'll do it. Tell you what, though, you don't come, I'll knock your ass right into Wednesday."

He turned and headed down the hall. It didn't feel good being threatened by someone who I considered my best friend. But I understood.

Lucky for me, I was completely serious and would stay firmly in the designated weekday.

Now, in the lake, I stopped where the pastor was standing and placed myself in the proper position beside him, facing toward the crowd.

And he began, "The Lord your God will set you high above all nations of the Earth!"

"Preach!" the dozen assembled parishioners yelled.

"Now, in front of the eyes and ears of these witnesses, I baptize you …" He stopped and looked up, as blind eyes sometimes do. "What's your name, son?"

"Yosef," I said shivering. "Yosef Bamberger."

The pastor's eyebrows lifted so high I thought they might leave his face. I'm going to guess he never baptized a Bamberger.

Boone yelled from the grassy knoll, "It's all right, Pastor Loy! Young Yosef wants desperately to be saved by Jesus Christ, our Lord!"

The pastor nodded toward Boone. "All right, then."

"Praise Jesus!" Calvin yelled, jabbing his pointer finger at me in excitement.

"Yosef Bamberger," the pastor continued, "in the name of the Father, of the Son, and of the Holy Ghost …" he paused, putting his right hand on my back and his left arm in front.

"Take hold of my arm," he said gently.

I did.

"Take a deep breath and hold it."

I did.

And with that, he pushed me carefully down into the water. It was cool and immediately energizing. I could hear him, muffled by the water, "… and in the name of Jesus Christ!"

The crowd praised loudly, "Hallelujah!"

As he pulled me back up, I opened my eyes, and the first thing I saw was a water-blurred Calvin, jumping up and down like a pogo stick, and screaming, "Praise Jesus! Praise Jesus!"

Boone was on his knees, shouting to the sky with open arms, "Hallelujah! Thank you, Lord! Thank you, Jesus! Thank you, Lord!"

The energy was contagious, and I ran out of the water toward them, lifting my knees high, and splashing wildly. "Praise Jesus! Praise Jesus!" I shouted.

With Boone still on his knees, the three of us fell into a tight, dripping, group hug. We swayed back and forth, praising Christ. It was incredibly emotional, my heart full of comradery and love. Even Boone was weeping, a man so hard he could've been declared official state rock.

"I'm so proud of you, boy," Boone said, standing up and collecting himself. "I am happier than a possum eatin' a sweet tater!"

"Me, too, man," Calvin added, punching me lightly in the arm.

"Thanks," I said, catching my breath from all the excitement.

The pastor was baptizing another believer. "The Lord your God will set you high above all nations of the Earth!"

"Daddy, I got a big hankerin' for Pizza Pete's," Calvin said.

"Hell, yeah!" I screamed in my best hillbilly. "I'm starvin'!"

Boone laughed. "Sounds good! Let's go."

As I put my Converse back on, something occurred to me. There was something I still needed to do. And I needed to do it while wet. I figured the chilly, fall temps should keep me damp for a while.

"Actually, guys," I said, finishing tying my shoes, "I wonder if you could take me home."

"Ah man!" Calvin said, displeased. "You want to skip pizza?"

"Sorry, I really need to go home. Maybe I can come by later."

Calvin was about to protest some more, but Boone put a hand on his shoulder. "It's okay, Yosef. Whatever you want. Let's get you home."

He said that last part with a smile and a wink, like he knew what I was planning. It unnerved me. I realize now - he might have had an inkling of what would transpire next, and the last thing Boone would want was to keep me from it.

As we headed up the hill toward his truck, I noticed my Baptism elation had diminished my Jewish anger quite a bit. I would have to dig that back up.

❦

I stunk like gasoline, carp, and just a hint of wet Irish Setter. The smell of purification in a speed boat lake. The smell of fuck you Jewishness.

I stood, once again angry, and successfully still wet, at the top of the stairs, the same landing I stood on when I returned from camp, more Jewish than I had been in Brooklyn. The contrast was striking and, admittedly, potentially deadly to aging grandparents.

But this was necessary.

My family needed to know that I had forsaken Judaism. I needed them to be sure of it. If there was any question, they might've sluffed it off as some kind of adolescent dippiness, continuing to force me to go to Shul, celebrate Hanukkah, Sukkot, and Pesach. They would continue to separate my milk from my meat and make me study for my Bar Mitzvah that now, I was sure I would never have.

"What happened to you?" Gram asked from the sofa, her nose turned up.

Her and Gramps were the only ones there. I needed the whole family. I wasn't going to repeat this. "Mom! Dad! Susan! Come into the living room please!" My voice was still unsteady, that part of puberty, relentless.

Dad walked in from the kitchen, immediately retracted from the smell. "*Oy gevalt.*"

Mom came out from her bedroom, still in her nightgown at 2pm. "What's going on? What stinks?"

Susan came upstairs from her room. "Jesus Christ, what smells?!"

"It's me! Okay?! I stink! Can everyone sit down please?"

Dad did as I asked. Mom and Susan stayed standing, now with hands on hips.

"You piss off a skunk?" Susan asked.

"Everyone … I just got baptized," I said, proudly, vindictively.

"What?!" said everyone.

"Baptized! I've been purified, and I am now a Southern Baptist! A proud Southern Baptist! I am not Jewish anymore! It's done! The Bar Mitzvah is off! Just wanted y'all to know! I will not be eating bagels anymore!"

Jaws in carpet.

Heads cocked.

Eyes bulged.

Rapid blinking.

Nausea.

Never has so much disbelief, frustration, and bewilderment lived in one room at the same time. What they had feared was the case with my botched Bar Mitzvah was now, a reality.

Gram put her head in her hands, and started crying, mumbling. "What kind of *shanda* is this? *Oy gevalt*. Oy, oy, oy...."

"Jesus Christ," Gramps said.

"Take a shower, dumbass," Susan said shaking her head and going back downstairs.

"Yosef!" Mom shouted, "you can't *not* be Jewish! It doesn't work that way!"

"Yes, I can," I argued.

"Everything we've been through?!" she asked. "I thought you were healed! I thought you were fine!"

"This, you got from our talk?" Gramps asked.

"Murray! Say something to your son! Say something!" Mom yelled at him.

Dad was gobsmacked, staring at me like I was some stranger who just broke into the house.

"Such a *shanda*! Such a *shanda*!" Gram was screaming it now, non-stop.

Mom was yelling over her. "You are Jewish, young man! You are Jewish! You are Jewish! You are Jewish! It is not just a religion! It is a race of people! You cannot *not* be Jewish! Do you understand me?! Forsaking your Jewishness is forsaking your family! Us! Do you understand that?! I am your mother, and I am telling you, you will get your Bar Mitzvah! And it will be beautiful! Beautiful! It will be beautiful!"

"No," I said adamantly to Mom.

Finally, Dad spoke. "Go to your room," he said, bluntly.

"That's it?!" Mom thundered. "Go to your room?! You are so weak! Goddamn you! Goddamn you!"

As I headed down the hall to my room, I heard Gramps trying to console Gram. "We can say it was *Tvilah*. No one has to know otherwise."

Tvilah is the Jewish purification ritual; you might say the closest thing Jews have to a baptism. Gramps - always thinking.

Okay, maybe I didn't plan it out very well. And I truly hated hurting Gram like that. But how do you tell your Orthodox Jewish family that you've chosen not to be Jewish anymore at thirteen, while living in a small, highly racist and bigoted Tennessee town?

I'll wait.

Hint: You don't.

But I had to. In my selfish, pygmean brain, doing it this way was the only way I was going to fall out of love. I was desperate. If Mom and Dad knew I was close to killing myself if I hadn't proceeded this way, they might've agreed with my approach. At least I didn't choose to do it over Hanukkah or some other holiday, like Passover. *Hey! The Jews escaped Egypt! I'm escaping Judaism! Makes sense, right?*

Seconds later, I was standing by my bedroom window, happy to have gotten it over with, when Mom suddenly charged into my room, crying and screaming unintelligibly. I'm surprised the door didn't come off the hinges.

Speaking of unhinged …

She lurched at me, smacking me hard with both open palms: on my face, my arms, everywhere her hands could land, over and over. It felt like a thousand scorpion stings.

I put my arms up to protect myself, begging her to stop.

But I was fighting a hurt, rabid octopus. She would stop only when she was done.

After what seemed like an hour, really a minute, she turned and stomped out, leaving the door open.

I tottered, screaming and punching out at nothing a few times, trying to grasp what just happened. I slammed the door, and dropped onto my bed, shaking and crying with agonizing, asthmatic-like gasps.

How could she do this to me?!

My skin burned. She had spanked me a couple times as a kid. But this ... this was an act of violence.

Unforgiveable. The furthest thing from love.

Through the tears and cursing, my rage toward her grew and expanded with every moment. Every hour.

Midnight. I was cried out. Hadn't slept. Except for the hushed hum of the central heating, the house was silent.

As I started to get out of bed, I realized I didn't know where my glasses were. Focusing the best I could, I found them in a corner, undamaged. She must've smacked them right off my face.

Doing my best to be quiet, I pulled my suitcase out of the closet and threw in two pairs of pants, a handful of underwear, socks, and a few redchecked, flannel, button-downs.

I put on my Converse, then with my suitcase in hand, opened my bedroom door slowly. I slipped into the hallway, and without a sound, tiptoed toward the front door.

At the landing, I was about to hit the stairs when I remembered it was getting colder. Not New York cold, but still. I put my suitcase down, opened the coat closet, and pulled out my winter jeans jacket from between the other heavy coats. I put it on, descended the stairs, and left.

The row of house lights shined through the trees, helping me see, but slowly fading as I made my way. I'd never been in the woods this late. A silver coating of frost covered every branch and colorful leaf. With every step, I crunched. A couple squirrels scurried here and there. Had I not been full of fury and, most likely, in shock, I might have noticed how beautiful it was.

Mom's attack on me was the stuff supervillain origin stories are made of, and although unaware of its magnitude at the time, it would take me years to fully understand it.

✻✻✻

I arrived at Calvin and Boone's a few minutes later, relieved, and exhausted from carrying my suitcase. Trudging my way up into their backyard, a neighborhood dog started barking, and I saw a light go on in another house, so I made haste.

I hurried up to Calvin's window and tapped with my finger a few times (Lower level - no rocks needed). The dog kept barking, so I used my fist, making more of a knocking sound.

Nothing. I did it again, louder this time.

Finally, a corner of the sheet lifted, and he peered out, squinting through sleepy eyes.

"Yosef?" He mouthed through the window.

"Can I come in?"

He looked down at my suitcase, then back at me and half-smiled. He pulled the sheet back, opened the window, and I climbed in.

We sat on his bed and I spilled the whole thing. Thank God, I was all cried out from before.

Afterward, I told him I couldn't live with Mom anymore, and he seemed to understand. We stayed up the rest of the night talking, listening to music down low, and laughing about farts and vaginas. Of course, Calvin smoked his pot and drank his shine.

When the sun rose, Boone came in to wake Calvin. He practically jumped out of his overalls when he saw me. We all had a laugh, and after telling him what happened, he said I was welcome to stay as long as I like. It was probably better this way, he said, as I could now be bathed in the light of Jesus, around the clock. Also, he added, Calvin would be happy to have someone help with the chores.

When Boone left the room, I remembered the murder, or suspected murder, I should say. I hadn't thought about it in a while, nor had Calvin brought it up. The thought was fleeting, as it was becoming harder and harder for me to see Boone in that way. Right now, he was saving my life.

That day, Calvin and I went to school together on his motorcycle. That was fun and crazy and helmetless and scary and illegal, and I had to hold on to the seat below me as putting my arms around Calvin was not going to fly.

Once we got to school, it was a struggle getting through classes. I was exhausted and I couldn't help but wonder what everyone at home was thinking. What was Dad's reaction when he came in to wake me in the morning? Did he scream? Was he naked? Did Gram faint? Did I cause Gramps to have a heart attack or stroke? Did Susan roll her eyes and call me a dumbass in absentia? When Mom saw I was gone, did she feel guilty for beating me? One thing was irrefutable: it was definitely Bamberger bedlam that morning.

Throughout the day, I kept waiting for Mom and Dad to come to school and see if I was even there. But they didn't.

School finally over, I met Calvin outside. As we mounted the Honda, I spotted Mom's car parked on the street in front of the school. Mom, Dad, Gram, and Gramps were all sitting inside, watching as we sped away. I didn't mention it to Calvin.

Okay. Now they know. And probably what they expected.

Years later, I found out that once they knew who I was with - they had assumed correctly - they had agreed it would be a good idea to give me time to cool off. Imagine that? My parents and grandparents all agreeing on something.

So, Calvin and I went to school together all week. I had my meals with him and Boone. I watched Calvin and Becky smoke and drink. I stayed sober, the future designated driver.

I felt bad about the extra money Boone was spending on food, but he didn't seem to mind. I guess the tree stump business was booming. Every night, their beat-up living room sofa became my bed. It was on the springy side, but I didn't care. At that point, this felt more like home than home did. If it wasn't for my time at camp, the accommodations might have been overwhelming, but Calvin and Boone were good roommates. And I had packed plenty of socks to do my business into. Each night, I still thought of Sarah and I longed to be with her, but amazingly, thankfully, that feeling was slowly fading. It was being replaced with hatred for my mother. I wondered if she regretted what she did, or did she feel justified?

⁂

It had been a week and I was beginning to get used to my new life.

One cold, rainy Tuesday, around dusk, we were at dinner and we'd just finished saying grace when there was a loud, angry knock on the front door. I jumped.

I knew exactly who it was.

Boone knew too. "Calvin, answer the door," he said, digging into his mashed potatoes.

"Okay, Daddy," Calvin said, standing up and giving me a what-the-fuck face.

I followed him to the front, staying a couple feet back.

Calvin opened the door wide.

Standing there, shivering in the cold wet, were Mom, Dad, and Gramps.

Mom looked past Calvin, at me. "It's time to come home, Yosef," she said, her voice weak and hurt.

"He lives here now," Calvin said, puffing out his chest.

Mom took a deep breath. "I am talking to Yosef."

"He told me what you did to him," Calvin responded.

334

"Calvin, don't," I said over his shoulder, not wanting more of a confrontation than we already had. Mom tried not to respond to Calvin's comment, but her trembling lips and speed-blinking eyes gave her away.

And judging by the curious looks on Dad's and Gramps' face, I don't think they knew.

That meant they thought I ran away just simply because I wanted to live with the Macafees.

"What, you gonna slug me, old man?" Calvin asked Gramps with a chuckle.

Gramps didn't move, but kept looking back and forth between Calvin and me. He was ready. Ready for something.

I heard Boone approach behind me.

"Y'all get on out of here 'fore I call the po-lice. You trespassin.'"

Dripping with anxiety, Dad stepped closer to the doorway. "Zees, enough. You're coming home. Period."

"I said, beat it," Boone said, stepping closer to Dad.

Surprisingly, Mom took a different approach. "Please, Mr. Maccabee," she said, smiling, "we just want our son to come home, that's all."

I wondered if Gramps was actually going to hit Boone. If he did, the situation would definitely escalate, and Boone would likely be the winner of that bout.

Local Man Beats the Crap Out of Trespassing Jews!

Not the screaming headline I wanted to see.

I did learn, years later, that they'd concocted a plan before they came over. If I wouldn't come peacefully, Gramps would, indeed, slug Boone, Mom would grab me, and they'd take off. Simple enough.

And not at all how it went down.

"Yosef," Boone said without looking back and keeping an eye on Gramps, "you wanna go? You wanna go home? If so, go on. We ain't stoppin' ya."

I didn't. I did. I didn't. I did. I was confused and still angry at Mom, and Judaism, and Sarah, and the universe, and everything, and everybody in it - except for the Macafees. If I did go back, did that mean I was telling Mom it was okay for her to beat me silly like she did? If I didn't, how long could I really stay at the Macafees? It was starting to feel unsustainable. I didn't know what to do. I had to say something. Everyone was waiting. It was up to me to diffuse the situation.

"I want to stay," I finally answered Boone, still unsure.

"Are you sure?!" Mom asked me, tears gushing now.

I looked down, thought about it another moment, then answered, "For now, yeah."

"You know, Yosef," Mom said, finding her fury. "We could forcibly take you. You are a minor; it's the law! We've been kind enough to let you ... let off some steam here! It's time to come home!"

"I don't care! I'll just run away again!" I screamed, this time looking her square in the eye.

Suddenly, out of nowhere ... pop! Boone was punched in the face.

Stunned, he stumbled backwards.

"Dad!" I shouted, shocked.

"Murray!" Mom and Gramps both yelled, angrily.

"Take that," Dad said to Boone, trying to cover his fear with bravado.

Apparently, when faced with losing his only son to rednecks and Jesus, my father, yes, that father, my overweight, scared to fucking death of everything Dad, found bravery. Actual balls.

He had slugged Boone somewhere in the face - it was hard to tell. This was the first punch my father had ever thrown - quite likely the only one. Because of that, it was wild and weak, like a toddler swinging his fists in excitement over a new Slinky.

When her surprise subsided, Mom reached out to grab me, but I was out of reach as I had dropped back toward Boone to see if he was okay. Not only was he fine, he had grabbed his shotgun and was pointing it at Dad.

"Try it again!" he yelled. "Go on, try it again!"

"Boone!" I shouted. "Don't!"

Tough to say who among us peed ourselves in that moment, but Mom, Dad, and Gramps did immediately start walking backwards, terrified, with their hands up, and shouting a thousand *Don't shoots!* Honestly, a small part of me wanted to go with them at that point.

"You better go!" Boone fired into the sky, the blast cracking through the air. With that, they turned to run. I could hear the buckshot falling into the yard like hail.

"Yeah! You better run!" Calvin repeated.

I was motionless. This couldn't be happening, but it was.

Boone lowered his weapon as we watched them jump into the car and peel out.

A few seconds passed, and Boone said, matter-of-factly, "Who wants dessert?"

"Me," Calvin said.

"Me, too," I answered, lying.

We went back in and settled back at the table.

I had Maalox for dessert.

I was relieved no one was hurt and that the debacle was over. But that night on the couch, I couldn't help wonder if Dad may have just started our own version of the Hatfields & McCoys. The Bambergers & Macafees … doesn't quite have the same ring to it.

❧

A few days later, after school, Calvin and I were getting on his motorcycle when I heard a familiar voice behind me.

"Yo-yo."

I turned, excited to see my ornery sister. It had been a while.

"Hold on a second, okay?" I asked Calvin.

"That your sister?"

"Yeah, I'll be right back," I said, walking over to where she was standing a few yards away.

"Hi," I said, trying to act normal, and failing.

There was a mix of frustration and apathy in her voice. "Listen, you need to come home. You're being stupid. This is a real drag, man. Mom and Dad have been, you know, really patient."

"I can't just ... it's not that easy."

"Yeah it is. You come home. There. Easy."

"You don't get it," I said.

"They're talking about telling the police you were kidnapped."

"That's not true."

"Your buddy's dad shot at them! Jesus Christ, Yo-Yo! What is wrong with you?!"

"He didn't shoot *at* them," I corrected.

"Look," she said, her exasperation growing, "I talked them out of the kidnapping thing cause it'd probably just make things worse. Just come home." She paused, then said, "I actually miss you."

I stared at the chewing gum-covered sidewalk. "I want to come home, kinda, but things have to be different. I'm not Jewish anymore, and I want to go to church with the Macafees."

"Far out! Go to church! I don't care!" Susan screamed at me. "But you gotta come home. They're driving me crazy!"

"Yosef!" Calvin shouted over his now running engine. "We gotta go!"

"Be right there!" I shouted back. Then to Susan I said, "See you later."

I ran back to Calvin before she could say anything else.

I jumped on the bike. And as we took off, I looked back, but she was gone. My breath suddenly caught, and a fear came on me like a blast wave from a nuclear bomb. She had simply left quickly, got in her boyfriend's car maybe, but it was a strong blow, almost knocking me off the bike. I tried to convince myself it was just motorcycle exhaust.

I saw a pattern forming. First, there was Lynn, my original soulmate. Then, Sarah, my first true love. Then, of course, dichotomy personified: Mom, good and evil mashed into one, rageful, moo-moo wearing monster mother. And now, Susan, the latest to abandon me.

That makes four the number in the long line of rejecting females, each one before making the impact of the latest worse.

Although life patterns build to get our attention (a pile of crap smells a lot worse than a turd), I was a mere thirteen, so I wouldn't understand that for years.

I held on tight to the motorcycle, burying those refreshed, now stronger emotions with the questions that had been ricocheting through my mind for days. If I did go home, how would Boone react? If I told him I planned to stay a Southern Baptist, he might be fine with it. Or, he might blow my brains out over chicken fried steak one night. And what about Mom? Could I forgive her? Would she finally accept my new religion? How about everyone else? It was hard to imagine Gram ever being okay with it.

Whatever the answers, a plan was forming in my head - I would eventually go home. I just needed more time to think things through.

You've heard the famous saying: Make plans and God laughs. Well, in my case, God happened to be drinking milk when he heard *my* plan.

RUNNING AMUCK

IT WAS A FRIDAY NIGHT. BOONE, CALVIN, AND I WERE PLAN-
ning on waking at 5am to go fishing. We hadn't decided where exactly,
as there were dozens of creeks and lakes full of fish: bluegill, trout, shad,
catfish, smallmouth bass. We were well into November, and the mornings were getting chilly. Of course, old man winter wasn't about to keep
Tennesseans from their fishing. As someone once said, *Tennessee fishing
season is March 1st to February 31st*.

I'd gone fishing with Calvin a few times after school. With stoned
impatience, he would show me how me to bait the hooks and use the
reel properly. Our last time out, I had somehow managed to catch a tiny
Bluegill. I acted like I just won the Daytona 500. Bring on the champagne!
The trophy! The girls!

Calvin was unimpressed.

We'd usually bring the catch home, and Boone would fry 'em up in a
pan for dinner. Once, Calvin caught a giant carp, and we brought it home
for the neighbor cats to eat. After tossing it in his backyard, it turns out
the flies and maggots were more interested than the kitties. Eventually, it
became so nasty we had to bury it in the woods. Good times.

I was excited for our little excursion. I was hoping it might take my
mind off of all the *tsures* with my warring families (Cue *Dueling Banjos*).

A loud knock on the door awoke me. I don't recall the time, but it
was still dark and felt closer to three than five. I sat up, and as my mind

cleared, I assumed it was the police. Mom had finally convinced them to get involved.

Dressed in shabby long johns, Boone stumbled past me and headed right for his shotgun.

I jumped up, standing terrified in my tightie-whities, my heartbeat quickening.

Calvin, also in his underwear, walked into the living room. "What's goin' on?"

I shook my head.

Was this the end of it? Were we about to be taken down in a gun battle, our bodies unmoving, underpants blood-red? I was ready to grab Calvin and run out the back, but Boone had already opened the door, after which he quickly positioned his weapon for shooting.

A figure stood in the doorway. Just one. No SWAT team. Someone I didn't know. A woman, judging by the ample curves. She was slightly swaying from side to side.

"Boone," the woman said, boldly and uneasy at the same time.

Boone lowered the gun slowly.

Suddenly aware of my state of undress, I grabbed my jeans from the floor and threw them on.

"Who is it, Daddy?" Calvin asked, trying to get a better look at her and feeling no need to cover himself.

"Hi, Calvin," she said. Her Southern accent was melodic, drowsy. There was a longing in her voice. That's when I realized who she was. Calvin just stood beside me, a pale blob, blinking at this unknown woman.

"You not gonna shoot me, are you?" she asked Boone as she scratched a place on her arm.

"What the hell you doin' here?" Boone said, his mouth locked in anger.

She walked past him and into the living room. Dorothy Macafee was rotund and freckled, with watery eyes, flushed skin, and dirty, dirty blond hair. Her dress: Goodwill, head to foot.

Calvin stepped back a few inches.

"Don't be scared," she said with a light laugh. She tried to put her hand to his face, but he pulled away.

"Daddy?" Calvin said, confused, shaken.

Dorothy looked at me suspiciously. "Who are you?"

"Yosef. I'm Calvin's friend."

Boone kept his distrustful eyes on Dorothy. "I asked you a damn question, woman. Why you here? I ain't got no money."

Dorothy turned toward Boone, really laughing now. "I think I know better than that!"

She scratched her arm again, this time the other one.

Boone shook his head in disgust. "You need to get the hell out of here." I could tell he was about to blow, and I found myself, again, calculating my escape. But I could tell Calvin needed me, so I stayed put.

"What the hell's going on, Daddy?!" Calvin shouted.

"I'm your mama! That's what's goin' on, child!" Dorothy screamed, more at Boone than Calvin.

Calvin's ears turned red. He pulled his head back on his neck, wary of this strange woman. "What?" I could barely hear him.

"That's right," Dorothy said, inching closer to Calvin.

His eyes started fluttering. Tears were flowing now like a broken rain gutter. He didn't want to believe it. But he knew it was true. Even if they have no memory of them, children know when they're in the presence of their mothers.

He looked over at Boone. "You said … you said she was dead. You said she died in a car crash!"

"Oh my fuckin' God! You told him I was dead?!" Dorothy shouted at Boone, her body language shifting into fight mode.

"You left, bitch! You fuckin' just left! Walked right on out of here!" Boone screamed back.

"Cause I married a fuckin' wife beater! How long's I supposed to put up with that?!"

"Just get the fuck outta here!" Boone yelled, moving closer to her, his gun resting on his arm.

"You tell your precious son? Huh? Did ya? You tell him you beat up his mama?"

"Shut the fuck up!" Boone yelled, now pointing the shotgun at her. "I'll do it!"

"Daddy, don't! Please!" Calvin yelled.

Dorothy thrust her chest out at Boone, challenging, provoking. "Oh! Big man! You gonna kill me for real this time? In front of your own son? Go ahead. Go ahead now!"

"Keep on, you fucking whore. Keep on!"

Unafraid, she turned away from Boone and took a few steps toward Calvin, toddler-talking now. "Oh, little Calvin, sweetheart, I'm your Mama. It's me, baby. Why don't you come live with me? You don't need all this. I got us a nice place in the Garden Apartments. You'll love it."

"Don't listen to her, Calvin! She's a damn lyin', drug addict! Why you think she's been gone so many years, huh?"

"That's bullshit!" Dorothy shrieked.

"He lives with me! You need to go!"

"He is fourteen now! He can make his own decisions!"

Calvin watched helplessly, in shock, as his parents engaged in verbal combat, a fight he never thought he'd see. I put my hand on his back, also helpless, having zero experience in the business of comforting, but doing what I could. Then, suddenly, he grabbed my arm and pulled me toward his room.

"Ah, don't be like that, Calvin," Dorothy begged.

We ran in, and Calvin slammed the door shut, locking it.

He pulled out an ash tray from under his bed. In it was a half-smoked joint and some matches. He lit up and toked hard, as he paced back and forth. I sat on his bed, steeling myself for the coming gun blast.

"Calvin!" Dorothy shouted, jiggling the doorknob, trying to get in. The house construction was so cheap, her voice was hardly muffled.

"You think we should call the cops?" I asked. "What if he shoots her?"

"Let him," Calvin said.

Dorothy pleaded, crying, "Calvin, sweetheart! Please! I'm sorry. Let me in! We can talk about it."

"Get away from that door!" Boone shouted.

Dorothy stopped trying to get in, but the circular, verbal sparring continued.

Calvin kept pacing, the weed not calming him down.

"Why would he tell me she died?"

I shook my head, wanting a good answer. "I don't know."

"Where she been? How come she shows up now?!"

Calvin put the roach out and put on a pair of jeans and T-shirt.

"You remember her, at all?" I asked.

"Naw. All I remember's when he told me. I's like ... six, I guess. Car crash, my ass. Had fucking nightmares about it for years."

Suddenly, we heard a loud slap, and Dorothy screaming in pain.

"Goddamn it," Calvin said, pained and under his breath, as the shouting outside his room escalated.

I expected he might join the fray, but instead he looked at me and said, "Let's get outta here."

"You sure?"

"Definitely," he said.

I was beyond terrified. "What if he ... what if he ... you know ... ?!"

"He won't. If he wanted that, she'd been dead long time ago." Calvin grabbed his heavy coat and threw me mine. Luckily, we kept all my stuff in there.

"You want to go to my house?" I asked.

"Naw, let's just ride for a while."

I nodded, not thinking things through, but happy to get the hell out of there. We put our coats on, grabbed our helmets, and climbed out the window.

That night, Calvin was hit with a twisted truth he'd managed to escape his whole life. Unfortunately for Boone, his lie was the highest level of betrayal, not easily resolved, not by faith, or blood, or anything else. It was the kind of deception that fixes itself as a whole new foundation, where everything, from that point on, is built upon it and affected by it.

⁂

Before I knew it, we were flying down the Turnpike, the motorcycle's jumpy headlamp the only light for miles. There was no one else on the road.

The wind chill was better suited for penguins than runaways. I was shivering more every minute, and my teeth were chattering uncontrollably, even with my new coat and gloves Mom had ordered me from Sears. My feet were even less happy, as I had on normal cotton socks and Converse. Hardly winter wear. Then there was the fact that I was really never comfortable on the motorcycle in the first place - even on the short trips to school and back.

Born to be mild, that's me.

And now ... now we were doing sixty.

And Calvin was upset.

Not the safest combo.

My only consolation was that I didn't imagine we'd ride for long, as his outfit was worse than mine; his coat was old and ratty with rips that revealed its white innards. His gloves had holes. Worse, being in front of me, he was getting the brunt of the wind. He had to be close to numb.

After a few miles of steady riding, I screamed into the wind, "Where are we going?!"

"Just filled up the tank yesterday!" he screamed back, not helpful at all. I'm not sure what he thought I said, but I let it go.

As we took a right onto Illinois Avenue, we had to slow down a bit, so that was nice. But we kept riding, and I was becoming more and more agitated. Were we just going to keep at it until we ran out of gas? We'd be blocks of ice by then.

It was still dark as we passed over the muddy Clinch River and onto the Pellissippi Parkway, a winding, new highway that eventually intersected with Interstates 75 and 40 in Knoxville. I'd only been on the Parkway a few times, but I knew one thing - it wasn't in Oak Ridge. I couldn't figure out what Calvin was thinking - he rode as if we had a destination. Or maybe he wasn't thinking at all.

As we merged onto I-75 North, the sun was rising and would start to warm things up a bit. I might have noticed if I wasn't panicking. The Interstate?! Seriously?! Speeding cars and mac trucks ... and us on our little Honda 125?! We'll be crushed! Dead statistics.

All I could do was hold on tighter - as if that would help. At least there still weren't too many other vehicles on the road, so that would keep things safer, for a while. Making matters worse, my butt and back were getting sore. I really just wanted to stop and turn around. Maybe there were surface streets.

"Calvin," I yelled. "I got to pee!"

I felt his body shake with a chuckle. Then he nodded.

As Calvin merged to the right to take an exit, I thanked the Lord, all of them.

Coming off the exit ramp, we pulled into a Rocky Top Market, a small convenience store/gas station. He parked alongside the building and we dismounted.

I found the bathroom, went in, and pretended to pee. The toilet was so filthy, I was grateful I didn't really have to go.

A few minutes later, I joined Calvin back at the bike. He face was bike rider red, but he didn't seem particularly cold.

"You got any money on ya?" he asked.

"I think so," I said as I dug into my pockets, finding five quarters. "You got any?" I asked, handing him the money.

He fished in his pockets and pulled out three dimes. "$1.55," he said. "'Nough to get some gas."

He went inside the market to pay. I took the time to stretch and pound my buttocks with my fists.

He was inside longer than I expected, maybe five minutes, but then came out and started pumping the gas. It was so cheap in '74, a buck fifty-five almost filled the tank.

Calvin put his helmet back on, hopped back on the bike, and waited for me. Instead, I stood beside him.

"You ready to head back?" I asked.

"Naw. Let's just ride, man."

"What?" That surprised me, and it also didn't. "Calvin, we can't just keep riding. Where would we go? We've got school Monday. We're going to run out of gas. And money."

Calvin looked at me, thinking, then cocking his head, and shouted, "Canada!"

I didn't understand him at first. Can of what? He saw the confusion on my face.

"Canada," he repeated. "Let's go to Canada, man. Supposed to be really cool up 'ere!"

I felt myself step back a bit, my face screwing up like a birth defect.

"Calvin, we've got to go home."

He looked down a moment, then straight ahead. "I ain't goin' back there, man."

"What?! What do you mean?" He wasn't making any sense. We had to go back.

"You heard me," he said defiantly, with maybe a hint of hostility.

"What are we going to do about food, gas? Where would we sleep?"

"Wait a minute!" Calvin said, excited, his eyes, full moons. "Didn't you tell me you got a sister in Detroit or somethin'?"

A little surprised laugh came out of me. "Yeah."

"How far's that?"

"From Oak Ridge?" I asked, thinking it absurd. "508 miles."

"Perfect, man! She'll feed us. Give us a place to stay. Right? She's your damn sister!"

"That's far! I don't know. What about school?"

"Fuck school, man!" Calvin said, nodding for me to get back on. "Come on. It'll be fun! You always said how cool she was."

I glared at him, my discomfort and fear likely informing my facial expression. These conflicting Calvin scenarios were starting to grow tiresome.

Should I shoot a helpless little animal?

Should I be a peeping tom in a tree?

Should I study the Bible?

Should I investigate a murder?

Should I risk being flayed alive by asphalt?

Of course, I had the option not to go. But that meant I'd not only have to call Dad to come get me, I'd have to be okay with going back home - and I didn't feel ready to forgive you-know-who. The idea that I would be doing to Calvin what I had suffered so greatly from myself - abandoning him - well, that escaped me entirely.

Or I could look at it as an adventure. Why should *Scooby Doo* and the *Six Million Dollar Man* have all the fun? This didn't have to be about me doing what Calvin wanted me to. Also, it would be really great to see Lynn.

It turned out though there was one reason, and one reason only, I got back on that motorcycle. Something I'm sure I was not aware of at the time:

I wasn't finished punishing my mother yet. Apparently, I needed to keep hammering that nail.

Calvin was beaming as I put my helmet back on and mounted the bike once again.

"What'll we do about money and food?" I asked.

"Well, shit, I just stole two Snicker bars. So we're all right for a bit!" He laughed, kick-starting the bike.

"Calvin!" I yelled at him.

"Which way?!" he screamed back at me.

"Seventy-five, same highway, north!"

❧❦

We'd been riding for a few hours, and I was really jonesing for that candy bar. My hands and feet were cold, but it did seem a bit warmer, making things more tolerable. There were more cars on the road, and they caused us a significant wobble when they passed. After each time, I thanked God we were still upright, and I'd reposition slightly. No idea why.

Finally, around Johnson City, Tennessee, Calvin pulled off the interstate and into a gas station. We passed through the main service area, around to the side of the building.

Once we dismounted and took our helmets off, Calvin pulled out the stolen property, and we devoured them.

"We're 'bout out of gas," he said, his mouth full of chocolatey goodness.

I nodded. "We can't exactly steal that, can we?"

"Nope," he said, putting his helmet on the handlebars and walking toward the highway.

"What ... where are you going?" I said, chasing after him, still holding my helmet.

"We got to hitch," he said, not stopping.

"Hitch? What's that?"

"Hitchhike, dumbass. You know ... " he said, sticking his thumb out showing me how it's done. "Come on. Might as well ditch the helmet. Don't think you're gonna need it in a car or a truck." He laughed.

"Is that safe, hitchhiking?" I asked.

"Sure, man. People do it all the time."

"We're just going to leave the motorcycle here?"

"Well, Mr. Shithead gave it to me, so ... y'know, fuck him."

We were on the sidewalk now in front of the gas station. Calvin stuck his thumb out, bounced it along with the dozen or so cars and trucks that went by.

"Have you ever done this?" I asked, trying unsuccessfully to hide my nervousness.

"Naw. Seen it on the TV, movies, somethin'."

Just then, a long, rusty, white Caddy pulled over. Sitting inside was a pleasant, young woman with bottleneck glasses and a zig-zaggy Christmas sweater. She looked at us through the passenger side window.

"Where y'all headed?" she asked with a dignified, Southern accent. I'd heard the type before, sweeter sounding than the East Tennessee version. Carolinas, Georgia. She was looking at us strangely, perhaps thinking it odd that I felt the need to be hitchhiking with a helmet.

"Detroit," Calvin answered her.

"Oh. Well, I'm goin' up to Dayton, Ohio. Part of the way there. Could use the company."

Calvin didn't hesitate and jumped in the front. I realized I was still holding the helmet and, not knowing what to do with it, laid in on the sidewalk. I got in and we took off.

"I'm Kathy," she said.

"I'm Calvin, that's Yosef."

"Hi," I said, waving to her in the rearview. I was happy to be out of the constant wind. So far, this wasn't too bad at all.

"Well, y'all definitely aren't brothers. I can tell that," she said laughing. We chuckled along cordially. "Nah," Calvin said.

"Kinda young to be hitchhikin', though. I mean, no offense or anything, but you look like you should be in school. I know it's Saturday and all, but ... where y'all from?"

"Oak Ridge, a ways back," Calvin said. "Our motorcycle just ran out of gas."

"Y'all runnin' away from home? Hey, if you are, I'm groovy with that, you know. None of my business what makes boys want to leave home. Wasn't a lot different for me, you know. I ran away once when I was twelve ... I think. Maybe thirteen. I made it from Lexington, North Carolina

- where I'm from - all the way to Winston-Salem. Twenty whole miles!" She laughed and we joined in.

"It was rainin' and cold. I got homesick. This nice trucker man picked me up and took me to a diner. I called my folks to come pick me up. Never ran away again, I'll tell you that. Unless you call going off to UT runnin' away. It is, kind of, you know, cause as soon as I was accepted, I ran as fast as I could out of Lexington!" We all laughed again.

"Well, drove, I guess, not ran. Either you boys have any ailments? I have somethin' called Diabetes Insipidus. It makes me real thirsty, and I have to pee a whole lot. That's why I keep a lot of water in the car." She pointed with her head, toward the backseat. Indeed, next to me were four-gallon, plastic milk jugs, now full of water.

"It's caused by a brain tumor. It sounds worse than it is, cause it's not growin' or anything. But I have to take shots in my butt, makes it all lumpy under my skin. I had a boyfriend for a while and he gave 'em to me, the shots I mean, but now I give 'em to myself. Sometimes I even wet my bed, probably cause I drink so much water durin' the evening and it doesn't collect enough in my bladder for me to have to go before bed, you see. The disease is what made me want to study Biology. That's my major, Biology. At UT. University of Tennessee, Knoxville. I really love it there. Such a good school. And fun, too."

I don't know if it was the *Gomer Pyle* quality to Kathy's voice or because boredom is a potent tranquilizer, but I fell asleep. When I finally awoke, we were heading into Dayton while she was going on about her brother's vast collection of TV Guide magazines.

She pulled off at a gas station and filled up her tank while we waited in the car. I was about to say something to Calvin, but then I heard him snore slightly, so I kept quiet.

A few minutes later, when she got back in the car, Calvin awoke. She had some corn nuts and Pepsi and shared them with us. Salt and sugar, that's some good runaway food.

"Okay, fellas," she said. "This is it. Really glad to meet you both. Good luck and don't feel stupid if you feel like calling your folks. It's okay."

Calvin and I smiled, got out of the car, thanked her, and she took off.

"I fell asleep," I said as we stood, looking homeless on the gas station pavement.

"Me too."

"You think she kept on talking the whole time - to no one?"

"Prob'ly," he said, laughing, as we headed back to the main road.

❧❧❧

It was dusk, drizzly and chilly. I thought about my twilight evenings with Sarah on the lake, and how things right now couldn't be more polar opposite, not the least the company I was with. I couldn't imagine Calvin in a yellow one-piece, and I was grateful for that.

We were standing at the entrance to an on-ramp with our thumbs out. After a half hour of steady non-stoppers, we were soaked, shivering and pissed off. Not that I would've known if someone did stop - thanks to Mother Nature endlessly spitting on my glasses.

"Shit!" Calvin said suddenly, pushing my arm down, and pulling me down the sidewalk, away from the on-ramp.

"What are you doing?" I asked, confused.

"Just keep your arm down, and walk," he said, quietly.

We walked maybe 10 yards before he stopped us. "Okay, let's go back," he said, heading toward the ramp again.

"What was that about?" I asked.

"You didn't see that Highway Patrol car?" Calvin asked.

"Oh, no, I didn't. Is hitchhiking illegal?"

"I don't know, but he's prob'ly gonna stop a couple of kids, gonna figure we're runaways."

"Yeah," I said, nodding, partly happy Calvin kept us from being taken in and partly unhappy that he kept us from being taken in.

Calvin could be a smart kid, for sure. When he saw the cop, he turned us around, making it look like we were taking a little walk through the outskirts of Dayton, Ohio; wouldn't have been my first choice for a stroll, but it worked.

Back in our spot now, we stuck our thumbs out yet again.

Fifteen minutes later, still no ride. And it was dark. The drizzling like kittens and puppies had turned to raining like cats and dogs.

Miserable.

"What do ya say we call it a night?" Calvin pointed to the cement underpass a few yards away. "We can camp under there - at least it'd be dry."

I was as uncomfortable as he was but setting up camp on a slanted slab of concrete was worth delaying, at least for a little bit. Earlier, I had noticed a restaurant not far away. I took my glasses off, wiped them (smeared them) on my shirt, then put them on again.

"There, look," I said, pointing down the main street, "a Denny's restaurant. Why don't we warm up, go to the bathroom first?"

Calvin sighed, frustrated. "Yeah, okay."

We started off.

Denny's was hot, fluorescent, and smelled like bacon and coffee. Only two booths were occupied. Two waitresses stared at us suspiciously. A cook with a tall white hat glared at us from under the heat lamps. Without stopping, we headed towards the bathroom, went in, and peed.

When we came back out, we practically bumped into one of the waitresses. Shirley, her nametag informed us, was African American, mid-40s and skinny, with makeup thick like a seven-layer cake, under a high and wide, perfectly rounded afro.

"Now that you've used the bathroom, you gonna eat somethin'?"

Calvin and I looked at each other. Should we just walk out and not answer her? Run, maybe?

"We don't have any money, or any place to sleep," I said. I think the desperation was coming through loud and clear.

She nodded, her fake eyelashes dancing along. "I think you should call your folks. They got to be worried. I'll give you a dime, you can call collect."

Before I could object, Calvin said, "Yes, ma'am. Thank you." Then to me with shut-the-fuck-up eyes. "It's the right thing to do."

"Okay, then," Shirley said, pulling a dime out of her apron pocket and handing it to Calvin. She pointed to the payphone in the back.

"Thanks," I said, as Calvin and I went over together, and Shirley went to check on another table.

At the phone, Calvin pretended to put the dime in the slot and dialed "0." He waited as I stood by, trying not to burst into laughter.

He spoke quietly so only I could hear. "Hi, collect to ..." he looked at me, thinking, then ... "collect call to ZZ Top please."

I lost it and had to hide around the corner by the bathroom to make sure Shirley didn't see or hear me.

A minute later, I rejoined Calvin and we headed toward the exit. Shirley approached us again.

"They comin' to get you?" she asked.

"No one was home, ma'am," Calvin said, frowning.

Shirley nodded skeptically. "Mmm-hmm. Well, why don't you both sit down, I'll bring you somethin' to eat. You can try again when you're done."

"We don't have any money," I reminded her.

Shirley looked over her shoulder to see who might be watching, or listening in.

"I know," she whispered to us.

"Very kind of you, ma'am," Calvin said, smiling.

"How about a couple Super Birds?"

We both nodded excitedly, as if we knew what she was talking about. She went off and we sat in a nearby booth. The corn nuts were a distant memory, so as long as it didn't come with a side of feathers, I was good with a Super Bird, goooneybird, jailbird, whatever.

Turns out it was turkey, bacon, swiss cheese, and tomato on grilled sourdough. Best sandwich I ever had for the hungriest I've ever been.

After our meal, Calvin went back to the phonebooth and pretended to call again.

When he returned, Shirley joined us.

"Still no luck," he said. "I guess we'll be headin' on. Thanks again for the food." Calvin gave me a head nod signal and I stood up.

Shirley blocked our way. "I know you haven't been calling. I should call the police. Your folks got to be worried sick."

She eyed each of us, waiting for some kind of response, but we had nothing.

It was then I realized - my folks probably didn't even know we'd left town. Of course, Boone did, and he might've called Mom and Dad or even went over there, but I can't imagine they would have had much of a conversation, considering the feud and all.

Shirley calling the police seemed like an empty threat, and we could've easily run past her, and back out into the cold, dangerous dark - not that there was much motivation for that. And as you know only too well at this point, I, mostly, took cues from Calvin on those types of things. I was there to support his every move. I was Robin to his Batman. Sam to his Rick. Barney to his Andy. Whatever Calvin thought best.

He was silent and unmoving; he just stood there, slumping with fatigue.

"You got somewhere to sleep tonight?" Shirley asked.

"No," Calvin and I answered simultaneously.

She gazed at us both for another moment, then said, "Wait here."

We watched her head toward the back, then walk through the double swinging doors with the port holes.

"You think she's calling the cops?" I asked, half-worried, half-relieved.

"Shit, man, I don't know."

"You think we should bolt?"

"Naw, she seems nice. Let's wait a minute, see if she comes back. If she doesn't pretty soon, we'll take off."

Shirley was back out in the dining area before we knew it, but now in a big coat with a fuzzy hood.

"You'll come home with me," she said as she fished through her giant purse, looking for her keys. "I live in a trailer park with my husband. There's no room inside, but you can sleep in the car once we get there. Clear?"

"Great. Thank you," I answered, grateful for the shelter.

With that, we left and all piled into her royal blue, '67 Cutlass Supreme. The interior was white and pristine and there was black fur glued to the dashboard. Calvin took the front as was our new routine. Me, the sidekick, sat in the back.

The trailer park was only a few minutes away. It was quiet and clean with perfectly spaced trees between each trailer. A planned community. Shirley parked beside her trailer.

She turned to us, her face serious and highlighted by moonlight. "Here the rules: Don't break in anyone's trailer. Don't steal anything. Be on your way in the morning. My husband's got a gun."

"Got it," Calvin said. "Thanks again, ma'am."

"Good luck," she said, her last words to us as she got out and slammed the door shut.

The Cutlass wasn't the worst accommodations considering the nippy Ohio weather. It was a Supreme, after all. Although it would've been nice if the dashboard fur was a big blanket instead of gratuitous decoration.

I stretched out in the back. Calvin did the same up front. We said our good nights and nothing else, both of us too tired to muster any comments about our adventure so far.

About an hour or so later, the heat we had from the ride over had dissipated, and the wee hours were made up of off-and-on, shivering shut-eye.

Making sleep all the more erratic - for both of us - were Calvin's nightmares, explosive nonsensical bellowing, interrupted with short bouts of weeping. I stared helplessly at the back of the front seat leather and tried to imagine what he was dreaming.

I closed my eyes, and first saw reality, when Calvin and I were in his bedroom, and he was smoking and pacing back and forth. But instead of fretting and listening to his parents go at it, he storms out of the room, walks right up to his dad and, Cousin Kevin style, burns the arson end of his joint right into papa's face. He holds it there, grinning as his dad flails and yells in pain. Calvin does his best Muttley, then brings a knee into Boone's crotch as Tchaikovsky's Nutcracker Suite suddenly starts playing loudly throughout the house. Boone falls to the floor, writhing in agony. Calvin then moves to his mom, who's been watching in delight while gnawing on a Super Bird, covered in feathers. Unfortunately, for her, that chewy smile distorts with pain when Calvin grabs her by her nasty hair and pulls her to her knees. The sandwich disappears, then Calvin moves behind her and pushes her down to a prone position. Laughing at his confused and terror-filled mother, he jumps onto her back and begins dancing, air-guitaring, and singing Creedence Clearwater Revival's *Fortunate Son*.

Of course, I'm watching the whole dream from the bedroom, applauding at the appropriate times.

⁂

The next morning, I opened my eyes to see Calvin staring back at me from the front seat. I guess he said something that woke me. The sun was low, but bright. The car windows were frosted outside, and we were both shaking from the cold.

"Let's get out of here," Calvin said.

I sat up, and we climbed out of Shirley's frozen Cutlass Supreme.

After the few feet to the gravel, main road, we started our journey back toward I-75.

Everything's a journey when you're on foot.

"Thanks, Shirley," I said, twisting my head back toward her trailer.

"Yep. She was cool," Calvin added, nodding.

It was a half-hour walk back to the interstate. Moving was helpful as it warmed us up a bit, yet we could still see our breath, and of course, we were starving, all of which naturally led to grumpiness. But I kept quiet. *Kvetching* would've been too much like my mother.

Calvin wasn't talking much either. Ever since his mother dropped in and blew everything up, he had become more and more quiet. The fun-loving, silly, red-headed rebel was now only showing up occasionally.

As soon as we hit the on-ramp, we hit the jackpot. At least, it seemed so at the time. A brand new, fresh from the carwash, '74, rust BMW pulled up alongside us.

A man in his early thirties cranked down the passenger window. He was muscular, with a tight, pink T-shirt, tanned skin, and a face full of fur: a massive, black mustache, and sideburns that came halfway down his face, then took a sudden turn toward his nose.

"You look freezing!" he said, flashing his blinding, white teeth.

"We are," I answered, returning the smile.

Calvin nodded. Or was it a shiver. Hard to say.

"Well, get in," the man said.

It was a four-door, and this time I went for the front seat. Calvin didn't seem to have an objection so we loaded up.

We took off with a jolt and my head banged against the headrest. As we merged, I peeked at the speedometer: seventy-five. Alarming, but anything was better than standing out in the cold or riding on the back of Calvin's bike. Calvin's ex-bike.

"I'm Donald," wannabe Mario Andretti said as he released a hairy right hand from the steering wheel. I shook it quickly, hoping he'd go right back to ten and two, and he did. He also went faster.

"I'm Yosef. That's Calvin," I said, getting nervous.

Calvin nodded again.

"Well, nice to meet both of you."

"You too," I said, realizing he hadn't asked us where we were going. "We're going to Detroit. Are you going that far?"

"Detroit? No, not quite. I'm going as far as Findlay. Just a couple hours from Detroit. Ever heard of it? Findlay?"

"No. We're from Tennessee," I replied, peeking again ... seventy-seven, seventy-eight.

"Tennessee. Far out. Beautiful country down there. I've been through on my way to Florida. I drive down to Lauderdale a lot. I enjoy the ride. I run a pretty big company, so it's hard to get any alone time. It's good for that."

He glanced over at me with an arrogant nod. I think I was supposed to be impressed with the running of a big company.

Highway terror was more on my mind, as he continued to accelerate, swerving between sluggish mac trucks and other inferior vehicles. My heart hammered against my chest. My skin was hot, and I'm sure my breathing was apparent. And, as it was the custom back then, none of us had our seatbelts on. Although the Federal seatbelt law had been in effect for several years, it was still highly under-utilized. I thought about putting mine on, but I was worried Donald might take offense, that clicking-in meant I didn't consider him an excellent driver. It's similar to failing to burp after a good meal in China.

I wondered at what point would we crash and be ripped into hundreds of pieces some poor coroner would have to put back together. I could see it inspiring a new jigsaw puzzle. They could call it *Multiple Fatalities*. Families would gather around the table, laugh, and drink various beverages while a kid tried to fit my spleen where my armpit should be. I'm sure it'd sell millions.

I looked back at Calvin to see if he was concerned at all. He was just looking at Donald, no expression really.

"You think ... maybe ... we could maybe ... slow down a little bit?" I asked, each word coming out more jellylike than the last.

"Oh, we're fine!" he shouted, laughing. "Don't worry. I always drive like this. So what's in Detroit? I mean, besides Smoky Robinson."

"My sister lives there ... waitress ... at a Thai food restaurant,"

"You know," he said, with yet another chuckle, "you're lucky *I* picked you up instead of the highway patrol."

"Yeah? Why's that?" Calvin asked, suddenly interested.

Donald looked at Calvin in his rearview and made a humph sound.

Hitting 100 mph now, he appeared to settle there, and turned on the radio. I don't recall the type of music. I'm going to guess Motown because he started dancing in his seat.

That was when I saw a sign; a glorious, thank you Jesus, Yahweh, Buddha, whomever sign: Findlay: ten miles.

We ought to cover that in under two minutes.

Then, oddly, he slowed down.

The terrain was still mostly rolling hills with a few scattered, small homes, but there were also patches of trees here and there. Donald pulled in front of one and parked. Being further up north now, fall had mostly fallen, so you could see well into the woods. I was grateful to be stopping, and I thought he was going to tell us to get out.

"Why we stoppin'?" Calvin asked, his head between the front, bucket seats. "We still got ten miles 'fore Findlay."

"Sorry, fellas," he said, turning the car off. "I've got to drain the lizard, really bad. Look, I know this is freaky, but do you mind coming with me? I don't really know you, and well, I don't really want to leave you alone with my car. No offense."

"Sure, I guess." Calvin said.

I shrugged, fine.

We got out and followed him up the hill and into the trees.

It made sense at the time. In hindsight, if he'd just taken his keys with him, we wouldn't have been able to steal the car. Not that we could drive anyway, but ... as I said, it *seemed* logical.

About twenty yards in, Donald sidled up to a giant Red Oak and proceeded to do his business. We stopped about ten feet behind him and busied ourselves with the wet leaves, kicking them, sliding on them, really just trying not to laugh.

"Boys," Donald said, with a weird tone to his voice.

We turned to see him, now facing us, but still holding his penis. I can't speak for Calvin, but it took me a few seconds to register what I was seeing. At first, I thought he was doing what teenage boys sometimes do - trying to pee on your friends when you're goofing around in the woods - but he was no longer urinating. His massive mound of pubic hair also threw me. Apparently, the Black forest ain't just a mountain range in Germany.

Then I realized ... Donald was hard, and he was masturbating.

"Can I get a hand over here?" he said nonchalantly.

"What the fuckin' hell?!" Calvin half-screamed, half-laughed.

I made a screeching sound, something resembling a barn owl with a touch of Robert Plant.

"Come on," Donald pleaded, seemingly unfazed by our reactions. "I gave you a ride. It's the least you could do."

Wrong! We bolted, beelining back down the hill, screaming and doing our damndest to stay upright.

When we hit the pavement, we kept going, running north up the shoulder of the interstate. Cars flew past us. Trucks blew past us, each threatening to send us sailing toward the motorway ditch. But we managed to keep going, our laughter and heavy breathing clouding the air with condensation. Evidently, your lungs can be on fire and freezing at the same time.

I finally stopped and bent over, trying to find my wind. Calvin followed suit. I looked back to see if Donald was chasing us. He wasn't. I didn't really think he would be, but I had to check, just to be sure.

As we finally caught our breath, Calvin and I looked at each other with our best *what the fuck* looks and burst out laughing once again, throwing our arms on each other's shoulders for balance and camaraderie.

We couldn't find the words, nor did we really need to. I guess that's how it is with best friends who are offered homosexual sex in a tree cluster just outside Findlay, Ohio.

Our next ride arrived only a few minutes after we stuck out our thumbs - a glossy, new, white Lincoln Continental Mark IV. Inside was a sweet, old Q-tip couple from Bloomfield Hills, a moneyed, Detroit suburb. They reminded me a bit of Gram and Gramps, but older, pushing eighty.

Planted firmly in the right lane, they drove so slow I was afraid we'd get pulled over for impersonating a giant snail.

Calvin had come out of his earlier funk, and when they asked where we were from, and where we were going, his answer was Detroit. We knew we had to lie this time, otherwise we'd be taken straight to the police. So the story was we were cousins, both sixteen, and his uncle (my dad) had a business emergency back in Findlay. We had to go with him, but, then he had to stay, so he told us to hitch home - about as plausible as a couple of Gurkha soldiers, turned zombie - but they seemed to buy it. They nodded and smiled. Nothing else was said about it.

As a matter of fact, I don't think they said much of anything else the whole rest of the trip. Fine by me.

Eventually, Calvin fell asleep. No audible nightmares this time, thank God. I stared out the window and thought about Lynn. I couldn't wait to see her. I'd gotten so caught up in my own shit over the last year and a half or so, I hadn't really thought about her much. All the better, considering the pain she put me through initially.

Then I realized something.

I had no idea where she lived in Detroit, nor did I have her phone number. We couldn't exactly stop in at every Thai food restaurant in town and see if she worked there.

I dozed off myself, not sure for how long, but when I awoke, I saw buildings on the horizon. City buildings. Glorious, ascending, cloud-kissing buildings. How I missed you so, concrete, steel, and glass. Granted, it was no Manhattan skyline, with its beautiful, new World Trade Center towers, but it was a downtown.

We exited the Interstate and wound our way through a number of turns, eventually pulling in front of a tall and majestic church.

We got out and thanked them. Before they took off, the man lowered his head, looking at us through the passenger side window. "You should go in, boys. You'll find what you're looking for, in there."

"Praise Jesus," Calvin said.

"Praise Jesus," the couple said in unison, smiling.

As they pulled out, I realized it was odd that they didn't ask us for our address. They just decided to drop us at a church?

They knew, just like everyone else. We were obvious runaways. And, I have to say, Mario was right: We *were* lucky the police hadn't caught up to us. In that respect, I suppose you could argue getting rides from a sympathizer, a predator, and a religious couple were fortunate. None of them even considered turning us in. Things were different in the early '70s. Kids hitchhiked. So did adults. So did escaped prisoners - happily, their numbers were fewer.

"We made it," I said to Calvin as we watched them turn the corner and disappear.

"Hell yeah," he said as he stared, mesmerized, at the towering church. "Big ass church, man."

"I'll say," I said.

It didn't occur to me at the time, but I imagine Calvin was more than a little uncomfortable in the city. He'd never even been to Knoxville. Cities can suffocate country folk. Too loud, too many people, and too many walls.

Surroundings aside, we were both hungry, and tired, and really just wanted to settle - somewhere, anywhere.

"So," he said, turning toward me, "where's your sister live?"

"I don't know, exactly" I said.

"Shit. What? Well, you got her phone number, right?"

"Uh-uh," I answered, shaking my head.

"Damn, man."

"Well, it was your idea in the first place. I didn't say I had her address or phone number."

"You might'a mentioned it," he growled.

"Oh, c'mon," I said, getting more and more irritated.

"Damn't," Calvin said, just as irritated. He started looking around, as if he might spot her walking down the street.

"I know!" I shouted. "I'll call my parents and ask them."

"I don't think that's a good idea," Calvin said. Of course, he had a point.

"There," I said, pointing at a phone booth just down the street. "I think we got to try it."

"All right, man," Calvin sighed. "But you can't tell 'em where we are."

As we walked toward the phone, a plan started formulating in my mind.

When we arrived, I opened the folding door and stepped in. Calvin waited outside but held the door open so he could hear. I picked up the receiver and dialed the rotary phone.

A musical voice came on the line. "Operator."

I raised my voice to sound feminine. "Hi, I'd like to make this a collect call, from Lynn." I sounded ridiculous. Calvin was snickering, but I had a plan.

"Hold please," she said.

After a couple rings. "Hello?" It was Gram.

The Operator came back on. "Collect call from Lynn. Do you accept the charges?"

"Oh ... I suppose," Gram said, unexcited.

Apparently, Gram was not the best person to answer the phone as she hadn't completely forgiven her granddaughter for deserting the family. But there was one family member she had an even bigger problem with.

"Gram, it's me, Yosef," I said, now in my regular low voice.

There was a pause, then in a slow, deep, disappointing tone, she said, "*Shanda eyngl.*"

Translation: *Disgraceful boy.* Even with the insult, hearing her voice caused a pang of homesickness - the kind of pain that makes you want to fall to your knees and weep. But you don't because of a thousand reasons.

"Are you hurt?" she asked.

"No, I'm fine. Gram--"

"Good. I'm not ready to speak with you. Goodbye," she said, her last word trailing off as the phone left her mouth.

"Wait! Gram! Please don't hang up!" I shouted as loud as I could.

"What?" She asked, bringing the phone back to her face.

"Gram, I need Lynn's phone number. I really miss her. I just want to call her. Please, can you find it for me?"

There was another lull. I could hear her breathing. It was labored, choppy. She seemed older.

"Why are you calling collect? I thought local calls were free."

I had to think fast. "Uh, yeah, well, not in Oak Ridge, Gram."

"This place," she said, sighing. "Where is it, the phone number?"

"On the bulletin board," I said, "above the phone, right in front of you."

"Hold on," she said.

I grinned silently, nodding to Calvin, mission almost accomplished.

She read it slowly. "313-555-9090."

I repeated it aloud so Calvin could hear and hopefully memorize it. "313-555-9090."

"313-555-9090," Calvin said to himself, quietly. We didn't have anything to write with, so he kept repeating it over and over.

"Thanks, Gram," I said, anxious to hang up and call Lynn before Calvin forgot the number. He was pacing in front of the phone booth. "313-555-9090, 313-555-9090."

"Yosef, you need to come home," she said, her voice breaking.

"I will. I will, Gram. Just … not yet. I'm sorry."

She was crying now. "How can you keep doing this to us, Yo--?"

"I have to go, bye," I interrupted, and hung up quickly.

Calvin rushed over. "313-555-9090."

I started dialing, then stopped and turned to him. "Can you do a collect call if it's local?

"What?!" Calvin asked. He had no idea what I was talking about. "313-555-9090," he repeated to keep remembering it.

I read the writing on the phone as Calvin kept reciting the number.

"I think we need a dime!" I yelled.

"Shit!" Calvin shouted back, then, "Wait, got an idea."

He ran over to a half-grass/half-dirt area on the other side of the sidewalk, bent down, and carved the phone number into the dirt with his finger. 3-1-3-5-5-5-9-0-9-0.

"Good thinking," I said, coming out of the phone booth. Now all we needed was a dime. There weren't a lot of people out, but I figured we could ask the next person who walked by.

Calvin had another idea.

"Be right back," he said, as he ran back down the sidewalk toward the massive church, and went in.

I stood anxiously in front of the phone booth, imagining Calvin asking a priest for the dime. They'd exchange some type of Jesus pleasantry, the priest would give Calvin the coin, and he'd be out of there. Even in the early '70s, a dime wasn't a big deal, so ...

Two minutes later, Calvin ran out of the church, and back over. "Here ya go," he said, handing me a dime. "Donation box."

"Great!" I shouted, laughing.

"That's what it's there for," he said, shrugging and smiling.

With that, I stepped back into the booth, picked up the phone, and put the dime in.

Dial tone! "Okay, read me the number," I yelled to Calvin.

He was already kneeling by the dirt number and repeated it once more.

I dialed ... waited ...

"It's ringing!" I screamed, putting my palm out for Calvin to give me skin.

He came over and slapped me back hard.

"Hello?" A warm, but very male voice said.

"Oh, hi." I was taken aback. "Is Lynn there?"

"Oh, sure. Hold on."

"Some guy answered," I whispered to Calvin. "He's going to get her."

"Hi, this is Lynn," she said, in that entrancing voice I loved so much.

"Hey, it's Yosef," I said timidly.

"Yosef! What it is, brother of mine?!"

"Hi John-Boy," I said. Calvin looked at me cockeyed.

Lynn laughed. I knew she thought I was calling from Oak Ridge, so I decided I should just spill it.

"Lynn, I'm in Detroit. I mean, we're in Detroit. Me and Calvin."

"What?"

"We rode up on Calvin's motorcycle, but then it broke down. Then we hitchhiked. We made it! We're here. In Detroit."

She was completely silent for a few seconds, clearly processing.

"Are you goofing with me?" she asked.

"No! We're here. Downtown, I guess."

"Yosef, this is ... do Mom and Dad know you're here?" Her voice was turning punitive, less loving.

"They don't know. We just took off. We needed to, okay?"

"You needed to? You're thirteen, Yos!"

"No duh."

"Jesus, Yos, you ran away?!"

Not the reception I'd hoped for.

"I can't believe this," she said, exasperated.

"We came here to see you."

There was another pause, then, "All right. Where exactly are you?"

"Woodward Avenue, I guess. Right near a big church."

"I'll see if I can borrow someone's car and come get you."

"Oh, cool," I said, more relieved than excited at this point.

"I need a cross street. Woodward and what?"

Calvin helped me figure out the cross street and I told her. She said she'd be there in ten minutes, then hung up without saying goodbye.

A half hour later, she pulled up in a rusty, brown Chevy Impala.

I was thrilled to see her. "Hi!"

"Get in," she said, not thrilled.

I sat in the front, Calvin in the back.

She looked like she did at my Bar Mitzvah, but that lightness, that joyousness was gone. She stayed quiet as we drove the short distance to her home. I could tell by her angry glances in the rear view she was blaming Calvin for our little excursion. She had never even met him, but I'm sure she had only heard bad things from Mom.

With each passing, silent minute, I was becoming more and more uneasy. And so was Calvin, I could tell. This cold reception was jarring. We had gone through hell to get up there. All for ... this? Lynn always supported me - in everything - but clearly, our encroachment was the furthest thing from cool.

Lynn lived in one of Detroit's oldest neighborhoods known as the Boston Edison district. In 1967, the Detroit riots threatened to destroy the neighborhood, but it survived, it's affluence helping to keep it afloat. The houses were palatial, home to Joe Lewis, Berry Gordy, and Henry Ford. And now, evidently, Lynn Bamberger. At the time, I didn't think it odd at all. I had very little awareness of what things cost, as Dad hadn't taught me much about money.

Snow flurries were starting to fall as we pulled up to an enormous, mid-'20s, red brick house. It was in good repair. A long porch swing hung from chains and there were several cars in the long driveway. All American, of course.

As we parked in front, Lynn turned the car off and turned in her seat to face both of us. Her anger seemed to be gone now, but it was replaced with something else: apprehension. Her eyes darted toward the house, then back at us. House, us. She was composing, starting and stopping a couple times before she said actual words.

"All right ... here's the skinny. So ... this is, my house here, but it's not just a house. It's what's called an ashram. I live here with 10 other people. You know what an ashram is?"

Calvin and I shook our heads.

She spoke slowly, for our benefit, yes, but it was clear she'd never had to articulate any of this before. "An ashram is a place for spiritual discovery. This one, ours, is called the Divine Light Mission. We follow the Guru Maharaji ..." She paused, becoming emotional, her eyes welling with tears. "He's this beautiful, young Hindu man. He teaches us a meditation practice. It's called Knowledge."

She gazed at both of us, letting that sink in, then continued. "The whole thing is based on connecting with one's inner strength. It's about choice, and appreciation, and hope. We're trying to create more compassion. I love it. I love him."

My face must have been pretzeled, and slightly deformed, because she started laughing.

"I know, I know, it's ... weird ... to most people," she said.

"Cool with me," Calvin said, hardly giving a shit.

"What's a Hindu?" I asked.

"Someone who believes in Hinduism," she answered, unsarcastically. "It's a religion. There're, like, a billion Hindus in the world."

My mouth flung open, and if I was a cartoon character, my eyes would've stretched out from my head before they snapped back. "You're not Jewish anymore?!"

Lynn sighed and slumped back against the car door.

"Seriously?!"

She didn't answer.

I looked over at Calvin, to see his reaction. He was just grinning.

"Yos," Lynn started, "I haven't really felt Jewish in a long time. I don't know why, exactly. I mean, yeah, I'd go to shul with you guys, but, you know, just to make Mom and Gram, happy. Jacob, too."

She turned bittersweet. "It's why we broke up. I met a few people from the Mission in New York. I really liked them, and they were so groovy. They invited me to stay here, work and meditate. One of my housemates got me the job at the Thai place. I donate my money to the ashram, and we all live peacefully together. It's really beautiful."

I was stunned.

Possibly drooling.

Jesus-Lord-God-In-Heaven - it wasn't just me!

Even Lynn had fallen out of love with Judaism. Her reasons were obviously different than mine. But, all this time, I had a partner in crime and didn't know it?! We shared a journey. From one religion to the next, whatever worked in that moment of time. It was amazing. I should've known. Lynn and I always had an extraordinary connection. I don't think I could've loved her more at that point.

I reached over and hugged her as tightly as I ever had.

I could hear Calvin repositioning, and sighing, likely uncomfortable with the show of affection.

Lynn whispered in my ear, "Feels good not to be lying about it anymore."

"Can we go in?" Calvin asked. "Gettin' kind of cold."

"Listen," Lynn said, pulling out of the hug, "you guys need to go home. Mom and Dad have to be so worried."

"They don't even know we're gone," I said, reassuring her.

"By now, they must. And what about school? Calvin, what about your folks? They have to be worried, too."

Calvin swung his head around and stared out the window.

"Do you have any money? Where will you sleep?"

"We thought we could stay with you for a while," I said, using my best baby brother pleading.

Her head fell onto her shoulder, her eyes shutting with aggravation.

"Look," she said, slowly opening her eyes again, "Before I picked you up, I talked to the other members. They agreed, if you guys do some chores around the house, maybe for a few hours, we can all have dinner together, but you can't stay. They're really strict about non-Mission people camping out."

My eyes met Calvin's and we nodded in agreement. "Okay," I said, frustrated.

"Okay," she said. "After dinner, we need to figure out some kind of plan. You can't just stick your thumbs out and end up who knows where."

She was right, of course. But when you're thirteen, fourteen, and both you and your best friend have mother issues, sometimes you're just going where the wind blows you. It's about the running. The destination is irrelevant, because there isn't one.

"So, what kind of chores?" I asked.

�֍֎֍֎

The house interior was cherry wood, floors and walls, with shadowy nooks and crannies and '60s, space-age furniture throughout. Lamps were on in every room, as the cloudy day demanded.

It was dark out by the time we finished the bathtub scrubbing, floor sweeping, leaf raking (front and back), and bathtub scrubbing again because, according to Lynn, we didn't do a good job the first time.

Exhausted, we settled down to dinner at a long table in the dining area. A glittery chandelier with pointy bulbs shined a warm, yellow light on the table full of food. Lynn sat next to me. Calvin across. Next to him was Richard, an ancient man with John Lennon glasses and a crocodile smile. Across from him was Madeline, the house mother, a loud-eating, forty-something mesomorph. Next to her was Stan, a young, upbeat Asian-American surfer with what he said was a shark bite scar on his arm. There were other members, but they were at their jobs.

Everyone was pleasant, happy to have some new, young minds to enlighten. Conversation first revolved around Satsang, associating with true people. Then we talked about service. Aka bathtub scrubbing, twice if need be.

The housemates weren't particularly heavy on the proselytizing, but there was some odd behavior. Retracted glances. A couple uneasy chuckles. Lynn, in particular, seemed unsettled, sitting on her leg. Not sitting on her leg. Getting up several times for this or that. I had never been around cultists, or believers, or whatever your descriptive inclination would be, so I didn't know if it was their manner and temperament, or something else.

You know that feeling you get when you know something bad's about to happen, but let it go because you're famished from hitchhiking all weekend without money and all you want to do is ensconce yourself in the gastrointestinal gifts bestowed before you?

Well, that's where my head - and stomach - were at.

Even with the vegetarian menu: Lentil salad, white rice, an assortment of nuts, and raw green beans that I picked from the garden in the back.

I looked at Calvin to see how he was tolerating the meal. He was gnawing on a handful of beans like a bloody-mouthed hyena. If he was pining for biscuits with sausage gravy, it didn't show. I forked a giant spoonful of rice and shoved it in my mouth, imitating him and making sure he saw me. We were having a grand ol' time.

That is, until Lynn, apparently unable to hold it in any longer, looked at me and blurted out five words that changed everything.

"I called Mom and Dad!"

Everything stopped, including the rice in my throat, stalling painfully as it has in the past, when food and anxiety have a head-on collision.

"What?" I said quietly.

You're not choking if you can talk.

"Please tell me you didn't." I was staring at my plate. I couldn't look at her.

"I'm sorry, Yos. I had to," Lynn said, beginning to cry. "They wanted me to get you guys on a bus home, but I told them that wouldn't work, that you'd just take off."

"That's true," Calvin agreed. I looked up at him, mouthing my own *sorry*.

"We had to think of something else," she said.

"What do you mean?" I asked.

Then I heard a sound coming from the front of the house:

The death rattle of another betrayal from a beloved female.

Specifically, the fuzz. Two Detroit police officers entering the dining room. I guess they were instructed to let themselves in.

Calvin swallowed audibly, his ears burning red.

I shot up, throwing my chair back, screaming at Lynn, "I can't believe you!"

Lynn stood, her hands up, trying to calm me down. "They're just going to hold you guys at the station until Dad can fly up to get you. I'm sorry! You can't stay here! It's for your own good."

"Lynn Bamberger?" A stocky, female cop with short hair was asking. Next to her was a male officer, Black, bald, and smiling, with his arms crossed against his chest.

Two police officers vs. two kids.

My palms were sweating.

I'd like to say the decision was fight or flight, but the idea of taking down two badass cops, two armed badass cops, didn't really appeal to me.

Nor did it Calvin, apparently, because when I looked at him to coordinate a run for it, he was already darting past our dinner companions and heading for the kitchen.

"Wait for me!" I shouted, as I took off after him.

"Hey! Get back here!" the cops yelled.

"Yos! Come back!" Lynn joined in.

Calvin and I shot through the kitchen, then flew out the backdoor.

The earlier flurries had turned to a steady snow. Stupidly coatless, and immediately freezing, we ran as fast as we could. I could hear the cops close behind, and Calvin was a good fifteen feet ahead of me, not at all slowing down for me to catch up.

Getting caught and being sent home would be different for Calvin. He'd be sure to get a massive whoopin'. *You better give your heart to Jesus, 'cause your butt is mine!* I could see Boone angry enough to put him in the hospital, maybe even kill him.

For me, it'd probably be another maternal slap fest, but murder was most likely off the table. Maybe there'd be a send-away to Israel for a year, or military school, perhaps. At the least, a good grounding, with a no-go-zone at the Macafees. It was always their fault. The only good news was I think my folks were running out of punishments.

Running through the vegetable garden, my foot crashed and squished into a massive pumpkin. Calvin was turning a corner, now racing around to the front of the house, instinctively knowing, I suppose, that going through backyards would require a myriad of fence jumps and barking dog dodges.

The police were gaining on me, the rays from their bouncing flashlights getting brighter. My heart was beating up into my cheeks. And I'm sure my lungs were forming icicles. I couldn't believe I hadn't collapsed.

Now beating it up the street, the distance between Calvin and I was increasing. And the streetlights' gray glow were only helping our pursuers.

Then, a God-send: The female cop slipped and fell on the snowy pavement.

"Fuck!" she screamed.

Whoo-hoo!

Her partner stopped and ran back to help her up. Calvin heard, looked back, then signaled to me with his head. He took a sharp left into someone's front yard and I followed. We were out of their sight now, at least temporarily.

We bolted around to the back of the house. Calvin took another sharp left, heading the opposite direction through the backyard, then, left, back toward the street again.

That's when I realized what he was doing.

Somehow, he had managed to work our way *behind* the cops.

Once we hit the street again, he dropped, crawling under a pickup truck that was parked in a driveway, and I joined him as quickly as I could.

We laid face down on the cold asphalt, gasping for air. My Maalox bottle, as always in my front pants pocket, was jamming into my thigh. Yay, let's add poking pain to all the other discomfort. The more the merrier.

Staying as still as we could, we could hear the cops continuing their search, their feet crunching like Corn Flakes in the snow, and cursing, calling us *little fuckers*. Their flashlights were shooting this way and that. And I thought about what I would do when they finally found us.

Struggle and scream? Or rejoice?

⁂

A beam of light lit up Calvin's face like some kind of ghoul. I figured that was it, we're done, caught, It was time to go home and begin the groveling while I packed my bags for Jerusalem.

But they went right on by. They didn't think we'd climb under some nasty ol' pickup truck, I guess. That, or they were cold and tired and pissed off. Also, we weren't exactly a danger to society. Just ourselves.

Within a few minutes, the flashlights were gone. The footsteps, gone. We listened for a while - just to make sure. To this day, the sound of fat snowflakes on tree branches takes me back to that very moment. Every time.

As we crawled out from under the truck, we stood, surveying the worsening blizzard.

"What now?" I asked, barely able to form words I was so cold.

Calvin started down the sidewalk. "Back on the road, I reckon." I could hear the fear in his voice. It was contagious. Freezing to death was a real possibility now.

"But, where?" I asked, catching up to him.

"Shit, I don't know," he said, shaking the snow off his face.

"Maybe we should … maybe we should go back to the house. Lynn can call the cops, if she wants. Police station has heat. Right?" I chuckled, trying to lighten things.

"What?!" Calvin said testily, his teeth chattering. "I ain't goin' back home, man. We'll get a ride, warm up in the car. It'll be fine."

So, there it was. We'd walk back to the highway through an early, Michigan snowstorm, without proper winter wear, and once we got a ride and they asked us where we were going, we'd say, *oh, anywhere but Oak Ridge, Tennessee.*

Solid plan.

About fifteen minutes later, we were still trudging through it, each step harder than the previous one. I couldn't feel my feet or my hands, and we were both shaking uncontrollably. Suburbia had morphed to industry, with soaring, brick and concrete car business buildings. In dark alleyways, dangerous looking homeless men warmed their hands next to flaming trash barrels, and stray cats raised their body temps under cardboard shanties.

We were finally coming up on the interstate, thank God. It had to be close to 9 or 10pm. With so few cars getting on the highway, we figured we needed to stand on the shoulder this time, so we kept walking until we hit the interstate itself.

At last, we stopped and planted our feet, squinting into the glacial abyss that was I-75 North. We stuck out our purple thumbs - not that there was any reason to. I imagined someone would eventually drive by and have mercy on us. It was obvious we were in dire straits.

But every minute or so, a car would speed by, probably not even seeing us. Or, worse, a mac truck would blaze past, throwing a flood of grimy slush in our faces if we didn't turn away fast enough. I had read stories about people losing various appendages to frostbite, fingers and ears snapping off like propeller blades in a helicopter crash. I was becoming more and more certain, that by the time we were picked up, we would leave a toe or two behind.

My God, what kind of morons were we, hitchhiking, outside in this weather, without coats?!

Desperate ones, that's what kind.

And you know what they say: Desperate morons call for desperate measures.

"This isn't working!" I shouted, shivering and stuttering. "There aren't enough cars!"

Calvin didn't respond. He just kept staring down the interstate, waiting for a wing and a prayer. Even another wooly, gay man would suffice at this point.

My pain and fear were turning to anger. And it was pointed at Calvin. Hard to blame Mom, or Judaism, for this one. How could I let him talk me into this? Sure, he was best friend, but was our friendship worth turning into a human ice cube?

Leave it to getting stuck in an epic Midwest snowpocalypse to separate one from childish notions. Survival instinct will do that.

"Calvin!" I screamed. "This is stupid! I'm going back to Lynn's! Come with me!"

"Naw! Hell naw!" He crossed his arms in defiance. "You better not go, man! You can't leave me out here!"

"Well, come on then!"

"We ain't goin' back!"

I was trembling, a combination of cold and fury. "This is your fault! I thought we were just going for a ride, not to run away! Now look! We're about to die out here!"

He glared at me, his anger matching mine now. "It ain't my fault you're such a wus!"

A truck barreled by, throwing up another blanket of icy hell. I screamed in pain.

"I am not a wus! Maybe I just don't want to freeze to death!" The tears started flowing, first warm, then quickly turning frigid.

"Chicken! Bawwwk, bawwwk, bawwwk, bawwwk!" Calvin squawked, just like he did that first time in the woods.

"At least my dad's not a murderer, and my mom didn't leave when I was a kid!"

I expected Calvin might lunge at me, but instead, he turned away. I was about to apologize when he spun quickly back around. He had tears in his eyes and was oddly calm. He came closer to me.

"You want to know a secret? I never wanted to be your damn friend. Daddy made me."

It didn't register at first.

When it did, I figured I misunderstood. It must be the wind and the traffic and anything, anything else but what he was actually saying. But whether I wanted to or not, I had heard him, and it began to soak in, slowly, like a rag dropped in a pan of motor oil. Suddenly, I couldn't feel the bitter cold anymore. It was replaced with something worse. He might as well have tossed a live grenade at my feet.

"Yup," Calvin said grinning. "That's right. I told him about the new Jew at school, and he said I should be friends with you - just so we could convert you to Jesus. Then, you'd stop being a damn Jew. And it worked, man! Even got you baptized. Hahahahahahhahahahahahhahaha!"

He pointed at me as he laughed, like I was some moronic clown, only there to be ridiculed. It was as if were back at that first day in the cafeteria, like nothing had happened between then and now.

Fuck you, Muttley.

"But you know what, man? Doesn't matter. Even Jesus can't keep you from being a goddamn kike."

The grenade exploded - blowing me up into a thousand pieces, all falling with a splat onto the icy asphalt. Dizziness kicked in, and a new lump in my throat appeared, unmotivated by its usual catalyst. My heart and head were pounding so hard I couldn't tell which was which. I started crying, loudly, uncontrollably. Still, without words.

And so it came down to it again - fight or flight?

I took off running, toward the on-ramp, my frozen legs kicking up snow behind me, and somehow, moving as fast as I was telling them to.

When I hit the surface street, I kept going in the direction of Lynn's house, my phlegmy sobbing and gasping, making me cough and gag - a moose dying from nerve gas poisoning, if you heard from a distance.

Regardless, five inches of snow wasn't going to stop me from the unconditional love of my big sister. I may have even increased my speed, and I almost fell several times.

Until I did. I tripped, or slipped, and went crashing face first into the snowy sidewalk.

I laid there, not moving. My glasses were jamming into my head, and my breathing was labored, but something was working against my instinct to get up.

My pubescent pendulum had swung in the other direction. Yo-Yo Bamberger. Susan had it right all along. As driven as I was a moment ago, my defeatist side took hold now. I was realizing something.

They were right. Everyone. The kids on the bus, in the schoolroom, around town. Me and the other thirty-six Jews from shul were inferior (Damn you, Gary!).

Anti-Semitism has been based on the same principles for centuries: Jews can't be trusted. They want everyone else's money. If they could, they'd take over the world and make everyone pray to only their God. They're not even human. The list goes on.

In Boone Macafee's eyes, with my age and the tools at his disposal, I was the perfect project. A nasty tree stump was inside me that needed to be removed, so something righteous could be planted in its place. In his view, I should've been thanking him.

New York? That was just a fantasy: a miniature, segregated paradise, where we had convinced ourselves we were worthy, while being completely unaware of the real America.

And so it was, as I laid there, I began to see it their way. From freak-azoid to kike, I was all those things and more. How can you trust a Jew who see-saws between Judaism and Southern Baptist and has even considered Hinduism?

Maybe this, this Mr. Freeze ending, would be the proper end to me. As the seconds ticked by, it was becoming increasingly clear: I didn't deserve to keep living.

So I stayed there. Not moving. Letting everything go.

I even stopped crying.

The parts of my body that weren't already numb were becoming so now.

I thought, this was really it.

But then it hit me.

It was something heavy. Some kind of cover thrown on top of me. It shocked me at first, but then I could feel its warmth. Was this death? Was this the loving embrace of one of my Gods? Maybe both of them.

It was neither.

I decided to move my head, just slightly, just to see what was going on.

It appeared to be a big, wool blanket.

Someone had actually put a blanket on top of me. I had to see who it was, so I sat up. Through my dripping glasses, I squinted in every direction. It was still snowing, but less, so that helped.

There. About twenty yards away, walking down the sidewalk. It was one of the homeless men we had seen in the alley. He wore a thick, super-hero cape, his own blanket.

I stood up, keeping the blanket wrapped around me, and stared at him as he meandered on. Guess he had a spare.

His kindness and generosity struck me. I felt that, even if he knew of all my faults and inconsistencies, he would've still done what he had.

There's no doubt he could've used two blankets for the coldest Michigan nights still to come. But he gave one up. Perhaps to save a life.

Shivering, I watched him until he eventually faded away.

I thought about going back to be with Calvin. Maybe we could act like everything he said was a lie. Or didn't happen. He'd probably be happy to see me.

Then, I thought about tossing the blanket aside, laying back down in the snow, and continuing my melodramatic death march.

After another minute of contemplation, I turned, put one leg in front of the other and headed back toward Lynn's house.

❦

It was close to midnight when I finally made it back to Lynn's neighborhood. Even with my new winter trappings, I was trembling uncontrollably, and I ran the last block.

After I knocked, a sleepy-eyed Madeline, the house mother, opened the door an inch. She was in a drab, tan nightgown, and an even worse mood. But, being a woman of grace and peace, the new Hinduism, she told me to wait in the living room while she went to get Lynn.

A minute later, Lynn ran in, dressed in her red and white pj's.

"Oh, thank God!" she screamed, before grabbing me, and pulling me into a tight hug.

We cried together for a few minutes, then sat on the sofa. I was beyond exhausted, and thought I might pass out, but I wanted to keep looking at her face. It was so comforting.

"Are you OK?" she asked, rubbing my hands to warm them.

I nodded. "I'm sorry. We shouldn't have come. I'm ready to go home."

She smiled slightly. "Good. Where's Calvin?"

"He's hitchhiking," I mumbled, not wanting to think about him.

Lynn took a deep breath. "Come on," she said, standing up and leading me upstairs.

Her room was the size of an 8-track tape, with a twin bed, a small, knitted blue and green area rug, and a dresser drawer with a lava lamp on top. She pointed to the small floor space between the dresser and her bed.

"You can sleep here tonight. We'll figure it out tomorrow."

I laid down, putting my blanket over me and noticing its smell for the first time: a combination of burnt wood and sweat. I didn't care. Lynn handed me one of her pillows, then turned off the light and got under her covers.

She was, of course, breaking the ashram rule of no guests, but it's not like she was going to be punished with a sacrifice into a Satan pit of hell flames. It wasn't that kind of cult.

"Good night, John-boy," she whispered.

"Good night," I replied as a yawn hijacked the rest of my reply.

I was asleep before my eyes closed. In a sense, I was home.

BLESSED BE THE ONE TRUE JUDGE

LYNN WAS FRANTIC AND KNEELING BESIDE ME, HER HAND shaking my shoulder. "Yosef, wake up. Wake up!"

I pulled my eyelids open and was accosted immediately by the morning sun. I didn't immediately remember where I was. "What? Lynn?"

"Wake up. We have to go home." She seemed panicked.

"We?" I asked, sitting up.

"It's Gram. She's in the hospital," she said with a tremble in her voice. "She had a heart attack."

I gasped, doubling Lynn's fear with my own.

She stood up, went over to her dresser, and started rummaging for clothes. "I just hung up with Dad. He bought us both plane tickets. I called a taxi. We're going now."

"Okay," I said, getting up.

Lynn pulled out a pair of dark green elephant bells and a tan V-neck sweater. "Go down to the bathroom, get cleaned up a little. I'm going to get dressed."

I was in a daze. Last night, now this. No one close to me ever had a heart attack or anything close, but I knew they were serious. My clothes were smelly, wrinkled and filthy, so besides peeing, and throwing water in my face, there wasn't much I could do to get ready.

As I hurried down the hall to the community restroom, Lynn closed the door behind me. I noticed the wood floor creaking underneath me.

It made me think of our home in Brooklyn.

The Delta flight took off on time. Hour and a half to Knoxville. Small plane. Uncrowded. Two seats on each side. Lynn and I sat about ten rows back. We didn't talk much. All I could think about was Gram, a not at all welcome respite from everything else. A heart attack at sixty-four. I wondered if it was due to her arduous life. Poverty in Poland. The Holocaust, of course.

Suddenly, the plane shook like a directly-over-the-subway apartment. I gasped. I wasn't comfortable with flying yet, that would come much later in life. Needing a distraction, I started imagining Gram and Gramps back in the day. First, I had to do some historical math.

Gram was born in 1910, in Poland. That meant she was twenty-nine when Germany invaded in 1939. So in 1942, she was thirty-three when her, Gramps, and Mom were all taken to Auschwitz. They were there another three years or so until they were liberated in 1945 and eventually came to America where relatives took them in. Curiously, I hadn't heard much about these relatives. Maybe they were dead by the time I came around. It would be nice to know more. Without them, I might not exist.

Wait a minute. Mom was born in 1936, so she was six when they got to the camp and nine when they left. That didn't make sense. She had always said she had no memory of Auschwitz; or maybe she just never wanted to talk about it. Then something else struck me: Gramps' boxing career started in the '20s. *America* in the '20s. Was he going back and forth between the U.S. and Poland, then in the '30s got stuck there during the war? I feel like I would've known if that was the case. It was all so confusing. I figured I had my years and ages wrong. Although, I was pretty good at math. I had just never thought it all through before.

The plane trembled again, this time more sustained. I white-knuckled the seat sides, just as the stewardess rolled her cart beside me.

"Do you have Tab?" I asked.

"Of course, sweetheart," she said, smiling. She popped one open and poured my drink.

Dad would've had to leave Mom in order to pick us up at the airport, so we had to take another taxi to Oak Ridge. It was close to 2pm by the time we got to the hospital.

Oak Ridge Hospital attracted some of the country's most brilliant minds for the same reasons the government labs did, so it was safe to say Gram was in good hands. I was comforted by that. I had had a good experience (as good as could be expected, of course) when I got my arm cast.

The hospital was big for Oak Ridge, all brick, architecturally vanilla like the rest of the town. The cab dropped us at the main entrance, and after the receptionist pointed us toward the ICU, we followed the signs from there. We walked briskly through the long, cold, white halls, breathing in the alternating smells of 409 and biscuits.

Finally, we spotted a low-hanging ICU sign, and beside it, a small waiting room that might have once been a broom closet. Lynn went in before me.

Sitting all in a row were Mom, Dad, Gramps, and Susan. They all shot up when they saw us. Mom came to me first and pulled me into a suffocating hug.

"Yosef, oh Yosef," she said, weeping.

There were more hugs all around. Of the kids, Lynn started crying first, then Susan, then me. In the order of our births.

I remember being amazed. In that thirty-four seconds of love and grief, it was as if I had done nothing untoward in the previous eighteen months. From screwing the Bar Mitzvah pooch to risking my life hitchhiking, none of it mattered now.

Thanks, Gram, I'll take it. You get better, okay?

"Where is she? Can I see her?" I asked.

Like a Jewish cocoon, the family was surrounding me and Lynn. Mom was now squeezing my right hand. They all looked at each other: Who was going to tell us?

"She's gone," Gramps said emotionless. "Died about an hour ago."

My breath caught. "What? No."

Lynn's tears turned to convulsive sobbing. Dad led her to a chair and they sat, holding each other.

Gramps sat back down and stared straight ahead, his championship belt digging into his gut as it always did. Even though he was the one who just told us, I don't think it had hit him yet. He could verbalize it, agree that it happened, but those were just words. I think a majority part of him assumed she was still alive. He had been with her, and in love with her, for over forty-five years. At her funeral, he would even throw rocks into her grave, as is the Jewish tradition, but as we know, Gramps wasn't one to move on quickly. He changed nothing in his life after her passing. He spoke to her empty chair at meals. Shared laughs with her watching Archie Bunker. Even had conversations with her before nodding off to sleep.

I was angry and feeling helpless. My head was jerking, almost Parkinson's like. No one had prepared me for this. If we'd known the heart attack was a major one, we'd have run over after the taxi dropped us. I needed someone to blame, yet there was no one. Mom led me to a chair and sat me down.

"I have to say goodbye," I whispered. "I have to say goodbye."

"I'm sorry, Yosef. They've already taken her."

The memory of the last time I spoke with Gram shot through my brain like a pinball headed for the gutter. It was that collect call. I was demanding and unpleasant. I hung up on her. The guilt and the sadness were overwhelming. I exploded into a thunderous wailing. Mom pulled me into another hug, and we cried in each other's arms for a long, long time.

❧❧❧

We flew Gram's body, and ourselves, up to New York, and had the service at our beloved Ahavath Synagogue. Rabbi Berkwitz presided. The two meshuggeners came and just about everyone else we knew in New York. Bittersweet, in that respect.

The burial was at Brooklyn's Washington Cemetery, where Gramps, Mom, and Dad also had plots.

Finally, for a full week, we sat Shiva at Cousin Michael's apartment in the Bronx. One evening, suffocating under my hot, black suit, I excused myself and went outside.

I found a space between two parked cars and sat on the curb.

Suddenly, a hand was on my shoulder. "May God console you among the other mourners of Zion and Jerusalem."

I turned to see a young, Hasidic couple I didn't know.

"Thank you," I said quietly. They nodded and walked on. Religious Jews will often come to funerals to pray and mourn with the family, even if they didn't know the person who died. That's some serious compassion.

It was almost Thanksgiving. Below freezing gusts were throwing trash in all directions. Cars were honking. Goyim drug deals were going down in filthy alleyways. The New York therapy I was needing. God, I wanted to stay. So badly. Get back to our synagogue, the meshuggeners, the neighborhood. Find another Sarah. Have Gram still with us.

Of course, none of that was possible.

"*Du Zol Nicht Vissen Frum Tsores*," I whispered to myself.

The building front door opened, and I turned to see who it was.

Mom sat beside me on the curb, squeezing into the small space I had commandeered. Her hair was a rat's nest, her eyes were droopy and glassy from little sleep. And she had a bit of schmutz on her black dress, mustard I think.

"You're going to get your dress dirty," I said, as she put her arm around me.

She nodded in agreement. Such were the consequences of loving your family, I suppose.

"Mom, did Gram say anything, you know, before she died?"

"Not exactly. It was a regular day. Her and Dad were watching the television when she screamed out in pain, grabbing her chest. We rushed her to the hospital. A little while later she went into a coma. A few hours after that, she ... she died."

She took a deep, painful breath in, no doubt re-experiencing it.

"Did she tell you I called for Lynn's phone number?"

"She did," Mom said, matter-of-factly.

I looked down at the gutter. "I hung up on her. I didn't mean to. We didn't have anything to write with, and we didn't want to forget the number ... and ..."

"She didn't mention it."

"Oh. Good," I said, relieved.

"If it was a big deal, she would've mentioned it. Right?"

"Right."

Ever since Gramps told us of Gram's death, I had been thinking about our last exchange, aching for a proper goodbye. But, according to Mom, no one had gotten one. That made me feel a bit better.

Still, I felt like I had fallen into a massive hole. I was barely holding onto the ledge, my fingernails filling with dirt as I slowly lost my grip. I couldn't imagine life without Gram. It's not that we spoke very often or that we had much in common, but she was just ... there. Always there. Even after she lost her finger and stopped cooked, and even after the move when she became more introverted, she remained a pillar of the family, just by her presence.

"You haven't said anything about staying with Calvin," I said, "or how we got to Detroit or anything."

"It doesn't matter," she said, shuffling her feet. "You're here now. We'll all go home together. Family needs to stick together, what we have left anyway." Her voice broke.

I nodded rigorously.

"Mom?"

"Yes?"

"This is kind of weird, but something's been bugging me."

"Tell me," Mom said.

"Well, it's about Gramps," I said, slowly. "Did he have all those boxing matches in the 1920s, here in America, then move to Poland in the 1930s? Then he met Gram and they had you and then, you know, the Holocaust?"

Her face tightened, and now, she looked down at the street.

"I suppose it's the right time," she said. At least that's what I think she said, as her volume was low and the words slightly garbled. A combination of grief and valium.

"What? Right time for what?"

"Your Gramps had an amazing boxing career," she said, looking up at me again. "Afterwards, he got a good job, ran the printing press at the New York Times, right here in New York."

"Duh. Mom, I know all that."

She nodded, pausing, deciding how to say what she needed to say.

Finally, she said, "He never went to Europe. Your Gram ... was never in Europe. Of course, neither was I."

I was mystified. What's next? The sky isn't blue? Taxis aren't yellow?

"I don't understand," I said, stammering. "The Holocaust was in Europe. Poland. Auschwitz."

She nodded, pained, then continued with sigh-filled pauses between sentences.

"Your *great*-grandparents were born in Poland. But Gram and Gramps were both born here. They were here during the war. Your father's parents were born in Russia. You never knew them, very nice people. Of course, we did have many relatives die in the ghettos, and the camps, but none of our immediate family - *du Zol Nicht Vissen Frum Tsores*."

I finally got it, and it hit me hard, like she was slapping me all over again. This time with words. They stung just as badly, maybe even worse.

"But ... Gram. She talked about it! There were horrible stories!" I shook with frustration.

Mom nodded, cupped my hands in hers. "And those stories were true, for some. After the war, we took in quite a few survivors: cousins, aunts, uncles. The house was full for months. We helped them get on their feet, get jobs, homes. Gram would cook for them, and they would tell her about the terrible, terrible things that had happened. What no one realized was that she was feeling so much guilt that she wasn't there. In many ways, she felt that we *should've* been. Sharing the misery. That's what Jews do. Then one day, she, she just started talking like ... we were there. She told their stories as hers."

I pulled my hand away, my whole body jerking with outrage.

"I know this is hard," Mom continued, "but try to understand Yosef ... it was a lie she ended up believing. She needed it, and we gave that to her. Understand?"

No, Mom. I don't *understand* how my own grandmother could lie to me about something so important, so life-defining. I wore her experience like a badge of honor, every day. When we discussed it in school, I shared her experiences every time. I talked about it with my friends. We prayed together about it. I had nightmares about it. I was there with her. Because of Gram, the Holocaust was a major part of my identity - even when Jesus came into my life. She had survived the Nazis, and, by proxy, so had I.

Suddenly, on a filthy Bronx curb in November, it all disappeared.

I wanted to throw up. Suckered again, that's me. Yosef Bamberger, available 24/7, for all your lies and deception!

Mom leaned in. "She loved you. Deeply. You know that, right?"

"I know," I said quietly, giving her what she wanted to hear.

"That's what's important. One day, Yosef, you'll understand."

I looked off. The wind had stopped, and it was getting dark. Across the street, the dry cleaners and the electronics store turned on their lights.

Mom was right. I would understand one day, but that was many years off.

I turned back to her. "Does Susan know? Lynn? Dad?"

"Everyone knows," she said, standing up, then brushing the dirt off her butt with her hands. "Come on, come back in."

I couldn't move and had nothing else to say.

"When you're ready then," she said, as she turned and went back inside.

BOONE BURNS

BOONE HADN'T SLEPT FOR TWO DAYS, EVER SINCE THAT night when Dorothy crawled back into their lives like some kind of strung-out cockroach. After he finally got her out of the house, he went to check on Calvin and Yosef, but they had disappeared. He saw the motorcycle was gone and figured they probably just needed to blow off some steam - they'd be back.

But by dawn, he realized they might have had other plans.

That day, Boone checked everywhere: the woods by the pot plant, a couple favorite fishing creeks, even the Bamberger house. All he had to do was spot the motorcycle - he didn't have to actually speak to anyone, and that was fine with him.

With every new place he checked, he got a little angrier, wanting to punch someone a little more. Finally, he checked one last place: the Garden Apartments, where Dorothy had said she was living. The rundown complex had been around since the war, and Boone knew of it. When he arrived, he walked the whole perimeter of the place. Nothing but dead grass, blaring TV sets, and raccoon-stormed garbage cans. No motorcycle. No Calvin.

Boone was boiling over. He would skin that boy's hide when he got a hold of him.

It was nightfall by the time he got back to the still empty house. He decided it best to do some praying, have something to eat, then try to get some sleep. If they weren't back by the next morning, he'd call the

Bambergers to see if they knew anything. After that, he wasn't sure what to do. The last thing he wanted was a conversation with the police.

The praying went fine, as it always did, but he could barely get down the can of pork and beans he opened. He was just too agitated. And he could definitely forget about sleeping.

When he laid down on the sofa for some shut-eye, pictures in his mind's eye started coming at him like a hive of rageful bees; first his ex-wife screaming at him; then Calvin on the motorcycle - riding who knows where; then, all of Yosef's kin when they were at Boone's front door, but this time, in his imagination, they were laughing at him.

That last image forced Boone's eyes open. They reminded him of something he'd been trying to figure out before all this Dorothy nonsense started. This was good. It gave him something positive, useful to think about. For a while now, he'd been trying to find the right kind of revenge on that kike asshole, the one who slugged him in the face. Just like a dirty Jew, Boone thought - hit him when he wasn't ready. But he'd get his. Oh yes he would.

But what exactly?

Boone had run through several options: Destroying the family car with a baseball bat. Shootin' out their house windows late at night. Comin' up on Murray unexpectedly and cold-cockin' him - just like he did to Boone.

But no. None of that was good enough. He had been humiliated in front of his own son. You just don't do that to a man and get away with it. Not around these parts, you don't. He had to come up with something bigger, something better, more meaningful.

The good news was that if Boone could figure out something quick-like, it was actually a good thing that Calvin wasn't around. He didn't want him accused of anything. Boone was always good at that, he thought, making the best of rotten situations. Takes shit to grow flowers, he heard someone say once. He liked that. When Dorothy left them years ago, Boone decided he'd be the best dad ever. When his ministry career didn't pan out, he created a successful stump-pulling business. And when a young Jew came into Calvin's life, Boone would convert him, slowly, and steadily, with the force of Jesus' love always moving him forward. Turning a Jew. Shit to flowers.

Then, of course, there was the icing on the cake: The ultimate act of redemption.

Boone needed some fresh air, so he got up off the couch and went onto the back porch. The cold air felt good on his face, and he could smell a nearby fireplace burning. He took a deep breath in, then out, and stared out into the black woods.

Suddenly, something overwhelmed him. It was sadness, and it hit him like a wrecking ball. Boone couldn't remember the last time he was sad; maybe when he was a young'un. Anger, love, passion, sure, all the time. But despondency, no way. That kind of crap was for wussies.

But he couldn't help it, not this time. It was only a few years ago that he used to stand in that exact place, staring out at those same trees, and behind him, Dorothy was still adorable, still sexy, still funny. Still his wife. He remembered taking care of her when she was pregnant, especially those last weeks when she could barely get around the house by herself. He felt needed. Then Calvin came around, and eventually, grew to be a good-looking, strappin' boy, did what Boone told him. Sure, he got into trouble, but only the good kind.

Perhaps common for people who don't endure sadness well, the feeling was quickly replaced with something else. For Boone, it was that oh-so-comforting feeling of vengence.

He finally knew what he was going to do to the Jews on Newell Lane.

Boone smiled, nodded to himself, and whispered, "Damn straight."

Now, in the quiet, early morning hours, Boone drove his truck down the dark, empty Oak Ridge turnpike. On the passenger-side floorboard, a chipped and rusty gas can rattled and sloshed with the occasional pothole. He chuckled, not because of the sound, but because he suddenly realized something: his retaliation would be yet another feather in his redemption cap. From shit, flowers.

DELIVERANCE

I SAT NEXT TO SUSAN ON THE PLANE BACK FROM NEW YORK. She had the window seat and was staring quietly out at the sea of sun-drenched clouds. I asked her what she was thinking about and she just shook her head. I'm going to guess it wasn't secret boyfriends.

We were taking Gram's death equally hard. Whether it's a relative dying of natural causes, or a classmate killed in a car accident, your first loss is always a shock. It leaves you bewildered and unprotected, like you're standing where your house used to be after a tornado.

But since Gram always lived with us, it went deeper than that. In large part, we were who we were because of her. She rocked us to sleep, and changed our diapers, and chased us down as toddlers before we ran into traffic. She taught us our manners and how to be Jewish. Regardless of whether we have memories of these things, we know them to be true. (There were also pictures sometimes.) In our early life, she was as much our mom as Mom was. We humans tend to love those who help create us. It's impossible not to.

"Susan."

She turned toward me. "What?"

"Mom told me about, you know, Gram not being at Auschwitz."

She nodded. "Right. You know, all you had to do was look at her left arm. She didn't have a number, concentration camp number."

She turned back toward the window.

Of course, I was well aware of the Nazis tattooing prisoners with numbers as they arrived at the camps. But I never noticed Gram's arm - obviously. Probably because that would've meant I didn't trust her completely. I wondered why she didn't try to keep her arm covered to hide the truth and how she could keep a straight face when she talked of the horrors. I wanted so badly to confront her. I started going over what Mom had said. I could imagine Gram sitting with survivors around the dinner table, listening to their stories, and wondering why she was spared the terror and torture. But why would anyone want to be part of that? It made no sense to me. Possibly because I didn't understand the concept of guilt and all its complicated tentacles. If I had any guilty feelings at that point in my life, they were fleeting.

It was after midnight when we arrived back in Oak Ridge.

As I lay in bed that night, the faces of everyone in my life, from Gram to Calvin to Sarah, darted through my mind like shooting stars. But I felt content, oddly. This was new, surprising. Suddenly, I didn't mind the ugly carpet, or my curtainless view, or even knowing I had to go back to school the next day. It felt good to be surrounded by family. Unconditional love. There was no need to be anywhere else.

That's when it struck me, like a thunderbolt without a lightning warning: I never really took responsibility for my Bar Mitzvah, not internally anyway. I hadn't thought much about what it did to my family, or our people back in Brooklyn. Sure, there was the humiliation, and the crying, and the letters of apology, but all that was because it was what I had to do to get out of the situation, to move forward. Not because I felt any real remorse.

Maybe it was due to Gram's departure, or the truth about Boone and Calvin, or simply maturity, but I realized that, everything in my life, I didn't have to do for me.

Whatever reason or reasons, it was time now for real redemption.

Time for a flawless, uninterrupted, do-it-for-Gram-Mom-Dad-and-Gramps Bar Mitzvah. I was truly ready.

The next morning at breakfast, I announced my renewed intentions to everyone. I didn't make a big deal out of it this time. I sensed that would've set it up for ridicule and disbelief, so I just said I was giving it another shot.

The responses were varied. Gramps was enthusiastic and acted as if there was no previous failure at all. Dad was skeptically encouraging. Mom was cautiously ecstatic. Susan mumbled something about the Jew who cried wolf.

The phone rang.

I got up to answer it.

"Hello?"

"Oh," a man said. "Yosef ... hello."

I didn't recognize the voice, but he was clearly unhappy I answered.

"This is Rabbi Brenner," he continued.

Ah, now I get it - not his favorite person.

"Rabbi, hi." I wanted to tell him the good news, but he cut me off before I could.

"May I speak to your mother or father, please?"

"Sure," I said, "Mom, it's Rabbi Brenner."

Mom got up and took the phone.

"Hello Rabbi," she said. "Funny you should call--"

He cut her off too. As he spoke, her eyes bulged, and she threw a hand over her mouth. To stop from screaming, I assume.

After another moment, she started crying and muttered, "What will we do?"

After the Rabbi's short answer, she said, "I'm so sorry. Thank you for calling, Rabbi."

We were all staring at her as she hung up. She looked at us, silently.

"What is it?" Dad asked.

"What?" Gramps asked.

"Mom, what?!" I asked.

Finally, she said, "The synagogue burned down."

❦

The fire happened late at night while no one was there, and the Rabbi surmised that he or Cantor Gary must have left a candle lit overnight.

I couldn't believe my bad luck. Somewhere along the way, I figured I must have been cursed. It was likely Mom's fault; on the subway, probably when I was a toddler, she took the seat of some toothless, old Yiddishe woman who smelled of rotting cow. And the woman retaliated with a curse. There are actually quite a few she could've chosen from:

He should have stones instead of children!

He should drink too much castor oil!

Leeches should drink him dry!

He should laugh with lizards!

He should grow a wooden tongue!

He should get the only hernia in town!

Venereal disease should consume his body!

He should crap pus!

He should never be a Bar-Mitzvah!

I should've been happy it was just that last one. So far.

Regardless, I was once again lost. My anxiety was at Woody Allen levels. Every meal now, lumps of food stuck in my throat. My stomach hurt often, regardless of what I ate. I felt small and lonely again. I had no friends, no Gram, and no way of redeeming myself.

At least school was a little easier since Calvin was still AWOL, and it was only a week before we were out for the December break. I did wonder where he was and how he was doing, and as far as the whole Boone converting thing, I had slipped into denial. It was considerably easier acting like it didn't happen. Denial saves lives.

At the house, Gram's absence changed the vibe completely. Gramps napped more. Mom hardly left her room - when she did, it was a groggy stumble to the kitchen for a nosh, then back to bed. Dad went to work earlier and came home later. Susan was either at school, or with some boyfriend.

I suggested we go back to Brooklyn and do the Bar Mitzvah there (my original want, of course), but Dad said he couldn't spend the money with the high probability that I would fuck something up again (my expletive). Also, we had just spent a lot of money traveling there for the funeral. Rabbi Brenner suggested we consider shuls in Knoxville, but I was too uncomfortable with that. He did tell us there'd be a rebuilding of the Oak Ridge shul. Unfortunately, that would take months, maybe even a year.

So, it was looking like we'd just have to wait.

Hopefully, I could.

Then, one night, I got a very unexpected phone call.

I answered again. "Hello?"

"Yosef?" said a man with a familiar accent.

"Who's this" I asked, excited.

"Hey, it's Pizza Pete."

"Oh, hi Pete." I couldn't imagine why he was calling.

"Listen, Yosef, I heard about your, uh, place of worship burnin' down, so sorry about that. I called your Rabbi, told him if anyone needed Pete's place for anything, I'd be up for it, you know? So he told me you were planning a … sorry, what do you call it again?"

"My Bar Mitzvah?"

"Yeah, yeah, yeah. Of course. Listen, if you want to have your service and party here at the restaurant, I'd be okay with that. I know it's, uh, whaddayasay, uh, non-traditional, and maybe even non-religious, but what the hey. This ain't New York, right?"

I laughed. "Right."

"Well, think about it. Talk to your folks about it. The Rabbi said he was fine with it."

I didn't know how to react. It seemed so odd. "Okay, well, thanks Pete."

We hung up and I stood there a few moments. The central heat from the floor vents kicked in and warmed my toes as I stared out the sliding glass door into the bare-treed woods.

A Bar Mitzvah at an old-timey pizza place. Nothing kosher about Pizza Pete's, that's for sure. But, as he said, this isn't New York. When it came to Judaism, so many things were unconventional in this part of the country. Also, there were plenty of people who worshipped at the altar of Pizza Pete's! Gram would've been a hard no-fucking-way. And Gramps, Mom, and Dad would definitely have issues with it. But maybe it actually made sense. If we could have the Talmud there, the Rabbi, and the Cantor, and anyone who wanted to come, did it really matter where it was? It's not as if I ever liked our previous shul anyway.

I went into the living room where Gramps and Dad were watching TV, then called to Mom who came in from her room. When she came out, I told them what Pete told me.

Judging by their blank stares and gaping mouths, you would've thought I just told them I was moving to Detroit and joining a cult. (Which, by the way, they only found out about after Lynn left. But that's a story for later.)

"Pizza?" Gramps asked, confused.

"It's a pizza place, right near Blankenship Field where they play the high school football games. It's called Pizza Pete's. He's from New York!"

"I think that's sacrilegious," Dad said, clearly uncomfortable with the idea.

"Well, the Rabbi's okay with it."

"What about the Knoxville shuls we were looking at?" Dad asked.

"I just ... I don't want to do it there. I don't know anybody, and they said we'd have to use their Rabbi and Cantor."

Dad nodded with a frown.

"Your grandmother would hate it," Gramps said, quietly.

The dead elephant in the room.

I figured that was the end of it, and Mom would put the final nail in the blasphemous, pepperoni coffin. She was sitting between Dad and Gramps and had been, surprisingly, silent. We all looked over at her, waiting.

She stood up and spoke slowly. "I don't care if it's at a Goddamn laundromat. If it'll get you to finally have your Bar Mitzvah, we'll have it at Ned's place. We won't have to cater. We'll keep the pizzas meatless. Done."

And with that, she walked out. leaving me with a smile as wide as the Mason-Dixon Line. Not sure how Pete translated to Ned, but I didn't care.

❧❧❧

It was the last day of school before the break. Gym class had just wrapped. I was dressed and at my locker, just about to take off for lunch. I'd actually become used to the group shower. Coerced, covertly homoerotic, group showers - what's not to love?

I turned to go when someone entered my narrow locker corridor.

Calvin.

I flinched and felt myself recoil.

In jeans and a flannel, his face was puffy, and he held a hang-dog posture.

"Hey," he said, quietly, unsure.

I didn't say anything at first. So many possible responses were swirling through my head, it was impossible to pick just one.

"Hey," I finally responded, keeping my eyes on my locker.

The denial I'd been so happily ensconced in like a warm cloud suddenly evaporated. Everything came rushing back: What was said on the interstate that night. What it actually meant. How I almost froze to death. How I wanted to punch him hard in the face. I might've learned something from Gramps, or even Dad. I could give it a try. But I didn't. The ability to overcome my inherited physical cowardice wouldn't come for years.

"What do you want?" I asked.

"Ah, hell, man. I just wanted to say ... you know ... sorry. Sayin' that stuff on the interstate ... I's really wantin' to get high and didn't have anything. I's just feelin' like crap."

I nodded slightly.

He went on. "All that turnin' you Baptist shit ... it's true, but it was all Daddy - not me. I don't care. Jewish, Irish, foolish, don't matter to me."

He cracked a tiny smile.

Hearing that felt good. I wasn't ready to laugh the whole thing off, but I could feel something building inside me, something I was only slightly familiar with: compassion.

This was hard for him. Sure, I was unsure ... about everything. I didn't trust him in the least. But I wanted badly, so badly, to have my best friend back. Was that what was happening? It seemed like it.

"How'd you get back?" I asked.

Calvin smiled, realizing I was letting him in, if not just a little.

"Ah, man, it was crazy. After you took off, I stood there, a minute I reckon. Fuckin' freezin' to death! And I's just thinkin' ... maybe I could go live with my mama. You know? Maybe it wouldn't be so bad. I didn't know what else to do. Couldn't go back to Daddy. Couldn't go to Canada, or wherever the hell I was headin'. So, when all the traffic was gone, I bolted across the interstate to the other side! Hitched back home. Took a lot of rides. No homos at least!"

We laughed, and Calvin, in his regained silliness, knocked his head several times on one of the lockers.

"So how's that going? Living with your mom?" I asked.

"It's fuckin' weird! Little apartment. She ain't workin' or anything. She's always mad about somethin'."

"What about your dad?"

"I ain't seen him, but Mama called him, told him I's livin' with her now."

"My gram died," I said, suddenly, needing some of that sympathy coming my way.

"Ah, shit, man. That sucks. How'd she die?"

"Heart attack."

I wanted to share with him how that collect call was the last time I spoke to her and how hanging up on her made me feel, but you know, teenage boys ... they can only go so deep.

"Well, that sucks," Calvin repeated.

"I decided to try my Bar Mitzvah again. We're doing it at Pizza Pete's. You want to come?"

"Wait a minute! Pizza Pete's?! What the Hell?!"

"Our synagogue burned down."

Calvin was about to say something, apologies, condolences perhaps. But then his expression changed. Part knowing. Part fear. I didn't get it at the time.

He shook it off and said, "Sorry about that, man. Yeah, hell yeah, I want to come!"

"Cool. It's January 4th. We better get to class," I said.

As we headed out, we talked about my adventure when I ran off that night, the joy of hand jobs, and the classwork we missed. You know, regular stuff.

And there it was - the bond was back. Extra Crazy Glue was applied, our falling out only strengthening what we had.

They say *Third times a charm.*

They also say *bad things come in threes.*

Naturally, for me, it was both.

My Bar Mitzvah day had finally arrived - again. I had OD'd on Maalox instead of LSD, and I was well into it when suddenly, the front door swung open, hard, hitting the side of the building.

Before that, everything had gone mostly as planned. I had studied hard over the holiday break and barely saw Calvin. Lynn decided to stay in Michigan. Mom was furious with her, of course, but Lynn told us she couldn't keep going back and forth and she couldn't really trust that I would actually do it this time. I know, I know: boy crying wolf etc, etc… I was obviously disappointed, but she had a point.

Also, Mom, Dad, and I all agreed it was best not to invite any of our New York friends or family. Our relationships were already strained with them, and we just saw them all at Gram's funeral anyway. Of course, it would've been amazing to have the two meshuggeners there with me, but Calvin was coming, so I was happy about that. Mom, not so much. But she decided it wouldn't harm anything, as long as he kept his mouth shut. I assured her he would. We also invited the Temple Beth El congregation, and a couple dozen showed up. Devin among them. I was sure they missed their synagogue, and this was as close to it as they could come without traveling to Knoxville. Once the big day arrived, we all got busy. Me and Mom helped the Rabbi and Cantor bring the Jewish texts to the restaurant. We had decided the ceremony would be at the back of the dining room, so to create a space, Dad and Susan helped Pete move the tables to the rear parking lot. After that, they rearranged the wooden chairs in rows to face the makeshift bimah. Pete had a dozen cheeseless, hamburger pizzas ready to go for the reception, and there would be plenty of soda pop and water for all.

The place was the furthest thing you could get from a Shul. The joint was dark and covered in checkered plastic with the smell of yeasty, beer backwash everywhere. But - this was *my* Pizza Mitzvah. No one else's. And I embraced it like a boy and his boner.

I would soon, finally, finally be a man.

There were a couple glitches in the beginning. As the Rabbi sermonized, the phone rang. Pete answered it quickly; it was someone wondering if they needed reservations, he told us afterwards laughing. They didn't. Also, when I brought the Torah onto the table we had arranged, I tripped on the jukebox power cord, dropping the giant scroll onto the greasy floor. I recovered it quickly, and besides the mild heart attacks, we were soon on our way.

Mom, Dad, Gramps, Susan, Devin, and Calvin were all in the front row, Calvin at the end, hugging the wall. I read and chanted with passion and purpose. I was back, and it felt good, and right. I knew the material so well, at one point, I actually closed my eyes while chanting and imagined I was at our old shul in Brooklyn. I could see Mitchell and Micah in the pews. Lynn and Gram, still the Holocaust survivor, were both there. Everyone was smiling, being Jewish with me. Feeling Jewish with me. Tribal.

That was when the crazed hillbilly came flying through the door, huffing and sweating like he was hopped up on pork rinds and fury. The place erupted into a collective, convulsive gasp. I stopped and whipped open my eyes, wondering ... what this time?

I guess Pete didn't bother locking the door once we got started. Who comes in for pizza before noon?

"Calvin!" Boone shouted, as he walked further in, looking through the rows of parishioners. "I know you're in here! I saw you go in."

The congregation was full of shocked whispers and fear-filled moans, a couple even escaped out the front door. Calvin had gone pale when he saw his dad. I was too stunned to say or do anything.

Mom and Dad were on their feet now.

"You! Get out of here, or we'll call the police!" Mom yelled.

"Sir, you need to get out of here. Period," Dad joined in.

"Or what?!" Boone shot back. "You gonna take another swing, Jew? Guarantee you won't be so lucky this time."

Pete approached Boone. "Boone, listen, this is a private affair. Why don't you--"

"This ain't none of your business, Pete."

"Well, sure it is," he said, smiling "My house, my rules. Right? Why don't you go on, come back later for a large pepperoni. It'll be on me. Whaddaya say?"

Spotting Calvin, Boone brushed past Pete and stopped at the end of the front aisle while Mom, Dad, Devin, and Gramps all scrambled for the back rows, leaving no one between Calvin and his father.

At the same time, Pete and another man from the congregation were slowly surrounding Boone from behind. I was terrified for Calvin, but I remained paralyzed, like I was watching a movie I was starring in that ended up on the cutting room floor.

"Come on, boy. Don't make me go over there and get ya."

Calvin stood up and faced his dad. "I don't live with you no more," he said, his voice defiant, but jittery. "Leave me alone. You heard him, it's a private affair."

"Don't you talk to me like that, boy," Boone said, inching toward Calvin, his rage building. "You're comin' with me, right this second. Now, come on."

"I ain't livin' with no damn murderer," Calvin said, just loud enough for everyone to hear.

The place filled with more gasps and scattered *oy gevalts*. I couldn't believe he said it, but as everything went quiet, Boone's demeanor did slowly shift. He moved closer to Calvin, but instead of more anger, as I expected, he morphed into the eye of the hurricane: calm, almost relaxed, even smiling a little. I had no idea what to make of it.

"I think you and me should just go outside and talk," Boone said quietly. "I ain't gonna beat ya. Like you said, this here's a private thang. Matter of fact, I apologize to everyone." He looked around and settled on me.

I nodded, hoping my faux apology acceptance would defuse the situation.

Calvin had turned completely toward his dad. "It's true, isn't it? I know it is."

"Where you hear that?" Boone asked, chuckling.

"Just tell me the truth."

"Boone, I'm 'bout out of patience here," Pete said, still right behind him.

Boone turned toward Pete and nodded silently. "All right," he said, quietly, putting his hands on his hips.

He spun back toward Calvin and stared at him, his eyes watering now, blinking.

"I tell you the truth, you come along without a fight?"

Calvin thought about it a moment.

"Sure, Daddy."

All eyes were glued to Boone as he took a deep breath and shared his story - pretty sure, for the first time.

"Okay, then. Well, one night, I was with your great Uncle Muir. You never knew him, but he ran with them KKK boys. Lot of folks did back then. There was uh ... this Black boy ... and he was to be ... you know, lynched that night."

Mom put her hand over her mouth, trying, unsuccessfully to stifle her revulsion. Susan was shaking her head with disbelief.

Boone went on, slowly, methodically, and yes, full of remorse, a steady regurgitation that suddenly couldn't be held back, after keeping it in for decades.

"Muir and some other men had corralled the boy, tied the rope around his neck, then ... you know, threw the other end up over the tree branch. The way it worked is, you grabbed the other end and pulled, you know, lifting the ... lifting the boy up by the neck. Muir gave me the rope to pull ..." Boone stopped, swallowed once, then continued.

"But I couldn't. I couldn't do it! I wasn't strong enough! I was only seven years old. Seven, Calvin! I's just a child, barely knee high. When he seen I couldn't do it, Muir came in, grabbed the rope and, well, we done did it together.

"That's the truth," Boone said, shaking his head in self-disgust. "That was the way it was back then. I prayed more times for that boy's soul than you know. Prayed for mine, too."

Sadness, contempt, repugnance, resignation. Every emotion was fully represented that day at Pizza Pete's. For Boone, he was only speaking to his son - and maybe Christ - but the rest of us were unintended casualties. Unfortunately, it was a truth we were deeply familiar with. The difference between the hatred and murder of Blacks and the hatred of murder of Jews was a matter of nuance and timeline, a different verse in the same sad, universal anthem.

Mom, Susan, and Gramps were side-huddled, folding into each other.

"I come clean, Calvin," Boone said. "In front of all these people, too. Time to come home, son. Let's get on out of here."

Calvin glared at his dad a moment, his face all twisted up with disgust. "You go on," he said hesitantly.

Boone stood up straight, surprised. "We had a deal, boy."

"I ain't goin' with you."

Boone nodded ... then struck.

Lightning fast.

A rattlesnake or a fist, it was hard to tell. He connected with Calvin's nose, splattering blood high and low, with the force throwing Calvin hard against the wall. And that was just the first of many punches Boone intended.

Maybe, after all these months, seeing his rage finally materialize made me act - I have no idea. But I darted from the bimah and started punching Boone in the back and head, screaming at him to stop.

As you might expect, Pete, the other man, and Dad beat me to it. But that didn't stop me from piling on and doing what I could to halt the attack. It was bedlam. Everyone was screaming.

Pete was the one who knew what he was doing. He grabbed Boone's slugging arm, his right, yanked it behind his back, then grabbed the other arm, and shoved them both up toward his head. Boone roared in pain as Pete took him face down onto the floor.

"Someone call the cops!" Pete shouted.

"We already did," the Cantor answered from behind me. Apparently, him and the Rabbi had gone out the back earlier and called the police from the next door movie theatre.

I went to Calvin. He was dazed, close to comatose. "Are you okay?!"

No answer. I grabbed a cloth napkin from a nearby table.

"Here, put this on your face," I said, handing it to him. As he did, he looked down at his father struggling under Pete's bulk.

"What the hell, old man?" he asked rhetorically.

The front door flew open, and this time, it was the police. Two of them rushed in and took over for Pete, handcuffing Boone and pulling him to his feet.

One of the cops said, "Boone, you're under arrest for disturbing the peace."

"And assault," Pete added.

"What?" the cop asked. Pete pointed to Calvin.

The cop looked at Calvin. "Oh, shit. All right, let's go."

Boone finally stopped fighting, but he did take one last look at his boy as they read him his rights and led him out. Calvin turned away, falling back into his seat, the wooden chair thunking loudly on the floor.

After a couple minutes of headshakes, family hugs, and lots of relieved chatter, me and Mom went back to Calvin.

"Pete called an ambulance," she told him. "We'll wait till they get here, but then you," she turned her eyes toward me, "you, will finish."

"No," Calvin said, muffled under the napkin.

"Excuse me?" Mom asked, looking like she was about to finish what Boone couldn't.

He looked up at me, wincing in pain. "Get 'er done, man. I want to see it. The whole thing. I'll go to the hospital after. Hell, it's just a broken nose."

Mom shrugged; she couldn't give a shit.

I smiled. Macho Southern man. Hell yeah.

Just to be clear, I didn't need Mom to tell me that I should finish.

There was no way in hell I was going to let Calvin, Boone, the horrific memory of Uncle Muir, or anyone or anything else ruin my Bar Mitzvah!

Not this time, motherfuckers.

So I got back up there ...

... and on January 4ᵗʰ, 1975 around 1:36 pm, in front of two glowing parents, one grandparent, one sister, one bloody best friend, and a couple dozen Oak Ridge sorta-Jews, I, Yosef Bamberger, finally, decisively, and with conviction, became a Bar Mitzvah. It was outtasight.

I joined everyone on the floor. Mom was weeping. Dad beamed with pride. Gramps pretend-jabbed me with a few pulled punches before he nodded off. Devin was supportive, but obnoxious. I hugged him anyway. Susan rolled her eyes, but then pulled me into an extended embrace. Rabbi Tower and Cantor Stinky shook my hand hard and pummeled me with Mazel Tovs and insinuations that I was now a man.

Pete shouted, "Kosher pies and Tab for everyone!" And everyone celebrated.

When the ambulance arrived, Calvin came over to me and said one thing before he left:

"Matzel Tove."

I exploded into laughter. The Southern accent combined with the mispronunciation: So completely appropriate.

I'll never forget that Calvin sat through the rest of my Bar Mitzvah in obvious pain. Only a real friend would do that.

SHALOM Y'ALL

SO - THAT EUPHORIA I WAS FEELING FROM BECOMING A BAR Mitzvah?

Lasted maybe a couple days.

By the next weekend, I was back to the regular, Tennessee teenagery of the day: school, doing yard work for money to buy records, hanging out with Calvin, and plotting new ways to see girls without their clothes on.

But, as the months went by, Calvin and I did begin to hang out less and less. It wasn't intentional, just natural.

By the next year, I had fallen in with the brainy, nerd crowd. Some Jewish, some not. One of them was David, a goyim son of an engineer. We became best friends and are to this day. Calvin started buddying around with a couple troublemakers, and by our senior year, we both finally got girlfriends. He and Becky were an item. I dated a sweet, Jewish, Southern girl named Marni.

On occasion, I would meet Calvin in the woods and we would smoke pot. Yes, I finally inhaled, thank you for asking. I think, though, when it came to drugs, my acid trip really formed me, spoiled me in a twisted way. Compared to LSD, the marijuana high was meh at best.

The rest of the '70s went about their groovy business. Like many parts of the conservative South, change is the enemy, crawling sloth-like with nails digging into the dirt, fighting all the way. Eventually, though, Oak Ridge did start to change with the times. Unfortunately, in the '80s and '90s, the town began to lose some of its government projects, which in turn diminished the population considerably.

Today, Oak Ridge has made quite the comeback, all while continuing to embrace its scientific origins. Oak Ridge National Lab, a major division of the Department of Energy, is now home to two major scientific endeavors. The Spallation Neutron Source is a facility featuring pulsed neutron beams for worldwide research and development and Titan, one of the world's most powerful scientific supercomputers, is there.

And growth coming from Knoxville has spread into Oak Ridge. With it have come several contemporary, even artisanal, restaurants, a ballet company, a bustling playhouse, museums and more. The population today is back up to 1970s levels.

And what of that fascinating dichotomy between the highly educated and the lesser than? Still there.

But my favorite part of Oak Ridge today is the 8,000 lb. bronze bell known as The International Friendship Bell. It's a monument that was built in the mid'90s to symbolize everlasting peace and goodwill between Japan and Oak Ridge. You can see it, and even ring it, the next time you're in Bissell Park on the Secret City Commemorative Walk.

❧❧❧

Sometime in 1984, while at a Divine Light Mission rally in Chicago, Lynn met a man dispatched by a local church to convince the *Knowledge* seekers to leave the Mission and come to Jesus.

Sound familiar?

As the story goes, not only did Cliff talk her out of the DLM, they fell in love and married a year later. Somewhere along the line, Lynn had started playing piano, and after moving to Oregon with Cliff, she got a bachelor's in music education from the University of Oregon. Today, they live in Eugene as born-again Christians. They have a twenty-six-year-old son, my nephew, Ricky. Lynn and I talk once a week or so. It's always fun and fulfilling. And each time, right before we hang up, we say good night to each other in exactly the same way. Even if it's broad daylight.

※※※

Susan got a bachelor's in Sociology from the University of Tennessee/Knoxville. And soon after, she moved to the desert area of California. Today, she's married to a lovely, Latina named Margueritta. They both work in health education.

Yes, you read that right.

Turns out, in her youth, with her wide slew of boys, Susan was simply doing research. Her ultimate findings, she realized in college, was that she didn't like the opposite sex as much as she did her own. Apparently, that whole Cybil Shepherd thing was more a crush, than idolatry.

They have no kids, but Margueritta's extended family makes up for that nicely. And they are not Jewish. I know - shocking.

I spent some time with them recently, and Susan, who has somehow become a very decent cook, baked a chicken. We made a wish on the wishbone.

And, no, I did not cry!

※※※

After Gram's death, I figured Gramps would be close behind. In some ways, you could argue he did stop living. He rarely spoke, hardly moved, barely ate. We ceased having our morning boxing ritual, as well as any real heart-to-hearts.

It wasn't until his 95th year that the 1926 Bantamweight champ finally left the arena. And that was only because Mom had climbed into his bed one day, snuggled up behind him and whispered that it was okay if he was ready to go.

And so he left the next day - after fifteen years of being barely alive.

Late to his own death, you might say.

I could just see God or St. Peter or whoever quizzing him on why he was tardy. They waited patiently, then impatiently for an answer. And when he finally came up with a decent response, they had moved on to more pressing business.

I still have that amazing boxing poster on a wall in my den. It's tattered and bending up in places in shouldn't be, but that matters not to me. I'm actually looking at it right now.

Dad remained distant most of my life, with the exception of the major milestones, of course. College graduation, wedding, Pizza Mitzvah; good or bad, when it was vital, he was there.

As I stretched into my later teens, and continued to emerge from my self-important bubble, I realized that my stress was also his, in that he felt it as deeply as I did. He was the same way with Lynn and Susan. That was why he could be so quiet during our personal dramas - he was just as upset as we were. Extreme empathy. Also known as love.

In the thirty or so years he had been in Oak Ridge, Dad ended up working at all three major engineering plants, K-25, Y-12, and X-10, as well as ORNL (Oak Ridge National Laboratory). He managed to keep whatever job he had for a while, then he'd find something somewhere else he felt he was better suited for.

Finally retired at age sixty-five. It might have even been the actual moment - 5pm on his sixty-fifth birthday. He couldn't have gotten out of wherever he was at the time faster. There was no retirement party, no big send off. He just left work like any other day, except for one stop before heading home. A visit to see Roger, his first Oak Ridge boss.

Roger was also retired, but Dad knew where he lived. According to the story as Mom tells it, Dad finally decided to confront Roger about the anti-Semitic crustaceans he endured at K-25. Apparently, Roger was appalled and disgusted, and asked Dad why he didn't say anything at the time. Dad had no answer, and just turned and left. When we were kids, he had shielded us from the disgusting gesture, rightfully so. It definitely ranks up there with one of the most baffling things about our experience.

After Dad's Roger encounter, he drove home, picked up Mom and Gramps, drove to the airport, and boarded a flight to LaGuardia.

Never looked back.

They had sold the Oak Ridge house, and the movers had come that morning. All three of them moved in with Cousin Michael in his dusty, roachy, dark, three-bedroom Bronx apartment. It was vile, but it was New York. And that was all that mattered. When I would visit, I could see the joy on their faces. They had made it home. Naturally, they spent a lot of time in Brooklyn and visited our old synagogue every Friday.

When Dad was seventy-five or so, he started writing a novel. The premise was what if Hitler didn't actually die. He wrote about half of it and, suddenly, stopped. He just put it down. One night speaking on the phone, I asked him why he quit, and after a few moments of introspection, he said: *If I don't finish it, no one can hate it.*

It was a concept I was familiar with, but I'd never heard him say something so honest, so revealing. And that was just the beginning. The comment seemed to open up some kind of ancient Murray portal. For the next thirty minutes, he wouldn't shut up, telling me all about his stories. Over the years, he had written a dozen movie screenplays, spectacular non-achievements, all of them. He had poured everything into them, and was devastated each time a script was rejected. For years, writing movies was all he wanted. Engineering was only supposed to be a sideline until he made it big as a Hollywood screenwriter.

I think his devotion to film writing, that passion for the movies, was why he lost his engineering job in Brooklyn in '73. And why he was consistently demoted and put on lesser projects in Oak Ridge. He thought it was due to anti-Semitism, but I don't think so. Maybe partly, but I think it was mostly cause he never really had heart for engineering.

I had no idea of these things. It's amazing the things you miss when you're a self-centered, punk-ass twelve-year-old.

Dad became ill around 2003. Multiple myeloma and congestive heart failure. Like Gramps, it was a slow going, much of it due to his weight. He and Mom had daily caretakers, and when it looked to be time, hospice came in.

When I got there to say goodbye, he was sailing on morphine, one foot in this world, the other in another. Rabbi Berkwitz was there, as were Lynn, Susan, and their partners. I held Dad's hand for an hour, and every once in a while, he'd raise his slumped head to smile at me with wet, sunken eyes. He knew I needed that, still, always about us.

He died quietly the next morning, just barely eighty years old.

I don't think Mom ever completely forgave Dad for the move to Tennessee. On a scale of one to ten, maybe a four.

A five for just a moment when he popped Boone in the face.

But, apparently, it was nothing hightailin' it back home couldn't remedy. I heard from reliable sources at the time that, once they moved back, Mom had actually started singing again. Understandably, she was stuck in the '70s with her choices - Three Dog Night, Rod Stewart, Carole King. If I'd been around, that would've been just fine with me. I even considered visiting just to hear her voice in that way again, but since I ended up coming only for funerals, she was never in the right mood.

For over thirty years, Mom was a functioning drug addict. Prescription only, of course. And sometimes non-functioning, one might argue. She did eventually make a friend, Alice, from the synagogue. Alice brought Mom into a mixed-religion knitting group, as well as a book club. She eventually left both groups. Probably not whiney enough. I did get a winter scarf out of it. Still have it.

Once they were back in New York, she started a rehab program, visiting AA meetings and NA meetings regularly, and eventually controlling the urges. Interestingly, the *headaches* disappeared, as well. Through all of it, Dad managed to remain in denial. Knowing him, he probably thought he was doing that for her.

My relationship with Mom improved in later life, slowly but surely, reaching previous Brooklyn levels by the time she reached full sobriety. We had forgiven each other for a lot. It was a relief, and it allowed me to embrace other things in my life.

On the first evening sitting Shiva for Dad, everyone had left but me. We were on the sofa. It was late. I stuck around because Mom had begun bursting into these frightening and explosive fits of wailing. They would last a few minutes, then she'd calm. Then another would come, then subside.

In between one particular outburst, she told me something that didn't surprise me, though I guess I only knew it subconsciously: I was always her great Jewish hope.

Early on, even before we moved, she realized her daughters were breaking away from Judaism. But me, I was different. I was like her and Dad and her parents: Jewish through and through, no matter what. Her assumption was that I would carry the Bamberger Semitic torch into the next generation. The girls had had their Bat Mitzvahs, and they went off with neither hallucinations, nor Jesus rants. But once they did it, that was it. It was like they had fulfilled their religious obligation, and it was time to move on to more 1970s *Me generation* things.

It was supposed to be different for me, Mom had said.

I pulled her into a long, tight embrace. No apologetic, guilt-ridden explanations or excuses. Just hugging. After a minute, we leaned back on the couch, still wrapped around each other. She became still, quiet, and eventually, both of us fell asleep.

I woke a couple hours later, and left, doing my best not to make too much noise on Michael's creaky floor.

The next few years were subdued for Mom. She was very much alone. Although Michael was still around, they kept out of each other's way. He thought she was arrogant. She thought he was a moron. When I would call to check in, she'd go on about the latest disgusting thing he did, or the nice thing he didn't do.

A few years ago, she had a stroke during Friday night services and passed right there in the pews. It was horrible, I'm sure, for those around her, but I was grateful she could pass surrounded by her beloved orthodoxy. She was eighty-five.

Susan decided she would be fine with traveling back to New York to get Mom's things in order. Ship whatever we wanted to keep. Sell what we didn't. Throw away what didn't matter. One day she called me when she found several old letters. They were addressed to Mom and stuffed inside in a shoe box with some other random papers.

It appears there was another man. His name was Burt, someone who Mom had fallen in love with when she was very young. It didn't last long apparently, but once we moved to Oak Ridge, he came back into her life. It wasn't clear who instigated that, but judging by his letters to her, there hadn't been a rekindling, although it seemed they came close.

At first, I told Susan it was something else. The letters had to be to someone else. This was not the Sandy Bamberger who we all knew: a Jew, a wife, a daughter, a mother who never uttered a word about another man. Ever. But there it was, black ink on parchment. Was she actually close to breaking up the family? I couldn't imagine.

Judging by the post mark, and his opening line, this was Burt's last letter:

Dearest Sandy,

As I have apparently written into the postal abyss for several months now, I will finally let this correspondence be my last. As difficult as it will be, I will stop pestering you. And no more surprise visits, I promise. I want you to know that I understand your decision to keep me at bay. I really do. There were three other women in my life beside you. They all lasted years longer, yet I pine for none of them as I have for you. Such as the mysteries of the nature of love, I suppose. Our last kiss in the parking lot, while frustrating, is a beautiful, enduring memory. I will take it to my grave. I will always love you, dear Sandy, desperately. But I know that that is not always enough.

> *All my love,*
>
> *Burt*

❧

Not long after my Bar Mitzvah (the sober one), someone - I'm going to guess his son - ended up telling the authorities about Boone's murder confession that day. The story was in the local newspaper, and everyone was talking about it. Tennessee had (and has) no statute of limitations for 1st degree homicide. But since Boone was a minor, and it was mostly committed by men long passed, the district attorney never pressed charges. I imagined Chief Kitchens pounding on the inside of his coffin, screaming in frustration.

But Boone *was* convicted of arson and sentenced to fifteen years at the Southeastern Tennessee Regional Correctional Facility. Although the Rabbi assumed the synagogue fire was an accident, after an investigation, the fire department realized it wasn't and managed to track the crime to Boone. He wasn't the only religious bigot in the Oak Ridge area, but none of this surprised anyone.

On our high school graduation night, Calvin and I were hanging out in the woods, reminiscing and laughing about my chaotic, temporary conversion. He said he thought the whole reason Boone attempted it was to be redeemed in Jesus's eyes for the murder.

You save me, I'll save a Jew.

Quid pro quo.

Calvin knew him better than anyone, so ... I'll give him that. Made sense to me.

During his incarceration, Boone lost the house to the bank. When he got out of prison, he kicked around Knoxville for a few years before he ended up homeless.

Once in 1992 or '93, he left a phone message for Calvin, asking for money. Calvin never returned the call, and no one heard from Boone after that.

⁂

The last time I face-timed with Calvin, I got the usual update. He was still living in the nice house in Knoxville he bought decades ago. He still went to church every Sunday and prayed for his dad who was probably in heaven by now (Debatable). And he was still sober.

The major news was Calvin was now the *former* head of Wendy's Hamburgers Eastern US operations, having finally retired after thirty years. He had worked his way up from grill cook. Pretty impressive for a kid whose Dad was an ex-con and Mother, a heroin addict. Oh, and also, the kids were fine, except for Cameron, who had been arrested again for drunk driving. The ex-wife (not Becky) was finally leaving him alone, and his new girlfriend was twenty years younger than him - did I want to see a nude picture?

Yes, but no thanks.

I told him a bit about my life. He sang some old Southern rock tune, and did air guitar, and we laughed about the same things we always did.

Me and Muttley. I get goosebumps every time I hear that guffaw.

Our friendship might have started from a lie, but it had turned into a true brotherhood. Because what it was really borne of, like all friendships, was a shared need. I wasn't the only one who needed a friend. Sure, Calvin had buds at school. But they were just that - only at school. As I came to realize in later years, Boone didn't let Calvin have any real friends; he wanted him all to himself. But the redemptive prospect of the new Jew boy's religious conversion was the perfect motivation for Boone to make an exception. Just that once.

How'd that go for you, Boone ol' boy?

Before we hung up, we both promised to call each other more often. That was the drill, once every five years. We have different political views. Different societal views. Different views on all things views. And that couldn't be more fine with me.

What Calvin and I share is history. A preposterous, excruciating, thrilling history. And it did nothing less than make me what I am today.

❈

I had a bizarre, but not entirely surprising, dream a couple nights ago. I was in a time machine built out of the old, flowery lounge chair we had in both our living rooms. It was cramped, but comfortable, and traveled the space-time continuum with very little turbulence. I eventually landed in the desert, where I got up and started walking. I had no idea where I was or where I was going, so I just kept trudging through the heat for a long time. Finally, I came across a towering, wooden cross standing upright in the sand. I was exhausted and thirsty, and I remember thinking: if this is my destination, there was plenty of parking. Why didn't my time machine bring me closer?

I walked around to the front of the cross and saw that Jesus was in the middle of being crucified. There were quite a few other people around: Jews, disciples, and a couple sheep who kept morphing into giant squirrels, then back to sheep. As I got closer, a bearded old man in rags handed me a hammer and nail.

"We saved the last one for you," he said, smiling.

I nodded, took the hammer and nail, and looked up at Jesus. We made eye contact. He looked more annoyed than anything, like, *can we just get this over with already?*

Realizing something, I shouted at the old man, "Wait! How am I supposed to get up there?!"

But he was gone. Everyone was, Christ, the cross, the enormous squirrels. I looked down at the tools the man had given me, then back up into the desert nothingness.

421

"What am I supposed to do with these?!"

I woke up, sweating and anxious, but happy to be in my home.

Me and my nightmares.

Something occurred to me. Recently, while trying to clear some junk from the garage, in an old box I found the cross Boone had given me. That certainly could've been the catalyst for the dream. It blew me away that I still had it after all these years. It's like it had a mind of its own and followed me throughout my life.

Creepy or spiritual - depending on how you look at it.

I shook off the dream as best I could and rolled over for my morning ritual: Checked my iPhone for texts, emails, the weather, the time, and any celebrities who might've died the previous night. There was nothing interesting.

Of course, my old bedside rituals were long gone: Reading from my Anne Frank book, checking growth with my ruler and flashlight, listening to that glorious cacophony of waking Bambergers. Some aspects of my youth simply morphed. Maalox to Pepcid AC. Yarmulke to hipster beanie. Short schmekel to gentle giant. The two meshuggeners were now my wife and daughter. (I lost touch with the original meshuggeners long ago).

It was 5:58 am.

I slipped slowly out of bed, doing my best not to wake my wife, Michelle. Bright, funny, expressive Michelle. You won't find any Rachel, Sarah, or Becky in her. Maybe some Mom. Okay, fine, plenty of Mom. Leave me alone.

We met thirteen years ago in Los Angeles at a U2 concert. We went out for a few years before we married on a beach on the Hawaiian island of Kauai. It was a small ceremony. A minister, a photographer, me, and the most *shiksa* girl you'll ever meet with the last name of Bamberger. Korean-American women are seldom Jewish.

We had moved to Denver from L.A. only a year before. We were in L.A. for three years, and before that, Detroit for four years. Before Detroit,

San Francisco for five. A month ago, the new Denver firm laid me off due to a sudden loss of business. Last in, first out.

Now we were stuck in a town we liked but that offered few opportunities in engineering. I had degrees in civil and mechanical engineering from the University of Tennessee. It was a great school for engineering, so I had done well over the years. But now, just over fifty, I was busy looking for work again. It stressed out both of us.

I tip-toed out of the room and down the hall to Ella's room. The door was open a bit, as we always left it, and I peeked in. She was sleeping soundly in her crib. Two years ago, we traveled to Vietnam to adopt her. Smartest thing I've ever done.

After getting coffee, I went out front, planted myself on our porch swing and gazed out at the rising sun. We're in a heavily treed part of the city, but close to a major thoroughfare. It either smells of crisp mountains, urine, or both. Colorado - fall's most yellow place.

A while back, I had an epiphany about those early Oak Ridge days. For many impressionable months, I had experienced two major religions, simultaneously. It was confusing, destructive, and infuriating to some. But that odd, spiritual soup allowed me to separate from the magnetic pull of the family religion. Most people grow up in one religion and carry it through their life. Not me.

In later years, this duality freed me to make up my own mind, unencumbered by personal history or familial pressure. It's not entirely surprising, perhaps, that each side pushed me to the middle.

Today, you might call me spiritual. Many religions resonate with me - really anything having to do with oneness, love, compassion. They all have some of that. Hell, even Jim Jones and the People's Temple believed in racial equality. True, they all ended up dead by the red hand of the Kool-Aid man - but there was love there.

And it's not only religion. My political, financial and social views are moderate, in the middle. That's me, Yosef Bamberger, the non-extremist.

It's been said that every day affects the next in one's life. Each day, you're just a little bit different than you were the day before. I often wonder what I would be like if we had never moved to Tennessee, if I hadn't spent ten years of my life there.

Ella's crying pulled me out of my thoughts. I shot up off the swing and went to her.